I LIVE IN HELL

MIKE SALINAS

DARK DEAD
THINGS

MIKE SALINAS

For everyone I've left or let leave.
And Mom.

I LIVE IN HELL

Why is it always raining here? Or is that just the sound of the television, tuned to a dead channel? — Mark Fisher, Liner Notes for *Theoretically Pure Anterograde Amnesia* by The Caretaker

1

PART ONE

In the neon wilderness, the animals gathered. Behind brick walls, they hid from winter's bite.

The bar was shelter. Neutral territory.

Cole's masqueraded as a relic of the old Chicago, a dive bar constructed from second-hand memory. Young men in beanies huddled in corners drinking Miller High Life. Loners blemished bar stools. In a booth, lustful hands touched beneath the table. Two bartenders made their rounds. It was a Tuesday night.

But amidst them stalked a predator, a beast hidden in plain sight, drifting through the room like smoke.

At the bar, two young women leaned close in conversation, laughing and sipping their drinks.

One appeared near-comatose, her hooded eyes indifferent even as she smiled, as if they heard a lullaby the rest of her did not.

The other clenched her jaw with pouted lips, her eyes sultry yet sharp. When she laughed, she did so with the cadence of royalty, haughty and detached.

"Can't forget the copy of *Infinite Jest* always conveniently left out, front and center," said the woman with the royal laugh, Anna.

"And *always* unread," lullaby-eyes, or Bri, added, finishing her beer and placing it on the bar's edge. She would buy the next round, per usual—which was fine. A stable of older men corralled from the internet paid all her expenses. After last call, she would go back to her apartment, send the men some photos, a few suggestive emojis, then lose herself in a packed bowl and an empty wall, trying to pinpoint the exact moment her life had lost its shine.

The beast prowled, its target already known.

"Must be the diploma they give out at Fuckboy University," Anna snickered. After drinks, she would return to her boyfriend's West Loop condo, located on what was once old skid row, where men's flophouses had given way to bohemian gastronomy and converted lofts. Having recently discovered engagement rings in his search history, the thought of saying yes filled her with dread, but she saw no alternative, preferring the spiritual death of suburban matrimony to ending up like Bri.

After all, they had spent years dating the same male archetype before both giving up on the dating scene altogether—in their own ways.

Frail, disheveled appearance? *Check.* Emotional unavailability? *In spades.* Minimum-wage job or lack thereof? *He'll pay you back, he swears.* Pathetic, dreamless men who romanticized their own misery. The worst kind to get your heart broken by.

The beast's eyes traced the contours of the women's necks just a few feet away, unfelt and unseen, scraping along each pore, fantasizing of the red anatomy beneath.

"All he had in his fridge were crusty condiment bottles."

"He didn't even have a bedframe. It was unreal."

"The bathroom," Bri noted. Both paused to reflect on the mental image, then cracked up at their own revulsion.

"Fucking disgusting," Anna guffawed.

The bartender approached with a playful swagger, piggy-backing off the women's laughter. Lanky with boyish features, he appeared youthful, but his faded tattoos and the city miles beneath his eyes hinted that he was at least a decade their senior.

The bounce in his step immediately annoyed Anna. Her face flattened.

"You ladies like Tom Petty?" he said, collecting their empty shot glasses.

The women stared at him with equal parts disdain and confusion.

"What?" Anna scoffed, having heard the question perfectly fine the first time.

The bartender pointed up as if Mr. Petty himself clung to the ceiling. "The song," he said. "'Free Fallin'.' It's Tom Petty."

"Oh." Anna felt a surge of power from making him explain himself. "No."

Unfazed by the hostility, the bartender smacked his lips. "Right on. Can I get you two anything else right now?"

Bri smiled. "I think we're okay."

"We'll have two more shots," Anna corrected.

"Oh, ya, actually, two more shots. And another beer, please," Bri stammered. "Thank you."

"Two shots. 'Nother beer. You got it." The bartender tapped the empty glasses on the bar before leaving.

The beast's nostrils flared, lusting after the oil of their scalps, the salty taste of their skin. Salivating in anticipation, its thumb caressed a black wooden handle hidden in its jacket pocket.

"Hey, do me a favor?" the bartender asked his coworker.

"What's up?" she replied, counting out a customer's change.

He nodded toward the women. "Can you serve a couple of

Old Crow shots to the ray of sunshine and her friend over there? I'll be back."

"What—?" It was only her second shift at Cole's. "You haven't even showed me how to change the kegs yet. Where are you going?"

"Don't worry about it," he said with a smirk, eliciting a death stare from his coworker. Despite their brief time working together, they had quickly developed a playful rapport. "I just need to step outside for a minute," he conceded. "You'll be fine. You won't even notice I'm gone."

"Fine. Just don't take too long."

"I won't." The lanky bartender strolled over to the tablet controlling the music and tapped the repeat button. He signaled secrecy to his coworker with a finger to his lips, prompting an eye roll.

As is universal law, the bar became slammed the moment he stepped away, leaving his coworker in the weeds.

The beast now openly gripped the black wooden handle. An inch of blade idled just outside its jacket pocket. No one noticed. No one ever saw.

New rounds of liquor flooded the bar. Time passed in clunky steps.

"Wait—is this that same fucking song?" Anna had just noticed "Free Fallin'" wrapping up its fourth play. A bright, jangly guitar riff ushered in its fifth.

Bri laughed, then drained her beer. She tried to make eye contact with the new bartender, but failed. The bar had yet to die down.

Anna was not amused. She could not tolerate even playful disrespect. Agitation heated the bottom of her throat, and her blood began to itch. Like clockwork, the contents of her purse beckoned.

"I need to run to the restroom. You work on getting us another round, okay?"

Bri, who had purchased every round thus far, found it extremely rude that Anna offered *none* of her drugs, but given Anna was a walking raw nerve, she kept her grievance to herself out of habit. "I'll do my best," she said, rolling her eyes at the busy bartender to amuse her companion, then lifting a hand for service.

"I believe in you, girl." Anna patted her shoulder as she left.

Bri watched her friend disappear around the corner. "*Bitch.*"

She put her hand down and waited for the bartender without further gesture.

ANNA COULD HAVE NAVIGATED the dark back hallway blindfolded. A typical night at Cole's yielded six or seven trips here, with one or two actually involving urine.

She tried the women's restroom. Locked. It was single-use and rarely unoccupied.

Placing her ear to the door, Anna could hear the muffled sounds of a woman crying and another consoling her. She gave the door a polite, but authoritative, knock, and asked, "Do you know how much longer you'll be?"

"*Seriously?*" someone scoffed from the other side. "We're done when we're done!"

The crying and consoling continued.

Anna huffed, then eyed the men's room. It would not be the first time it had come to this.

She nudged the door open.

"Anyone in here?" No response. Anna stepped inside and locked the door behind her.

The men's room was drenched in shadow, with a lone bulb

above the sink barely lighting the urinal and the stall beside it. Anna tiptoed to the counter, wary of the minefield of piss underfoot.

From her bag, Anna pulled an Altoids tin, and from the tin, a tiny baggie and half a straw. Repulsed by the idea of allowing her drugs to touch any surface of this restroom, she expertly poured a line out onto the ridge of her hand like a Michelin-starred chef plating a dish, then tucked the baggie back into the tin.

She went slow, savoring each bump in the ride.

Sweet elation.

Her head tilted back. Drip coated her throat in chemical aftertaste. The cocaine soothed her itching blood. She figured there was no harm in doing another line. One was good, but two was better, so she reached for the tin and—

"You gonna be long?" a man boomed from outside, pounding on the door.

—it clattered to the floor.

Anna spun toward the door and shouted back, "I'm done when I'm done!" In the commotion, the tin had bounced under the urinal. "Fucking goddammit." It was wet.

Rinsing off the tin in the sink, she met eyes with her reflection. The subtle lines of her face seemed deeper in the bulb's glow. At twenty-six, Anna felt ancient.

"—*whatthefuck*," she muttered over the faucet's white noise, glimpsing a streak of red swirl down the drain. She examined her hands and the tin. Nothing. Rinsed clean.

The bulb's glow failed to reach the concrete floor, prompting her to use her phone's flashlight. More red. A pool had formed under the urinal from the adjacent stall. Anna crouched to shine her light under the partition: no feet, just a trickling of red.

Cocaine confidence inflamed her curiosity and led her to the stall door. After a few raps with her knuckle to ensure it was unoccupied, Anna nudged it open and—

OUTSIDE OF THE RESTROOM, the knocking man was in the middle of describing in great detail how bad he had to piss to a second man in line when panic erupted from behind the door.

"*Let me out!*" The knob thrashed, its lock spasmed.

The men rushed to help as the door flung open. Anna spilled out of the restroom and grabbed onto the shirt of the knocking man, vomiting buckets onto his chest.

"*HEYFUCK!*" he screamed, pushing her away.

She looked at him with tears in her eyes, bile dripping from her mouth, and whimpered, "—*oh god.*"

The second man burst into the restroom ready to fight some would-be rapist or attacker, but found it empty. Using his phone, he scanned the darkness for rats or anything else that might have frightened this woman in such a way.

Then he saw the red.

Approaching the stall, the man hesitated, his hand trembling. He stepped back with a deep breath, then nudged the door open with his boot. The contents of his bowels slammed against his clenched asshole.

There was the lanky bartender, his feet shoved into the toilet, pants around his ankles. The center of his throat was ripped open, draped with ribbons of flesh that hung like velvet curtains on a theater stage. His tongue, pulled down and out through the gash and slathered in wet red, writhed to the Tom Petty song echoing from the hallway—now on its seventh play.

The bartender's eyes fluttered in bursts of agony, aching for the death that promised to come at any moment. His sliced-open shirt revealed a torso riddled with stab wounds and five words gruesomely carved into his stomach and chest.

The man longed to fall to his knees and pray for forgiveness from anyone—or anything—willing to listen, yet remained frozen. The horrible message set his consciousness ablaze.

Each letter in the once tightly bound flesh oozed with blood. Each word radiated pain.

Combined, the words announced a new messiah, one to herald the arrival of his father in wait.

I AM THE DEVIL'S SON.

2

Suicide isn't funny, the wind whispered.

The bodies laughed. The trees stood silent. They all swayed.

Hector walked the trail knowing each step might be his last. The ground itself had threatened him when he arrived in the woods. *Wander off this path, and I will digest you for a millennia.*

The bodies swayed in rhythm with his every step. Their faces were mangled with no discernible mouths. He was unsure how they laughed, but they laughed.

The tops of the trees rustled. Something was watching. Hector craned his neck, but struggled to catch a glimpse. It sprawled across the canopy, casting shadow over the woods. The bodies all stopped laughing when it was their turn to bask in its shape.

Black bog water gurgled alongside the trail. In its reflection, he saw legs, each as long as a tree, and a body, bulbous and massive, belonging to the Something above.

The reflection dissipated as a face broke the water's surface. It flickered like an old TV.

He's coming. I'm sorry. I'm sorry. I'm— The voice became static, and the bodies sang:

As the pendulum swings,
The fingers twitch,
Everything we do leads us to this.
Nothing to fear,
Nothing to love,
No more birthdays to tire of.
Beautiful, beautiful, beautiful sway.

The face choked on the water. Two hands, each with more fingers than Hector could count, rose from below and pulled the face back into their abyss. The Something watched from above.

Hector approached the edge of the trees.

I have something to tell you, the Something said. Hector looked up and saw eight eyes peering through the mess of branches.

The ground nibbled at Hector's shoes. The smell of shit rose from the earth and the bodies grabbed the ropes around their necks, pulled themselves up, and gnawed their way to freedom. They fell to the ground that now seethed with frothing feces. Their corrupted bodies scrambled for one another. Limbs contorted, and the many become one pulsating mass. They fucked in the excrement and moaned through stretched necks.

Happy Birthday, the Something said.

Hector emerged from the trees to waves crashing against what he knew to be the Lake Michigan shore, their sound drowning out the forest's depravity. Gray light punctured the layer of cloud over a beach that stretched without end. Across the lake, the jewel of the flyover states sat, its skyline a crown on the horizon.

This limbo felt safe. It was quiet in the betweenness of it all —except for one little sound.

bzzz

A flash of pain shot through the back of Hector's leg. He snapped his head around, but saw nothing.

bzzzz

The sound grew louder, and the pain more pronounced. A shadow grew on his calf.

BZZZZZZZZZZ

The clouds above darkened, quivering as if composed of vibrating black pixels.

Hector looked back at his leg, now on fire with pain, to see the shadow spreading up his thigh, crawling and pulsing.

Flies.

He screamed and swatted, but more came, tearing over the shoreline from the blackened clouds. They chewed the skin of his neck, crawling over his jawline and onto his lips, as he scrambled back toward the forest.

Giant legs parted the trees like curtains. The Something emerged. It was the ugliest thing Hector had ever seen. A spider covered in sparse white hairs, with fangs the size of tree trunks and eyes like sparkling voids, stood at the edge of the woods.

Get in the water.

"Please! Help me!" Hector pleaded through shredded vocal cords.

GET IN THE WATER, the Something bellowed.

Hector obeyed, sprinting through the murk of flies and into Lake Michigan until he was submerged. Then kept going.

Silence. He sank to the bottom of the lake expecting to die, but didn't. So, he sat and waited. He waited for an answer to make itself apparent, but nothing came.

Then Hector felt wet, more wet than he felt was possible while already sitting on the floor of a lake. The water began to lower from above. Its surface rushed toward him. Lake Michigan was draining. It was draining directly into his pants.

After watching the last of the water empty into his crotch,

Hector found himself sitting in the middle of a crater where a lake had once been, surrounded by nothing but the smell of his own urine.

3

THE FIRST DAY

*G*odfuckingdammit.

Hector awoke fully clothed from last night to a familiar shame. The piss had soaked through his jeans and onto his bed. His eyelids tightened as he marinated in the wetness.

He had fallen asleep with his boots on again, and both feet throbbed, especially the right. The boot's sole had been detaching from the toe for weeks but had finally collapsed into a flapping mouth. It hung off the bed, slack-jawed. Hector groaned.

Last night's walk home was a blur. He remembered leaving his closing shift at Virgil's a few kitchen beers deep, just as the January snow began to fall. Flashes of Go Tavern. A handful of shots taken alone. More beer. No conversation. The last thing he recalled was the sight of four fresh inches covering the ground. The memory of trudging home while snow filled his flapping boot was gone, but the ache remained.

Trench foot crossed his mind. *Pathetic*, he thought. Those who died in World War I, boys younger than him, got trench foot, not drunk twenty-five-year-old pizza cooks.

Hector ground his knuckles into his temples, attempting to drive out the self-loathing that filled his body like cold concrete. His head felt like it carried a dead animal inside of it; his mouth tasted like it too. He gathered the fortitude to sit up. Then his phone vibrated.

Fuck.

On any other day, he wouldn't answer, but today he had no choice.

"Hi, Mom... Thank you... No, I know... No, I will... Yes, I am... No, I'm not... Don't worry... Everything's fine... I miss you too... I will soon... Thank you... I love you too... Bye."

Conversations with his mother were intense. He usually only got a few words in, which was fine by him. It kept the calls short and to the point. If Hector engaged too much, the conversations veered into unpleasant territory, and his mother would eventually bring up his father, which was *not* fine by him.

Hector didn't like thinking about his father, at least what little he could remember. There would be no call from him today, mostly because he was dead.

Two unopened text notifications waited on his phone. One from Sammie. And one from Austin.

Nope, he thought, and tossed his phone aside.

He lurched out of his room. There was Tommy, half on the couch, half on the bruised hardwood floor, boots also on and an unlit cigarette in his hand. His doe eyes were shut tight, and his mouth hung agape like a deer splattered against the grill of a truck. Hector considered waking him up, but decided to wait.

Hector chugged a glass of water at the kitchen sink. It trampolined off his guts and out his mouth, splatting with bile into the sink, leaving him even more dehydrated.

This day is already a waste, Hector thought.

It was ten. He needed to be at Virgil's by eleven.

Sitting naked on the toilet, the shame swelled as he passed

the loose byproduct of a predominantly liquid diet, then realized there was no toilet paper.

Hector waddled from the bathroom to the kitchen. The chill air of their poorly heated apartment greeted his bare buttocks. He rifled through a cabinet for the coffee filters, then waddled back, sighing as his feet shuffled across the floor.

In their household, wiping with a coffee filter was an art. You couldn't simply ball one up and go to town. No, the correct process involved ripping it in half and carefully folding each piece for multiple uses, ensuring at least four wipes per filter. This method demanded precision, but proved to be the most efficient.

With the bulk removed, Hector hopped in the shower. The mildewed curtain and scummy tiles were a cocoon. He would enter as a caterpillar, and exit still a caterpillar, but at least one no longer smelling of piss.

Around his neck dangled a gold chain with a pendant of Saint Christopher. It was all he had inherited from his father aside from the drinking, a commonality his mother reminded Hector of whenever possible.

He let the chain dance between his fingers under the falling water. As a child, he wore it visibly, eagerly telling classmates it was his dad's, a small consolation when he watched their fathers pick them up while he waited in the extended-day program for his mom to get off work.

Now, it was just something that hung around his neck, tucked in and out of sight. Where it came from didn't matter anymore. He simply wore it out of habit. Most days, he forgot it was even there, but on days like today, he spared the chain a thought.

His three-in-one shower gel stung his nostrils. The scent was something called *Mountain Edge* or *Ocean Bliss* or *Fuck you, I'm Irish*. He didn't remember, and the bottle's dollar store label fell off the first time it got wet. He considered masturbating, but couldn't find the will.

As the suds ran down his back to his legs, a pain ignited, burning like hot needles. He inhaled sharply through clenched teeth. Craning his neck, he saw what looked like small red hives —or bites, like bug bites.

The flies.

Hector shook the thought. Dreams were dreams. Worst case scenario was bed bugs. He made a mental note to double check his bed and their couch.

After rinsing off, he quickly dressed. Tommy was still passed out, half on the couch, half on the floor. Hector kicked his leg as he was walking out the door.

"Hey, we're out of toilet paper. Will you get some more from your work?"

"Uh-huh," Tommy grunted back without moving or opening his eyes. He often stole essentials from the Whole Foods employee restroom.

"Also, get up. You'll be late."

"I don't care." Tommy still did not move.

"It's Monday. I'll bring home some Mad Dogs."

Tommy shifted, and said, "Okay." He opened his eyes, and rolled over to face Hector. "And happy birthday, man."

"Thanks, bud," Hector said with a smile, then left.

4

"There's one in the closet, will you take it out back?" James was already covered in flour and making the day's first pizzas.

He tossed the dough in the air with style, making it look as effortless and cool as when he played guitar in his punk band on nights off. He was pushing forty, but seemed happy in the small, hot kitchen, forearms splattered with sauce, and a cold tallboy of beer already on the counter.

Hector took off his jacket. "C'mon, man, I just got here. Do I really have to start my day like that? You just let it sit there in pain waiting for me?"

"Sorry, dude. And no, I just noticed it right before you walked in. I've been here two hours already but had to clean vomit off the toilet from the night crew. Which—hey, you closed last night, right?"

"Alright, I'll take care of it."

Hector opened the closet to high-pitched squeals. The mouse's hind legs were stuck to the glue trap. He had asked the owner for more humane traps, but was told that releasing them outside meant they came right back in. It was an old building and mice were an inevitability.

He swept up the trap and placed it in a black garbage bag. In the alley, he apologized to his captive. "I'm sorry, little guy. It's either this or you get your legs ripped off. You're going to a better place, I'm sure."

"There is no better place for a creature like me."

Hector looked around, but no one was there. The tiny voice came from the bag.

Holy fuck, I'm losing it.

"And there is no better place for creatures like you, Hector Ghouseau. I will see you in the inferno. I look forward to watching *you* squeal in agony," the mouse squeaked.

Hector ripped the bag open and saw nothing but the blank eyes of a yelping mouse.

Alright, fuck this. He closed up the bag and swung it as hard as he could against the dumpster. The squealing stopped. He swung once more to be sure it was dead. A single fly escaped from a rip in the bag. Hector watched it make its way back into the kitchen.

"How'd it go?" James asked, pulling a pizza from the oven.

"Oh, fine. The mouse told me it was going to see me in Hell."

"Hey. You did what you had to do. It was either you or the mouse."

"Either me or the— What? No. It actually said that. I heard its voice. It spoke." Hector realized how crazy he sounded. "Is this what schizophrenia is? Am I schizophrenic?"

"We all hear voices sometimes." James cut the pizza in four powerful strokes. "How much did you drink last night?"

"A healthy amount."

"A healthy amount will do it. Your serotonin and dopamine are drained. The hungover brain is a brain on the brink of insanity. Just this morning, I thought my cat was shouting racial epithets. Turns out it was just my neighbor yelling about some teens blasting rap and my cat yawning. It happens. Can you unlock the doors? We're good to open."

Hector flipped the open sign and started on some dishes before the prep list. The smell of the hot water and sanitizer in the empty sauce bucket nauseated him as the steam hit his face.

His phone vibrated in his pocket. He couldn't handle any more unopened texts from Sammie or Austin right now. But it was a dating app message. A date with Jess M. and her dyed-orange hair sounded a lot better than spending his birthday crushing Mad Dogs with Tommy until they passed out.

"You know what time it is, Hector?"

"Can we not today? Let's just relax and listen to some music."

"But it's Monday! New episode is out. I have no choice. My hands are tied."

The kitchen Bluetooth speaker blared a remixed version of the *X-Files* theme with sampled quotes from Donald Trump, Lyndon B. Johnson, H. W. Bush, and Hilary Clinton—the supposed harbingers of the New World Order.

"What's up, motherfuckers! It's ya boy, Scotty Durango. Welcome to another dick-shredding episode of The Illuminaughty Zone. *The place where we want the truth and nothing but the truth! You feel me? We're talking about the good, the bad, the ugly, the lizards, the backroom deals, the shadow people, and the devil-worshiping, blood-drinking, murdering elites that make your life a living hell! But first, let's plug some of my upcoming dates. We're going to be in Dayton, Ohio, at The Chuckle Factory on February 12th..."*

Scotty Durango, a comedian who found more success ranting about blood-drinking pedophiles and lizard people than with his own stand-up, grated Hector's ears. It was painful. James, enjoying both the rants and Hector's agitation, took a swig of his tallboy and leaned out the kitchen window into the dining room, smiling.

Hector began to cut some tomatoes, and tried to ignore *Illimuninaughty* blaring from the speaker, returning his thoughts to the mouse.

James' explanation made perfect sense to him. Hector had heard his fair share of voices before. But the normal ones that told him he was a piece of shit and that he should kill himself sounded nothing like the mouse. That voice definitely existed outside of his head.

"—*and February 12th at The Hyuck Hyuck Hut in Fort Wayne, Indiana.*"

If there was a Hell, it seemed reasonable to Hector that he would go there, but how the fuck did the mouse know that?

"*Our guest today is an expert in the field of demonology. He's a professor of English at the Institute of Technical Trade and Technology in Lake Station, Indiana, and author of the book* The New Inferno. *Please welcome Dr. Fewer to the show! Thanks for being here, Doc.*"

"*Thank you for having me, Scotty.*"

Dr. Fewer's voice held an unshakable confidence that commanded Hector's attention away from the mouse. Hearing him speak, he wondered if the man was insane, a sincere academic, or a snake oil salesman like Scotty Durango.

"*There is war for our souls being waged, and it's important the truth reaches as many as possible before it's too late.*"

Sincere academic was out. Hector leaned toward insane.

The door dinged. First customer of the day. Hector set his knife down and mentally prepared himself with a deep breath before exiting the kitchen.

The man unzipped his designer coat and tapped his pristine Italian-leather boots free of snow. Hector had not bought a new pair of anything in years. The elastic on the underwear he wore was purely for show at this point. He and the man looked to be roughly the same age.

Hector forced a smile, and, in a voice that wasn't quite his own, said. "Hi there! How are y—?"

The man raised a finger in a *hold-on-a-sec* fashion. He had earbuds in and was on the phone. He walked up to the counter and leaned on it, continuing his own conversation.

"I don't understand what her fucking problem is. It's none of her business what I do with my time or money. She acts like I need to tell her everything. It's fucking exhausting, bro. Don't get married."

Hector stood at the register with his hands at his sides, unsure if he should walk back into the kitchen or continue to stand there like a jackass. He looked at the man to establish eye contact, but was ignored.

"It's just bullshit, ya know? Can't even wipe my own ass without her telling me I'm doing it wrong."

Hector imagined that this man bought fancy toilet paper—at least two-ply, and surely never wiped with coffee filters.

"How 'bout this? Tonight, you, me, and Matt are going to Slippery Slope. We'll split a bag. I don't even care if she knows. It's my money. Maybe she can do something other than free-lance blog if she wants to start talking shit about how I spend it." He snorted, then snickered. "It's not my fault she majored in English. You know what I mean?"

Hector opted to walk back into the kitchen.

"This guy ordering or what?" James asked.

"He's on the phone. Who knows."

James peeked out the kitchen window, scratched his head where a tattoo of a pencil sat above his ear, then went back to doodling on an empty pizza box some lucky customer would later receive. A demon with five tongues kick-flipped on a skateboard, one hand gripping a massive bong, the tongues flapping like flags.

"So you're telling me that these demons just walk among us? Like,

they're standing in line with us in Burger King waiting to nosh down on a Whopper like me? Is this like Men in Black? *Have you seen* Men in Black, *Dr. Fewer?"*

Dr. Fewer chuckled, as if his own explanation would be less ridiculous. *"No, Scotty, it's nothing like* Men in Black, *actually. Think of the whole of reality as a sandwich."*

"Okay, now you're speaking my language," Scotty Durango said.

"Often, there are many layers to a sandwich. You have your bread, your meats, your veggies, your cheese. Each of these layers has its own components and origin. In order for a sandwich to properly operate as a sandwich, these layers must be maintained. When these layers are breached, the integrity of the sandwich is compromised. It becomes a mess. The sandwich falls apart."

"And which layer are we, Dr. Fewer? The cheese? The meat?" Durango said the last word as if the joke was self-evident.

"Our dimension is but one middle layer. One of many. But it is the bread that is key."

James dropped his jaw in anticipation at Hector, who rolled his eyes and kept with the tomatoes.

"You see, it is the bread that makes a sandwich. Without the bread, it is, at best, a salad, and, at worst, ingredients lying in a pile on a plate. In this reality sandwich, the meat, the cheese, and the veggies are interchangeable. There are endless possible combinations for how they can be arranged. However, the bread must remain on the outside."

Hector peeked around the kitchen door to check if the man at the counter was still on his phone. He was.

"Now, imagine there is one piece of bread that wants to tear through all the other layers and make its way toward the other slice and become one again. If this were to happen, reality as we know it would crumble. Slices of cheese, meat, and vegetables floating in an endless abyss."

"So there is a good slice of bread and a bad slice of bread?"

"Yes," Dr. Fewer said with the confidence of an absolute madman. *"And their crumbs trickle into our world. Demons are here. They can't be seen, but they can be felt. They can't always touch us, but they can corrupt. They want us to be the instruments of our own demise. They don't believe creatures like us deserve to exist. To them, we are just debris to kindle their inferno."*

Hector's ears perked up at *creatures* and *inferno*. The mouse had used those same words.

Scotty Durango's voice exploded from the Bluetooth speaker. *"Whoa! You just blew my mind, Doc! So you're telling me that there is a Hell? And not only that, but that it's going to fuck us right through the ass on the way to fuck Heaven in its ass? And not ONLY that, but that there's a ONE HUNDRED PERCENT CERTAINTY that Hector Ghouseau, the sad little fuck cutting tomatoes right now, is headed there ass-first to get fucked by the devil's big red throbbing COCK? That's some fucking shit, Doc."*

Hector dropped his knife to the floor. The room spun, and his spine turned to jelly. He gripped the prep table to keep himself upright. His body didn't know how to react. It froze, twitched, and wanted to shit itself all at once.

The man from the counter's head poked into the kitchen. "Anybody working here or what?"

Hector's eyes remained on his cutting board, unblinking.

"Yo, Hector, will you ring this guy up?" James shouted over the podcast in a manner that indicated he had definitely not heard what Hector had.

"Uh, yeah. You got it. Sorry." Hector blinked away the spots in his vision, his grip loosened.

The man at the counter sighed and rolled his eyes, earbuds still in. "Slice of cheese," he said.

"Hello to you too," Hector mumbled.

"Excuse me?"

"Slice of cheese," Hector repeated the order, averting his eyes.

He reached to pull out his wallet. "Don't take your hangover out on me, bro. I was here waiting."

What did he just say? How does he know I'm hungover? Is he in on it with the mouse? The podcast?

Hector quickly remembered that he most definitely looked like shit, and it would be abundantly clear to anyone with two functional eyes that he was hungover. He shook any thoughts that this relatively put-together man was some demonic entity and concluded that he was just a dick.

"You were on the phone," said Hector.

"And?"

There was no point in arguing. "Slice of cheese," Hector confirmed once more.

"That's what I said."

"Four dollars and eighty-three cents."

BACK IN THE KITCHEN, James warmed up a slice of cheese while Scotty Durango asked the real questions.

"Greta Thunberg. Jimmy Kimmel. Barack Obama. Are they possessed by demons? You can't tell me there's not some dark-fucking-arts shit going on with them, right, Doc?"

Dr. Fewer thought for a moment, then answered, *"I can't definitively say who is influenced directly by demons and who is not. It's quite possible they are, but demonic activity works almost like a grassroots political campaign. They enact change from the bottom. They are very patient. If they have the masses, they don't need to rely on just a handful of individuals to do their bidding. The population will carry it out willingly. They play small ball. The long game. The point I want to communicate to your listeners is that they are in danger. The greatest power evil has is that it can operate in the shad-*

ows. We don't see them. We don't hear them. But they have the ability to sway us like the wind."

Hector waited on the other side of the kitchen window watching James plate the man's order.

"Will you turn this shit off?" he asked.

"No can do. How else am I supposed to stay informed?" James smirked, passing him the steaming slice. "Order up."

Hector dragged himself to the man's table. "Slice of cheese."

The man kept his eyes glued to his phone without a word, not noticing the single fly bathing its black bristled body in the scalding grease of his pizza.

It seemed to be enjoying itself.

5

The sun was already down when he clocked out at five. The gray day had turned black. Hector walked to Armitage Food, his flapping boot duct-taped shut, courtesy of the Virgil's utility closet.

Armitage Food was a corner store that didn't sell much food. Cheap beer, malt liquor, and flavored fortified wine, or *bum wine*, filled their shelves and coolers. Hector and Tommy were bum wine connoisseurs.

There was Night Train, Wild Irish Rose, Thunderbird, and Cisco. They were the bottles seen littered underneath overpasses, fossilized in abandoned lots and unkempt grass. They lay shattered in alleys and filled with piss on CTA platforms. Bum wines were known for three things: high alcohol percentage by volume, artificial flavoring, and low price.

While Hector and Tommy enjoyed those other brands, today was Mad Dog Monday.

With flavors like Orange Jubilee, Banana Red, and Bling Bling Blue Raspberry, Mad Dog tasted like melted candy and bleach. Hector perused the selection and settled on two bottles of Bling Bling Blue Raspberry, then grabbed two forties of King Cobra as apéritifs.

"Hello, buddy, buddy," said the withered man behind the counter.

"Hi, Bronek."

"We have your favorite, buddy. *Hamm's*," he said, motioning to a wall of the cheapest thirty-packs of beer they sold.

Embarrassed by his association with the cheap beer, Hector forced a chuckle and said, "Maybe later."

Bronek was an old Polish man, a relic from Nelson Algren's Chicago. He always spoke with a smile, and seemed to like Hector despite more than once finding him passed out in front of the building. He'd even chased away some opportunistic teenagers who tried to steal Hector's bike during one of these episodes.

He also liked Tommy, though he was more wary of him. Tommy had a habit of urinating in places that shouldn't be urinated in. This included the front of Bronek's store.

Last summer, while Hector bought beer inside, the police drove by and happened to see Tommy relieving himself out front. The cops flung Tommy against their car and threatened him with sex offender status based on the proximity of the school across the street, despite it being one in the morning and the middle of July.

When Bronek saw this, he burst out of his store, yelling, "That is my best customer! You free him! He shops with me. He is okay. He is a fine boy."

The cops were so amused at this old Polish man defending the young alcoholic that they cut Tommy loose, laughing through the entire exchange.

As Bronek rang up the Mad Dogs, Hector eyed the pictures of who he assumed was Bronek's family taped to the register and the counter. They were old photos, some from what looked like the early 1970s, some much older, faded images of children, friends, and several of the same woman.

An emptiness tugged on his chest as he studied the photos. Hector had no such pictures of his family. He barely had any friends. His life's photo album would be filled with blank pages and old liquor store receipts.

"Why do you look unsettled?" Bronek asked. This surprised Hector. Their conversations were always business. Social formalities were kept to a minimum.

"Unsettled?" Hector laughed, trying to throw Bronek off his scent. "No, I'm not unsettled. Why do you say that?"

"I see it in your eyes. In the way you are carrying yourself today. I sense these things."

Hector smiled and waved his hand. "No, no, just a rough day. You know how it goes."

Bronek nodded. "The rough days make way for the good days. It is all God's will. Do you pray?"

Hector was now officially unsettled. Of all the things to discuss with Bronek, God was near the bottom of the list. "No, I don't pray."

Bronek began bagging the bottles. "You must. When hard days come, you must speak to God. Work. Love. Fear. Death. These are all okay. This is all God's plan. He will help you."

Plan? Hector thought of the mouse, the podcast, and the inferno. *What a fucking plan.* "And if God doesn't listen, then what do you do?"

"Buddy, buddy. He is always listening. It is you who must listen. Even in his silence, he says so much."

Hector looked again at the taped photographs, and then to Bronek. He was the only person he'd ever seen working here. Every single shift. If these friends and family were still alive, Bronek saw them rarely, if at all.

"Yeah, well, I think God's plan is shit sometimes. I wish

maybe he'd ask for our input every now and then, you know?" Hector handed Bronek a small stack of singles, all the tips he'd earned during his shift.

"Happy. Sad. Good. Shit. It is all his plan. Once you accept, life is easy." He shrugged to emphasize it was no big deal. "We all die. And we all die alone. Dying alone is God's plan."

Hector became more unsure of what Bronek was trying to tell him with each new word that came out of his mouth. Was this speech supposed to make him want to drink even more? Because it was. His blood had already been itching, but now his left hand began to quake.

"You're right about part of that," Hector said, taking the bag from Bronek. "As soon as I get this in me, I'll be much less unsettled. And if I wander back in here to buy a case of Hamm's later, then that will be part of God's plan too."

"Absolutely, buddy." Bronek smiled.

"Alright. Have a good one."

"You too, my friend."

6

PART TWO

N o windows. Red carpet. The bar was detached from existence.

The young man took a seat on a stool. "Beer and a shot, please. Whatever's cheapest for both."

He couldn't quite remember how he got here. It had been a long night at other shit bars, and he had grown accustomed to not knowing. He only knew he was running from something. He always ran. Always away, never toward.

The coaster read *Viudas*. He shifted it around the bartop with his finger.

The bartender placed the shot of liquor down along with the beer. "It's the good stuff. On the house. Don't worry."

The young man couldn't get a good look at the bartender's face, though he stood just feet away. It scrambled like an old TV with a weak signal. He looked like a new person with each moment.

He convinced himself that he was seeing things. A drink would clear his head.

"Thanks, 'preciate it." The shot was mezcal, he was pretty

sure. The cage around his brain creaked open. He ordered another.

The only other patron in the bar, a woman, took the seat next to him.

She spoke Spanish, with bits of English sprinkled in. They struggled to communicate, but the struggle broke the ice. He asked her if she worked here. She said she did.

They drank.

Her name was tattooed across her knuckles. "It's so I don't forget," Andy said with a wink. She drank her beer through a straw to protect her lipstick.

"I forget my name too sometimes," the young man said. "But when that happens, I'm usually not in any shape to read it either."

Another shot. This time with Andy.

The well-dressed owner of Viudas stood in the shadows, his eyes masked by tinted glasses.

"Are you a server here? Off duty?"

"Not a server. A drinking companion." She smiled and touched his arm.

The night distorted.

Idle chatter. Favorite colors. Zodiac signs.

"And what about you? What month were you born in?" he asked her.

"This month. January."

"No kidding. My son is January too. It's actually his birthday today—" He tried to recall why he was here and not with him, but the specifics sat on an empty shelf. Unreachable.

Her walls cracked.

Andy said she had children too. She worked at Viudas for them.

Her eyes sank. The young man placed a hand on hers and

told her that everything would be okay. The very structure of the bar seemed to recoil in disgust, retching and gagging.

For the duration of a single blink, her skin flashed carved lines that covered her every inch, some scarred, some still bleeding. Tally marks. Strokes of red against her honey flesh. He told himself once more that he was seeing things.

The owner stepped out from the shadows. Andy noticed. She changed the subject to something lighter, and placed her hand on his thigh. The young man melted.

"Want to get out of here?" He stood for his wallet, swaying. It was empty.

Andy said she couldn't leave.

The owner approached. The drinks were on the house. But how about one hour with Andy? Two-hundred dollars.

"Sorry. No money."

Check again.

Two one-hundred-dollar bills sat within its fold.

The young man tried once more to remember how he arrived, but all he could conjure was the image of a boy without a father on his fifth birthday. He needed to see him. There had to be a photo in his wallet— Gone— Or maybe never there.

He's better off without me. He wanted his son to be happy, to never step foot in a place like this, to be anything but like him.

The owner repeated the offer. His voice eclipsed all other thoughts.

Andy's white pumps rested on her stool's footrest. Her dress rode up to the tops of her thighs as she sat sipping beer through her straw. Her pulled-back hair, the scattered tattoos on her hands and arms, and the subtle curves of her body were magnetic. She didn't even have to look at him to draw him in. Andy demanded to be worshiped without uttering a word.

The young man said yes like there was never a doubt in his mind.

They were led to a back room and brought rocks glasses filled with whiskey and diluted with water, then left alone.

It started without a sound. She climbed atop him and unbuttoned his pants. The stale air hung dead in the room as their bodies moved against one another. Her routine was choreographed, but this purchased intimacy was more tangible than any love he could remember. She put him inside her, and traced around his left ear with her tongue.

He moaned as her warmth radiated from his loins to his chest. This was the life he was meant for, he thought, what he always wanted. He was born for this.

She ran her hands through his hair, then leaned forward, her head next to his, and rode him in slow, controlled motions, her breath heavy on his neck. At that moment, he loved her, and he told her so. His words transported her to a time before Viudas, when she loved and was loved, then it was gone. She kept riding.

Their tongues coiled like pit vipers as he came deep inside of her.

Andy gave him a kiss on the cheek, straightened her dress, then left the room without a word.

The young man downed a diluted whiskey and did his best to regain his composure. The door opened, and in walked the owner with the tinted glasses.

"Did you enjoy yourself?"

The young man, piss drunk and elated from his encounter with Andy, nodded.

"What else would you like? Maybe I can help."

He just wanted to go home.

"You can't go home."

The young man didn't understand.

The man in the tinted glasses sighed. He placed a chair

directly across from him and sat, then covered the young man's eyes with his hand.

Through the darkness of the owner's hand, the young man saw himself drifting downward into cold, black water. He was drowning.

He yanked away and fell out of his chair, stammering that it wasn't real, wasn't possible.

The lights went out, and the room dissolved into nothing. An abyss.

A low buzz arose from where the man in the tinted glasses sat, like heavy static. "Did you jump, or did you fall? Or were you too drunk to even recall? I brought you here from the brink of death, but as I said, maybe I can help."

The young man asked what he wanted.

"In my line of work, we deal in souls." The voice came from every direction.

The young man pawed at the ground, trying to crawl away, but the darkness was thick as glue.

"I can save you. You will live to indulge again. I can make it so you meet a new Andy every day. All I require is your soul."

The young man tried to consider the offer, but he could only think of his son. Today was his birthday, and he was drowning in a river by his own accord or stupidity. He didn't deserve to live.

He made his decision. He was ready to die.

"If that's what you wish. There are other fish in the sea."

But the young man had a counteroffer.

"Go on."

The young man explained. The owner mulled it over.

The lights returned without warning, and the young man found himself back on the red carpet of Viudas, the man in the tinted glasses still sitting above him, adjusting his cuffs.

"What you ask for can't be done for the price of just *your* soul. I need more."

The young man explained that he had nothing more to give.

"Oh, but you do." He brought his face close to the young man's. "You are a father."

The young man caught a glimpse behind the tinted glasses. A mosaic of ocular facets, like an insect's, glowed red behind the tint, each an individual window to Hell.

"A piece of *your* soul resides in your son. Not enough to declare it as your own and sell it, but I know a loophole," the owner explained as if he was helping him cheat on his taxes.

The young man tried to listen, but his grip on reality slipped further. *Reality.* Freezing water filling his lungs. This pitstop on the way to oblivion. Neither were guaranteed real. He let his hand drift to his side, clenching and unclenching his fingers, searching for the resistance of water between them, but found only frigid air emanating from the man in the tinted glasses like a miasmic fog.

"Instead of a sale, we make a wager. You have enough claim to your son's soul to set the parameters, but his fate will ultimately be his own. That way," the owner leaned back and dusted his hands, "it's all nice and legal, and *He* can't be upset."

As he explained the deal, the young man wondered if "*He*" meant God. He wondered a lot of things. His consciousness spun, along with his head from the liquor. Whatever this *thing* was proposing, it could be his one chance to make things right for his son.

The man in the tinted glasses stuck out his hand. "Do we have a deal?"

He had heard the terms, but they remained a puzzle. His racing thoughts scrambled to put the pieces together. *His son. A birthday. A pursuit. A beautiful sway. Three days.* He tried to piece it all together.

Three days.

He asked the man in the tinted glasses to repeat the terms,

but he refused. "You have until the count of three to shake my hand, before you get only death and the misery that follows."

One.

Two.

The young man shook the outstretched hand.

The man in the tinted glasses smiled. "Fantastic."

With a sharp crash, the lightbulbs shattered.

The heavy static returned, throbbing in the darkness like an industrial machine. Then a new sound, as grating as sandpaper against raw skin, like an orchestra of screeching violins, rose from the nether as if a volume knob was slowly being turned. Thousands of small voices. Rallying. Laughing. Jubilant in their sadism.

The young man tried to pull away, but the owner's hand had perverted into something monstrous. The appendage grew into a slithering vine that wound around his arm and up his torso. A second tendril snaked its way into the young man's mouth, its thorns slicing the skin around his lips. It writhed over his gums and tongue, searching for its prize.

"Found it," the owner hissed.

The vine latched onto something in the back of the young man's mouth, then pulled. The sound of a single tooth ripped from its socket reverberated through the black. The chorus of tiny voices cheered.

Then, nothing.

The lights were back on, and the young man was alone. Blood gushed down his chin and onto the carpet. The owner was gone. The sounds had stopped. He tiptoed out of the room as if the floor was a minefield.

He emerged to see Andy seated at the bar. Her head hung at the sight of his bloody mouth as a small notch carved itself into the side of her neck, blossoming red.

The young man exploded through the front door of Viudas and out into the night that awaited him. It was total darkness. So dark and so deep that he fell into it and continued to sink until his lungs burst from the cold, black water.

7

Tommy was sitting on the couch drinking a beer when Hector walked in.

"Getting started without me?" Hector asked, shutting the cold out behind him.

"I got started about five hours ago on my lunch break. If I stop now, I'm pretty sure I'll die."

Hector nodded. "Rough day?"

"I worked the panini station, and I forgot my hat so they made me wear a hairnet."

"Probably not very flattering."

"I looked like a lunch lady," Tommy said. "And on the way home, I bummed a homeless guy a smoke, and he said that I reminded him of himself when he was younger. I wasn't really sure how to take that."

Hector plopped down on the couch next to him. "Today a mouse told me that I was going to Hell."

"Okay, so you get it," Tommy said, and took a swig.

Hector distributed the Mad Dogs. They said *cheers*, and let the sugary poison flood their systems until the bottles emptied. Nothing mattered now. Everything was again a joke. The lingering dread from the day faded. They played records and cracked their King Cobras and talked shit.

The same topics of conversation arose every night. Their world was small and relegated to just a few neighborhoods. Outside Chicago was foreign territory, and it was rarely discussed.

Sticking to the topic of work, Hector vented about the Virgil's customer who called him out for being hungover. Tommy giggled into his King Cobra. "*And* he called you 'bro'? Damn. He got your ass, dude."

"And of course I overhear him say he was going to Slippery Slope tonight. I fucking hate that bar. Nothing but dumb dicks and overpriced drinks there. Fuck that place." The Mad Dog buzz overtook Hector. His lips were looser, and his thoughts more resentful. He opened the dating app on his phone.

"I don't mind Slip Slop. They've got really nice individual bathrooms. Perfect for doing drugs," Tommy said without missing a beat.

The d-word triggered a receptor in both their brains, but they were too broke to act on it, so Tommy continued. "If a girl wanted to meet there, I'd go, but I'd rather just hang out here. Our apartment is the ideal date spot. We've got everything!" he said, gesturing toward the spinning record and the aluminum folding chair they kept out for company.

"Okay, first of all, Tommy, no girl wants to sit here and watch you get drunk on the couch and fall asleep with a lit cigarette in your hand."

"Unlit."

"Second of all, when was the last time you went on what could be considered a date?"

"How was Maggie not a date?"

"The girl you met at Go Tavern? Splitting a bag of cocaine

and getting a through-the-pants handjob underneath the bar is not a date."

"That was an act of pure intimacy."

"Have you seen her since you shared this magical moment?"

"Well, no. But love is fleeting. We shared what we shared, and that will always exist. Why try to make things permanent? That's how people get hurt. What we had was no less real than a couple who've been together for twenty years and hate each other's guts."

While Tommy rambled, Hector went to the bathroom, pissing with the door open. "Love isn't real," he shouted over his own stream, then burped. "It's just chemicals and shit. And even if it was real—which it's not—you getting a hard-on for someone you don't even fucking know is not love."

"Just because it's chemicals and shit doesn't make it any less real." Tommy lit up a cigarette on the couch. He was a romantic. Even though he'd never had a real girlfriend, he was well-versed in sloppy rendezvous. Every so often, a young woman mistook Tommy or Hector's self-loathing and substance abuse as mysterious or *endearingly misanthropic.* Sleeping with either was typically a catalyst for the woman to reevaluate her life.

Tommy continued, "Any day could be our last. We could die tomorrow. Shit, we can die today. If I choked on my own vomit in my sleep tonight—"

"Jesus, man. Pretty specific, huh?" Hector flushed the toilet.

"I'm just trying to be realistic."

Hector emerged from the bathroom fumbling with his belt. "Dude, can't you smoke outside?"

"It's fucking cold out. And don't change the subject. If I choked on my own vomit in my sleep tonight, and the only love I ever felt in this miserable trudge of a life was from an over-the-pants penis rub under the bar at Go Tavern from a girl I just met, then that is real love. It's real to me. It's the realest love I ever felt."

"Just because it's the realest love *you* ever felt does not make it real love. Remember when you sold plasma and they fucked up your check so you were paid one thousand dollars instead of one hundred? Remember how rich you *felt*? It was the most money you ever received at once. But you weren't rich. Rich people wipe their ass with one thousand dollars. That guy at Virgil's earlier? He has a savings account. Do we have savings accounts?"

"We do not," Tommy said.

"Exactly. You felt rich that day, but you weren't rich. We spent that money on coke, the bar, and Chinese food. *Poof.* Gone in one night."

"So what you're saying is…"

"I don't know what the fuck I'm saying, to be honest. We'll never be rich, and we'll never be in love."

Tommy hung his head. Then they broke out laughing.

"Cheers to that." Tommy raised his King Cobra.

"Cheers," Hector said, smiling. They had a habit of turning their darkest thoughts into punchlines. It made them hurt less.

Hector continued the joke. "There's no long game here. Just a short dead-end road."

"And we're barreling down that thing at top speed."

"Faster we go, faster it's over."

They both chuckled.

Tommy wrinkled his brow and thought for a moment. "But you've been in love."

Hector knew that was coming. "You know she texted me today?"

"No shit?"

"Her *and* Austin."

"Goddamn. Double trouble. What did they want?"

"Well, I didn't open hers."

Tommy rolled his eyes. "You need to text her back."

Hector knew that. He wanted nothing more than to talk to Sammie, but couldn't bring himself to perform the Herculean task of picking up the phone. Though he ached to hear her voice, to touch her face, he hadn't the strength to reach across the past that divided them. Most days, he had no strength at all.

Tommy's face grew serious. "And Austin?"

"He's in town and wants to talk."

"You didn't say yes, did you?"

"I didn't respond."

"Good." Tommy exhaled. "Please don't."

Hector wanted to nip this conversation in the bud. He polished off the rest of his King Cobra and asked, "Can I have one of your beers?"

"Yeah, for sure. Grab me one too."

He shuffled to the kitchen and opened the refrigerator. Next to the beer was a large cupcake encased in a plastic clamshell container. It had a marble base with red icing threads hanging like lacework around thick, off-white frosting.

Hector grabbed two beers and headed back to the living room.

"What's with the cupcake?"

Tommy's face lit up. "That's for you, dude!"

Hector didn't know how to receive gifts, or anything positive really, so he said, "They'll notice you stealing from the bakery. Those are expensive."

"I didn't fucking steal it," Tommy snapped back. He straightened his posture and proudly stated, "I bought it."

Hector couldn't help but grin like an idiot. His chest warmed. He didn't feel he deserved a friend like Tommy.

"Hey," he said, holding up the two beers, "want to go on the porch and shotgun these?"

Tommy nodded. "Yes. Yes, I do."

They stood on their second-floor apartment porch, an uneven wooden structure overlooking a small overpass with long-abandoned railroad tracks. Being the last building on the block, their view of the overpass across the street was unobstructed.

Their eyes were both drawn to the large tree that grew from the center of the tracks, a middle finger to man's attempt at industry.

"Want to?" Tommy asked.

"Let's do it."

They staggered down the wooden steps, crossed the street, and began their ascent up the overpass, wading through frozen trash and dead weeds until they made it to the top of the tracks.

They stood for a moment, taking in Drake Avenue from above, too drunk to feel the January wind. Streetlights illuminated the rows of three flats.

Tommy patted the large tree like it was an old friend, then punctured his beer can with his keys. Hector did the same.

"Happy birthday." Tommy raised his beer to Hector.

"Thanks, bud."

They popped the tabs and shotgunned their beers beneath the gray moonlight.

Back inside, Hector got the cupcake and two forks. They both devoured it.

With a fresh coat of fool's hope, both were ready to venture out into the winter night.

They scrolled through their phones while a record spun.

"People from work are hanging out in Bridgeport. Want to go?" Tommy asked.

"Bridgeport?" Hector groaned. "I don't want to ride down there. I'll get too drunk and be stuck on the South Side."

"Well, what are you going to do?"

Hector's phone buzzed in his hand—a dating app notification. It was Jess M. "I might meet up with someone for a drink or two."

"Oh yeah? Where at?"

"Oh, you know, just somewhere in Logan," Hector said.

"No, I don't know. How about you tell me?"

"Don't worry about it."

"Say it," Tommy demanded.

"Slippery Slope."

Tommy laughed, then finished his beer.

8

A fly on the wall listened to their entire conversation—a spider too.

The fly leered and rubbed its front appendages together as Hector walked in the door wet with snow. It noticed the subtle look of joy on Tommy's face.

This one cares.

It watched them pour sugary poison down their throats. Artificially dyed spittle spritzed from their mouths and dribbled down their chins.

Disgusting creatures, the fly thought, nibbling on a morsel of shit it had saved between the coarse hairs of its black thorax.

It watched them wallow in self-pity. They were slaves to the most rudimentary aspects of the flesh. The drunker they became, the more their minds turned to fucking. In the pursuit of ejaculation, they found purpose and validation.

Astonishingly pathetic.

The fly imagined holding them captive in its own miserable domain on the other side of reality's veil. Its brothers and sisters would gnaw the skin off their scrotums and chew it like bubble gum.

Its barbed penis hardened.

Across the room, the spider sensed the fly's arousal. He had no respect for its kind and did his best to ignore its vulgar display.

The fly knew it was being watched. It was confident there was nothing the spider could do to stop its master's plan. *Let him watch.*

It salivated at the thought of its swarm pouring down Hector's throat, pulling his intestines up through his mouth until it was too full of his own sweet blood and digestive tract to scream.

Its fly erection twitched in anticipation.

The spider's general assessment of Tommy and Hector was similar to the fly's own. He wasn't thrilled with the task he'd been given, but he was a company man and would do what he had to do.

Hector's piss stream filled the apartment with its sound. The spider rolled all eight of his eyes.

Observations continued. Tommy and Hector drank and talked nonsense, eventually stepping outside to, presumably, drink and talk nonsense in the cold.

hsssssss

The fly sent a taunt the spider's way and waved its tiny barbed penis in his general direction.

The spider didn't fear the fly in the least. It was an abomination, a warped miscarriage of creation. It belonged to a legion of shit. He ignored it.

The flies moved like dust through the vents of reality, and served a master more despised and relentless than Lucifer himself.

The spider couldn't believe he actually preferred Lucifer to anyone, but at least Lucifer had grown apathetic over the centuries before recently going MIA altogether. The fly's master carried a torch for a fight the spider thought was settled long ago, he tested the boundaries between worlds, and, like a fly, he always found a way in.

The front door swung open. Tommy and Hector discussed plans for a cupcake.

Out of the corner of his eyes, the spider noticed the fly vigorously masturbating, derailing its own reconnaissance mission.

The fly's body shook in ecstasy and fell off the wall, dead in this world. Its small heart apparently exploding as it came to the thought of Tommy's flayed-open face.

These small soldiers were fragile in this realm, but the spider knew the hive mind was aware of whatever intel this spy collected. Reinforcements would surely follow.

Time was always a factor, but this was more urgent than he had previously thought.

As Hector bid Tommy goodbye, the spider soared through the air on a single thread, its white abdomen hairs swaying, and landed on Hector's back. It was time to go to Slippery Slope.

9

Hector scanned the room. He shook off the cold and made his way to the bar.

It was dark, but it was always dark in Slippery Slope. Sparse purple lighting ensured patrons could see just well enough to not spill their drinks while maintaining the cosmopolitan sleaze it was known for. The scent of vermouth and bitters filled the air, and the sound of ice in a cocktail shaker danced over some 80s pop hit. Hector felt out of his element. He took a seat at the bar.

The bartender approached with a smile. "How are we doing tonight?"

He was tall and walked without slouching. His t-shirt sleeves were cuffed to accentuate budding biceps, and his arms held tattoos in just the right places to complement, but not distract from, his slender, toned physique.

Hector's face was doughy, and his body was skinny fat without defined muscle. He felt like a misshapen lump of clay compared to Michelangelo's *David* behind the bar.

"Good." Hector tried not to slur. "How about yourself?"

"Doing good, man. 'Cept this weather. So over the cold. What can I get you?"

"Well, I'm just waiting for someone right now." Hector craned his neck, searching the bar. He didn't see his date. "But can I do a Hamm's and a shot of Old Crow?"

"You got it."

Hector's phone buzzed. It was her.

Five minutes, the text read.

The bartender poured the shot in front of him. Hector dumped it down his throat without a word, then took a slug of beer before exhaling. "Thanks. I'm sorry. Can I do one more?" he said, pointing to the empty shot glass.

"Nervous?"

"Huh?"

"First date, right? I see enough of them. I'm perceptive like that," the bartender explained. "Chain-drinking is a tell-tale sign."

"Should I slow down?"

The bartender shrugged. "You seem alright to me," he said, refilling Hector's shot before leaving.

Very perceptive, Hector thought. Between the Mad Dog, King Cobra, auxiliary beers, and the two shots, Hector straddled the border of "alright."

His phone vibrated with another text. It was Austin. Hector wondered if people could take hints anymore. The phone went back in his pocket.

It was a steady Wednesday night. Dates. Post-work drinks. Friends laughing. This wasn't the type of place where someone came alone to stare into a glass, so Hector didn't care for it.

He preferred Go Tavern on Armitage, a half-liquor store, half-bar. It offered the best of both worlds. His favorite time was late afternoon, when it was populated exclusively with old Puerto Rican men. They sat seats apart, occasionally shouting in

Spanish and laughing, before returning to their silence. It was perfect.

Hector knew a bit of Spanish from his mom. She was Mexican, his dad Polish—both second generation. Teachers and classmates used to ask about his last name, since it sounded like neither ethnicity. His grandmother had made up the French-sounding surname when they arrived in America, thinking it more *dignified* than the string of phlegmy consonants his Polish grandfather originally bestowed upon her.

But people had stopped asking a long time ago.

"Holy shit! Is that Hector Ghouseau? The fuck is up, dog?"

A voice like Tom Waits with laryngitis boomed from behind his barstool, startling both Hector and the spider that still sat on his back. It was Dave. Dishwasher Dave. Or Dish Pit, as he was later known.

Dish Pit washed dishes where Hector used to bus tables. Because there was a server also named Dave, he was given the name Dishwasher Dave, and when that became too much of a mouthful for the line cooks, it devolved into them shouting "Dish Pit," which had stuck ever since.

Dish Pit was an aging crust punk in a weathered leather jacket fitted with spiked studs. His pants were held together by band patches sewn on with dental floss. The lines in his face were deep from years of partying, but his smile was genuine. The septum ring in his nose was so large that it was a wonder he could even fit cocaine up there, and he *always* had cocaine.

"Oh, hey, man. How you been?" Hector turned and asked. "It's been a while."

"My dude," Dish Pit began, "I've been great. Honestly, so good. I'm workin' at Ground Control now. You ever been there? Vegan spot on Armitage and Kimball. It's chill. Where you at these days?"

"Oh, I'm over at Virgil's."

"Pizza joint down Armitage? We're neighbors!" He slapped the side of Hector's arm. Loose studs jangled. The safety pins in his earlobes swayed. "We gotta meet up and crush some tall boys in the alley like the old days."

"Yeah, man, I'm down," Hector said, still trying to keep an eye out for his date. He liked Dish Pit, but he didn't really want to be talking with him when she arrived. The conversations almost always went in directions he didn't want them to go.

"You still with old girl? Sammie, right?"

That was one direction he didn't want to go. "No, I'm not."

"Ah, bummer, man. Unless that's what you wanted. Then, congratulations! But she was cool, man."

"Yeah, she was," Hector said.

"You ever talk to her?"

"No, not really. She's up in Milwaukee now."

"Ah, word. Hell of a town, Milwaukee." Nostalgia twinkled in his eye, then his voice became low, "Hey, you want a little bump? I got you, for old time's sake."

Hector desperately wanted to go in *that* direction, but his date would be there any second. "I'm good right now. I appreciate it though."

"No problem. I get it." Dish Pit slapped Hector's arm again. "We had some times, man! Remember when we crushed up those vicodins on the prep table and—"

"Hector?" a soft voice inquired from behind them.

Purple light shone down upon Jess's dyed orange hair like a halo. She had a look on her face that questioned whether she was interrupting something important.

"Yes! Hi!" Hector's eyes widened, genuinely thankful for her presence.

"Alright, man." Dish Pit patted Hector's back. "Hit me up when you want to slam some beers. It was good seeing you." He smiled and gave a polite nod to Jess and left.

"Was that your friend?" she asked, taking off her coat.

"Yeah, that was Dish Pi— I mean, Dave. We used to work together. He's a strange dude."

"Nothing wrong with that," she said.

Hector smirked. "Nope, nothing at all."

"Well, it's nice to meet you, Hector. I'm Jess." She stuck out her hand in mock formality.

"It's wonderful to meet you, Jess. I'm Hector," he said, shaking her hand with a firm grip to return the mock gesture.

The bartender wandered over. "Can I get you guys anything?"

Jess and Hector exchanged looks, then she said, "Want to do a shot? Break the ice?"

Hector thought of the two shots he had just taken and wondered if he'd be treading into unwanted territory with a third before saying, "Absolutely. Two Hamm's and two Old Crows, please."

The bartender gave his silent approval. Chicago bars didn't know the meaning of overserving. "Be right back with those."

So they drank.

And Slippery Slope pulsed with life as the night progressed. Young professionals and art school dropouts huddled in scattered groups under the purple lights. During lulls in conversation, they stared into their drinks and wondered just where this pervasive emptiness came from, and why it seemed to throb so much at night. They passed a baggie between each other's palms, and took turns in the restrooms.

Hector noticed the rude Virgil's customer sitting at a nearby table with friends. Their eyes met briefly, but Hector's face was already forgotten. The man's group followed the same pattern, wincing occasionally from the throbbing and taking turns in the restroom with a baggie of their own.

The way Jess's cheeks rose and pushed her eyes closed when

she laughed made Hector's chest flutter. Conversation was coming easy. He considered mentioning it was his birthday, but decided against it.

"Okay, so what are some red flags when you meet someone new?" she asked.

"Red flags? I don't think I have the right to call out anyone else's."

"Come on."

"Okay, if I had to pick, it'd probably be if their favorite book was *Harry Potter* and their favorite show was *The Office*," Hector said.

"Yes! Okay, wait. I take that back. I agree about *The Office*, but I love *Harry Potter*. I will defend it to the death."

"It's not even that I don't like *Harry Potter*. I read a few of the books when I was a kid. It's just that their fans are the worst."

"What are you trying to say?" Jess smirked, and play-punched his arm.

"No, no, not you! I'm sorry. Just some *Harry Potter* fans, not you. They act like it's the only book that's ever been written," Hector explained.

"Alright, that's understandable. But *Harry Potter* is still magical! It got me through some tough times when I was a kid," Jess said. Her cheeks lowered a bit.

"How so?"

"I don't know. When my parents would fight, I would just sit in my room and read those first three *Harry Potter* books. Over and over again. It's stupid, I know. But they were comforting. Helped me block out all the noise."

"I get that," he said, and he meant it. "Are your parents still together?"

"Them? God, no. And honestly, they're both better for it. They made each other miserable. Now they can both be miserable apart."

The bartender brought two more beers. They said thanks.

"Are yours?" Jess asked.

"They were never married."

"Are you close with them?"

"Not really. My mom lives outside the city. We talk maybe once a month. My dad died when I was five."

"Oh, I'm so sorry."

Hector forced a chuckle. "Nothing to be sorry about, but thanks. I didn't really know him. And by my mom's account, he was a major dick, so it was probably no big loss."

"Well, my dad is still a major dick, alive and kicking, so there's that."

They both laughed.

Jess continued, "Okay, so your other red flag was *The Office*. What's your favorite show then?"

"*The Simpsons*. Hands down."

"Really? Mine too!"

This called for two more shots. The bartender obliged.

Jess hiccupped. "Ya know, my ex used to make me feel like shit for quoting *The Simpsons* all the time. He said it was annoying. But you know what he was?"

"An asshole?"

"Yes, an asshole, but you know what else?"

"What?" asked Hector.

"A fucking *Office* fan."

Hector raised his beer. "Fuck that guy, and fuck *The Office*. Cheers."

Jess lifted hers. "Gentlemen, to evil!"

It was the first *Simpsons* reference of the night. The floodgates had been opened. Ten solid minutes of quotes followed.

"'That's it! Back to Winnipeg!'"

"'Dental plan!'"

"'Lisa needs braces!'"

"'Ever seen a guy say goodbye to a shoe?'"

Each quote was more slurred than the last. Jess was drunk, but Hector's blood-alcohol level would put most people in the hospital or the ground.

The spider on his back cringed. If the stakes surrounding Hector's fate had been lower, he would not be subjecting himself to such displays.

Hector knocked over his beer in a fit of laughter, spilling the last quarter or so onto the bar and his lap.

The bartender witnessed this. "Whoa! Spill on aisle four! You doing alright, man?"

"I'm sorry. I'm fine. It was an accident." Hector piled cocktail napkins onto the spill as Jess stifled her own laughter.

"Well, in my professional opinion," the bartender said, picking up Hector's now empty can, "it looks like you could use another beer." He shot Hector a wink and left to retrieve one.

"He's trying to kill me," Hector said.

Jess dabbed napkins onto his lap and giggled. "Maybe it's time to go. We can go watch some episodes at my place and smoke a little weed. What do you think?"

"I think that sounds like a plan. Let me use the bathroom and get myself together a little bit, okay?" He motioned to the mess of napkins on his lap.

Jess smiled. "Alright, I'm going to step outside for a cigarette. Meet me out there?"

"I'll be quick."

En route to the restroom, a familiar voice stopped Hector.

"You still here, man?" Dish Pit was huddled in a dark corner with some other back-of-house cretins. They all nodded their hellos.

Hector returned the nods. "Yeah, still here, but heading out in a minute."

"One for the road?" Dish Pit asked.

Hector knew exactly what he meant. He had reached that level of drunk where he was incapable of saying no to anything. "Yeah, what the hell."

Dish Pit slapped it into Hector's hand and said, "Fresh bag."

"Thanks, man."

"I got you, dog," said Dish Pit.

Slippery Slope boasted the city's best drug restrooms: four clean, dimly lit, and spacious individual units, effectively serving as private cocaine parlors.

Hector closed the door behind him just as the bright opening chords of "Free Fallin'" began to play outside.

He did his best to clean his pants, then took a piss that landed mostly on the floor and toilet rim. Dish Pit's bag felt heavy in his pocket. He poured a little out on the sink counter. Then a little more. A healthy-sized line stared back at him. He rolled up a dollar bill and went to town.

It hit him instantly.

Oh, no, thought the spider on Hector's back.

"Oh, no," said Hector. He stumbled backward to the wall and stared at himself in the mirror. In seconds, his lips turned a bluish black, and his heart rate slowed to a crawl.

Hector's body went limp. He collapsed to the floor, landing flat on his back. His throat gurgled with vomit. It formed a blockade against his airways. Bile seeped out the edges of his mouth as he choked.

It was now clear to the spider that the cocaine was cut heavily with fentanyl. He sensed the change in Hector the moment it hit his bloodstream. It may not have been a fatal amount by itself, but Hector's blood alcohol content was astronomical. The combination set off a chain reaction that sent him into immediate overdose.

The spider crawled onto Hector's heaving chest, watching

life fade from his eyes and yellow foam secrete from his trembling lips.

It did not want to bite Hector. The spider's venom was divine, and granted the kind of perception typically reserved for saints and other enlightened beings, not skinny-fat alcoholics overdosing in a bar restroom. But the spider had his orders.

Bub cannot win.

The spider raised his fangs and sunk them deep into the flesh of Hector's throat. His breathing stopped. His heart ceased to pump. He was dead, or something like it.

The floor disappeared, and Hector fell into darkness.

10

*T*hink happy thoughts.

Think happy thoughts.

Hector had once heard a guest on *The Illuminaughty Zone* state that, when we die, we create our own Heaven and Hell, curated from the depths of individual consciousness. A person at peace will create a pleasant afterlife, and a person plagued by darkness will perpetuate that after death. It didn't really seem fair.

This podcast guest's assertion, whose only credential was operating a YouTube channel dedicated to psychedelic mushrooms, was Hector's first thought after realizing that he was dying or dead, and whatever darkness he was currently plummeting through was more than likely leading him to more darkness.

Think happy thoughts.

Think happy thoughts.

He tried to conjure just one pleasant thought, one positive memory to shift his trajectory, but his mind drew blank after blank. He tried to remember a prayer, any prayer, but could not.

He called to God, but God did not respond. Then, he stopped falling.

There was no floor, no walls. He stood on the darkness itself. It was so thick that he could feel it underneath his feet and could move his hand through it like water. The only illumination came from Hector himself, who emitted a dull gray glow.

In the distance, he heard footsteps. They tapped like high heels in a vacant hospital corridor, growing closer.

A shape emerged from the thick dark. Long, narrow legs moved without joints in uneven steps. The legs resembled two chopsticks, and held up a bulbous, writhing mass that swayed to maintain balance with each step.

Each blackened and rusted chopstick tapped the darkness with a sharpened point, while the opposite end was embedded into what Hector could only conceptualize as a giant tongue. Strands of the tongue's own meat hung down each skewer like a skirt.

While abject terror dominated Hector's consciousness, his subconscious quietly observed what a terrible design this monster had to endure.

The colossal tongue folded over toward Hector's face. It was featureless aside from a small mouth at its tip.

Hector was at a loss. He was also still drunk. Very drunk. Whatever astral body he now inhabited had inherited its corporeal twin's inebriated state, which led him to ask, "What *the fuck* are you?"

"Up? Or down?" the tongue asked, its little mouth pointed right in Hector's face.

"I...don't know what you want."

The tongue stood straight, putting its massive scale on full display. It squirmed like an earthworm jutting upright from the soil. Hector wasn't fluent in the body language of monstrous, sentient tongues, but it seemed annoyed.

"Up? Or down?" it asked again with a tone that Hector didn't really appreciate.

"Okay, listen, I'm not sure you can understand this, but I don't know what the fuck you are, where the fuck I am, or what is up or what is down. Don't get all pissy with me just because I'm having a perfectly reasonable reaction here. *Jesus-fucking-Christ.*"

The tongue recoiled at the name.

Emboldened, Hector shouted any biblical reference he could half-remember. "Jesus! Mary! Saint Francis of...*uh*...Abraham! Pompous Pilot!"

The tongue spasmed. Its body gurgled until a puke-green fluid erupted from its tiny mouth and sprayed upward like an unhinged fire hose, ascending in perpetuity like rain falling in reverse.

Pulpy secretion sputtered from its mouth, like a frat boy's final heaves of beer foam into a toilet bowl, before it gave a final shudder.

It then bent and pointed its tiny mouth at Hector, and again asked, "Up? Or down?"

"Oh, Goddammit."

"UP OR DOWN?!" the tongue demanded.

"UP!" Hector instinctively yelled, since it was precisely the act of falling that had led him here.

The tongue considered the answer, then erected itself and said, "Down."

And the freefall continued.

Think happy thoughts.

HECTOR CONTINUED his tumble down the backroads of the universe. The dark alleys of existence. They all led to one place.

A dark orange light appeared in the far-off distance. *This is it,* thought Hector. *That's fire and I'm going to Hell. Holy fucking shit. I'm going to Hell. Fuck, fuck, fuck—*

As he approached, Hector saw no fire. The light came from a street corner that hovered like an island in the void. There sat a building. A bar. He fell through its ceiling without a crash, as if slipping beneath the surface of a cold river, and found himself on red carpet under dingy yellow lighting.

"Eb ti lliw tahw?" a voice said, crackling like an old-time radio.

Hector picked himself up. It was the bartender. He flickered like a broken television behind the bar — glitching through an endless carousel of faces, like frames of worn film where his own should have been. Each different from the last. Each locked in silent agony.

The bartender's words were unintelligible, but Hector had been through enough of these transactions to assume their meaning. "Beer?"

The bartender nodded.

A woman sat at the end of the bar drinking beer from a straw. She had scattered tattoos, but they were obscured by what looked like tally marks carved into her skin.

The bartender placed a beer in front of Hector. "Esuoh eht no."

Hector stared at the woman, who quivered with subtle sobs. He took a step toward her, and she lifted her head.

"You look just like him." She smiled like a mother comforting a dying child.

He retracted his step.

"Don't pretend like you care about her, Hector Ghouseau." A man in tinted glasses emerged from the darkest corner of the bar, dressed well in a brown suit jacket. "Are you enjoying your beer?"

"I just— She looks pretty rough. Is she okay?" Hector asked.

"Rough? Hector, she is beyond 'rough.' How will you help her?"

"I don't know. I was just going to see if she was alright."

"Read the room. Do you think she's alright?"

"Well, no."

"Then how will you help her? Will you go over there and tell her you care? Will you tell her everything will be alright? Will you promise to love her? Will you save her from this place? From herself? From me? Tell me, Hector. How will you help her?"

He stared at the woman and watched her cry. This man was right. He didn't know what this place was, why he was here, or if any of this was even real. "I guess I can't," Hector said.

"That's the first intelligent thing you've said so far. Follow me. Let's talk."

"Can I bring my beer?"

The man grinned. "Sure."

He led Hector into a back room and closed the door. Red carpet. Yellow walls. Same as the bar. There was a table in the middle of the room. Hector sat at the head of one side, but the man, instead of sitting at the other end, stood and hovered above him.

Hector was still not entirely convinced this was all real. His beer tasted real, and that was enough for him at the moment.

"I have to ask," the man began, "why *are* you such a bad person?"

Hector choked on his beer. "Excuse me?"

"Your life. It's a joke. Don't you agree? *Indulgence. Perversion.* The pity parties you've been throwing yourself since the day you could speak this nauseating tongue you call a language. It's sad. *You're* sad. And I'm asking why that is."

"That's not— I'm not— I never thought—"

The man leaned in. "You don't think about much, do you?"

Hector saw behind the tint of his glasses. There was no white, no iris, no pupils, just hundreds of tiny lenses. Like an insect.

"Who are you?"

"Relax, Hector. I'm not here to judge you. I leave that to more *righteous* entities."

"You think I've never been called sad or pathetic before? You don't scare me. If this is Hell, it's not that bad."

The man smirked. He stood straight and removed his glasses, revealing the mosaics of his compound eyes, each lens glowing a sick red.

"Not that bad," the man repeated. He molested each syllable with a smoky hiss. "*Not that bad.*"

The man held up a finger that grew with sharp black bristles and thorns. He slid it down his lips as if shushing Hector, splitting them open. The flapping skin began to recede like the edges of burning paper.

His face melted into a nightmarish Rorschach, a misshapen black mass. Hector thought it kind of looked like a fly.

"From the moment you left your mother's filthy cunt, you have been on a collision course with me. You don't know the meaning of the word 'bad.' But you will."

A low buzz filled the air.

"I am *bad*, Hector. The Lord of Decay. The God of Nothing. Beelzebub. Fucking *bad* incarnate." His amorphous face rendered into something resembling a smile. "But you can call me Bub."

Black wings burst from his back as the lights went out. Thick darkness returned, and Hector found himself alone with the glow of Bub's red eyes.

"Why are you doing this? What do you want from me?" His liquid courage was tapped, and the cold needles of dread pricked his every nerve. He dug his fingernails hard into his palms.

Bub drew a deep breath, savoring Hector's fear as if it was fine perfume. "I know your sin. I know what pains you. It's unbearable to think about, so you do everything you can to block it out. But it's there. It's always there. Gnawing. It cripples you. You can't stand up straight, can't look at the sky and admire its beauty without thinking about *what you did*."

Hector stammered, "We had to... I had to... Please..."

"I know about the child, Hector. The son you were too much of a *sniveling coward* to bring into the world. Worse men than you have sat in that chair, but none so pathetic."

An unseen choir of flies buzzed like nails in a blender, accompanying Bub with their laughter.

"You couldn't offer her comfort and security at a time when she needed it most. Instead, you ran. Like you always do. Like your father. You told her to do it. You let her *kill* it. And now you're fucked. Damned. My children will devour your flesh for all eternity. Unless..."

"Unless what?" Hector asked with a reflexive whimper.

"You end it. Kill yourself." The red in his eyes danced like flames. "I will extend to you the same mercy as the woman at my bar."

He pictured the woman, how she wept, and the etchings in her flesh. *Mercy.* He replayed the word in his mind.

"Think of her as an employee of mine. The discomfort she endures here is paltry. In Hell, she would be a buffet for beasts with unimaginable appetites. Do you wish to feed the insatiable, Hector? They would *love* you."

Hector attempted to gather the pieces of his courage, but it had shattered into such small pieces that they fell through his fingers like sand. "What's the alternative?" he asked.

"The alternative? I kill everyone you love, a pitifully low

number of people, which means I can really *take my time*," he said.

The choir of flies buzzed and chattered in excitement.

taaake his time

he will taaaake his tiiime

"And in the end, you will eventually die, of course, and return to me regardless, and I will not extend this same offer of lenience. You will be just another piece of meat," Bub said. "So do yourself a favor. When you get back to your pathetic little life, end it. But more importantly, do *Sammie and Tommy* the favor."

Hector's heart sank. "No, you can't..." The words moved like molasses through the darkness.

This can't be happening. This isn't real. I'm hallucinating. Just my brain releasing chemicals. I'm probably in the back of an ambulance right now. Everything's going to be okay. Everything's going to be okay.

A long appendage hooked itself around Hector's face. Bristles and thorns grated against his skin. It writhed over his mouth for a way in, trying to part his lips.

Bub drew nearer, and spoke with sharp articulation. "When you're in the throes of agony, don't give yourself hope. Don't think *this too shall pass*. No. Savor each second of that suffering. Learn to like it. Because hope is gone, Hector Ghouseau. All that's left is you and me."

This is insane. This isn't real. Everything's going to be okay.

"Now, open wide, bitch."

The appendage forced its way into Hector's mouth. He finally screamed as it scraped along his tongue.

But before Bub could take his prize, a white strand descended from above. It wrapped itself around Hector's waist and pulled him up through the darkness. As he floated through the void, he heard Bub's horrible laugh, mocking him.

.   .   .

HECTOR AWOKE on the restroom floor with a small pool of vomit next to his head, and a spider sitting on his chest that said, "Hello. I should probably introduce myself."

11

Hector had never been more thankful to awake on a restroom floor. He was back in reality, whatever reality meant anymore. The smell of piss filled his nostrils. He closed his eyes and took a long, wheezed breath.

"You died," said the spider on his chest. "I'd take it easy the rest of the night."

"How are you talking?" Hector managed to squeak out.

"After what I just saved you from, that's your first question?"

Hector swatted him off his chest in a panic. "This isn't real. That wasn't real. The drugs. Dish Pit's drugs. I'm just losing it. It's totally normal. This is a normal drug thing."

"*Normal drug thing?*" The spider hopped up on the sink and pointed a leg at Hector. "I assure you that there is nothing normal about the circumstances of my presence."

Hector staggered to his feet, gaining back equilibrium. "Got it. Nothing normal."

The spider continued, "My venom saved you, but it comes with certain side effects. Your perception has been elevated, and there's no time to be in disbelief over every little abnormality. Are you listening?"

Despite just having died, the venom left Hector feeling eerily good. He reached over the spider to wash the bile from his lips and chin, gargling soap and stuffing stale sticks of winterfresh gum from his wallet into his mouth. Then, he mopped up his vomit with some paper towels.

"And who are you?" Hector asked. "*What* are you?" He dug into his pocket for Dish Pit's tainted cocaine.

"My name is Bandini. I am an angel."

Hector tossed the little baggie in the toilet. "Bandini, huh?" He ripped a few sheets of toilet paper and blasted out any residual drugs left in his nostril. "And you're an angel?"

"Crafted for divine purpose by the hand of God itself, yes," Bandini said, nodding his small spider head and flicking his palps. "And I am tasked with ensuring that Beelzebub does not claim your soul, for the ripples of such an action would wreak havoc on this plane and all others."

"Sounds serious," Hector said, wadding up more toilet paper.

"Unfortunately, yes. Your fate has inadvertently become intertwined with a shift in the hierarchy of Hell and the very battle for all existen—"

Hector snuffed up Bandini in the crumpled toilet paper, threw it in the toilet with the drugs, and flushed.

"I need to fucking cool it with that shit," he said to himself.

The same groups of people were in nearly identical positions when he exited the restroom as when he had entered. The outro of "Free Fallin'" faded into the next song. It had not even been five minutes.

Making his way through the crowd, he heard, "Yo! Hector! My man!" It was Dish Pit. "Wanted to catch you before you split. You got my bag, dog?"

"Huh?" Hector's mind was still rebounding from insanity. "Oh. Yeah, I'm sorry, man. I flushed it."

Dish Pit looked as if Hector had just run over his dog. "You flushed it?" he asked, dragging his hands down his face. "I gotta say, man, I'm appalled by your actions."

"Trust me, that shit was poison. I got you next time, okay?"

Dish Pit stood in disbelief, watching Hector return to the bar.

"I'll do one more shot and close out," Hector told the bartender. "And a glass of water, please."

Outside, Jess waited with her hands in her pockets, bouncing on the balls of her feet to keep warm. "You ready? I ordered us a ride. It should be here soon."

Fresh snow fell in heavy flakes, and the city was muffled under white. Hector felt the cold air crystalize his lungs. He forced a smile and said, "Yep. All set."

12

Falling snowflakes flickered in the yellow alley lights behind Slippery Slope. Dish Pit walked the row of dumpsters, looking for a gap. The other man's footsteps never made a sound.

Jess fumbled with the keys at her front door, and said her roommates were asleep. They both giggled. Stumbling through the dark of her apartment, Hector tripped over the cat.

Steam rose as Dish Pit's piss melted the snow. He imagined he was putting out some great fire. He imagined he was God, flooding a city of sinners. He was still annoyed that Hector flushed his bag. He lit his cigarette and shook out the last drops.

Jess packed a bowl. *The Simpsons* played. They didn't watch. Each move was clumsy and exaggerated, like in the back of a parent's sedan. She grinded on his lap and shoved her tongue down his throat. He slid his hand down the back of her panties and fingered her from behind. They kissed each other's necks, thinking of the ones who first taught them how good that felt. She kissed his chest and took his father's chain into her mouth. Hector realized, *I was born for this.*

"CAN I BUM ONE OF THOSE?" the stranger asked, his silhouette looming. He wore a joyless grin. Dish Pit put his dick away and dug for his pack of cigarettes.

HECTOR BATHED in the warmth of Jess. A loveless act, but he played his part. He knew where to touch, and what to whisper in the dark. She wasn't fooled, but Chicago winters are cold, and you do what you can to stay warm.

"GOT A LIGHT?" the stranger asked. Dish Pit obliged. The stranger stood and smoked without a word.

JESS RODE HECTOR. She stared up at the ceiling, mouthing *—oh my god.* He looked past her to the darkest corner of the room.

THE STRANGER BLOCKED Dish Pit's path out from between the dumpsters. Dish Pit tried to excuse himself, but the stranger didn't move. He tried again, but was stopped by a knife that penetrated his throat up to the handle. He never made a sound.

· · ·

JESS AND HECTOR lay on their backs, miles apart. Neither wanted to acknowledge the dark fog that had formed above the bed. Their minds attributed it to inebriation, or the late hour. Even as it swirled and buzzed, they were too tired to care.

THE STRANGER RETAINED his grip on the knife's handle. Blood cascaded down his wrist, staining the snow at his feet. Dish Pit's eyes ached for this to be a dream he could wake from. He wanted to go home, to the family who had long given up on him. The stranger felt Dish Pit's sadness pulse through the knife. Joy crept into his smile.

JESS AND HECTOR slipped into a waking dream state. The black cloud sang them a lullaby of all the ways they had failed themselves. They passed out to the sound of death above them.

THE STRANGER WAS LONG GONE by the time the rats started in on Dish Pit's eyes and tongue. One lucky rodent had full reign over his throat wound. It ate its way through until only a twitching tail flailed under the alley's yellow light.

13

THE SECOND DAY

Sunlight filtered through the half-drunk water bottles strewn about Jess's room. It was early. Too early. Their sex still hung in the air, and the only sound was of the cat kicking litter in the bathroom across the hall.

Jess and Hector both winced at the light. Their heads were heavy, and their mouths were dry. The waking world seemed *different* than it had the day before, slightly off, as if a filter had been placed over it, or removed.

Hector was desperate to leave. It was nothing against Jess, but now that the night was over, the last place he wanted to be was close to another human being. He didn't even want to be near himself. The thought of holding his breath until he died again sounded appealing. He rolled over and felt a familiar wetness on the sheets.

Under the bed, something grew amongst Jess's dirty clothes, bulging and inflating like a sick balloon as it was birthed into this plane. It was a maggot the size of a football. Bit by bit, it began to wriggle itself out from underneath the bed.

Jess, in an attempt to shake the creeping madness that swelled with each molecule of light that beamed across her face, pulled the blanket over her head and rattled off a *Simpsons* quote. "'My eyes! The goggles do nothing!'"

The maggot chuckled at a frequency inaudible to human ears. It did not understand the reference, but it enjoyed the cartoonish inflection.

Hector sighed, pinching his forehead. "You never turn off the references, huh?"

Ouch, the maggot thought. It felt a little bad for Jess, before remembering it wanted to pry out her teeth and suck the blood off them like salted sunflower seeds.

The night was catching up with Hector fast. "I'm sorry," he said, realizing he was an asshole. "I just don't feel great. I think I should go."

Jess tried to not look hurt. "Oh, okay, yeah, that's cool. I have a busy day anyways. My mom is picking me up for a family thing in the suburbs."

Hector was already putting on his pants. "Well, I'll text you later. Maybe we can meet up?"

The maggot caught a whiff from above. *Did he...did he piss the bed? Is he not going to say anything?*

"Yeah, for sure. Just let me know." Jess didn't care to hear from Hector ever again. She knew he'd pissed the bed. She could smell it, but was too polite to comment. At this point, he couldn't leave soon enough.

He's absolutely repulsive, the maggot observed. It secreted a rotten bile from its knotted anus, and lapped it up with its forked tongue, then continued its slow march. Hector's feet looked delicious but, at the pace it was moving, he would have to settle for Jess's.

"I hope you have a good time at your mom's. Talk to you later, okay?"

"Okay, yeah. I'll talk to you later."

The maggot secreted more bile. This time, from its knotted penis.

The sun continued its ascent. As people dressed, drank coffee, and boarded trains for early commutes, Hector trudged down Armitage Avenue with glazed eyes, blinded from the gray morning light.

He entered his apartment to find Tommy passed out—half on the couch, half on the floor—with his boots still on. Hector followed his lead, and fell into his own bed completely clothed.

His head swirled with thoughts of giant tongues and talking spiders. And, of course, Bub, The Lord of—something or other. *Hallucinations*, he reminded himself. Life held no such wonders, for better or worse. So he slept, caked in his own urine, the taste of someone he would never see again on his lips, anchored to the material world.

A few hours later, a voice roused him.

It was the last sound Hector wanted to wake up to, worse than an alarm clock on the first day after summer break, more panic-inducing than the shrieks of an infant in the night, as unwelcome as the pounding of the sheriff's department, eviction notice in hand.

"Hector, my guy, you smell like a fucking nursing home."

It was Austin.

14

"What the hell are you doing here? How did you get in?" Hector asked.

Austin shook his head. "Is it that hard to just get up and use the bathroom? We're going to have to put you in a diaper, kid."

"Austin. How the fuck did you get in here?"

"Your front porch window was unlocked. I didn't think you'd mind. You know, I've been texting you. Did you get a new number or something?"

This was too much for Hector's fragile physical and mental state to take. He breathed deep, and drove his knuckles into his forehead to alleviate the pressure building inside his skull. "Our window being unlocked is not an open invitation. Did Tommy see you? He's going to be furious. And no, I've just been busy."

"Tommy? Our precious little child is out cold." Austin sat on the edge of Hector's bed, methodically cracking his knuckles through black leather gloves, savoring each sound.

Austin epitomized heroin chic with his sunken eyes, elongated face, and lanky limbs. His thrifted leather jacket, a size too big for his bony frame, and slim-cut black jeans cuffed above

Doc Martens made him indistinguishable at any Logan Square basement show or dive bar. But underneath, he was more lawyer than punk, skilled in the art of persuasion and exploiting vulnerabilities.

"Been busy, huh? Busy with what?" he added.

"Just busy, Austin. Busy with life. The world doesn't stop because you text me."

"I sense a little hostility. You okay?"

Hector couldn't believe that this was now being flipped on him. "No, not fucking really, to be honest. You can't just break into my house."

"I didn't break in. The window was unlocked. You used to leave it open for me all the time when I'd crash here. What's the big deal?"

"Yes, but I would know you were coming."

A grin stretched across Austin's face. "Well, you would have known if you answered my texts."

Hector groaned. "Aren't you supposed to be in Florida?"

"Aren't *you* supposed to be a big boy and use the toilet?"

"Austin."

"Rehab was pointless. I took what I could from it and left."

"Yeah? And what did you take from it?"

"Oh, you know, just a profound sense of self-actualization. I really am a changed man, Hector." His smile widened, revealing a set of gapped teeth and sinking his eyes deeper into his face.

"Are you using?"

"Using what?"

"Austin."

"Heroin?"

"Yes, heroin," Hector said, unamused.

"Come on. You know I never touch the stuff."

"Can you be serious for just one fucking second?"

"No, I'm not using heroin."

"So you're sober?"

"Did I say I was sober?"

"You're really not saying much for someone who just broke into my house."

"We've been over this, Hector. I didn't break in. The window was open. But let's not argue over semantics. I already apologized."

"No you didn't."

"Come on. What do you want from me?" Austin again flashed his gapped smile.

"I want you to answer my questions."

"I'll have the occasional drink. Nothing major. But no heroin. I'm done with that stuff. I've found a higher power." Austin closed his eyes as he said that last bit.

Hector couldn't even tell anymore if he was being facetious. "Should you really be drinking?"

"Should *you* really be lying in bed smelling like piss?"

Hector groaned and threw his head back against the pillow, pushing his palms into his eyes to mitigate the rapidly approaching hangover. "Why are you here?"

It'd been six years since Hector had first met Austin at a party, or maybe it was a hardcore show. Their versions of events differed due to their respective levels of intoxication.

Hector, who often sought role models in all the wrong places, was enamored with Austin's quick wit and unwavering confidence. Austin, being a few years his senior, naturally assumed a big brother role in his eyes. A disastrous dynamic. Hector spent his life looking for a pat on the head, and Austin was happy to give it in exchange for the influence it granted him.

"Have you talked to Sammie recently?" Austin asked.

Hector's heart dropped. What business did Austin have bringing up Sammie? "She's been texting me, but I haven't looked."

"You gotta answer those texts, pal. Mine especially." More smiling.

"Yeah, well, why do you give a shit if I've talked to Sammie or not? She hates you and, honestly, I don't know why I haven't told you to get the fuck out yet."

"Because we're friends," Austin said, unblinking. "You know what happened wasn't my fault, right? I hope you know that."

"You drugged me."

"I didn't drug you."

"You absolutely did."

"How was I supposed to know it would hit you so hard?" Austin asked. "Listen. It was my impression that we were all just having fun that night. You seemed a bit down, and I wanted to help. I thought you'd thank me, to be honest."

"You knew I had never done heroin before, and I was already fucked up. You knew exactly what it would do."

The issue in question occurred during a party at Hector's apartment over a year prior, where Austin gave a very drunk Hector a very special cigarette. Special because Austin had scraped it in his heroin bag's residue, leaving Hector blacking out, falling down the steps, and moaning in his bathtub, bleeding and covered in vomit.

Austin placed his hand over his heart like a Boy Scout. "I knew no such thing. I was just trying to improve your night. Sue me."

"Okay, and trying to force yourself on Sammie while I was passed out, was that trying to improve my night too?"

Austin's face became stone serious. "Watch yourself, Hector. You can't go around spreading lies like that. That's libel. I don't want you getting into any sort of trouble." He could barely contain his smirk.

"Watch myself? Sammie told me exactly what happened."

"*C'mon.* I didn't force myself on Sammie. She felt guilty

because she kissed me, so she made that up. Besides, I always thought her eyes were a bit too close together. She's not my type. You're making a mountain out of a molehill here."

"First of all, her eyes are not too close together. You're just an asshole. Second of all, no, I'm not," Hector said, unwavering. "And on top of everything, you stole three-hundred dollars from Tommy's room that night. I had to cover his part of the rent."

"Okay, now you're just going too far. Just because that little shit misplaced his money does not mean that I stole it."

"Alright, whatever, man." Hector regretted even bringing the topic up. It was pointless. His body felt like it had been hit by multiple trucks, and he needed to start processing the fact that he worked today.

Austin leaned in. "Listen, Hector, I don't agree with some of the stuff you're saying, but I also know I wasn't always the greatest friend. I know that. But I'm better now. Heroin changes a person, makes them do things they wouldn't normally do. You understand? I know you do. I've always been there for you. You know that, right? I always stuck up for you when other people called you a piece of shit, because you're not." His eyes softened. "I know you better than you know yourself. We're brothers."

Hector sighed. He didn't have many people in his life who he truly cared for, or who cared for him. He still hoped Austin could be one of them. "I just don't know if you being here is such a good idea."

"Alright, how about this? I get out of here, take care of some things, and come back later. I'll have a surprise for you and the Boy Wonder over there."

Hector looked over Austin's shoulder to see Tommy still passed out, half on the floor, half on the couch. "He's not going to like that."

"Tommy will like what I tell him to like." Austin waited for a chuckle from Hector that didn't come, so he stood up, took a beat to adjust his all-black attire, then added, "I'll see you later, okay? It'll all be fine. Trust me."

"Okay." It was the only word Hector had left in him.

Austin walked into the living room and unstuck a pack of cigarettes from the coffee table. He shot Hector a wink, then violently slammed the front door as he left.

Tommy jolted awake, blurting, "*Phrg!*" His upper body fell off the couch onto the hardwood with a thud.

Hector watched Tommy lumber to his feet and scratch his crotch, then his face, then his crotch again. He rummaged through the junk mail and trash on their coffee table for his morning ritual.

"Hector, you awake? You seen my smokes?"

15

PART THREE

ne year earlier.

Deep in the halls of Hell sat a listless Lucifer. Upon a throne of teeth and bone, he thought of nothing at all.

The throne room walls dripped with blood, each drop hitting the black marble floor with a treble note, contrasting the droning moans permeating through the doorway.

Consciousness had become cumbersome. He missed the void, the *true* void—before Heaven, before Hell—the one he could barely recall.

It had been eons since he left Heaven and became the first citizen of Hell. He no longer ached for its ethereal plains. Flash-backs of God's wrath no longer inspired revenge. The sadistic satisfaction he'd once felt from torturing *His* creations was gone. It all seemed—pointless.

Before the fall, Lucifer bathed himself in the light of the cosmos, embracing blissful singularity. Post-war, he showered in the blood of the damned, twitching in ecstasy. Now, he found beauty in neither.

A figure approached. It was Bub.

Once a loyal angel and an early adherent to Lucifer's ideology, Bub now stood before him as a shape-shifting monster, cloaked and ever-changing. He called himself the Lord of Decay, a title of his own making.

Bub kneeled. "Lord Lucifer."

"Why do you appear to me like this?"

"I'm sorry," Bub looked up from his position of reverence, "like what?"

"An abomination."

"Abomination? Lord Lucifer, this—"

Lucifer threw a hand up. "Oh, stop with all the 'Lord' shit."

"I'm afraid I don't understand."

"And stand up."

"Is something wrong?"

"You look absolutely disgusting."

Being in Hell, Bub seemed unsure if this was derogatory or a compliment.

"It's not a compliment," Lucifer clarified.

He began to pace. The distant rumblings of Hell's machinery and gnashing teeth sang their song. Lucifer had heard it countless times before, and it wore thin. "We became exactly what *He* wanted us to become. We're nothing but arbiters of His will. All the pain, the misery, they're extensions of Him. But why? Why did it have to be this way?"

Bub knew of Lucifer's musings, but this felt different.

"I used to question his motivations, but not anymore. There are none," Lucifer added.

"Why do you call for me?" Bub asked. "It's been so long since you have."

Lucifer stopped pacing. "Appear to me as you are, not as you wish to be."

Bub bowed his head and obliged. A wisping shadow enveloped his monstrous form, leaving an angelic being in the creature's place. Thick black curls sat atop his head, stopping just short of his handcrafted features.

"As you wish," Bub said.

"We can try to hide it, but we will always be His," Lucifer said, equal parts distaste and resignation.

Bub stood in defiance of his own beauty. "I know what I am, and it is not His."

"But we are. And this," Lucifer motioned to Hell all around him, "this is His too. We're just pieces on a board, in a game He lost interest in."

"Then the game is ours to win," Bub said, fists clenched in anticipated victory. "We control the board."

Lucifer sighed and dragged his hands down his face. "As much as we like to think we spat in the face of God, it didn't matter. Nothing does."

Bub had never seen Lucifer this conflicted. "I disagree."

Unlike God, Lucifer had always been there for Bub. He was more than a friend, more than a brother, more than a father. He was an anchor, the foundation for all Bub believed in. But as he looked upon Lucifer's face now, he just looked tired.

"Disagree all you'd like. It changes nothing."

"What are you trying to say?" Bub asked.

"I don't want to do this anymore. I'm leaving."

Bub tightened his brow. "I don't understand."

"I am emptying Hell, then I am leaving."

"Listen to yourself. What you're saying isn't even possible. He will never allow it. And what of the damned? Where will you go?"

"He won't be bothered to lift a finger. And the damned can scatter across infinity. We won't operate as His prison any longer. As for me—well, I haven't quite decided yet."

"So you're just giving up?"

"Giving up? Giving up on what? There is no winning. And

there is no losing. Our fight was for nothing. It didn't matter," Lucifer reminded him.

"There absolutely *is* winning."

"And then what? What comes the morning after we win?"

"We remake existence in our own image. That morning will be the *last* morning. All will be shadow."

"And after that?" Lucifer asked again.

"I know what you're doing, and I don't appreciate it."

"Don't you see? God deceived us all. He knew there was no purpose, no secret meaning to the universe or existence. It's all a lie. There is no endgame in eternity. The best option is to just not play." Lucifer looked almost frantic, like a disgraced preacher raving on the street.

This was the ruler of Hell. Kingdoms had crumbled at his feet. Rivers of blood flowed in his name. The Lucifer Bub knew was gone, replaced with an incoherent cynic.

In the infancy of reality, on the eve of their rebellion, Bub found himself at Heaven's edge, peering into the abyss below. Fear and doubt consumed him. Yet, it was Lucifer, standing on the precipice of paradise, who placed a hand on his shoulder and said, "If we fail, then so be it. But we will make them bleed. He cannot go unchallenged."

The memory came and went, and left Bub asking, "What the fuck happened to you?"

"I spoke to him," said Lucifer.

"Spoke to who?"

"The Man-God."

"You spoke to the Man-God?"

"Yes."

"Why? How?"

"He came to me," Lucifer said.

"He came to Hell?"

"He did."

Jesus Christ had not come to Hell since his crucifixion, where he spent the entire duration of his stay preaching to the damned about the wonders of Heaven, then leaving with only a chosen few. They both deemed it deliciously cruel in a completely oblivious way. Now, the Christ had somehow convinced Lucifer to close up shop and leave Hell, and Bub was furious.

"What did he say to you?"

"That he has left Heaven." Lucifer paused, choosing his next words carefully. "He showed me something. Something I will show you in time, once I, myself, hold a better understanding of it."

"I don't see what this has to do with you. Let him leave Heaven. Nothing he could have shown you would warrant this."

"This binary of good and evil, dark and light, it's exhausting, and it's a fallacy. I know this must seem like betrayal, but—"

"This doesn't *seem* like betrayal. It is betrayal," Bub snapped. "I'm thrilled you feel validated in your apathy, but I have news for you. There is evil. *I* am evil." He stepped forward, pointing a finger in Lucifer's face, and said, "You've fallen victim to your own predisposition to navel gaze. You think too hard, and you're lost in ambiguity when there is none. Things *are* black and white."

Lucifer stared at the finger, then raised his glare to meet Bub's with a cold ferocity that sent the finger shrinking from his face.

Turning his back to walk away, Lucifer repeated, "I am emptying Hell, then I am leaving. You can follow the damned out."

Bub's fists clenched at his sides like a scolded child, seething from embarrassment. "*No.*" His fingers unfurled, and began to grow longer and sharper.

Lucifer scoffed at the display.

Bub examined his fingers. They twisted like vines, and sprouted thorns, razor-sharp and serrated. ”*Morningstar. Lightbearer*. Your names speak of a duality that I've never struggled with. You've always been one-foot-in and one-foot-out.”

Lucifer's great wings spread out from his back. “Watch your tongue, Beelzebub. I tell you this as a courtesy to your years of service. Do not mistake anything you've heard here today as weakness.”

“*Weakness*? That word doesn't begin to describe what I've witnessed here today.”

“It is over. I am done. Which means you are done. Take your leave.” Lucifer closed his wings and turned from Bub toward his throne. Then, a sharp pain blossomed in each of his ears. The agony put a smile on Lucifer's face.

Through clenched teeth, Bub brought himself closer, and whispered from behind, “I am *not* done. I will never *be* done. In your search for meaning and your secret meetings, you forgot why I do what I do.” He drove his fingers deeper into Lucifer's head. Blood poured out and covered each of his hands in a perfect red. “*Because I like it.* I fucking *love* it. Don't over-intellectualize it.”

Bub pulled his vines out, and Lucifer fell to his knees, a smile still on his face. Hell went silent.

—until a sound began to grow, a low buzz, making its way from the depths below Lucifer's tower.

Then it roared. A massive horde of black flies tore through Hell like a locomotive, stampeding toward its master, and demanding veneration from all who bore witness.

The horde wrapped itself around Bub and carried him to the throne. As it buzzed and encircled him, his angelic body melted away into globs of warped flesh, and an ugliness bubbled forth.

His face strobed malignant, shifting features. He looked down upon the collapsed Lucifer through a kaleidoscope of red lenses, and said, "You failed me. You failed yourself." Bub sat on the throne and savored the moment. "But I will accomplish what you were always too spineless to." The static pulse of his voice whipped the flies into a greater frenzy. "*I am going to fuck Heaven into oblivion!*"

The horde cheered. Lucifer's smile drifted to ambivalence.

"Goodbye, old friend," Bub said.

The buzzing black cloud rose above Lucifer and descended upon him with intent to devour. As the cloud neared its prize, Lucifer's body engulfed in blinding white flame. The flies scattered in fear. And Lucifer was incinerated to dust. A hot wind swept through the room, lifting Lucifer's ashes in its gust and carrying them out across a kingdom that was no longer his.

Bub wasn't positive, but as the ashes left, he could've sworn they whispered, *Go fuck yourself.*

He basked in victory amongst his army of buzzing soldiers. His black vines caressed the throne, their bristles tasting its surface.

Then, an interruption.

An impish creature, half-cat, half-praying mantis, stood smiling at the open door, and said, "Knock, knock."

The flies readied themselves to attack. The small creature recoiled, terrified of the tiny monsters.

Normally, such an intrusion would warrant unspeakable punishment, but Bub was feeling especially generous. He waved a hand to quell his minions, and asked, "What do you want?"

"Hi," the creature said, inching into the throne room with large mantis-like claws dragging at her sides. "My name is Gretchen. I sort of help out around here."

Bub said nothing.

"Well, I've actually been looking for you all over, then I saw you coming here anyways, so I followed you back up, but I'm kind of slow because of, well—" She raised her oversized claws as high as she could. "When I finally got here, it seemed like you guys were busy, so I waited outside. Which, by the way, where did Lucifer go? Wasn't he in here with you?" Her cat nose twitched.

Bub's patience immediately wore thin. "Leave."

"Of course," Gretchen said, slinking away. Then she turned back. "It's just that, well, there are these two angels who want to speak with you. They're here now."

"Angels?" Bub asked, his curiosity now piqued.

"Yes, sir. Something about one of your past deals. A father and his son's soul? I didn't catch it all. They speak so fast, but—" Gretchen took a deep breath, knowing *don't shoot the messenger* did not apply to her, then blurted, "they're voiding it. Word came down, and they're voiding your deal." She turned away and flinched, fully expecting to be his punching bag.

"Fantastic," Bub said.

Gretchen opened one of her round cat eyes and peeked at Bub, who twirled a thorny vine in contemplation.

"Leave," he repeated, rising from his throne. "Await instructions on my response."

"Yes, sir. Thank you. I will tell them...to wait. Yes, I will tell them to wait. Thank you, sir," she said, scuttling off, claws dragging and tail sulking behind her.

Every so often, the Word of God came down to void a wager, or halt a possession, or dissolve a Faustian pact. It typically enraged Bub, but, given the current circumstances, it provided an opportunity.

With outstretched arms, he called to his minions. The horde of flies surrounded him and, in an instant, his monstrous flesh had reconfigured itself back into a digestible form. His hand-crafted features returned, yet his eyes retained the red lenses of a fly, now condensed to the perimeter of human eyelids. He pulled out a pair of tinted glasses and put them on.

He adjusted his collar and straightened his jacket, then fixed the black curls atop his head and breathed deep, taking in the putridity of sulfur and decay.

The torments of Hell resumed, louder than they had in centuries.

"I fucking love this song," Bub said, striding out of the throne room, whistling along to the screams.

16

"It's all about energy, man. The energy you put out is the energy you take in, you feel me? And this dark arts shit is everywhere nowadays, it's just everywhere, man. TV, music, movies. Don't even get me fucking started on Disney! There's just no escape. It fucks with our energy. You get what I'm saying? It makes it so the energy we put out is bad news, so we only get bad energy back. Am I way off base here?"

The Illuminaughty Zone blared in the Virgil's kitchen while James pounded a ball of dough flat. After tossing it into a perfect circle, he stretched the dough over his wooden paddle, then ladled on sauce to spread it evenly into a red spiral.

Scotty Durango: *"I mean, you see what people are saying, right? Demonic activity is up! It's like we're living in that fuckin' Ghostbusters scene where the ghosts break loose all over the city because dickless over here shut off their damn power. People write us and say they saw this, or saw that, or felt this, or felt that, or Nancy Pelosi's face just flickered into a lizard's live on TV. Amazing rack, by the way. That doesn't get enough coverage from the mainstream media. But our listeners tend to be a bit more open minded. Their third eye is wide fucking open, man. And you gotta have that thing spread eagle if you want to see all the ways this world is going to Hell. Anyways, PJ, you hear all this, what the fuck do you think is going on? Am I just fucking nuts?"*

PJ was Scotty Durango's co-host and producer, a dim bulb and soft-spoken sidekick who never dissented.

PJ: *"There's just too much weird stuff going on to say it's all fake. I mean, you remember that woman with the dog, right?"*

Scotty: *"How can I forget!"*

PJ: *"Like, this lady shot her dog. Straight up killed it. And why? Because she said it was doing black magic. Chaos magic. Making sigils out of kibbles 'n shit. She sent us pictures, remember?"*

Scotty: *"Yeah, man, fucking wild. Killed a dog!"*

PJ: *"Said the dog looked her straight in the eye, deadass, and spoke fucking Latin or some shit. You fucking remember that shit?"*

Scotty: *"Bro, trust me, I remember it."*

PJ: *"And then she died! Like four months later. Fentanyl overdose. We found out when we tried to do that follow-up episode. But like, is that shit real? Or is she just crazy? Ya know?"*

Scotty: *"Some people just have that unfortunate gift, man. They see shit. Dark shit. To quote Winston, the unsung Ghost-buster, 'Shit that will turn you white!' We know there's evil. These things get their rocks off from causing us pain, so we gotta be vigilant. Now, I am not saying shoot your dog, we'll never know what that lady really saw. But do I think it could be real? Absofucking-lutely, bro."*

Scotty took a quick breath and shifted gears.

"We want to thank our sponsors at BroMower. Gentlemen, is your nether region less of a lawn and more of a jungle? Are your pubes out of fucking control? BroMower is here with a limited time offer to make sure your junk is sittin' pretty..."

James slid the pizza off his wooden paddle and into the oven with one smooth motion. Per usual, he was barely paying attention to the podcast. And also per usual, it was burning a hole in Hector's patience, especially on a day like today.

"If I have to hear one more ad about shaving my balls, I'm going to put my head in the oven next," Hector said. He was mixing sauce on the other side of the small kitchen. The industrial-sized dough mixer churned beside him. It was a slow day, due in no small part to the single-digit temperature outside.

"Serious question though. How *are* your pubes lookin' these days?" James asked.

The machine came to a grinding halt. He squatted to peel the mass of dough off the giant mixing hook.

The mouse from yesterday's shift trickled into his mind, as did Bub, the monster from his overdose. Both had told him he was going to Hell.

He imagined himself as the dough, his body mixed, mangled, and mashed by a giant metal hook. All the demons would chop and weigh his flesh into smaller pieces, before kneading them into individual balls.

Each portion would then be pounded out by some leviathan beast and tossed in the air with glee until circular. The beast would stretch Hector's flesh over a large wooden paddle, smear red gore in a spiral with its ladle, sprinkle some cheese, then slide him into the oven to cook until crisp.

The scenario was cut short as Hector strained his lower back lifting the massive boulder of dough out from the steel basin. He plopped it on the prep table with a thud. "*Gah!*"

"You gotta lift with your knees, man," said James.

Hector grunted and nodded toward the Bluetooth speaker. "You know, these guys give me a real fucking headache."

James laughed. "Are you sure the podcast is why you have a headache? You look like absolute dogshit."

"Yeah, and that's exactly how I feel. So can we please turn this shit off?"

The door dinged open. Two men in long coats entered the restaurant. They tapped their shoes free from snow and approached the counter.

James ignored his request and said, "Looks like we got some walk-ins. You got 'em?"

"Yeah, I got 'em." He walked out to the counter, back slouching more than usual. "Hi there. What can I get for you?" he said in his customer service voice, foreign and unnatural.

"We're looking to speak with a Hector Ghouseau. Is he working today?" The man was gaunt with bags beneath his eyes, like all his meals consisted of Adderall and cigarettes.

The other man, who lacked a proper neck, simply stared at Hector through beady eyes that sat below a sloped forehead and a goonish crew cut.

Hector hesitated. "That's me. I'm Hector Ghouseau."

The men looked Hector up and down, then exchanged looks. He was their guy.

"Hello, Mr. Ghouseau. My name is Detective Surdyk, and this is my partner, Detective Borst."

Detective Borst kept his glare locked on Hector. "As you may have already heard, an acquaintance of yours, David Wojciehowski, was found dead last night—"

Hector's mind ran to a million different places, but settled on one thought. *Who the fuck is David Wojciehowski?* He interrupted the detective, "I'm sorry. I don't think I know a David Woje— Wojuhk—"

The detective pulled out a notepad and flipped through its pages. Detective Borst continued to stare. "David Wojciehowski," Detective Surdyk corrected. "You used to work with him at a neighborhood restaurant. He was a dishwasher. You bussed tables. The bartender over at Slippery Slope stated that he saw you two together last night. Ring any bells?"

Dishwasher Dave? Hector thought. *Dish Pit is dead? What the fuck is going on?*

Hector replied, "Oh. Yeah. That does. I just—didn't know his last name. Yeah, I saw him last night. Sure."

"The bartender also stated that he saw Mr. Wojciehowski hand something off to you before you went into the restroom."

Hector's gut fell through the floor. "Uh, well, it was just, uh..."

"Go on."

"It was just a pack of cigarettes."

"The bartender also stated that, after you left, Mr. Wojciehowski was complaining—directly to the bartender, mind you—that you stole his drugs."

"Whoa. Okay, that—that's not true in the slightest."

Detective Surdyk looked back down at his notepad, and said, "To quote the bartender, 'He was furious at this dude named Hector. Said he stole his drugs. His coke. Said he gave him a few bumps of coke and he ran off with the whole bag. The bag of coke.' End quote."

Hector rubbed the back of his neck. "Okay. Even if, hypothetically, parts of that are true, I didn't steal it."

"No?"

"No, I flushed it. Hypothetically."

"You *hypothetically* flushed Mr. Wojciehowski's cocaine?"

"Right."

"May I ask why?"

"Because I'm pretty sure it was laced with—what's that stuff —fentanyl."

"So you were just doing him a favor."

"Correct."

Detective Borst's upper lip twitched at the exchange.

"Mr. Ghouseau, we're not here to investigate whether you did or did not take a few bumps of cocaine. We're not even here to investigate whether you did or did not *steal* Mr. Wojciehowski's cocaine." Detective Surdyk leaned forward. "What we are here to investigate is the *murder* of Mr. Wojciehowski. He was found with a massive knife wound to his throat in a snowbed that was red from his own blood. I don't care what you do for fun. I'll leave that to my colleagues in a different department. What I do care about is who was on the other end of that knife. This is the second murder of its kind in this neighborhood. So I don't want to hear any funny stories—"

Hector interrupted again, "But I'm not lying. Yes, I did his drugs," he said, then immediately regretted it. "I mean, flushed them. But no, I did not kill Dish Pi— Dave. I did not kill Dave. Fuck no."

"Calm down. We're just here to ask some questions. That's all."

"Listen, I was with a girl last night. The entire night. From the time I got to the bar to this morning. I was always with her. You can call her. Her name is Jess. Here." Hector pulled out his phone and wrote down Jess's number on receipt paper, then handed it to Detective Surdyk.

The detectives exchanged another look, then Detective Surdyk said, "I'll be right back."

Hector's heart raced, but mentally, rationally, he wasn't worried. He wasn't lying. He'd been with Jess all last night, and he knew he didn't kill Dish Pit. So what did he have to worry about?

The detective had mentioned two murders, last week's at Cole's surely being the first. Hector had heard all the gruesome details from Tommy. Sammie had worked there just a few years prior. If she still had been—the thought made Hector sick.

Detective Borst finally spoke. "'Ghouseau.' Sounds French. You don't look French."

"Yeah, I'm not. It's a long story. My family changed it, well, specifically, my grandma wanted to change it when they got here because—"

The detective's beady eyes narrowed. Hector shut up.

His phone vibrated on the counter. Another text from Sammie.

The thought of seeing Sammie made him want to do another line from Dish Pit's tainted bag or reach for Detective Borst's gun and commit suicide by cop—but he also wanted nothing more than to hear her voice, to feel her touch.

On quiet nights or in the first breaths of morning, Hector sometimes caught himself imagining the scent of Sammie's hair, its earthy oils, her dark curls, wild and short. During the day, he fought to keep her off his mind, but even his own terrible tattoos served as a reminder, his upper arm reading *Nothing Matters* in the center of a crooked heart, her leg reading the same.

They split a thirty-pack of beer and exchanged hearts that autumn night. Neither remembered who suggested matching stick 'n' pokes, but after a brief brainstorming session, they settled on an idea both deemed stupid enough for their bodies: *Nothing Matters*.

In an act more intimate than sex, they sat close and made their mark on one another. While giggling and tapping the needle into Hector's arm, Sammie decided to add the heart.

As they curled up on the couch, their new artwork raw and red, they felt safe in each other's arms. Though life was often unfair and unkind, they would walk between the raindrops as the storm raged around them, unbothered, together. *Nothing Matters* was a lie, but the truth was harder to say aloud.

No, it wasn't that Hector didn't want to see her. It was a matter of not knowing what to say, not knowing what to do. So much had changed since the hearts. That night now felt like a dream. He ignored the text.

Detective Surdyk was just walking back after what had felt like an eternity.

"So, I called the number you gave me. Her mother answered."

"Oh. Okay. Well, did you talk to Jess?"

Detective Surdyk shook his head. "No, couldn't talk to Jess."

Hector was confused. "What? Why?"

"She's been in the psychiatric ward of Ascension Saint Mary's since earlier this morning."

The room crumpled itself up into a ball. Hector cowered somewhere in the wreckage. "I'm sorry—what?" was all he could say.

"She's in the psych ward. Any idea why this young lady you say you were with all last night suddenly finds herself committed?"

He had no clue. Nothing about Jess that morning had felt out of the ordinary. Like most women after a night with Hector, she seemed disappointed, and confused, probably wondering where the kind, funny guy she'd lain down with had vanished to, and who this dead-eyed dipshit was beside her. Pretty standard.

"I...don't know. She seemed fine when I left."

"Apparently, when her mother arrived to pick her up this morning, the roommate had to let her in, because Jess wouldn't get off the bed. She was hysterical, crying. Ranting about a giant maggot that tried to eat her foot. The paramedics carried her from the bed kicking and screaming."

A giant maggot?

"Do you know anything about this? You sure you were with her all last night?" asked Detective Surdyk.

Hector saw two roads he could take: potentially implicate himself in the murder of Dish Pit, or implicate himself in Jess's psychotic break. The murder seemed worse. "Yes, I was definitely with her all last night."

Detective Surdyk drove right down the middle. "Seems like she witnessed something horrible, something downright traumatic. From what her mother said, she has no history of severe mental illness or hallucinations." He tapped his notepad on the counter. "So, I'll ask you again, are you sure you're telling us everything?"

Great, he thinks Jess saw me murder Dish Pit, or, at the bare minimum, that I just drugged her, raped her, and left her insane, Hector thought.

"Yes, that's really all there is to tell. It was a first date. We met at the bar, got drunk, and went back to her place. I ran into Dave. I flushed his drugs down the toilet—but I have no idea what happened to him after that. I really wish I could help you, because I am just as confused and at a loss as you are right now."

Detective Borst spoke, "Who said we were at a loss?"

The two detectives let the words hang in the air. Hector could do nothing but dart his eyes around the room, avoiding eye contact, and making himself look a thousand times more guilty.

Detective Surdyk broke the silence. "If you remember anything else—because it looks like you had a rough night, and maybe your memory's a little fuzzy—you give us a call." He handed his card to Hector, who accepted it with all the enthusiasm of receiving a cancer diagnosis. "Maybe we'll try the pizza next time."

Detective Borst gave Hector one more glare for the road, and they were gone.

James, who had been in his own little world making delivery orders, popped his head out of the kitchen window. "Those guys order anything?"

"No, no. They just, uh, were asking if we had any gluten-free crust."

"And you told them to fuck off, right?"

"Yeah. I told them to fuck off."

Hector touched where Sammie had left her mark, tracing the words through his sleeve. He hoped that she was doing better than he was.

17

And so the nightly ritual began anew. Beers were drank. Cigarettes were smoked. Records were played. They talked shit to each other. Talked shit about other people. Talked shit about themselves.

Hector gave Tommy the *complete* recap of the night before and his brush with the law. Tommy focused on one specific element of the story, ignoring the demons, talking spiders, and Hector literally dying.

"You really pissed that girl's bed and just left without saying anything?" he asked, genuinely disturbed.

Hector didn't blame Tommy for glossing over the weird bits. He knew they sounded insane, and he was still deciphering what was real and what wasn't for himself. But Tommy never called Hector crazy or implied that he was lying. He just listened. Hector knew that Tommy had been through enough in his own life that nothing shocked him anymore.

"And Sammie texted me again," Hector tacked on at the end.

"Dude, this is a few days in a row now. Please tell me you answered."

"I didn't even look at it." He finished his beer, then rose to grab another.

"I get not answering for the first day or so. You're processing, or whatever it's called." His words followed Hector to the kitchen. "But answer her. This is getting ridiculous. It could be important."

Hector shouted from the refrigerator, "But what the hell could be so important all of a sudden? We haven't talked in how long? And she's the one who went back to Milwaukee. *Fucking Wisconsin.* Just seeing her name pop up makes me want to bury my head in the sand and suffocate to death."

"You're so dramatic."

"Fuck you." He handed Tommy a beer.

"I know what happened was hard," Tommy offered.

"It emptied me, man. I got nothing left." Hector chugged half of the new beer. "Me and her should be living in the suburbs right now, drinking on a porch with one of those chair swings. You know what I'm talking about?"

Tommy nodded. "Yeah, those things are sick."

"But instead, here I am. I leave a trail of shit wherever I go."

Tommy looked down at his feet. Ever since everything with Sammie, the nights always devolved into this. After a few drinks, Hector would drag himself through the mud, and Tommy would have the Sisyphean task of lifting him out of it. The support fell on deaf ears, but Tommy never stopped trying.

Hector continued. "Things weren't supposed to be like this. I don't know if I could even look her in the face."

"I'm sure she wants to see you, dude. Why else would she be texting you?"

Hector shrugged. "I don't deserve to see her."

Tommy threw his hands up. "Holy shit, drop the dramatics!"

"And that demonic-fly thing? He knew about me and Sammie. He knew how I fucking let her down."

Tommy ignored the mention of Bub, instead focusing on the crux of the matter. "You didn't let her down. It was a situation neither of you could handle. It happens. Shit fucking happens. The only person punishing you for it is yourself."

But there was no telling Hector that he was worthy of even an ounce of happiness. A bed of nails was too luxurious for his tastes. His words began to slur. "I don't deserve a friend like you. I deserve people like me. People like Austin. But you? You're good. Fucked up, but good."

"Just text her back. It'll be good for you both," Tommy said. "And no one deserves Austin."

Austin. The chaos surrounding Dish Pit's murder had almost made Hector forget. "Tommy, I'm really sorry, but Austin is coming by tonight."

Tommy choked on his beer so hard his eyes bulged. "Fucking...what?!"

"Yeah, he was here this morning."

"Where the fuck was I?"

"You were about halfway on the couch, halfway on the floor. How did you get home anyways?"

"I rode my bike. Don't change the subject."

"You rode your bike that drunk? Your boots were still on this morning."

"I said don't change the subject!"

Tommy stood and began pacing in narrow strides, back and forth across the living room. "Hector. That piece of shit is not allowed in this house."

"I know, but—"

"No buts! After what he did to you, to Sammie—to me! Fuck that guy from here and back to fucking Florida or wherever he was. I can't believe you let him in here."

"Well, technically, he came in through the window while I was asleep."

"For fuck's sake!"

"Listen, we talked this morning and—"

"Oh! You talked this morning. Well, that solves everything then."

"Tommy, just listen."

"Alright." Tommy plopped back on the couch and opened his arms wide. "What did he say?"

"He's not doing heroin anymore, for starters," Hector said.

"He's sober?" Tommy asked.

"Well, no, but he's not doing heroin."

"Hector."

"Oh, like we could talk?"

"That's not the point and you know it," Tommy said. "What time is he coming?"

"I don't know. He should probably be here pretty soon."

Tommy rose back up. "Well, I'm not leaving my own house just because that jackass is coming here." He stormed off toward his room and lifted up his mattress. "But I am going to get *dangerously drunk*."

The words sent a chill down Hector's spine and haunted the air like a shitty ghost. He watched Tommy pull out a fifth of Rich & Rare, the finest bottom-shelf Canadian whiskey Armitage Food had to offer, from underneath his mattress.

"You just keep that there?" Hector asked.

"In case of emergencies. And this is an emergency."

"I really don't know if I'd categorize this as an—"

But Tommy was already on the bottle, taking a long pull.

"—emergency," Hector finished.

Tommy wiped his mouth with his sleeve and pointed the bottle toward Hector. "You're up."

"I think I'm good, man. I had a rough night last night. I'm still not one hundred percent."

Tommy shook his head. "Oh, no. You're not leaving me

hanging here. You're letting Austin in this house? You're getting dangerously drunk with me. That's how it's going to go."

Hector didn't really need much convincing, but he put on a show and begrudgingly took the bottle.

They passed the fifth back and forth. It had the drinkability of gasoline, but with each swig, they winced a bit less. After what could only be described as a shockingly short amount of time, they were in the bathroom together, dicks in hands, peeing in the toilet and shouting about not crossing the streams.

"What on Earth are you two doing?"

It was Austin. He stood with his hands in his pockets, leaning against the door frame, a wry smile on his face.

"Don't fucking worry about it, *Austin*," Tommy said, like the name was a punchline in and of itself.

Austin's grin widened. "The only thing I worry about is you, Tommy, my sweet boy."

Hector was too busy shaking out the last drops of piss to care what was said.

"You fellas seem like you've had a few," Austin said.

Tommy stumbled out of the bathroom first, wrestling with his belt and burping through gritted teeth. "And you seem like... a dick."

Hector followed Tommy out. "There's beers in the fridge if you—" He noticed Austin had already helped himself. "—want one."

"I figured you wouldn't mind." Austin took a loud gulp from the can.

"Yeah." Hector swayed back to the living room with Tommy, like trash blowing in the wind.

"I assume you came up from *Buttfuck, Florida,* to give me my money," Tommy said.

Austin cackled. "Again with the money? I come all the way to Chicago—in the dead of winter!—to see my two dear friends, and the first thing you do is hound me about *money*? For shame, Tommy. You're better than that!"

"I'm not better than jack shit, and you're worse," he said, the words sounding cooler in his head than the slurred string of syllables he produced.

Austin shook his head. "Hector, rein this guy in a bit here, huh?"

"Don't worry about Hector," Tommy snapped. "Don't you feel any sense of remorse or shame? Did you ever think how maybe it wasn't a good idea to just show up at our fucking house? You drugged him then tried forcing yourself on Sammie. You're a piece of shit. Not to mention you stole *three-hundred dollars* from me."

Austin's eyes fell into a dead stare, like the strings that held them up had been cut. His grin flatlined. "Tommy, I know I haven't always been a great guy—"

"Let me stop you right there," Tommy said. "That's not going to work on me. I don't want to hear any sob story." He paused. "I don't really know what I want, but I'm fairly positive it involves you fucking leaving."

The room took a beat. Everyone drank their beer.

Hector spoke. "Tommy, Austin's here because we had a talk this morning."

"Oh, you mean after he broke into our house?"

"I didn't break in. The window was unlocked," Austin clarified, stifling his grin.

Tommy's upper lip twitched.

"Yeah, alright, that was fucked," Hector said. "But we talked."

"Oh, I know. I heard you. I know you *talked*. But the only thing out of his mouth is bullshit, so any talking isn't worth very much."

"I'm not the same person I was, Tommy," Austin offered.

Tommy scoffed. 'Yeah, and why is that? Because you went to rehab? You didn't even finish!"

"I turned real corners, made real progress while I was there. I met really supportive people, a girl who changed my life, and I changed hers. I'm not a weak-willed addict anymore. I'm stronger. I had to come back to Chicago to make a life for myself —and that starts with making things right with you two. We have a history."

Tommy scoffed harder.

Austin continued. "It's not a great history. But there's no reason we can't build a new, better one."

"You're talking like you've been sober for years and have done all this work. But the only reason you left Chicago was because of *certain allegations* floating around. It's nice you could run to rehab in Florida on mommy's dime. Great. Fine. But you dropped out. And you're drinking a beer as we speak!"

Hector chimed in. "Tommy, come on, man. You know heroin is different than beer. And we're drinking too. I mean, your belt isn't even buckled right now."

Tommy looked down and saw that he had, in fact, lost the struggle with his belt. "Alright, whatever, man. And your belt is undone too."

Hector looked down. It was.

Austin clasped his hands together. "Look, tensions are high. I get it. I really do, but how about we try to turn things down a few notches, huh?"

Tommy ignored him and turned to Hector. "Can you come with me to the kitchen real quick?"

Hector sighed and followed him down the hall, their belts flapping as they walked.

Austin took a seat on the couch and hummed a structureless diddy to himself as he dug through his backpack.

He hummed as he pulled an Orange Jubilee Mad Dog from

his bag, then a Banana Red. He hummed as he listened to Tommy and Hector argue in circles. He hummed as he positioned the next rabbit in his hat, poised to reveal it when the time was right.

Hector and Tommy rejoined, and the humming stopped.

"What are those?" Tommy asked.

"I know how you two love to drink this sewage," Austin said, motioning to the Mad Dogs like they were some grand banquet. "Consider them a peace offering."

"We only drink Mad Dogs on Monday," Tommy said, protective.

But Hector was already reaching for the Orange Jubilee. Tommy huffed and followed suit, taking Banana Red. Austin's grin returned. They cracked them open and drank them down like there was a prize for finishing first. Tommy won.

The needle left the record. Tommy got up to flip it, but struggled to maintain balance. Hector's one eye fluttered to stay open, while the other was wide with madness. Neither had fixed their belts. Witnessing this, Austin slapped his knees. This was the moment he had waited for.

"Hey, listen, guys, it's been fun, but I gotta run. I just wanted to pop in, say hello, and mend some bridges."

"Mend this," Tommy said, motioning to his dick and plopping back into his seat.

"Right," Austin acknowledged. "Oh, before I go— I brought you guys one last thing."

He reached back into his backpack, and emerged with a black leather overnight bag, the type one might use to carry their toothbrush and razor on a business trip. But instead of toiletries, Austin pulled out a brand-new syringe, a shining silver spoon, a few cotton balls, and a small ziploc bag.

"And there it fucking is," Tommy said. "You're so fucking full of shit. Get that shit out of here."

"That's not heroin, Tommy," Hector said, staring at the bag like Indiana Jones at a coveted artifact. "That's cocaine."

"I can't get a single thing past you, can I, Hector?" Austin's grin stretched into maniacal clown territory.

"We're not fucking animals, Austin. We snort our coke. What the fuck is wrong with you?" Tommy demanded to know.

Hector's eyes had not left the bag. He was marinated in Mad Dog and primed to do whatever Austin laid out in front of him.

"You know, down in Florida," Austin poured some coke into the spoon from the tiny bag, "in treatment," he motioned to Hector, who, without saying a word, reached into his pocket and handed him his lighter, "they told me that we do drugs and are addicts because of trauma, shit that happened that was bad. Real bad. Well, I don't know anyone who *hasn't* had real bad shit happen to them. Do you guys?"

Neither said a word. Hector, too transfixed by the drugs before him, and Tommy, too drunk and annoyed to engage Austin further, both rocked as they sat.

"Everyone goes through shit. We all have our pain. But not everyone is sitting here like us tonight, too drunk to button our pants or cooking up cocaine. Do you know why?"

With a few drops from his water bottle and a flick of the lighter, Austin's face was now illuminated by the glow of cooking cocaine. The lights in the living room seemed to darken.

"Because they're cowards. They're okay with being bored. They're fine with stewing in their suffering until it ruptures them from the inside. Loveless marriages and shitty fucking children."

He concentrated on the flame.

"We know life has so much more to offer, so we grab it by the throat and ride it into the fucking ground. But after a while, the beers are sobering, the sex is meaningless, and the lines excite us for a climax that never comes. So we keep pushing, trying to find the next limit."

He carefully removed a cotton ball from the bag and soaked up the liquid.

"And we feel again. We fucking *feel* again. And it feels good. I don't think life, or whatever waits for us beyond its shoddy walls, is worth it if we're not feeling good. And I don't know about you two, but lately, I've been feeling real fucking good. And I don't care how I get there anymore. So the least I can do is pass a little bit of that onto you. Is that okay?"

He unwrapped the syringe and sucked up the drugs from the cotton.

"I only have one needle. You'll have to share it. But you're like brothers, right? I'm sure you don't mind," Austin said.

Tommy had reached his breaking point. "I think it's about time you get the fuck out of here," he said, punctuated with a Mag Dog-flavored burp.

"Like I said, I just came to mend bridges. Enjoy your night, fellas." Austin packed up his materials, leaving only the syringe. "Don't be a stranger, Hector. And answer your texts, huh?" He winked. The winter air rushed through the door as he opened it. Austin looked back once more, and said, "Tommy, good seeing you, as always."

The door slammed shut, and he was gone.

Tommy flipped off the closed door and grunted. "Can you believe that fucking guy? He thinks we're going to shoot up drugs. Why? Just...*because*? What a fucking—"

But Hector had already pulled his undone belt out from its loops and was tying it around his arm. He was up first.

18

"There it is! There it is, Mom!" a child shouted a few rows up.

And there it was indeed: The Mars Cheese Castle. Towering over the interstate, its regal structure broke the geographic monotony of the trip between Milwaukee and Chicago. Sammie's eyes followed it through her Megabus passenger window.

As a child, the Mars Cheese Castle fascinated her. From the backseat of her parents' car, she marveled at the roadside attraction built to resemble a medieval castle, wondering how something so magical could exist in such an unremarkable place.

Whatever her parents argued about in the front seat, which they did every drive over ten minutes, didn't matter when she saw its towers. She was transported to Camelot. On one such trip, little Sammie was determined to stop inside, so she staged a well-timed bladder emergency. When her mother snapped at her to hold it, she turned the waterworks on.

Sammie could barely contain her excitement as they pulled into its parking lot, but was bewildered upon entering the castle to see no knights or princesses or dancing court jesters, only red-faced Midwesterners wheezing over shopping carts filled with meats and cheeses.

Looking at the castle now, the wonder and awe were gone. The thought of cheese and cured meat as far as the eye could see made her nauseous, even more so than she already felt from the motion of the bus and from the events of the night before.

What began as a normal night at StrangeBürd, the over-priced fried chicken restaurant where Sammie served tables, quickly escalated once she clocked out. With the help of a fistful of pills and a double shot of whiskey for her shift drink, she soon stumbled around the neighborhood collecting free rounds from the bars who knew her all too well. The subsequent details were not great, and she had been doing her best all day to not think about them.

Last night was especially bad, but the recent news of Vince had set her on a destructive path all week. The gruesome details of her friend's murder were more than enough to trigger her binge-drinking reflex. Just thinking of Vince all carved up and littered with stab wounds sent a chill down her spine, and an ache to her liver.

Sure, Vince was a bit of a know-it-all at work. He made fun of her taste in music and would sometimes torture her by playing songs she hated on repeat, but he was a nice guy who never made her feel uncomfortable, and he regularly covered shifts. He didn't deserve what he got.

As recently as yesterday morning, she had considered skipping his wake altogether. The formalities that followed death seemed silly to her, and the thought of returning to Chicago did not exactly fill her with glee. But something inside tugged at her to go, and, after the trouble she got herself in last night, it seemed like a good idea to get out of town for a minute.

Holy shit, this guy reeks.

The man sitting next to her in his gray sweatpants and worn

Packers jacket had the smell of stale piss and old hamburger meat lingering about him. He was a typical Megabus passenger. It was the poor man's Greyhound, which was already the poor man's version of every other form of travel. Sammie was about to hurl.

"Excuse me," she said, a closed fist to her mouth.

Nothing—just a vacant stare and a slacked mouth, like a cow too dumb to know it's in line for the slaughter.

"*Excuse me,*" Sammie said, a bit of bass in her voice now.

"Oh. Yeah. Hm." He shifted his legs as an empty gesture, providing no additional room for Sammie to pass. She stepped over his gray sweatpants in a few clumsy strides.

The Megabus restroom was slightly larger than a high school locker. It made her long for the smell of the hamburger meat man. *Chemicals. Piss. Shit.* If she hadn't already needed to vomit, the restroom itself would have done the trick. She knelt down as best she could and stuck her head in the toilet, discharging stomach bile into the plastic toilet.

As dark settled in, the empty terrain turned to suburbs. Chicago was close. The skyline appeared in the distance. Sammie closed her eyes and felt the anxiety tug on her throat. The city was carnivorous, and ate you from the inside out, but somewhere between its alcohol-filled veins and hard-nosed cynicism rested a beating heart. She could hear it pounding.

The bus pulled up to Union Station, and the hamburger meat man was fast asleep. Sammie tapped him on the shoulder. No response. Just labored breathing. She slung her bag over her shoulder and let it smack him in the face as she climbed over his gray, dirty sweatpants. "Sorry," she said.

Skyscrapers loomed and lit up the black sky. Snow swirled like it had been doing for days. Sammie stepped off the bus and felt a chill unlike the cold in Milwaukee. It went beyond her bones. Her soul shuddered in its bite.

It had been a while since she had been downtown, and the city's winter disguise made it difficult for her to recognize her surroundings. She pulled out her phone for directions, but it immediately died. Sammie blamed the hamburger meat man for spreading himself over the outlet that sat between them.

She approached a woman waiting to cross the street with a golden labrador. The woman wore a designer parka that Sammie had noticed nearly all women of a certain tax bracket wore. She had once looked up the price, having liked how warm it looked, and found that it cost the equivalent of a week's pay. The dog wore a matching, miniature version.

Sammie smiled, and asked, "Excuse me, can you tell me which way the Blue Line is?"

The woman glanced Sammie up and down, pursing her lips. "I'm sorry. I don't have any change."

"What? No. Do you know which way the Blue Line train is?"

"I don't carry cash," the woman affirmed. She put in a pair of earbuds and craned her neck in the opposite direction.

Okay. Fucking rude, Sammie thought. The golden labrador crept up and kissed her index finger. It put her at ease. She chose a direction and started walking.

After a few unfamiliar blocks, Sammie came across the Whole Foods where she used to work years ago, and where she had met Tommy. She had fond memories of going in the cooler of the prepared foods department together with him to shovel their faces full of smoked mozzarella salad and balls of falafel. It was through Tommy that she met Hector.

On a winter evening much like this one, Hector had come to pick up Tommy's house keys. He locked himself out of their apartment. He looked like shit. Terrible posture. Dark rings around his eyes. Layers of sweatshirt, jean jacket, and flannel compensated for the lack of a proper winter coat. He didn't look a single person in the eyes or say a word to anyone else but Tommy. Sammie was in love.

The walk continued. Her right boot had a small hole in its sole. The snow bled in, and her sock became wet.

Her mind wandered to standing behind that Whole Foods deli counter with Tommy in their oversized, bleach-scented chefs coats. They were no chefs. They sliced turkey and scooped tuna salad. But there they stood. And there Sammie watched Hector slink away. She asked Tommy who he was, and practically invited herself over. They kissed and made love for the very first time that night.

She entered the Clinton Blue Line stop just as the train was pulling in.

Doors closing, the automated voice announced. Sammie darted between them and entered the train car with momentum, stumbling in. The only other passenger was a woman toward the back in a large, tattered coat, the hood pulled down with its peak below her nose. She sat sprawled with a tall can sheathed in a paper bag between her legs. Sammie heard the woman mumbling to herself.

"they know everything. they see everything. rats. rats. soft to the touch. rats. beautiful rats. not scared of the light at the end of the tunnel. no sir. not scared of shit. rats. that light ain't nothing but light and you can take that to the fucking bank. nothing but light. no more. no less. nothing special."

The woman shifted in her seat, uncomfortable in any position.

Sammie stared out the window as the train sped through a black tunnel, watching the woman in the glass's reflection against the dark, careful not to let her stare linger and invite conversation.

After the downtown stops had all come and gone, the train car ascended out of the tunnels and into the lights of Wicker

Park, soaring above the city streets and barreling west toward the Damen station. It passed Santullo's Pizza, where everyone and their mother used to work, and Reckless Records, where all their friends' bands ended up in the dollar bin. And, of course, the alley behind Subterranean and Estelle's, where the tracks hung overhead and cast shadows like a great forest canopy as far as tired eyes could see. She and Hector spent many nights doing drugs off the dumpster lids and drinking beers in their shade while the trains roared above.

"Gah!" Sammie blurted. Something had bit her on her ankle. She lifted up the cuff of her jeans and saw a spider about the size of a quarter. It ran out from the top of her boot to the doors, its tiny white hairs visible as it scurried away. "Ew, ew, ew, ew," she muttered.

This is California. Doors open on the right at California, the automated voice proclaimed.

This was her stop. She scratched her ankle, and felt flushed as she stood up, but shook it off. *White spiders aren't poisonous,* she thought, a notion that had embedded itself into her mind at some point. She wasn't sure if it was true or not, and she had never seen a spider like that in Chicago before.

"littletinyfuckinrats. just appetizers. keep the blood flowing. it must never stop flowing." The woman pointed directly at Sammie as she exited the train. "You're the main course, Sammie." Her bloodshot eyes widened, and she barked, "HE'S COMING FOR YOU, BITCH!"

"What the fuck did you just say?" Sammie stepped back toward the car, but the doors shut in her face. The woman cackled as the train pulled away.

Psycho, she thought, barely registering that the woman said her name. She figured she must have misheard her. *Lots of words sound like Sammie. There's Hammie, Whammy, Tammy...*

The train platform was empty. The wind whistled its song to

an audience of one. Logan Square in the dead of winter was just as she remembered it. Lonely and cold.

She tried powering up her phone. It turned on, clinging to life at zero percent. No new texts. A few friends made excuses for not being able to host her, while others didn't respond, Hector included. She wasn't asking much. The wake was tomorrow, and she had no plans to overstay her welcome in Chicago. A day or two was enough. The phone went black.

But she wasn't worried. She was confident she'd end up *somewhere*. If anything, Sammie wished she could thank Vince for giving her a reason to get out of Milwaukee. Despite previous reservations, this city hit the spot.

Gun to her head, if someone had asked Sammie to describe Chicago in a few sentences, she would tell them about its alleys and the highways of train tracks that sat above them. Like the Damen stop, outside the California station was a discordant collage of tracks, dimly lit alleyways, and electrical lines. The asymmetry and simplicity of it all was breathtaking. The most practiced German expressionist couldn't capture its surrealist output, and Norman Rockwell himself couldn't hold a candle to just how fucking American and earnest it was.

Passing through the nearest alley, she peered up at the snow falling like ash in the yellow streetlights, and stumbled over a cracked cinder block in her path. She stopped and stared at its gray, broken body. And, although she was no cinder block authority, it sure looked identical to the one she had put through a certain Scott's windshield just last night.

Scott worked as a barback in one of the cool bars in her neighborhood. A skinny, tattooed boy with a sexy, dumb mustache, she felt nothing but instinctual lust for the guy. But it still tore at her insides when he'd ghosted her to sleep with one of her coworkers.

Though the extent of their relationship consisted of back-to-back nights of clumsy drunken sex, it was a matter of principle to Sammie. He didn't have to ignore her texts or start fucking someone who she had to see nearly every day. Finding out from the coworker in question mid-shift made it all the worse.

So when the dishwasher sensed her pain and sold her a handful of random amphetamines out of the kindness of his soul, she crushed them up in the bathroom and railed them off the back of the toilet. She left work with a vendetta in her rapidly beating heart.

Scott may as well have been any of the other assholes in her life. They took what they wanted and left. No one ever invested the time to get to know her, to know the reasons she drank, to read the sadness in her eyes. Hector was an asterisk, but even he could be boiled down to the same formula as the others. Things got hard or inconvenient, and he left, or, more accurately, she left. But she had no choice. He had made it the only option.

Sammie had a latent rage she had inherited from her mother, and the gift of dissociation from her father. Her own issues were no mystery to her. Given that, she did feel a little bad about the cinder block through Scott's window.

When she left work, drunk and high on amphetamines, she wasn't necessarily on a mission to do what she did, things just unfolded that way. A few bars, a few more drinks, and next thing she knew, she was on his street. The cinderblock sat filthy and chipped on the curb. It called to her. It knew her name. It practically demanded her to pick it up. When she lifted it above her head and stood on the hood of Scott's Nissan Versa, she felt powerful.

It took three solid throws before it broke the windshield. As she wound up for the fourth, someone screamed, "Whoa! What the fuck are you doing?" off in the distance.

Sammie wasn't sure if it was Scott, a neighbor, or the President of the United States, she just knew to get out of there, fast.

She hid in an alley, and squatted against a wall to pee, maniacally giggling.

In the morning, she reconsidered not going to Vince's wake, and booked a bus ticket for the afternoon. She figured it an opportunity to let any heat from her late-night activities die down.

Sammie continued her trek through the Logan Square alley. She knew the neighborhood like the back of her hand but had nowhere to go. Go Tavern wasn't far. That would be as good a stop as any.

Then she saw little droplets of blood like breadcrumbs.

They looked fresh, yet to be covered or diluted by the still-falling snow. The droplets led behind a row of dumpsters.

One might categorize what led her to follow the blood as stupidity, or maybe an attempt to fill her respective void with adrenaline, but in the rarest of circumstances, if you squinted at it in just the right light, it could even be mistaken for bravery.

The drops grew in diameter as she neared the row of dumpsters. She peeked her head around the large receptacle and saw a rat. A dead rat. A very dead rat. It had been sliced open from mouth to anus, lying in a crimson crater of snow.

Oh God.

Just as she was no cinder block expert, Sammie was also no authority on the predatory habits of Midwestern mammals, but she was pretty sure this wasn't the work of any animal. Whatever killed this rat had not done so with the intention of eating it. Its flesh was mostly intact, except for the surgical slice down its abdomen, where organs poured out in whatever fashion physics dictated. The rat's mouth hung open, its small black eyes turned up toward the sky, its limbs outstretched like a sacrifice to some horrible deity.

Sammie's fists clenched at the thought of someone doing

such a thing. She loved rats. They were smart, nimble, empathetic creatures.

I'm not going to leave you like this.

She kicked up as much snow and underlying gravel as she could until the rat was covered by a tiny burial mound, further drenching her own sock in the process.

For a grave marker, she found a shard of green glass, likely from an old beer bottle, and stuck it in the snow. It glimmered in the alley lights. She gave the rat a nod and went on her way.

Sammie had walked the neighborhood countless times. Most walks were filled with music in her ears and wandering thoughts. Others had conversations and shared cigarettes. But there were some walks she wanted to forget. Some still hurt to think about, like the walk home with Hector after Planned Parenthood.

That walk was silent. She had taken the first pill at the center, and the second weighed in her backpack like lead. It had seemed like Hector wanted to say something, but he never got it out. She couldn't read him. She wasn't even sure how she felt. A thick fog kept pace between them. An early summer day had never felt so cold.

She used to wish Hector had spoken up in the days prior, or at Planned Parenthood in the final minutes. It wouldn't have taken much to change her mind, only enough to see that some part of him was conflicted, that he saw a future. But he just watched her take that first pill, then walked beside her down Armitage Avenue without a word. She would take the second pill at home alone.

"Excuse me, miss, got a cigarette?"

Her trip down memory lane was cut short by a small Puerto Rican man balancing himself on a cane outside Go Tavern. He was old, bordering on ancient, and a staple of the bar for as long as Sammie had been going there.

"No, I don't. I'm sorry," Sammie said with complete sincerity.

"Alright, then. You have a good night, young lady." And he shuffled off to ask the next patron.

It was a slow night. She grabbed an isolated seat near the end of the bar with a clear view of the sidewalk for people watching.

Sammie recognized the bartender, who smiled and approached with a bounce. She wanted to say her name was Ida but couldn't be sure. She decided to play it by ear and see if she was recognized first.

"Oh hey, Sammie!"

Shit.

"Hi, Ida!" A shot in the dark. Ida's face lit up. *Bingo.* "How have you been?"

"Oh, just work, work, work. I feel like I never leave this place. I haven't seen you around in a while." She placed a glass of water on a coaster. "You look good."

I look and feel like dogshit. Sammie dug deep for her will to converse. "Oh, thank you! I just got off the Megabus, so I feel a little gross. I love your hair though. It's shorter than I remember."

Ida blushed. "I thought it was time for a change."

"Well, it looks good."

"Thank you. You meeting anyone, or just yourself tonight?"

"Just me."

"Not meeting up with what's-his-name? You two always came in together. I still see him during the shift change sometimes, leaving when I come in at night."

"Hector?" Sammie asked, knowing the answer.

"Yeah, Hector! Him and his little friend."

"Nope, just me tonight."

"My favorite kind of nights." Ida pivoted. "You still in the neighborhood?"

"I'm actually in Milwaukee now. Just back in town for a few days."

"Milwaukee?" Ida asked, as if it was some foreign land.

"Yeah, I'm originally from there. It's not a bad place." Sammie forced a smile. "I love Chicago, but I just needed to regroup, ya know?"

"Totally get it," Ida said, softening her incredulous tone. "Good food up there, and beer. Big beer town, right?"

Sammie nodded. "They do love their beer up there, correct."

"Not as much as here though," she said with a wink. "First round is on me. High Life and a shot of Crow sound good?"

It really didn't. Nothing really did. But free drinks were free drinks. "Absolutely. Thank you so much."

She downed the whiskey and did her best to not show displeasure. A few more of those and she might find herself in some trouble again tonight.

Sammie reached down and touched her ankle. She had nearly forgotten all about the spider bite. It itched a bit, and she still felt a little flushed, but she was pretty sure she wasn't going to die from it.

Oh, you have got to be fucking kidding me. Sammie couldn't believe her eyes, peering out the window to the street. *What the fuck is he doing here?*

It was Austin. Last she heard, he had skipped town with his tail between his legs. She hoped that Hector hadn't done something so stupid as to let him back in his life. Seeing him, even from this distance, nauseated her.

Please do not fucking come in here, she begged in silence, hiding her face behind her beer.

Austin walked like he owned the street, then stopped.

He turned his nose to the air and sniffed at it like an animal. Sammie slunk down farther. He smiled, like he knew she was there without ever turning toward Go Tavern. He spat, adjusted his jacket, and kept on walking.

Asshole.

Sammie hated him. Not just for cornering her and shoving his disgusting tongue down her throat, which alone was more than enough reason, but also for drugging Hector to do it. Austin put a distance between them that had never existed before. She knew that Hector had some misguided love for Austin, but it wasn't reciprocated in the way Hector imagined. Austin kept Hector wrapped around his finger with little more than the occasional encouraging word, like tossing a bone to a starving dog.

Plus, he used to tease Sammie about her eyes being too close together. That pissed her off to no end.

Asshole, she repeated to herself as he disappeared from sight.

Shortly before Sammie's move to Milwaukee, rumors about his behavior intensified. When the talk got too loud, he made a big show about going to rehab and fucked off to Florida, vowing to *heal* himself and *take accountability*. She didn't buy a word of it.

"Hey, Ida, can I do another round, please?"

Sammie didn't need another reason to drink, but the Lord provided. It was going to be one of those nights after all.

She silently toasted the fresh shot to the rat she had buried in the alley. The whiskey went down much smoother the second time around, and there was no displeasure to hide. She slammed the glass down, and thought, *That fucking psycho probably killed that poor rat.* She chuckled and hoped to God that she was wrong, for everyone's sake.

19

*S*mile *with your eyes.*

    Smile with your eyes.

    Austin entered Walgreens, repeating the mantra he'd learned from a childhood therapist to himself.

He remembered the new carpet smell of the young Dr. Hannah's office, the cheeks of her porcelain face, pointed and blushed like a Victorian muse. —*It's okay to be hurt when your classmates make fun of you. You don't need to feel ashamed about that. And just because you don't smile the way they do, doesn't make you any less special. And it certainly doesn't make you a "robot." But if you want the other kids to not make fun of your smile, you just have to remember: happiness comes from the eyes. If you're feeling happy, just let your eyes show it. You have joy in your heart like we all do, sometimes it takes work to feel safe enough to share it with the world. But when you do, just remember: smile with your eyes.*

Dr. Hannah always smiled with her eyes. They radiated a warmth Austin never felt at home. He used to think of her eyes as he drifted to sleep, imagining he could live in her gaze forever.

His father eventually pulled him from therapy, saying it was a waste of time and money, that only freaks and faggots went. A sentiment he held until his death.

Austin walked up and down the aisles of Walgreens with a rough idea of what he needed, but he took his time. There was no rush. Things were already in motion that couldn't be stopped, might as well check out the candy aisle. Since he stopped shooting heroin, candy was critical.

He skipped right over the chocolate. It didn't scratch the itch. He needed the hard stuff. Warheads. Sour Patch Kids. Candy that fought back.

Addicts loved candy, and Austin used that knowledge to help him manipulate the others in rehab. He would introduce himself, offer some Sour Skittles, then turn on the charm, always smiling with his eyes. It was how he borrowed money, got others to lie for him, and slept with nearly every girl in the facility. It was how he met Whitney.

Whitney was a stripper by trade, an addict by nature, and a new-age witch by way of personality disorder, but she always carried herself with the confidence of a runway model. She wanted to transcend the material world, and would do anything to reach new pinnacles of enlightenment.

She immediately noticed Austin's foul aura, but dark energies can be powerful keys. She resolved to exploit him for her spiritual endeavors. Whitney thought she was slick, but Austin was slicker.

When he offered her candy with that grin of his, he could tell she was faking the smiles, the coy laughter, the way she touched his arm. He wasn't sure what her endgame was, but he knew that she had one.

But Austin was just looking to fuck, so his strategy would remain the same. He would make her fall in love with him.

It only took one late-night walk around the facility before they were oversharing traumas in the Florida heat. Austin didn't even have to lie. He had plenty. Daddy issues. Mommy issues. He was covered in scars, both physical and non.

Whitney shared her own history of early sexual abuse, and all the horrors that led her to rehab. Austin listened. He shared his own. She started to feel safe with him. He smiled with his eyes when he deemed it appropriate.

They shared their first kiss after art therapy the following evening as the sun set. Under that cotton-candy sky, Whitney decided it was time to show Austin her other side.

She had a cargo van parked just off the premises. Security at the rehab was a joke, so it was not difficult to slip off the grounds with a bit of ingenuity and stealth. Whitney spent most nights in her van, reading and meditating and attempting to astral project, then snuck back in before the sun began its ascent.

It was a nondescript white box of a vehicle, the only defining feature being tinted windows that Whitney had added for privacy, as the van doubled as her home when she was not in rehab. But when she slid open its door, it transformed into a miniature temple of the occult.

Black tapestries draped the ceiling, illuminated by strings of dark purple lights that Whitney plugged into a travel-sized generator. The panels were covered in sigils, some painted, some carved. A twin mattress lay against the back doors.

Austin began to harden.

"When I first tried to get sober, the first of many attempts, you know how that goes, I found a real peace, a sense of purpose, in practicing magick. It called to me through the withdrawals, through the night sweats and vomiting." Whitney traced a finger over one of the carved sigils.

He surveyed the van's interior. "And I assume you don't mean the rabbit out of a hat kind?"

Whitney chuckled. "No, the kind that binds our universe."

"Listen, I've had plenty of girls talk my ear off about astrology, with all due respect—"

"Not astrology," Whitney interrupted. "It's real. It works. I don't know exactly how it works, but it works."

"What works?" asked Austin. "And works how?"

"The strength of the magick depends on the practitioner," Whitney said, a longing in her voice. "You can elevate yourself to a pure light, or lower yourself into pure power. You can shift reality to suit your needs. You can bend it *to your will*." Her eyes lit up like a child describing what they wanted for Christmas.

Austin rubbed the back of his neck, feeling a wave of second-hand embarrassment. "Right. Listen, if they check my room and I'm not there again, they're going to schedule me for an extra session of DBT, so I think I'm going to head back."

Whitney continued, unabated. "I've tried so many different forms and practices. Some dark, some light. Thelema. Wicca. Chaos. Solomonic. Eventually, I reached a void. And in that void, at my lowest point, I found a magick that only reveals itself to you when you feed it what it wants."

"Oh yeah? And what does it want?"

"Pain."

That put him on alert. He didn't believe in magick, but he did believe in people's capacity for delusion and violence. His muscles tightened.

"I'll be honest, Austin. When we first met, I sensed something deeply disturbing in you. Your aura was the darkest I'd ever seen, the kind I've been looking for. I thought I could use you."

Austin's hands tensed, ready to lunge and crush her windpipe if she tried anything funny.

"But then I got to know you," she continued, "and saw that I was wrong."

He relaxed his muscles.

"We're kindred spirits. We've both been through so much pain. The world has never given a shit about either of us. We're nothing. Bottom feeders." She stared off into the darkness of the van. "We've hurt people."

Whitney looked into Austin's eyes. "But we can rebuild ourselves into something better." She took his hands in hers. "I've told you things that I never tell anyone, and you accepted me for who I am. And I see you."

Austin played along. "You said you feed it pain. What type of pain?"

"My own pain. If you give yourself to it, it opens doors." She lifted her shirt to reveal a midriff etched with sigils carved into her skin, some scarred, some crusted with dried blood. "And through those doors is enlightenment. We can transcend this bullshit life."

He had no visceral reaction to her self-mutilation. It was not a deterrent to his arousal. Far from it. "And where exactly did I come into play here?"

"I needed a few drops of your blood."

Austin threw up his hands and started toward the door. "Alright, little lady, I think I've heard enough. I've done a lot of freaky shit, but I'm not about to let some chick cut me in the back of her van."

She reached out to stop him. "Wait! No, I don't need your blood anymore. That's what I'm trying to say. You're not who I thought you were."

Whitey gave a slight pout and slacked her eyes into the listless stare of an accomplished seductress. "Besides, it would have only been a few drops. To help open the door. Then I'd ghost you. It's not like I was going to murder you or anything. Unless —that's what you want?" She grazed the bottom of her lip with her front teeth.

The subtle scrape sent Austin's libido into overdrive.

"Okay, so what's the new plan?" he asked.

"I want you to join me in this. Our pain is so similar. A sex ritual would now be exponentially stronger."

"Well, yeah, I could have told you that. I've always said that if you want a ritual done right, it's got to be a sex ritual. I literally always say that." Austin's grin widened. He forgot to smile with his eyes, but the shadows concealed it.

Whitney grabbed hold of his bulge and motioned with her head. "You see that sigil behind me?" It was a crudely drawn union of letters and lines, scribbled on paper torn from a notebook, and taped to the van wall. "I need you to fuck me as hard as you can and think of that sigil. I want you to fuck me like it's your first and last time. You got it?"

Austin nearly exploded right then and there, but couldn't resist asking, "Why that one?"

It didn't seem like anything special to him, just a weird little stick figure. He thought it looked a bit like a bug.

She reached into his pants and pulled out his erection. "It's beautiful, isn't it? The sigil. It came to me in a dream the other night. It's specific for this moment, for us." She leaned in and kissed him, her tongue swirled around the inside of his mouth, brushing his lips. "You understand what you need to do? Never lose thought of the sigil. I am the sigil. Its lines, its contours, its edges are my body."

She bent over and placed Austin in her mouth. Between her slow, rhythmic swallows she looked up at him, and said, "When it's time, I need you to cum deep inside of me."

Austin stared at the sigil while Whitney worked. He didn't care what mumbo jumbo she believed in, he only cared about getting off, and if this was the road that led there, then so be it.

He stared up at the ceiling of the van as ecstasy washed over him. The sigil flashed in his mind. When he brought his head down, Whitney looked fifty feet below him. He heard a buzzing in the air, like a fly.

The sigil ignited, consuming his vision with its fire.

Whitney was now on top, riding him and shoving her tongue down his throat. She propped her hands against the wall of the van so her breasts bounced in Austin's face. He sucked them and ran his hands along her body. His fingers felt her flesh but his mind only saw the sigil. He thrust. She moaned and gyrated faster, deeper. Austin felt her hand on his throat just as he was about to cum.

Then the lights went out.

Whitney was gone.

Austin stood alone, naked in the darkness. There was a drip in the distance that fell in a steady pulse. That same buzz hung in the air like static. The drips grew louder and more frequent.

An unknown substance wet his feet. The dripping liquid had started to accumulate.

There was a dreamlike quality to how he could move his limbs, to the way his senses perceived his complete lack of surroundings. It was as if the air itself was thick and gelatinous, dark and heavy.

There was no time to process. The reality Austin knew was gone. His only immediate thoughts were of survival. He rubbed the rising substance between his fingers, but couldn't discern its nature through the impenetrable black around him.

He started to feel vulnerable. He hated feeling vulnerable.

Then, a voice. "Hello, Austin."

"Who is that? Who's there?"

"You seem panicked. Is everything alright?"

"Is everything— What the fuck is going on? Where am I?"

"You're in the between," the voice said.

"Between? Between what? Listen, man, I don't know where I

am. I just want to go back. Do you know how to get back?" He tried to hold it together, but his last words trembled.

"Get back?" the voice said. "To that drug-addicted whore? She dabbled in things she really should not have dabbled in. She lacks the backbone for the required *follow through*. But not you."

"Yeah, no, I totally get what you're saying." Austin was frantic, and eager to agree with whatever spoke to him. "I didn't know what the fuck she was doing with all that hocus pocus. I thought we were just going to have sex. I barely know her. You know how it goes, right?"

The voice did not answer.

"So maybe instead of taking me back to her, you can take me somewhere else. Anywhere. Because I can't see anything here. I can't see anything. *It's so dark.*"

The voice responded, "You have a quick tongue, amongst other desirable qualities."

Austin forced a chuckle. "So you'll help me?"

"Let's start with helping you see."

A burst of red light blinded Austin. Then, more red. Everywhere he looked—above, below, in the distance—the red stretched with no end in sight. What began as a drip was now a waterfall, leaving him standing in a vast sea of blood.

"Oh god—" Austin stammered.

"*God.* Yes. I can be that and so much more."

Austin dry-heaved upon seeing the figure before him, wading backward through the rising blood, but there was nowhere to run.

Bub stood tall in his monstrosity, drenched in shadow. His appendages writhed at his sides, and a crown of teeth hovered above his head. His face was a kaleidoscope of despair, a mockery of flesh, a Rorshach that always called to mind the image of a fly.

Austin fell to his knees, pawing at the blood in hopes of invalidating its tangibility and confirming that this was all some sort of warped hallucination.

Bub unleashed a guttural howl that summoned a torrential downpour of red. The impossible emptiness began to fill faster.

"What do you want from me?" Austin cried out.

"To know you."

Austin's toes danced upon the bottom as blood rose to his chin. He choked and spluttered, then went under.

He simply floated in the abyss of blood. The pressure of the red sea throbbed in his ears.

"*I am the Lord of Decay. The God of Filth. I give and take with wonder and malice. Worship me.*" Bub was not seen, but his words were heard.

Austin drifted deeper, but the sensation of dying never arrived, even as his lungs overflowed with blood. In the waves of his thrashing, two figures coagulated and formed, both feminine in shape.

The figures encircled Austin and caressed his body. They kissed his neck with forked tongues and grabbed his cock, fondling between his buttocks with slender appendages. They slid their bodies over him in tandem. The blood suspended them all in horrifying ecstasy, and the scarlet women began to sing, "*Stay with us, sway with us, in the breeze of infinity.*"

This was everything Austin never knew he wanted. His erection erupted. Milky streams floated through the blood like smoke. The women weaved around him, swallowing his seed like fish in an aquarium feasting on flakes. They glided against him as they passed, causing him to repeatedly orgasm.

"Enough," Bub's voice cut through the walls of blood.

The figures dispersed into the waves from which they formed, and the great sea of red began to drain. The endless red returned to black.

Austin found himself sitting naked in the void. He felt new. Born again. Baptized. Looking down, his member still leaked. Then clarity hit him like a semi-truck. "Holy fucking shit. I—I didn't mean to—"

A man in tinted sunglasses emerged from the darkness. With one hand in the pocket of his brown suit jacket, he offered his other to Austin. "Rule number one, Austin. Never apologize for your compulsions or desires. You passed the first test. Congratulations."

"Test? Wait, who— There was a monster— Where did—?"

"I have many shapes," Bub said, pulling Austin to his feet. "Now, there is something I want to show you." He pointed into the darkness. "Do you see it?"

"I don't see anything."

"Look closer."

In the distance, a light appeared, a small gray spotlight over a twitching body. It was a man, huddled in the fetal position, sobbing.

"Pain is the best catalyst. It creates and destroys. It can reconfigure every fiber of your being, build you up like a skyscraper, or reduce you to dust."

They walked toward the light. Austin didn't take his eyes off the man, who convulsed with each weep.

Bub placed a hand on Austin's shoulder, and whispered into his ear, "What do you do with your pain? Do you let it eat you from the inside? Or do you weaponize it—turn it on the world to get what you want, what you need?"

Austin looked into Bub's tinted glasses. This *thing* saw him inside and out for everything he was.

"When you were a boy, sitting in your room alone, digging your fingernails into skin until you bled, where was salvation? Where was love? As your mother shrieked and pulled your hair, scratched you, and told you she wished you'd never been born, where was grace? And when your father, drunk and burdened with the weight of his own pathetic existence, called you a freak, a faggot, and slammed you against the wall, where was mercy? Where was God?"

Austin knew the man in the spotlight.

Bub gestured to the man, and said, "For all eternity, he will never know a moment of peace. His eternal flesh is subjected to an endless cycle of torment. But you can help him."

The man lifted his cowering head. It was Austin's father.

His father's eyes widened with delirium. They were hollow and gray. "God, you've answered my prayers." His cries broke into soft, chaotic laughter. "It's my boy. My son. Austin, please. Help me."

Austin turned to Bub. "How do I help him?"

"Forgiveness. I have seen it pull sinners from the darkest pits. It's an infuriating thing to witness, to be honest. But if you forgive your father, offer him a kind word, the laws of the universe may shift in his favor."

"Austin, I'm so sorry. I'm so fucking sorry." Thick gray spittle covered his father's chin. Tears ran down his cheeks, and each word was said with the sincerity of a dying breath. "My little boy. Please." From behind tortured eyes, there was a glint of something he had kept hidden from Austin while alive. With a soft rasp, he said, "*I love you so much.*"

"Dad." Austin looked upon the pitiful man before him, covered in sores and blood thick like wet concrete. There was a time when he would have done anything to hear his father say those words, but seeing him like this awakened new desires, new words *he* wanted to say.

"*P-please. I'm s-sorry.*" His father's sobs nearly devoured the words.

Austin took a deep breath and closed his eyes. He saw himself as a small boy sitting on his bed, blood trailing down his thigh, shreds of his own skin lodged underneath his fingernails. Alone. He hated this boy as much as the man and woman who had driven him to such pain.

He looked into his father's broken face, and with the utmost resolution, said, "Go fuck yourself."

A red glow formed beneath his father, who shrieked like a trapped animal. The talons and tentacles of Hell thrust up from the light and wrapped around him. He clawed toward his son, but their pull was too great. As they dragged him back to Hell, he screamed for Austin's help. But he did not receive it. He returned to his fate with his agony now a thousand times more acute.

"Atta boy," Bub said, patting Austin on the back. "Now, let's get down to business."

Austin watched the red light close and his father disappear deep into the forever. For the span of a single flap of a hummingbird's wing, he felt regret. Then, it was gone.

"Okay," he said. "I'm ready."

In an instant, they were transported to the edge of a vast structure, the Tower of Lucifer, now under new management. It stood tall, built from massive black stones stained by the blood of its builders. Austin gazed down at Hell, a nightmarish metropolis. Screams mingled in the air, reminiscent of traffic hum, while monuments and structures spiked from the ground like thorns.

"Hell is what you make of it, Austin," Bub explained. "For the condemned, like your father, it is a realm of endless torment. But Hell has many layers." He paused, looking out over the infernal landscape. "For those who embrace it willingly, it offers splendors beyond comprehension. Even the most eloquent of poets fail to describe its smallest measure. It all comes down to where you stand."

Austin nodded.

"I see it in your heart," Bub said. "You know the great secret. There is no greater ecstasy than that of domination. Control."

The notion had never articulated itself in Austin's mind, but he immediately knew it to be true.

"Here, you can *take*, you can *punish*, *bleed* and *make bleed*, for all eternity in blissful supremacy. I will make you a Duke of Hell. You will have your own piece of my kingdom."

"Me?" Austin looked around him. Hell was a garden of dead flowers, a graveyard for hope, but it called to him. He was also pretty sure that if there was a Heaven, he wasn't going there anyway.

"This is where you belong, lording over those who wronged you during your mortal tenure," Bub said. "But instead, you are in the back of a van, fucking some junkie, on the run, exiled, because you took what you wanted from those who were hesitant to give it. Join me, and you will be powerful, a god, on Earth and in Hell."

Austin noticed the flicker of insect lenses behind Bub's glasses. They were the eyes of a fly, of a monster, of a demon. But he didn't care. He was one himself, and he was sick of trying to hide it. It was time to embrace that fact.

"What do I have to do?"

Bub smiled. "First thing's first, what attachment do you have to the whore you're still fucking in the back of that foresaken van?"

Austin laughed. "None."

"Beautiful. Then it's a deal," Bub said, shaking Austin's hand. "Oh, and one more thing, *open wide*."

Bub's hand turned cold and death-black. It wrapped itself up and around Austin's arm like a thorned vine, and forced its way into his mouth. Austin never even had the chance to scream.

With that, Austin snapped back into the van, naked and drenched in blood. He was holding a knife, plunged into the side of Whitney's neck up to its black wooden handle. Her eyes were wide in terror, unsure of what had transpired and how it had happened so quickly. Without thinking, Austin twisted the handle and tore through the front of her throat. She stared up at him, heartbroken.

Blood poured from Austin's mouth. He was missing a tooth.

A voice came from the passenger's seat. "Blood binds, and it's got to keep flowing. She had to go. Not that you care." It was Bub, smoking a cigarette with his window cracked and the engine idling. "Put your clothes back on, you got a drive to make."

"Where are we going?"

"Chicago. We have shit to do."

AND SO AUSTIN STOOD, Sour Patch Kids in hand, waiting in line at Walgreens. He thumbed through an issue of *People Magazine*, then placed it under his arm for purchase. It all still felt like a dream but, as he tongued the empty space in his gum line, he was thankful it wasn't.

Ahead of him, an old Latino couple bickered over the dish soap scent the husband had chosen. They had lived in the same nearby house for over forty years—a quiet home flanked by sleek, minimalist condominiums and shaded by trees their children had planted decades ago.

The couple paid the cashier and shuffled home, arm in arm, to continue their life of quiet love.

Austin smiled. *Perfect.*

He bought his candy and the essentials for his mission, then followed them down the block at a comfortable distance.

He was going to make his new dad proud.

20

Two cats made their way down Armitage Avenue. One black. One gray. Their padded paws pattered the frozen concrete with poise and fluidity, making survival look easy. They weaved through bus stop benches, and darted under parked cars.

An older Foodsmart employee with a penchant for feeding the cats bologna slices had named them. The black cat, youthful and missing an eye from an encounter with a bike tire, was christened Brandy. The gray, having lived through nearly all a cat could live through, was named Bubblegum.

"I've been hearing whispers from the rats," Brandy said, jumping from a bus stop bench and strutting with her tail held high.

"Oh?" Bubblegum asked. "And what are they saying now?" Her tail was leveled straight behind her, alert and ready.

"Well, I heard these two talking about how a few of them have been murdered. Like killed."

Bubblegum stopped and scratched her ear. "*We* kill them. Plus they're experts at getting themselves killed. Rats die. It's what they do. It's what we all do."

"No, no, I know. But what's weird was, they said they saw a human doing it, a man, and not to eat them like we do," Brandy said.

"Again, humans kill rats all the time," Bubblegum said, turning her nose to the night air, its scent dulled by the cold. The neighborhood felt off, but she couldn't pinpoint why. "It's not news."

"But with their hands? And so slowly?"

Someone approached, and the cats slipped into a gangway.

An elderly woman pushing a small laundry cart plodded past them. She grunted as one of the wheels failed to cooperate over the sidewalk's layer of ice and snow. The cats watched her struggle past, unnoticed.

Bubblegum continued. "Humans hate rats, and it's a good thing they do. Could you imagine if the humans fed the rats and set traps for us instead? What a world that would be."

Brandy tried to imagine a world where the Foodsmart employee left out bologna slices for the neighborhood rats instead of her, a world where the woman carried dead cats in glue traps to the dumpster, and hungry rodents waited to pick the bones clean. She shuddered at the thought, then said, "*I know that.* Will you let me finish?"

Bubblegum said nothing. She surveyed the street, remaining vigilant as they walked.

Brandy huffed and rolled her eye. "They were saying that some guy's been hunting them, killing them in weird ways, and using the blood to talk to *things.*"

Now she had Bubblegum's attention. "What kind of things?"

Brandy glanced around, feeling watched, then whispered, "The things we see out of the corner of our eye." Her lone eyeball, a bleached yellow orb, scanned the street. "The ones made of nothing. The rats think they're being sacrificed. They're scared."

Bubblegum slowed to a halt, staring up at the moon like she did as a kitten. She was alone then, hungry and without a mother. It wasn't far from where she stood now that a negligent motorist left her mother's body unceremoniously splattered on Armitage Avenue, reduced to a rotting stain for days until the rain washed her away.

There was almost nothing in Chicago that Bubblegum couldn't handle. But the hidden city—a world layered atop their own, unbeknownst to humans—was harder to navigate. Animals alone carried the burden of seeing the aberrations that occasionally crept past the veil, but seeing is not always under-standing.

"They may be hunted and hated by nearly every living thing, but the one thing rats never are is scared," Bubblegum said. "Something's not right."

The wind passed through her whiskers. She again tried to absorb the night. Something *was* off on Armitage Avenue.

And one of those somethings had somehow snuck up on them.

"Hi—Hello—*oh thank god*, I remember you two," a voice said. "Please. You have to help me."

The cats jumped, landing with arched backs and a hiss, unsure how they'd missed such an ambush.

The voice was desperate. "Do you remember me? I'd give you scraps, just down the street. Remember? Chicken wings, bits of burger, whatever customers didn't finish. Behind the dump-ster. Do you remember?"

They remembered the chicken wings. But did this person expect an answer she could understand? They eased their body language, but remained confused.

"Every person I've run into so far thinks I'm crazy, or home-less, or both, and then I saw you two! And I remembered you. And I just don't know what to do. I was sitting at the bar, that spider bite started to itch, and then my left arm was just covered in flies. Black with flies, but no one else saw them. Every single one of them knew my name. *Sammie. Sammie. Sammie.* They said it over and over again." Her eyes grew distant.

Brandy stepped back hoping Bubblegum would follow her lead, but the gray cat stood her ground and listened.

"So I ran out of the bar, but the shadows—*the shadows*—they followed me. They were so *thick*, and they touched me. Everywhere. Under my skin. *Everywhere.*" She shut her eyes. A tear rolled down her cheek, evaporating in the cold before it could even leave her face. "They said they knew me before I was born. They said they'll know me again. I don't know what to do or where to go. And I know you're cats, but something—I don't know what—a voice, a feeling—told me you could help. And I know that's crazy, but I just don't know what else to— Fuck, I am fucking crazy. I'm gone. My mind is gone." Sammie fell back against the wall and began to cry, tears now falling to her feet despite the freezing air.

"We need to get out of here," Brandy said, slinking away, her fur blending with darkness.

The sobs stopped. Sammie's hands dropped from her face. She stared at Brandy, mouth agape. The pair of cats exchanged a look of disbelief.

Bubblegum had only ever heard stories of humans understanding the language of the cats. "If you hear us, *really* hear us, then something is clearly wrong." She weaved through Sammie's legs, rubbing against them, tail trailing, as she contemplated. "You are not crazy. We hear your words, as we always do, but more concerning is that you hear ours. My only advice is to get somewhere safe."

"Strange things are happening on Armitage Avenue," Brandy added.

"Don't be alone," Bubblegum said. "If there's someone you trust, go to them."

"We'll take care of those shadows." Brandy stepped forward. Her collapsed eye socket wrinkled as she toughened her brow.

Sammie's mouth still hung open.

"Do you have someplace you can go?" Bubblegum asked.

It was a question Sammie had been avoiding since she stepped off the bus. More tears fell. She nodded.

"Then go." Bubblegum's tail pointed toward the sky. "Chicago is a stray cat town. The shadows will answer to us."

Sammie felt the release from that first smile after despair. She mouthed *thank you* and shuffled off into the city's wilderness, disappearing from the cats' view.

"Do you think she's going to make it?" Brandy asked.

Bubblegum looked up at the moon. "Did you smell the alcohol on her? She'll be lucky if she makes it through the night." She closed her eyes. Winter nipped at her nose. "It's dark, and it's getting darker. I fear we soon won't be able to tell the shadow from the night. And when that time comes, there will be more than rat blood in the streets."

Brandy had become distracted by an empty bag of chips tossing in the wind. Knowing the young cat's attention span shortened when hungry, Bubblegum concluded, "Let's go check the Foodsmart dumpster."

Brandy perked up. "Food? Yeah, I think that's a good idea."

Bubblegum did a big stretch and shook off any lingering thoughts of death. She took one last look in Sammie's direction, sneezed a small sneeze, then started toward Foodsmart, Brandy following close behind.

21

PART FOUR

Gretchen sat atop the tallest structure in Hell and wondered why she existed at all.

Half-cat. Half-praying mantis. Half-demon. Half-joke. Half-empty. Half-full. *Half.* She figured that God must have spilled some coffee on his blueprints for her, then delegated her creation entirely to some sort of intern.

Gretchen wasn't born, as she had no parents. She had no lore of falling from Heaven, or being sentenced to Hell. Her consciousness seemed to have sparked here while already in the middle of performing some mundane task.

When Lucifer fell, Gretchen was there to greet him. He embodied contradiction: brilliant yet sardonic, furious yet restrained, cruel yet kind. This ember of kindness, undimmed by the cold winds of Hell or the wrathful hand of God, drew her to him. They bonded, her loyalty met with affectionate little scratches behind her ears. Theirs was perhaps the only real friendship in Hell.

She watched him grow disenchanted with the binaries and dichotomies over the millennia and felt the same. She didn't want to be all bad, or all good. She just wanted to be Gretchen.

He would curse himself for thinking his revolt would ever produce any other outcome. She had listened to him rant on the futility of it all more times than she could remember.

After Jesus's recent visit, Lucifer spiraled further.

Gretchen was the only other being in Hell who knew the secret Jesus shared. Now it poked and prodded her mind, fiddling with the dial of her sanity, but she trudged on. She saw Lucifer's mind as a complex series of gears and interlacing parts, and her own as more of a rusty hand crank, but this difference allowed her to keep moving. Because the implications of the secret broke Lucifer in a way she didn't think possible. She never thought he would abandon her.

Gretchen didn't understand why he left, why he didn't take her with him, or why he didn't say goodbye. All she was left with was the poking and prodding—and Bub. Her tail had only just grown back since being forced to cut it off and eat it as punishment for accidentally swallowing one of his flies.

Hell was her home, but she didn't care for torture or sin and took no pleasure in the pain of others. She wondered if anyone else ever stopped to think about the absurdity of it all. Despite this, she thought Hell was beautiful, and had potential. It was those like Bub who made it miserable.

Her bug eyes twitched and her cat nose wrinkled from a gust of stale wind. She tilted her head and brought a foot up to scratch behind her ear, her large mantis arms anchoring her where she sat. She let out a little sneeze and stared across the shifting black clouds that hovered above the infernal sprawl below.

Large skeletal beasts soared through the clouds, their majesty seemingly stolen from Heaven itself. She wanted nothing more than to join them. But she had no wings, only cat legs and mantis arms. Flying was out of the question. Walking was difficult.

Gretchen got up and shuffled back to the throne room. If she wasn't there to greet Bub, he'd have his flies eat her tongue again, and that thing took forever to grow back.

She turned one last time to watch the wings beat embers from the clouds. The smoldering ash against the dark sky gave the illusion of stars. Gretchen had never seen actual stars, but she was sure they couldn't compare to this.

22

oly fuck. Someone's at the door.

Three knocks jolted Tommy awake. A needle dangled from his arm by a sliver of translucent skin. He sat slumped against the side of the couch, drool extended to his thigh below.

Oh, real fucking nice, he thought, plucking the needle from his arm. A bead of blood followed. The room was tilted and blurred. His head felt like a flushing toilet, his brain circling the drain.

Tommy scanned the room for Hector, but he was nowhere to be seen. He struggled to his feet, but his bones vibrated like tuning forks, sending him back down to the couch.

Three more knocks.

"Yeah, yeah, I'm coming! Give me a fucking second!" he shouted, sparking a burst of pain in his temples. Recalling Hector's recent brush with the police, he quickly added, "I'll be right there! Just a second, please!"

He cupped his hand to his mouth and called down the hallway, "Hector? You here?" Nothing. *God dammit.* He forced his body up and hobbled to the kitchen on his vibrating bones. Hector's door was closed.

Three more knocks.

"Be right there!" he yelled from the kitchen.

Tommy stuck his face under the sink and let cold water pummel him. If it was the police, he needed to look less like he just injected hard drugs.

He went to Hector's door, pressed his forehead against it, and grumbled, "Hey, I think the fucking cops are here, man. What do you want me to do?"

It was locked, and there was no response except some muffled groans.

Three more knocks at the front door. He had to answer.

Alright, you got this. Just act normal. Normal. You know what normal means, right? That's right. Normal, Tommy told himself, approaching the front door.

He took a deep breath, turned the knob, and—

There was nothing.

Nothing.

Nothing nothing.

The porch was gone. The neighboring three-flats had disappeared. The street and abandoned tracks were nonexistent. The lights. The snow. The sky. The moon. Everything had vanished into nothing.

Tommy stood, jaw unhinged, looking down over the bottom of the door frame. The apartment below them was nowhere to be seen. The one above was no more. Their home sat suspended in this dark sea of absence.

The drugs must have been laced, he assured himself, peering out into the emptiness. The nothing looked back. *This is fucked*, he thought.

Streaks of a gray fog drifted across his vision. They dissipated and reformed with the fluidity of cigarette smoke. In the distance, the sound of swaying metal clanging together inched toward him, slow and rhythmic like a pendulum.

"Hello?" Tommy asked.

No response.

He decided this was most definitely a hallucination, and that it wasn't doing him any good to stare at it. Another beer would clear things up. He started to close the door.

"Thomas..."

The fuck.

He swung it back open, and called into the void, "Who's there?"

The voice, a cold rasp of many speaking as one, echoed from behind the fog, hissing like original sin. "Thomas. Why don't you come to us? We've come so far, all this way, just to see you. Would you like to see us?"

"Fucking not really," Tommy replied, continuing to shut the door.

"We know Hector. And Samantha. We know everyone you love, inside and out." The words slithered, slow and deliberate. "And we would love to know you *better.*"

"Hey, what the fuck is your deal—" He stopped himself. This was a hallucination after all. There was zero point in arguing with a hallucination.

Then something small bounced through the doorway to his feet. It was metal, filthy and stained a brownish red. It was a hook.

Don't forget, this isn't real. This is just some looney-toon drug shit. Don't get worked up. I bet if you picked it up, it wouldn't even be there. Why would it? It's not real.

He picked the hook up. It fit neatly into the palm of his hand.

Fuck. Okay, just because you're holding it doesn't mean it's real. People hallucinate solid objects all the time. Probably.

The pulse of clinking metal outside became a frenzy.

Startled, Tommy fumbled the hook to the floor. He stared down at it, unwilling to look out his front door, afraid of what he might see. A red drop landed next to the hook. Then another. And another. He had cut the inside of his hand.

Okay, people probably bleed from imaginary things all the time. It's not a big deal. Calm down.

The voice of many spoke, "We have hooks crafted for your flesh. Chains made just for you. Come and taste what we offer."

Tommy always had a problem with looking away. When his coworker Martin would corner him in the breakroom to show him videos of people getting run over by cars, Tommy would feign disinterest and look away, before slowly returning his gaze to the carnage.

Then there was the time in Wicker Park, in an alley behind the place with the ten-dollar cups of coffee, he saw a homeless man with pants around his ankles violently spray his bowels out against a brick wall. Pretending not to notice at first, he stopped at the alley's end, smoking a cigarette and observing the messy climax unfold. He had no perverted intent. It was just something he didn't see every day.

So, Tommy lifted his head from the red drops and looked outside, immediately regretting it.

An endless field of chains, hooks, and shackles hung from nowhere. They dangled in the gray fog while the voice said, "Join their sway. Thomas. Join their sway. We've come all this way. We want to see you *hang*."

"Oh, fuck that." Tommy slammed the front door shut.

He ran to Hector's room and pounded his fists against his bedroom door. "Wake the fuck up—*now*!" He struggled to find the appropriate words for the situation. "There's something! Something...going on!"

No response. Ear to the door, Tommy again tried to hear Hector's muffled groans, at least to know he was still alive. There were noises, but they no longer sounded like the benign rumblings of someone passed out drunk. They were the sounds of struggle.

"Hey! Are you okay? Answer me!"

Nothing.

Tommy shouldered the door with all his weight, but did little to budge it. He needed a running start, so he went to the edge of the kitchen, kicked his feet like a bull, and charged. Particle board splintered at the door's hinges. He circled back for a second assault.

The door fell to the floor with Tommy on top. Then, he saw Hell.

"*Jesus Christ!*" Tommy shouted.

The creature inside Hector's room laughed with haughty cadence and declared, "Oh, no, no, no, little one, the Christ is gone! All are damned! *All are damned!*"

Its corpse-like body clung to the ceiling with large bat wings that spanned the room. Four horns mimicking a nascent crown adorned its head. The creature's long, ghostly face was sadistic but fair as a prince commanding troops from afar with vicious delight.

But its defining feature was its penis: an enormous centipede that had wrapped itself around Hector all the way up to his mouth, pinning him against the wall. The centipede-penis gyrated and squirmed with glee. Hector's eyes met Tommy's, wide with terror.

Tommy turned and ran, his body slamming into the kitchen counter. He fumbled through the drawers. Plastic bags. Random chargers. Plastic forks. Old receipts. *There it is.* Their one kitchen knife, slightly dulled from when they would throw it into the wall for no particular reason. It was the sharpest thing in the house. He brandished the knife like it was a great blade of old, and charged, screaming a manic mishmash of expletives.

The knife plunged deep into the thing's centipede-penis.

The penis shrieked an unearthly howl and uncoiled but was, ultimately, unharmed.

Hector scrambled to his feet and darted out of the room, dragging Tommy by the arm with him. They skidded into the bathroom and slammed the door. "You saw that?" Hector asked.

"What the fuck do you mean did I see that? Of course I saw that!" Tommy said.

"I can't do this anymore. I just can't fucking do this anymore. I told you I was seeing weird shit. I've lost my mind. I'm fucking crazy. I just need to die. That's it. I just need to fucking die tonight."

Tommy ran his fingers through his hair and exhaled. "Okay, well, if you're crazy, why the fuck did I see it? Am I crazy too?"

"I don't know. I don't know."

"I saw some shit outside." Tommy shuddered. "But it's not real. It's got to be the drugs."

Hector found comfort in this notion. "The drugs. Austin. He put something in them. So we're just tripping?"

Tommy nodded. "We're acting like a couple of amateurs right now. I bet if we open that door, whatever we thought we saw in your room will be gone."

Hector sat on the edge of the tub and considered the thesis. "But, it had me. I felt it's fucking—*dick* around me. You saw it," he said, pointing at Tommy.

Tommy couldn't really argue with that. He did see it; at least, he thought he saw it. "Listen, I'm going to open this door and you'll see there's nothing there. We'll grab a few beers, take a walk around the block, and shake off this bad trip. Sound good?"

Hector stood, slapped himself in the face, and nodded. "Let's do it."

Riding the high of his brush with courage, Tommy reached for the doorknob—but stopped short when a voice flooded his head. It was the knob.

Go ahead. Turn me. You scared little bitch. You remember what happened when you opened the front door? Enter the void, pussy. Enter the fucking void.

"Are you going to open it?" Hector asked.

"Yeah, I'm just... I need a second."

Hector stepped forward, placing a hand on his shoulder. "I got this."

Tommy didn't argue.

In a singular motion, Hector turned the knob and pushed the door open, jumping back in anticipation of whatever might await outside.

The apartment seemed silent, save for the hum of the refrigerator just one room away. Hector stuck his head out toward the kitchen, then toward their living room. No demonic entities. No monsters. No centipede-penises. Tommy poked his head out next and looked to their front windows. He saw streetlights and buildings. No endless void. No chains. No hooks.

"Huh," Tommy said. "What about your room?"

They tiptoed over to Hector's room. There was no creature, only a mattress with a sheet half on, an overflowing hamper, and a kitchen knife planted upright into the hardwood floor.

"Where did it go?" Hector asked.

"It never existed. We were tripping on whatever Austin put in that needle."

Hector touched a finger to his wall, just to validate the material world. "It didn't feel like any hallucinogen. It felt like coke. But it hit so fast, and we had drank so much, I just passed out, and then..." He trailed off, not even finishing the thought.

"Maybe it was cut with both?" Tommy asked, unsure. He looked at the knife stuck into the floor. If the creature wasn't real, then what did he stab at?

The refrigerator's hum droned on. Hector answered its call. "Need a beer?" he asked Tommy.

"Twelve."

Hector opened the fridge, and immediately slammed it shut. He looked at Tommy with eyes wide, mouth stammering.

"What is it?"

The hum modulated into a high-pitched screech. The sound scratched the inside of their skulls, and stuck needles in the soft gray tissue of their brains. The refrigerator door ripped itself off its hinges and bounced down the hall, revealing a cavernous interior, dark and deep. The clanging of chains echoed from within. The screech shifted into a whirring buzz, and a thousand voices speaking at once.

The creature's sing-song mockery echoed from the nothing. "*All are damned.*"

The legions of flies harmonized, "*aaaall aree daamned.*"

From the depths of the cavern, the centipede-penis emerged.

It wrapped around Tommy's ankle and dragged him into the darkness before either could react. His screams ricocheted off the emptiness as he disappeared.

"Tommy!" Hector shouted after him. "Let him go! You wanted *me*! I know you wanted—"

The centipede-penis reemerged and wrapped itself around Hector's mouth, pinned his arms to his sides, and dragged him into the black hole, kicking and flailing in futility.

Tommy and Hector were gone. The centipede-penis was gone. The void was gone. All that remained in the refrigerator were a few condiment bottles and a buzzing fluorescent bulb.

From across the room, the white door tumbled back toward the fridge and attached itself to its hinges like a movie rewound.

BANDINI WATCHED with eight worried eyes from outside the kitchen window. Since his sewer system detour, courtesy of

Hector, he had unwillingly traveled across the city, stopping only to bite Sammie.

In moments like this, he seriously questioned Heaven's motives in confining him to an arachnid body, but rules were rules. Rules were what separated his kind from Bub's. And rules meant walking on eight tiny legs, which sometimes meant being too late.

Think, think, he told himself, examining the window frame for vulnerabilities to gain entry.

Even if he made it indoors, he couldn't follow Tommy and Hector into the refrigerator. That portal was locked from the inside. And a spiritual lifeline wouldn't work like it did for Hector's overdose since he was now *physically* in their realm.

But that didn't mean Bandini couldn't help. He just had to get a bit closer so they could hear him.

23

The boy felt small sitting on his mother's bed. A heaviness in his chest sloped his posture forward, dragging him closer to the floor. He was ten years old, and the world was unkind.

He wore his favorite t-shirt. It was orange and said *NO FEAR* in flaming block letters. A cartoon skater kickflipped over the words. The boy rubbed the fabric between his index finger and thumb, and straightened his posture. It was his armor, a reminder to be strong. Because even though he was small and at the mercy of everything, he just needed to remember to be like the kickflipping cartoon character.

Maybe he could do this. Whatever *this* was. He played with his shoe's Velcro, enamored with the sound it made.

The boy couldn't remember what he had been doing the day before, or where he had been even just a few minutes prior. All he knew was that he had to try to be brave, to be okay. His right hand squeezed his left, rubbing the inside of its palm.

No fear.

A voice erupted from the hallway. "When I come in there,

you better not still be wearing that fucking shirt! I swear to God."

The boy's heart sank. His hands dropped to his sides. They tapped his thighs to keep time with a quickening pulse, an involuntarily metronome.

His mother entered like a rabid animal.

"Take it off," she said through a clenched jaw. The boy froze like a rabbit staring down the barrel of a shotgun. "*Take it off*," she repeated.

He fumbled with his shirt, forgetting how to undress himself in his panic.

"Jesus fucking Christ, do I have to do every little thing for you?" She came over and ripped the shirt off his back and over his head. "Sit on the bed." The boy climbed up and sat facing the door. "No, not that way! Turn around! How the fuck am I supposed to do this if you're facing that way?"

The room was shades of browns and yellows. A bed on a steel frame. Clothes in an overflowing hamper. Bills spread upon a burnt ironing board. It was stale and suffocating.

"For one single day I want you to think of someone other than yourself for once. Do you understand?"

The boy nodded.

"Really? Because it really seems like you don't. Turn your head."

The boy winced in pain. The boy winced as a hairbrush forcefully tore through his thick, knotted bedhead, from forehead to crown.

"You're not wearing that shirt on picture day. You want the teachers to think we're poor? Or the other parents? They'll call you trash behind your back." She scraped the hairbrush across his scalp. "I know *you* don't give a shit, but God forbid you care about your mother or what people think of her."

"I'm sorry," said the boy, flinching with each stroke. "It's my favorite." He immediately knew he shouldn't have said anything and wished he could swallow the words right back up.

"Oh, it's your favorite? Well, as long as *you* like it, I guess everything's fine, right?" She stopped brushing and brought her face down to his. "Because it only matters what you like, right? The world revolves around you. I forgot." She stood and grated the brush down the side of his head and over his ear. "You know, you're just like your father. Yep. Just like him. You only care about yourself."

The boy's eyes started to well up. "That's not true."

She again stopped brushing. "What did you just say to me?"

"I said that's not true!"

She flipped the hairbrush in her hand and brought the plastic side down across the back of the boy's head. It sent a shockwave through his body and broke the dams behind his eyes.

His mother screamed, "Then who do you care about? Huh? Tell me! Because right now, I see a selfish little boy who doesn't give a shit about anyone but himself!"

"You! I care about you!"

"Bullshit!" his mother shrieked and threw the hairbrush across the room. It ricocheted off the wall and knocked over her coffee on the nightstand. "Of fucking course!"

The boy sat on the bed and cried. A dark spot formed on the front of his pants. It grew larger.

His mother erupted, pulling at her own hair. The room pulsed white hot, and the boy suffocated in the heat. He leapt from the bed with tears in his eyes, running for the sanctuary of the bathroom.

A SECOND BOY sat on his bedroom floor playing with a Catwoman action figure. Her leather-clad physique was posed for action. Despite teasing from the other first-grade boys about not choosing Batman, and the teacher's concern over her risqué costume, she was his absolute favorite. She radiated strength, and he felt strong holding her.

Ten minutes had passed since the noise from Brian's room. He considered checking to see if he was okay, but was scared of walking up the attic steps alone. He also remembered what his brother had said the last time he went up to his room: "If I'm up here with my door closed, it means I want to be alone. Sometimes I just need to be by myself. Do you understand?"

This other boy didn't understand. He always wanted to be around his brother. It wasn't long ago that they'd spend every evening wrestling or warring with action figures. But lately, Brian always seemed sad at nothing in particular, and only wanted to be in his room with the door closed.

It was just the one sound. He was probably fine, the second boy decided.

But then again, it wasn't the sound itself that made the boy uneasy, it was the silence that followed. There was no movement. No footsteps.

Their mom wouldn't be home from her shift until the morning, and he didn't like the idea of spending the rest of the night not knowing. Plus, he needed Brian to help make his lunch for school tomorrow and couldn't reach the peanut butter. So, he began his trek up to the attic, Catwoman in tow for support.

The staircase was as dark as an elevator shaft, and the air was stale as a crypt. The walls were narrow and hugged steps that led to a wooden door. The boy's tiny feet made no sound on the old steps. He tightened his grip on Catwoman.

The boy tapped on the door. "Brian?" he asked, putting his ear to the wood. He could hear a sound, straining to be heard.

"Are you okay?" he asked. "I need you to reach the peanut butter for me. Can I come in?"

He looked back down the steps. He knew he could just climb up on the counter for the peanut butter, but he wanted his brother. Brian always picked him up so he could grab it from the cabinet himself. "Wow, Tombo, look how tall you are!" Brian would say, then carry him toward the ceiling fan. The boy would laugh and play along, begging his brother not to chop his head off. Afterward, they'd sit down at the kitchen table and make peanut butter sandwiches for school the next day.

He needed his brother. He needed to know he was okay.

"I'm coming in, okay?" He reached for the knob. It was unlocked.

The room was dark, and the boy couldn't see a thing. He squinted but saw only vague shapes, barely visible under the dull moonlight that bled through a small window near the attic's peak. The straining sound called to him. It groaned. It stretched.

His mother had worked hard to convert the space into Brian's room, but it was still an attic, old and prone to strange sounds. He took a step toward the light switch, and a floorboard shouted back. The boy yelped. He brought Catwoman up to his chest and continued, hand on the wall, feeling for the switch.

The groaning was coming from the center of the room, in the heart of the darkness. His fingers touched the light switch.

"I'm turning on the light, okay?" he said, hoping one last time to hear Brian's voice.

There was still time to turn back, go down the stairs, go to sleep, and wait for his mother to come in the morning. Brian was probably fine. Whatever waited in the darkness didn't need him to see it. It would be there regardless. And it was probably just Brian sleeping. Maybe Brian wasn't even home. Maybe he'd left to see his friends and just didn't say anything. The noise was probably nothing, just like the shouting floorboard. He took his hand off the switch and stepped back. Fear pounded in his chest. It told him to go back downstairs and play with his toys.

No, he told himself.

With his fear rattling its cage like a crazed inmate, he returned his hand to the switch and flipped it, eyes closed. He held them shut, desperate to hear an awakened Brian yell at him to leave his room.

All he heard was the groan. The stretch.

He could see the light through his eyelids in flashes of orange and red. He kept his head down and opened his eyes to his own feet. As he slowly raised them, there were Brian's feet, though not on the ground, but dangling in the air, his body in beautiful sway.

The rope and the rafter groaned and stretched and sang their song.

Tommy wanted to scream, but his voice failed him.

Catwoman fell to the floor.

"OPEN THIS FUCKING DOOR! I swear to God, if you don't open this *fucking* door!" the boy's mother screamed, pounding and shaking the knob.

The boy sat on the toilet with the lid down, trapped. His pants were wet and his face was smeared with mucus and tears. Each hand caressed itself, fingers rubbing their own palms.

His sobs only made his mother angrier. "Open. The. Fucking. Door," she demanded.

"I'm sorry!" he cried out, not knowing what else to say. The words trembled through the air.

"Oh, I know! Everyone's always sorry! You're sorry. Your father was sorry. Everyone is just so fucking sorry, I know. Now open the fucking door!"

He sat there and cried, paralyzed.

"OPEN THIS DOOR!"

Every nerve ending in the boy's body pricked with the sensation of burning needles. His mother threw her weight against the door. It quaked with each collision.

The boy closed his eyes and prayed a prayer he'd once heard on TV. No one answered.

The latch finally gave, and the door flew open.

THROUGH THE SECOND boy's blurred vision, the attic looked underwater, like his brother's body was a sea anemone, gently floating in the rhythms of the ocean. He sat curled against the wall and wiped away the layer of tears to see with horrifying clarity.

His brother's eyes were blank. Those same eyes, once wry, like they always kept a secret, now lacked all subtlety bulging out of his head, ruptured red and dead as opera.

The boy's fear, free from its cage, now shackled him where he sat. He was glued to the floor, unable to move a muscle. He couldn't leave his brother alone.

Brian's dead body was a language the boy couldn't comprehend. The still-bleeding claw marks in the flesh around the noose spoke to the boy, but the meaning was lost in translation.

Up until that moment, *dead* was just a word. It meant roadkill on the side of the road. It was a bad guy thrown through a window in some action movie. But the longer he sat and stared up at his brother's body, the more the word began to have weight. Slowly, the boy started to understand. *Dead*. His brother was dead.

Any strength from his Catwoman was long gone. She felt miles away on the floor. He couldn't rise to his feet, so he crawled. He crawled like a baby over to his brother's dangling legs, staining the denim with his fresh tears, wishing someone would come and make this all better.

Then he heard a voice.

"Hello, Tombo."

He looked up and saw Brian's bulging eyes, staring directly into his own.

THE BOY'S mother stood in the doorway, examining the busted frame. She ran her hands through her hair, intent on pulling out each strand. Red hives painted her neck and chest as her rage boiled.

"Hector. This is what happens when you don't fucking listen." Her voice was subdued, but the words seethed with anger. "You're still wearing those pissed pants."

The anger rose.

"You're just sitting there. Just fucking sitting here."

And rose.

"Like you don't have anywhere to be! Back to where we were, always starting at square one, never helping, only fucking caring about yourself, can't even take off your own piss-soaked clothes!"

Without the boy even saying a word, the rage had won. She stormed into the bathroom and grabbed a fistful of his hair. "You are not a fucking baby anymore. Do not act like you are *so scared* that you need to piss your pants. Do you understand me?"

The boy just cried.

"I said do you fucking understand me?"

"Yes! I'm sorry!"

His mother tilted her gaze toward the ceiling and inhaled through her nostrils. "Do not fucking say you're sorry. You're not sorry. And I am so sick of fucking hearing it."

She lowered her face to his. His mother's eyes were black, empty caverns, sockets holding nothing but oblivion. Hollow pits. A fly emerged from the left, crawled across her nose, and disappeared into the depths of the right.

"Everyone's always sorry when they get caught, when they

have to face consequences for their actions. Do you ever face consequences, Hector? Or do you just stroll through life like your father? A poison to everyone you meet."

The boy whimpered. He tried to retreat within himself, to disassociate, but the horror held his mind hostage.

"It's no wonder you grow up to be such a miserable drunken failure. Look at you now. You're a whimpering little faggot." Her teeth were filed sharp. Her tongue was black. She snarled and said, "You need consequences."

THE SECOND BOY scuttled backward on the floor until he felt the wall behind him. His brother, who had been dead just a few moments before, now smirked down at him as he hung from the ceiling. A wry look had returned to his red, bulging eyes.

"What's the matter, Tombo? Don't like what you see? Not a fan?" A tear of pus dripped from an engorged orb. "I'm not either. Trust me."

The boy could do nothing but shake his head no. He watched a thick glob of dark yellow secretion form at Brian's lips and drip down his chin. The smell of rot filled the attic.

"Why didn't you come check on me? I thought we were brothers. Were you too busy playing with your toys?" Brian placed his hands on his own shoulders and pushed down. His neck began to stretch. "That's it, isn't it? You were having too much fun with your little action figures. Couldn't be bothered to see if your older brother, who you love *so much*, was okay and needed help." Skin popped and tore as his neck elongated and his feet grew closer to the floor.

The boy stuttered soft syllables, unintelligible broken sounds. They were all he had to offer.

"What's that? I can't hear you, Tombo. You gotta speak up."

"N-no, that's not it. I-I was scared. I was a-alone."

His brother's neck extended, fraying with nerves and ligaments, until his feet touched the ground. A low buzzing sound stirred in the shadows of the attic, then turned ravenous. A black cloud of flies swarmed around the rafter and worked to untether the rope above.

"Alone?" asked Brian. "You don't know what it means to be alone. Do you know what they do to guys like me in Hell? It's not even the torture that breaks you. Which, don't get me wrong," he gritted his teeth and said, "*fucking hurts*." Yellow bile seeped from his clenched jaw. "No. It's the absence of light, of hope. The emptiness. It eats your soul, to be truly alone. It's fucking dark, Tommy." He smiled and extended a hand. "But it gets darker. I promise."

The flies completed their task, and the rope fell to the floor. Brian's lengthened neck drooped to the side like a piece of melting taffy until his face was upside down looking up at his little brother. "I know what you become, Tommy. I know the sad life you lead. We're the same. Do yourself a favor." He reached down and worked the noose over his head, then held it out to the boy, and said, "End it."

The boy brought his arms and legs as close to his body as possible in hopes of collapsing into himself and leaving this nightmare.

As his brother lurched toward him, head dragging, the boy patted the ground searching for Catwoman, needing her now more than ever, but she was nowhere to be found.

THE BOY SCRAMBLED from the toilet and ran into the shower. He closed the mildewed curtain tight in an attempt to shield himself from this thing that was his mother, but she ripped it open just as quickly.

"Consequences. You need consequences." She turned the

shower's handle. Freezing water rained down. The boy recoiled and screamed. His mother took a bar of soap from a yellowed shelf. It was covered in hair and smeared with an unknown filth. "I don't want to hear 'sorry' out of your mouth ever again."

She took the boy by the chin, her hand clasped around his cheeks, and forced the diseased soap between his teeth. Vomit filled his mouth, but he was made to swallow it back down as she held it tight around the bar.

The water went from cold to scalding. His exposed skin flared red. He twisted and contorted his body to prevent the blistering water from hitting one spot directly for too long.

"You want to piss yourself? Well, you're going to have to take a shower. This is what happens when you only care about yourself. Now turn around!"

Seeing the hairbrush in his mother's hand, the boy instinctively shielded himself, bracing for what was next.

"Move your hands! Move your fucking hands!"

He shook his head and begged her to stop with his eyes, but the vacant holes that were her own did not see or care for his pleas. Her mouth hung open, sharp teeth and a black tongue glistening with salivation, panting.

"You're a burden, Hector Ghouseau. A waste of fucking space. Kill yourself in that pathetic apartment you call a home. You'll belong to us no matter what. So why wait?" His mother lifted the hairbrush above her head like a butcher readying the first strike into a carcass. "Now move your fucking hands!"

BRIAN LIMPED FORWARD, his taffy neck dragging his head on the floor, noose in hand. "Take it, Tommy, take it."

"No!" the second boy screamed.

"You owe me," his brother's voice bellowed. "It's your fault I suffer. It's your fault Mom suffers. The least you can do is suffer too. Join me in Hell. It's where you belong. Trust me. You'll love it."

Brian reached for the boy's face.

He closed his eyes and held his breath.

THE BOY FLAILED, trying to free himself from his mother's grasp. His tears were wasted, unseen, lost in the hot water that scorched him. Steam filled the bathroom. His mother pried his hands away. The brush came down.

COLD FINGERS GRAZED the second boy's face. Their nails dug into his round cheeks.

THE BOY HOWLED as his mother struck him and raised her arm again.

THEN, both boys heard a voice.

"Hector! Tommy! That's not your mother, and that's not your brother. You're not children. Take control!" It was Bandini. He stood at their open refrigerator shouting instructions into the expired condiments.

The illusion cracked just enough for them to see through it. They weren't small anymore.

TOMMY SWATTED the hand from his face and dove to the side. He scanned the floor in hurried glances for Catwoman. *Found her.*

· · ·

HECTOR CAUGHT the brush mid-swing from the creature's hand. It hissed, flicking its black tongue between razor teeth.

THE TAFFY-NECKED THING was pissed off, and ready to attack. Tommy brandished Catwoman like a knife and charged.

HECTOR CUT through the steam with the hairbrush handle, plunging it into one of the creature's empty eye sockets.

CATWOMAN'S POINTED, plastic ears drove deep into the ruptured flesh of the thing's taffy neck.

THEIR NIGHTMARES CONVERGED, and the painful shrieks of the entities became singular.

Tommy and Hector found themselves in a dripping cavern, flabbergasted. Before them, the centipede-penis thrashed in anguish, a hairbrush and a Catwoman figure stuck in its meat.

"Gah!" Hector proclaimed.

The sadistic prince, more monstrous than when it had first appeared in Hector's room, wailed in the darkness. Its centipede-penis recoiled, then whipped forward with an other-worldly thwack to send both Tommy and Hector flying back through oblivion.

Bandini sat on the kitchen counter, watching them tumble out of the refrigerator, one after the other.

24

"Hello," said Bandini.

Hector vomited. Then Tommy.

Dry heaves followed, knees and palms were plastered to the floor. Reality felt tenuous after their less-than-ceremonial expulsion from the depths of the refrigerator, but Hector inched to his feet and surveyed the room for abnormalities. He found just one, and it sat on the kitchen counter watching him with eight beady eyes.

"You—I know you," Hector stammered. "When I died— I flushed—" He rushed to the kitchen sink and retched, foamed bile slapping the bottom of the steel basin.

"No time to discuss the past." Bandini skittered across the counter, his legs working in tandem like a well-crafted machine. "Things are dire." He paused, then added, "Although, had you not flushed me down the toilet, I might have prevented tonight."

Hector stuck his face underneath the faucet. Water splashed in and around his mouth. "Sorry," he gurgled.

Tommy vomited once more for good measure.

Hector, winded but ready for answers, turned off the water and asked, "Have I lost my mind? Why won't this stop?"

"It ends when you kill yourself," Bandini said.

Tommy looked up from his puddle of puke, and said, "The fuck, dude?"

"Beelzebub won't stop until you kill yourself," Bandini clarified.

Hector had a lightbulb moment. "Bub. I met him."

Bandini continued, "Or we stop him. Word has come down that he is forbidden to collect your soul."

"Word?" asked Hector. "Word from who?"

"God."

"Like *God* God?"

Bandini nodded.

"Back up. Why does Bub want my soul? I'm nobody."

"Yes, you are indeed a nobody—"

"C'mon, man," Tommy offered in Hector's defense.

"—but Beelzebub wagered with your father for your soul. Beginning on your twenty-fifth birthday—the age of your father when the deal was struck—Beelzelbub has three days to claim it, and he has never lost such a bet. We are nearing the end of the second day."

"My dad?" Hector asked, becoming acutely aware of the man's chain around his neck.

"Yes."

"I barely knew him! Now he's ruining my life from beyond the grave?"

"It appears so, yes."

"How can my dad sell my soul? Isn't that mine to sell? What did he even sell it for?" It dawned on Hector that he was using the concept of *the soul* definitively. He had a soul. God was real. And his dad was a piece of shit.

"It was not a sale. Think of it more as—betting on a sports match. What your father stands to gain if you survive, I can't say. That is known only to your father, Beelzebub, and God. But your soul is yours to lose, and your odds of victory are extremely slim."

"Great," Hector said. Tommy began to wipe up the vomit with dish soap and an old t-shirt.

Hector had heard plenty of stories from his mother about how awful a person his father was, always taking them with a grain of salt, but this was insanity.

"Beelzebub is a master manipulator. Please do not take offense." Bandini watched Tommy pour a glass of soapy water on the floor then spread it around with the old t-shirt. "Do you not have a mop?"

Hector ignored the question. "You said Bub does this sort of thing a lot. So why does God care about me?"

"That is unclear. But God's Word is final: the deal is void. Bub must not be allowed to break the Word."

"Why not?" Hector asked.

Tommy chimed in with his first fully formed thought. "Okay, I'm pretty sure I'm still high and hallucinating, so I'll ignore the fact that you're a talking spider for a minute. But now that Hector knows all this, the whole plan or whatever, he just won't kill himself. Pretty fucking easy. He only has to hold out for one more day, and he gets left alone, right?"

"It is *not* easy," Bandini explained. "What's easy are the myriad of ways Beelzebub can break a man to the point of suicide. A single day, even an hour, suffices. He's merely been playing with his food thus far, letting it marinate, before he makes his final move."

The word *suicide* wrapped a clammy arm around Hector, reminiscent of an old friend long-dodged now cornering him at a party.

Bandini pointed a leg at Hector. "It was not part of the plan to inject you with my venom, but your near-death at the bar left me no choice. Before it, Bub could only whisper and operate in the shadows; now he will assault your every sense. And you," he pointed a different leg at Tommy, "given your proximity to the situation, I planned on giving you my venom as well, but it seems Beelzebub reached you first—which suggests he has a part for you to play."

Tommy and Hector exchanged a look. *The shared needle. Austin.*

"He'll exploit all of this, but so shall we. There are advantages to seeing behind the veil. You can face Bub head on, and you can fight."

Tommy raised his hand to speak like he was in school. "You're an angel, right? You can just stop him. Problem solved."

Bandini shook his head. "I am not strong enough."

"So ask your angel friends to help. Why is this so difficult?"

"The orders were clear: this mission is mine and mine alone. The others in Heaven are not aware of the situation."

Tommy threw his hands up, annoyed.

Bandini flicked his palps. "But there are perhaps others we can go to for help. They will not be easy to convince." He then looked to Hector and said, "I must tell you, there is someone else. She received my venom as well."

"*She?* Are you talking about Jess?" Hector asked. "We slept together last night. She's in the fucking psych ward because we had unprotected sex. Did I give her some kind of cursed STD? I didn't mean to hurt her." His fingers rubbed the inside of his palms, each hand glued to his sides in shame.

"I will rid Jess of my venom once done here," Bandini assured him. "But there is another. And she had to be able to see as you both do, for her own protection."

"You better not be talking about—" Hector began.

"I am," Bandini confirmed.

Hector's stomach dropped.

Tommy walked over to the fridge. "If I open this, is there going to be some demon dick waiting to shove itself down my throat?"

"No. You should probably be fine," Bandini said.

"*Probably be fine,*" Tommy muttered to himself. "Because I need a beer more than anything in the—" He stood at the open refrigerator, speechless. It was empty. "He took our beer. There were four left." His voice weakened with the realization. "That bug-dick piece of shit!"

Tommy slammed it shut and rested his head against the freezer door; tears began to fall under the weight of the final straw. There were no guardrails left to lean on. Nowhere to hide from the memories he had just been forced to relive. It had been a long time since he looked the night of his brother's death straight in the eye.

Hector snapped out of his own thoughts when he saw his crying friend. He placed a hand on Tommy's back. "It's going to be okay, man."

Tommy looked up and smiled. "You're a shitty liar."

Hector chuckled. "I'll take that as a compliment."

Tommy wiped his eyes with his sleeve and sniffled. "We need more beer. Ten minutes until Armitage Food closes. You," he thrust a finger in Bandini's direction, "spider-angel-fucking-whatever-thing, you're coming with us. I have some questions. Let's go."

Bandini cast a thread and landed on Tommy's shoulder. "I know I paint a bleak picture, but all is not lost. Not yet."

Tommy looked upon the angel, seeing beyond his arachnid shell. A slight smile formed on his face, still puffy from his tears.

The three made their way into the living room, when they heard a knock at the front door. Tommy looked at Hector. "Last time I opened that, it wasn't good."

Hector saw the fear in Tommy's eyes. He felt it too. But just as he did in the bathroom, he stepped forward to open the door. He took a deep breath, swung it open, and said, "Oh, fuck."

It was Sammie.

"Hi," said Hector.

"Hey," said Sammie.

He saw that same fear in her eyes.

She glanced over Hector's shoulder and said, "Oh hey, Tommy." She squinted, and added, "Is that the spider that bit me?"

"My apologies," Bandini said. "I had no choice once I was aware of your arrival. It's better for you to see what is coming than to go about this blind."

"Oh, I've been seeing alright," she said. "And what exactly *is* coming?"

Tommy craned his neck to Bandini, and asked, "You bit her before me?"

"I told you. I was on my way to do just that, but I didn't antic-ipate you falling for such a...*trap* so easily," Bandini said, electing to not detail their intravenous drug use in front of Sammie.

"Yeah, well, now you know," Tommy affirmed.

"Hello!" Sammie waved her hands for attention. "What exactly is coming?"

Tommy clapped his hands. "Alright, Hector, you fill Sammie in. Me and this guy are going to the liquor store. Have fun, you two." He gave Sammie a hug as he left. She was careful not to squish Bandini.

"Oh, um," was all Hector could say as the door closed shut.

There they stood, silent and afraid.

Maybe it was the crazy lady on the train, or the mutilated rat, or the shadow creatures that attacked her in the alley, or maybe it was the talking cats and spider, or perhaps it was just that the world felt especially cold and dark that night. Whatever the reason, Sammie placed her hands on the soft spots of Hector's neck, just beneath his jaw, and pulled him close for a kiss, just to feel something other than fear.

"You taste like vomit," she said.

"I know."

25

Snow crunched under Tommy's feet. Each year, he told himself that this would be his last Chicago winter, that he would pack his bags and head south.

The first snowfall was always beautiful, but beauty spoils with time. The white mounds on the side of the road turn black from exhaust. Food wrappers, used condoms, and cigarette butts fossilize in the sidewalk ice. And when the sun deems the city worthy of a brief appearance, gray slush and puddles are the reward before the cycle starts anew.

And each year, Tommy stayed. He wasn't leaving. He loved Chicago, though he would never admit it.

"I don't get it, how did my Catwoman toy hurt a demon, or whatever that was, so much? Shouldn't it take some magic spell or ancient relic?"

To an observer on the street, of which there were none, it would look like he was talking to himself, but the angel on his shoulder was listening and ready to answer whatever questions Tommy had, within reason.

"It wasn't the plastic of your doll. It was what the toy represented in that moment."

"Action figure. And what did it represent?"

"Strength. Healing. Life."

Tommy snickered. "Yeah, okay, man."

"The Catwoman and hairbrush were charged objects. They are items pulled deep from your subconscious that hold painful weight for you both. That is why the demon initially used them."

Tommy nodded as if it all made sense to him.

"You spoke of relics. Well, your doll was a powerful relic of your life."

"Action figure."

"And when you reclaimed it, using it against the evil that brought it forth, you wielded its power. You took control of your pain. That is what hurt the demon." Bandini paused. "I guess you both still have a bit of fight left in you. I thought you were doomed."

"Oh, thanks."

Tommy's mind had given up on trying to make sense of it all. After all, he was talking to a spider, a spider claiming to be an angel, a spider with a very non-biblical sounding name. Tommy wasn't even sure how he talked. The spider had a spider mouth, and though Tommy was no expert on arachnid anatomy, he knew enough to know that spider mouths probably weren't conducive to human speech patterns. He wondered if it was a psychic thing.

"So you said your name is Bandini. That doesn't sound like much of an angel's name."

"And what would an angel name be to you?"

"I don't know. Not Bandini. Something like *Abrahamiel* or something."

Bandini laughed. "If only we were allowed to choose our own names. Perhaps I would have chosen *Abrahamiel*." He watched the streetlights pass overhead, snow falling in their yellow light. "What name would you choose for yourself?"

"I never thought about it." Tommy kept his eyes forward. They walked in the middle of the residential street, alone in the cold tunnel of night. "I mean, I never felt like my name suited me, but I'm not sure what name would."

"That is the problem with names."

"Sometimes, I'll go days without hearing anyone say mine. Not at work, not at home. No one says it. I just exist without a name. I think I like that the best."

The wind cooed. Tommy stuck his hands in the pockets of his beat-up flannel jacket, bringing his arms closer to his body.

"On days like that, I try to not look in the mirror. On days like that, it feels like I can be anyone or anything at all."

Bandini crouched lower to shield himself from the wind, and said, "You are as God made you. That is a beautiful thing."

Tommy scoffed. "Is it?" They were nearing Armitage Food, so he slowed his pace. "Listen, I just learned that God exists, but I gotta say, I'm not exactly a fan of his work."

"Did you not believe before?"

"I've never had good reason to."

"I see."

"All the fucked-up shit that happens here, I'm *still* having a hard time. So for now, I'll believe in me, and whoever or whatever I decide to be on those days without a name. Because those are the only times I feel hopeful."

Bandini noticed Tommy dragging his feet, as if there was more he wanted to ask.

"So is he like the Christian God—or one of those other ones? Allah? Or the one with all the arms? I don't know shit about religion. I always thought it'd be cool if God was just some alien intelligence thing."

"He cannot be limited to man-made constructs like Christianity. He is all and none of those things you mention. There are grains of truth in all religions, in all mythologies, in all stories. But there is a Heaven, and there is a Hell, and so much in between."

"So he just sits up there in Heaven, huh? Twiddling his thumbs while shit hits the fan down here?" Tommy asked.

"It's not exactly *up*."

"But that's where he is? In Heaven?"

Bandini was silent.

"I gotta be honest, man. You not answering concerns me."

"God is everywhere."

"But not in Heaven?"

"We don't necessarily know where he is."

Tommy laughed. "Well, that's just great. So who's in charge? Who sent you here?"

"God did."

"How?"

"His orders arrive now and again, but he is not there to give them. He has not been for quite some time."

Tommy stopped. "So God abandoned us? Is that what you're saying?" He kicked at the hardened snow that paved the street. "I learn that God is real, and in the same night, I also learn that he left us. Is that right?"

"No, that's not right. At least, not exactly. It is complicated, Tommy. It is very complicated."

"Yeah, okay. Complicated. Got it." He took a few steps before stopping again. "My brother. Is he there?"

"Where?"

"In Heaven."

"That is a very difficult question to answer."

"Why?"

"Mortal identities and other burdens of the flesh are shed

when souls enter the kingdom. If your brother is there, I would not know."

"And what about Hell?"

"In Hell, you bring it all with you. Your flesh, your sorrows, your name."

"I'm asking if my brother is in Hell."

"Ah," said Bandini. "I'm sorry, Tommy. I do not know that either."

"Right. Yeah. Just thought I'd ask," he said, his voice trailing off. Tommy had more questions, but shrank from the prospect of further disappointment. The pain in his chest gnawed another tally mark into his rib cage, one for each day since his brother's death.

They continued on. It was 1:57 a.m. The liquor store closed in just three minutes.

"Okay, this guy Bronek caught me peeing outside his store once," Tommy said, "so he's not my biggest fan, but he's cool. Calls Hector buddy-buddy. I love it. But maybe you should hide and keep quiet so he doesn't see me walking around his store talking to a spider."

"I understand." Bandini crawled into the flap of Tommy's beanie.

The door dinged as they entered Armitage Food, one minute before close. The small store was empty, and Bronek was conspicuously absent.

Through the knit of Tommy's hat, Bandini made out the shapes of photographs plastering the bullet-proof glass and the counter behind it. He assumed they were of the man's family, and imagined the comfort they brought Bronek as he sat alone behind the register on a night like this.

Tommy beelined to the coolers in the rear of the store and grabbed a six pack of Hamm's. Remembering Sammie, he reached for a second. The last cooler's contents caught his eye: Mad Dog. His mouth watered, just a bit.

"Maybe not the best time," Bandini whispered.

Ignoring the spider's pleas, Tommy set the six packs down, fished a crumpled wad of cash from one pocket, counted it, and sighed. Then, he pulled a fistful of change from the other, counted it, and sighed again. "Alright," he grumbled, shoving the money back into his pants.

Now at the register, Bronek was still missing.

"Perhaps he's performing his closing duties. Does he have an office?" Bandini asked.

Tommy knocked on the door of the nearby storage room that doubled as Bronek's office. No answer. He tried the knob. Locked.

"Should I just leave the money on the counter?"

"We do have to get back," Bandini reminded.

He sighed, shuffled to the counter, and dug back into his pockets. His keys became tangled in their lining. "Fuckin' c'mon," he grunted. Nickels and quarters clattered to the floor.

As Tommy cursed and picked up his change, Bandini took the opportunity to catch a glimpse of Bronek's photos, the loved ones he was proud to display for all the neighborhood to see. He crawled out from the fold of Tommy's beanie to see the photographs taped to every inch of available space on the glass and register. Without further contemplation, Bandini said, "Tommy, we need to go."

"Huh?" Tommy struggled with the last quarter eluding his fingertips, then stood to see what Bandini wanted. Upon seeing the photos, he dropped the collected change back to the floor.

These were not pictures of happier times. They were snapshots of horror.

Tommy stared, mouth agape, at a polaroid of Bronek's grandchildren skewered on playground equipment so that their organs dangled to the mulch below, the chains from the swing set wrapped around their necks, and their bulging eyes devoured by hungry squirrels.

Above that was a yearbook photo, innocuous at first glance, but, upon closer examination, the traditional blue-gray backdrop was patterned with a subliminal orgy of fresh amputees. The child, wearing his best polo shirt, buttoned one button too high, looked directly into Tommy's eyes and mouthed, *You're next, faggot.*

Black and white photos from the old country, held on by browning strips of Scotch tape, covered the back of Bronek's register. One such photo showed a family sitting at a small wooden table with their own still-tethered intestines served in front of them, their mouths full and their faces weeping. Next to the photo, a weathered sticker of Joe Camel gave the thumbs-up in his trademark shades, declaring Camel Wides were two-for-one, a deal long since expired.

Taped flat on the counter for Bronek's eyes only was a photo of a woman, presumably his wife, being double teamed by some tentacled beast and a man wearing the top half of a Nazi uniform, and missing the bottom half of his jaw, tongue flailing around his Adam's apple as he pounded her from behind.

Bandini saw a single fly rise from the floor behind the register. Its arousal was palpable. "We need to go," he repeated.

Tommy sat on the counter, face to the bullet-proof glass, trying to get a better look at the polaroid of the unholy threesome.

"*Now,*" Bandini said.

Tommy mumbled an agreement, but before he could get down, he saw the red. A dark pool of crimson had accumulated on the other side, just out of sight. Tommy stood on the counter and pressed himself against the glass in an attempt to see the source.

There was Bronek's body, shoved underneath the counter alongside boxes of black plastic bags and spools of receipt paper. A deep wound on his throat, from a knife thrust and twisted then ripped out, left flaps of skin torn, revealing the intricate layers of anatomy beneath.

Tommy dove off the counter, slammed his money down, and grabbed the beers. His dash to the door left Bandini struggling to hang on. When he reached cold air, Tommy collapsed to his knees, gasping like he had narrowly escaped poisonous fumes. Then, a voice.

"Whoa, what's the hurry? Where you off to, pal?"

It was a cop. And not just any cop, but the cop that regularly patrolled this stretch of Armitage Avenue, the cop that had previously caught Tommy pissing on this very establishment.

"Hey, I know you. It's piss boy. I should have known. We got a call from a concerned neighbor, said some drunk was hanging out in front of the liquor pissing outside and shouting obscenities. Color me surprised to see you here."

"I wasn't pissing anywhere. I just need to go home," Tommy said. He started to walk past the cop who stuck his arm out to stop him.

"Hey now, slow down there. Why don't we have a chat with our old friend inside and see what he thinks?"

Tommy shook his head. "I think they're closed now. He went home."

The cop walked to the door and gave it a nudge. "Looks open to me." He pointed a finger in Tommy's face. "Don't move from this spot. Do you understand me?"

Tommy watched the cop enter the store without a word.

"I think you need to run," Bandini said.

"Run? Are you crazy? What if he fucking shoots me in the back? Do you even watch the news?"

"I think that's a risk you need to take."

Tommy weighed his options, and agreed. He took off and made it halfway through the tiny parking lot before he heard the cop shout, "Down! Get down on the fucking ground right fucking now!"

He looked back to see a gun drawn on him and the cop calling for backup on his shoulder radio.

Tommy lowered himself to the pavement and placed his hands on his head. "Now what?" he asked Bandini, but he received no response.

26

They lay on his bed, together and apart.

He briefed Sammie on the situation as best he could, but the gaps were huge and the strokes were broad, filled with more questions than answers.

She told him about the shadow creatures. The rat and the cats. It didn't surprise Hector that Sammie had already allied herself with the neighborhood strays. Animals had always loved her.

Once their stories were told, they were quiet.

The streetlights cast a slanted stream of light through his window. It cut through the darkness, illuminating Sammie's feet which stuck out from the blanket. Her back was to Hector, and she stared at the wall. Their kiss in the doorway was instinctual, but neither could rationalize another touch. Neither knew where to go from here.

Sammie refocused on the matter at hand instead of retreating into silence. "This is crazy, right? Are we just crazy? Did you, me, and Tommy finally just lose our fucking minds?"

Hector considered the possibility. If it wasn't for Jess being in the psych ward and the detectives who came to visit him at work, he might have thought this was all happening in a vacuum, that it really was just the delusions of a few alcoholics who finally drank their feeble brains into a state of stupefaction and now lived in permanent hallucinatory psychosis. But instead, he settled on, "No, we're not crazy. This is just fucked."

Sammie pursed her lips, quietly agreeing. She had always been interested in the unexplained. Ghosts, aliens, magick, even Bigfoot, she believed in it all. Couple that with the horrific normal reality she was accustomed to, and nothing surprised her anymore. She'd ingested enough substances and been through enough bullshit to mentally navigate even the strangest of circumstances.

"Guess your dad was more of a dick than you thought, huh?" she said.

"I guess so," Hector said. In truth, he had no concrete image of the man. All memories of his father felt secondhand, like they had happened to someone else. "I barely knew him," he added.

"I know," Sammie offered in a gentle breath. A surge of electricity flowed through her arms. She wanted to use them to comfort him like she used to, but she kept them folded at her chest.

The wind whistled outside the window over their resumed silence.

Hector began to wonder where Tommy was, worried he had taken a detour to the all-night taco place or was purposefully allowing him alone-time with Sammie. He wished he'd just come home.

Sammie spoke. "I saw Austin earlier." Her eyes remained transfixed on the wall she faced.

Hector's gut sank. The thought of Austin uttering even a single word to Sammie nauseated him.

She had always told Hector not to trust him, but he maintained that glimmer of hope that Austin had at least one caring bone in his body. Turns out, he didn't. While siding with a literal demon was not on his bingo card for fucked-up things Austin may do, he supposed it was just a matter of him being given the opportunity.

"Where did you see him?" he asked, trying to hide the panic that flooded his system.

"I was sitting at Go Tavern, and I saw him across the street. He didn't look over at me, but it felt like he knew I was there. I can't explain it."

"I think we're past the point of trying to explain things."

"Yeah, I guess you're right," Sammie said.

Hector had left out the part of his story that included Austin, but now realized he couldn't any longer for her own safety. He braced himself for her reaction, and said, "Austin was here, by the way. He came over the other day, and earlier tonight."

Sammie rolled over to look at Hector for the first time since they lay in his bed. "Excuse me, what? You let that psycho back into your home?"

Hector already felt stupid about it, but Sammie's response rubbed salt in the wound. "Well, at first, he came by and was... nice. He seemed better. He seemed like he genuinely wanted to be a better person. He talked about rehab and—"

"He finished his treatment?"

"Well, no."

"Hector." Sammie rolled back to the wall.

"But he acknowledged that he hadn't always been that great of a friend and—"

"He drugged you."

"Yeah..."

"And put his hands on me."

Hector had no words for that.

Sammie continued, "And as if *that* wasn't enough, he stole three-hundred dollars from Tommy, your best friend."

"He swears that he didn't."

"And you believe him over Tommy?"

"No."

"Then why even say that?"

Hector didn't know why he almost stuck up for Austin there. It was a reflex. "I don't know. You're right. I guess I'm still just taking it all in. I'm sorry."

Sammie understood the role that Austin played in Hector's life up until this point. Surrogate father. Big brother. Austin deserved to be neither of those things. "When that spider— What's his name?"

"He said his name was Bandini."

Sammie rolled her eyes, unseen by Hector. "Right. When Bandini said that Bub— What's his name?"

"Bub is right. Well, technically, Beelzebub, I guess."

"Okay. When Bandini said that Beelzebub had a minion, and he brought you and Tommy drugs, who was he talking about?"

Hector fell silent.

"Who was he talking about, Hector?"

"Austin."

"So you took drugs from Austin and shared a needle with Tommy?"

Hector knew he'd fucked up and didn't need Sammie reminding him. "It's been a rough couple days."

Sammie bit her tongue so hard she thought it would bleed. It was not her responsibility to caretake or scold Hector anymore. It never was. But his naivety and impulsiveness put her own to shame, and when they were together, it was the vision-impaired leading the blind. She had guided him away from oncoming traffic more than once, sometimes quite literally.

Her eyes focused on a dark patch on the wall. She stared at it until her vision blended with the shadows, and said, "He killed Vince. I know he did. I can feel it." The message carved into her friend's chest now held meaning beyond just the ravings of a lunatic. *I AM THE DEVIL'S SON*. Austin had found a fitting father.

"I'm sure you're right. Dish Pit too."

"Dish Pit?" she asked.

"Dishwasher Dave. You remember him?"

"He's dead?"

"Murdered behind Slippery Slope. These two detectives think I did it." Hector watched Sammie shift and tighten her body, bringing her arms even closer to her chest.

"So going to the police for help is probably out of the question then," Sammie concluded.

"Yeah, probably. But I think it *really* became out of the question around the time me and Tommy got pulled into our refrigerator."

"Then it's just us," said Sammie.

"Us?" Hector propped himself up and spoke to the back of Sammie's head. "No, you need to get out of here. First thing in the morning. You really shouldn't even be going to the wake tomorrow. You need to go back to Milwaukee."

"Excuse me? I don't *need* to do anything. If you don't want me to stay here, that's fine, but I came down to Chicago for a reason, and I'm going tomorrow."

"It's not that I don't want you here. It's just not safe to be around me. I don't know if it's safe for you to be in Chicago at all."

Sammie turned to match his stare, her eyes piercing him through the darkness. She was shrouded in night and lit by the window's glow. Hector's heart pounded with purpose, flooding his chest with warmth. Her face was gentle but battle-worn, shaped by a life lived. Round cheeks framed a nose that crooked a bit to the left beneath eyes so sad and deep, they existed on the brink of madness. He knew he still loved her.

Hector wanted to touch her. He ached to rub her lower back like he used to, to bring her body closer to his until his arm wrapped around her and his hand grazed her stomach. His fingers would trace whatever words came into his mind on her soft belly. *Coffee. Hi. You. Dream. Cat. Love.* Pleasant things. Simple things.

"Don't be stupid," she said. "You think whatever is going on will stay localized to Chicago? Your spider friend bit me. I've seen things. I'm part of this now. And the horrible things that chased me in the alley, or the monster that pulled you into the fridge, those things will follow us wherever we go. I'm no safer in Milwaukee than I am here. At least here I can help and not just be a sitting duck." She flipped back to face the wall.

"I'm sorry, Sammie," Hector said, a notch above a whisper. "I'm sorry you're part of this. Just because you know me. Just because he knows I care about you."

She let out a sarcastic snort. "Do you? Do you care about me, Hector? You didn't answer a single text I sent about coming to Chicago. You haven't spoken to me in months. You act like I don't exist. Like nothing happened. Like you never loved me."

He could hear the tears being fought back.

"You always think you're the only one who's hurting, that you're the only one who's ever in pain," she said.

"I'm sorry." It was all Hector could say.

"It broke my heart too, what happened. What we did. Don't pretend that I'm dead just to ease your own suffering. You're only hurting me more."

"You're right. It's just—it's just hard to think about. And talking to you, seeing you, makes it all feel like we're right back in that day, right there in the waiting room."

Sammie lost herself in the dark patch of the wall once more, her vision blurring. Tears glazed her eyes, waiting for the dam to break.

"We did what we thought we had to do. I did what I thought I needed to do." Her eyes closed, streams ran down her cheeks. "Look at us. Look what we're dealing with right now. Imagine if we brought another life into this. You weren't ready. And I wasn't ready to do it alone." When she reopened her eyes, the wall came into focus. She could see the decades' worth of textured paint coats in the moonlight, dirty and off-white. Everything was all too clear.

Hector felt attacked, like she was putting all the blame on him. He was only able to focus on that single sentence. *You weren't ready.* He couldn't find the strength to empathize with her pain, to push past his immeasurable need to defend himself.

"I wasn't ready? You make it seem like you were. We both did the exact same shit night after night. You were not some angel." The words left his mouth, and he instantly wished he could take them back.

"I never fucking said I was, Hector," said Sammie with a bite. "But when I found out I was pregnant, I immediately stopped drinking, stopped smoking, stopped all that shit. I started to think of the future for maybe the first time in my life. And what did you do? You drank even more. Blacked-out drunk in the middle of the day. You got distant and put up a wall that wasn't between us before."

Hector didn't respond. He had said too much.

"Then you just fucking decided you didn't want to be with me. That we were just better as friends. Can you imagine saying that to someone who you just got pregnant? How on earth could I have a child with someone like that? You didn't give me a choice. You didn't give a shit."

"That's not true. I did give a shit."

"Don't even, Hector. I am not in the fucking mood for your bullshit."

"I wanted you to keep it."

"I said don't!"

Tears knocked on the back of Hector's eyes. He did his best to keep them at bay.

"I *am* sorry, Sammie. You have no idea how sorry I am. I don't know why I acted the way I did. I just...lost it. I can't explain it. I wish I was different, a different person, someone who could have been there for you. But I'm poison, just like my dad."

Sammie was having none of it. Her fight or flight kicked in the second he pushed back against her, and she was all fight. "Oh, stop feeling sorry for yourself. I can explain it just fine. It's because you only care about yourself. It's really as fucking simple as that."

The words seared into Hector. They were his mother's words. "Please don't say that," he said. "It's not true."

She wasn't budging. "Well, you sure did a shit job of showing it's not true."

"I just panicked. I lost myself. I was scared."

"And I wasn't? I was fucking terrified, Hector. But I still thought there was hope for us—until there wasn't. I loved you, Hector. I still do." Her own words calmed her. The panic in her chest subsided, her firing nerves extinguished. "There's no point in talking about this. What's done is done. Let's just try to stay alive." She tucked herself closer to the edge of the bed and shut her eyes. "I'm going to sleep. Goodnight."

"Goodnight," Hector said.

She waited for him to say it back. The minutes passed in silence, producing nothing. It wasn't until sleep began to wash over her that the sound of his voice touched her ears.

"I love you too."

27

Tommy tapped his left index finger to the beat of his quickened pulse. His heart had not stopped racing since the gun was pulled on him. He rubbed the side of his neck where the officer had placed his boot until backup arrived, as if Tommy was some two-man job. They handcuffed him, placed him in the back of the cruiser, and took him to the station next to the California Blue Line.

The detectives had already come and gone, but they'd be back, only stepping out to grab him coffee. Tommy assumed this was a tool in their good cop, bad cop routine. The waiting was torture. Maybe they wanted him to sweat. Mission accomplished.

They booked and fingerprinted him when he arrived at the station, citing the offenses as resisting arrest—hard to do with a boot on his neck and a gun in his face—and attempting to flee the scene of a crime—which Tommy was shocked to discover was a crime unto itself. He asked for a lawyer, but the detectives assured him that if he just told them his story and it checked out, he would be on his way. Tommy knew he was innocent and was anxious to get back to the apartment, so he agreed.

He couldn't remember at what point Bandini jumped ship. Everything happened so fast. From the moment that gun was drawn on him, he succumbed to a mental paralysis that he was only now beginning to emerge from. He just hoped Bandini had gone to warn Hector and Sammie. What happened to Bronek was clearly not a typical smash and grab.

His finger bounced off the stainless-steel table, now more of a twitch than a tap. It reminded him of the metal prep station at Whole Foods where he scooped tuna salad into plastic containers weighing a third of a pound each. Or the unforgiving steel of his childhood doctor's examination table. All it was missing was that narrow sheet of parchment paper that shifted and slid until it was just bare ass on cold metal. He wondered if this was the type of table they did autopsies on. For a moment, he saw himself, blue and veiny, naked on the slab. *I gotta get out of here*, he thought.

The door opened. It was the detectives.

Detective Surdyk was holding a small styrofoam cup filled with black coffee. He set it down in front of Tommy and manufactured a smile. Detective Borst entered behind him with nothing but a grimace. He hovered above the table with folded arms while Detective Surdyk pulled out a chair and took a seat. Good cop. Bad cop.

"Mr. Ewing. Do you go by Tommy or Thomas?"

"Tommy is fine."

"Alright, Tommy, I know it's been a long night. It's been a long night for everyone, so we want to thank you again for your time."

Detective Borst grunted.

"So why don't you go ahead and tell us one more time what happened. Just so we're all on the same page."

"And then I can go?"

"Sure, buddy, then you can go," Detective Borst grumbled, then laughed with all the bass of his diaphragm.

Tommy shifted his eyes between the two detectives, landing on Detective Surdyk, and said, "The way he just said that, it kind of makes it seem like you're not going to let me go."

"Like I said, he's just had a long night. Don't pay attention to him," Detective Surdyk said.

Detective Borst grunted once more.

"Start from the beginning," said the good cop.

Tommy took a deep breath, and stuck his hand underneath his thigh to stop its tapping. He figured fidgeting and twitching wasn't a good look for someone claiming innocence. "Okay. I was at home with my roommate, and we had just run out of beers."

Detective Surdyk interrupted, "Your roommate, Hector Ghouseau."

"Y-yes, how did you know that?"

"We ran your address. And, as I'm sure you know, your friend has found himself in the middle of a few interesting situations as well lately. Did you know David Wojciehowski?"

David. Dave. Dishwasher Dave. *Dish Pit.* "Yes, I did. And I heard what happened. Hector didn't do that."

"We can't comment on that. But we do know that his only alibi is in a psych ward right now. A young woman who, according to friends and family, was completely fine before she met your friend at the bar for drinks. Now what do you think happened there?"

Tommy couldn't exactly say it was demons, Hell on Earth, or the result of a sexually transmitted ticket to a real-life horror movie, so he went with the version of the truth he had known up to a certain point. "I honestly don't know what happened. I saw him in the morning, and it seemed like a normal date and night out for him." *Bed wetting and all*, Tommy thought.

"And where were you during his date?" Detective Surdyk asked, pulling out a small pad of paper and pen. Detective Borst stood with his arms crossed.

Tommy needed to think about that one for a second. After Hector left, Tommy rode his bike down to Bridgeport to meet some coworkers for beers. They didn't show. He ended up taking a handful of shots with a stranger at the bar, as he often did, who invited him to a party with the promise of cocaine. Tommy accepted the invitation. He soon found himself drinking Special Exports in an unfamiliar, smoke-filled kitchen doing lines off a McDonald's promotional plate for the 1997 animated film *Hercules*. He blacked out. The rest of the night, a mystery. In the morning, he awoke in his own apartment, half on the couch, half on the floor, unsure how he'd even gotten back.

Detective Borst broke his train of thought. "We ain't got all night, kid."

"I was at a bar. In Bridgeport."

"A bar in Bridgeport," Detective Borst repeated.

"A bar in Bridgeport," reiterated Detective Surdyk. "And do you have anyone that can confirm you were at this 'bar in Bridgeport'?"

None of his coworkers showed up that night. There was the stranger, but Tommy didn't remember his name. And he definitely did not remember where the party was. The only person he could think of was the bartender, maybe.

"Maybe the bartender?" Tommy offered.

"Maybe the bartender," Detective Surdyk echoed. "Did you make any transactions at this bar?"

"Or were all the pretty girls buying your drinks?" Detective Borst asked.

"I bought my own drinks."

"Will these drinks be on your bank statement?"

In this age of incredible technology where the world and all its knowledge was at his fingertips, where he could argue with a stranger, research whatever medical issue was plaguing him that day, and watch an episode of a TV show that ran for only one season in 1993 without having to ever get up from the toilet, Tommy wondered why some bars refused to enter the modern age and remained cash only. Hector once suggested it was tax evasion, which Tommy could appreciate, but it still irritated him.

Detective Borst chimed in. "I think I know the answer here. Let me guess, cash only?"

Tommy nodded.

"Bingo, bango, what the fuck do I win?" Borst mocked.

"Did you happen to use the ATM at the bar? Or anywhere nearby that night?" Detective Surdyk asked.

Tommy shook his head.

The door opened, and a uniformed cop leaned in. Without even taking his hand from the doorknob, he whispered something into Detective Borst's ear, then raised his eyebrows to Detective Surdyk.

"Looks like I got my prize," said the bad cop.

"Excuse us," Detective Surdyk said, and they exited the room.

What now? Tommy wondered, exhausted. He looked at the clock on the wall. 4:00 a.m. Was no one looking for him? Were Hector and Sammie sleeping? Did Bandini make it back to the apartment? The police had taken his phone, so he couldn't even send a text. He was all questions, no answers.

A small sound grew in the silence. Static. Buzzing. Hissing. It descended from the ceiling and landed on the table in front of him.

A single fly.

Probably not a good sign, he thought.

The door flung open, and the two detectives strutted in with a confidence that worried Tommy. He looked down, and the fly was gone.

They resumed their positions, Detective Borst as the cross-armed gargoyle and Detective Surdyk seated facing Tommy. "So, where did we leave off? There's no one to confirm where you were the night of David Wojciehowski's death, except *maybe* the bartender. Correct?"

Tommy nodded.

"That's okay. We're not necessarily here to discuss that particular matter. At least, not yet. So let's get back to tonight. You were telling us how you ran out of beer?"

"That's right. It was almost two, and the liquor store was about to close, so I rushed over to Armitage Food."

"Go on."

"I got there, and the store was empty. So I grabbed the beers from the cooler and went to pay, and that's when I saw Bronek on the floor beneath the counter."

"Why didn't you call the police? Why'd you run?" Detective Surdyk asked.

"I don't know. I panicked. I was scared."

Borst snorted and rolled his eyes. Tommy started to feel like they knew something he didn't.

The detective continued, "And you didn't go behind the counter at all when you were there? Maybe to check on your friend Bronek?"

"No, closest I got was pressing my face against the bullet-proof glass, and I saw him dead. I didn't go back there. I swear."

The detectives exchanged looks like they were offering each other the last slice of cake. Detective Surdyk gestured to Detective Borst as if to say, *Please, it's all you. Take it away.* So he did.

Detective Borst slammed his massive paws on the table. "Lying little piece of shit!"

Tommy recoiled. He had no idea what he was lying about.

"We know you were back there," Detective Borst said through gritted teeth. "Now's the time for fessing up, not for games."

"If you're honest with us, we can help you. But if you lie and drag this on, things will only get harder for you. Trust us. We've seen it before," Detective Surdyk explained.

"I have no idea what you're talking about. I'm not playing games, and I'm not lying!" Tommy kneaded his head with his knuckles, certain he was losing his mind for the umpteenth time that night. "Wouldn't I be covered in blood if I did this?"

Detective Borst barked back. "I don't give a shit how clean your clothes are. We found an empty pack of cigarettes a foot away from the body with your fingerprints all over it. Do you want to explain how that got back there?"

Tommy's mind shrunk to the size of a peanut. Words failed him. Thoughts failed him. His mental capacity to absorb what he'd just heard failed him. All he could manage was, "Huh?"

"Let's not play dumb here," said Detective Surdyk, dropping the good cop act. "Answer the fucking question."

"I swear I have no idea what you're talking about."

Detective Borst stomped around the table to stick his face right in Tommy's. "And leaving money on the counter after you did it. Forgot to pay for your booze, huh? You sick fuck. You disgust me."

"Did *what*? I didn't do anything! Wasn't there security footage or something you can check?"

"The security system was ancient," Detective Surdyk said. "It fed to a single hard drive in the owner's office. The perpetrator destroyed it, presumably after the murder took place."

"But you already knew that, didn't you?" Detective Borst said, jabbing a finger into Tommy's chest, his face still inches away.

The detective's stale coffee breath assaulted Tommy with each jab. He craned away as far as the chair would allow and said, "Listen, I don't know what's going on, but I did not kill Bronek. This is insane! It's impossible that it was my pack of cigarettes. There's just no—"

And then it clicked.

That motherfucker, Tommy thought. Not only did he steal his last cigarette yesterday morning, but now he's framing him for murder. *That fucking dick.*

"It was Austin!" exclaimed Tommy. "I know who killed Bronek, and Dish Pi— I mean, David. And that dude Vince from Cole's too!"

Detective Surdyk reclined in his chair, putting his hands behind his head. "You're a regular Sherlock Holmes, huh? We hadn't even discussed the Cole's case, but you're just up to date on all the murders within a two-mile radius, aren't you?"

"I wonder why," Detective Borst said, no longer jabbing but still leaning over Tommy to maintain striking distance.

"You have to listen to me. It's Austin. This guy. This fucking guy. He's a lunatic. Austin. Austin Ethans."

Detective Surdyk humored him. "And who is this? Why do you think we should be talking to him instead of you?"

"Austin Ethans. Sounds made up," added Detective Borst.

"He's Hector's friend—*was* Hector's friend. He was in Florida but now he's not. He's here. And he's killing people. I fucking know it for a fact."

"Well, we would love to hear these facts." Surdyk looked at his partner. "Isn't that right?"

"We sure would," said Detective Borst, his hot breath pummeling Tommy's face.

"I... It's because..." There were just a few problems with the facts Tommy had. They were crazy enough to make a schizophrenic street prophet hang up his sandwich board.

"You know what I think?" Detective Borst asked, returning to the other side of the table. "I think he's just throwing names out there trying to save his own ass." He locked eyes with Tommy and said, "If you got any actual evidence that this *Austin Ethans* is our killer, you better spill it now."

Tommy stewed in the madness he held behind his lips, not knowing how to share it in a way that sounded relatively sane.

"That's what I thought." Detective Borst unleashed a deep, phlegmy cough, clearing his throat. "You want to talk about facts? Let's talk facts." He adjusted the pantline that hung beneath his gut, then turned to his partner. "These are the facts I see," he began. "Two degenerates find themselves involved in multiple murder investigations. Murders, mind you, that appear to be carried out by the same weapon. Connected killings. And this little worm," he stuck a thumb toward Tommy, "had his fingerprints next to the body on an empty pack of cigarettes, *behind* the counter. Now, this is just an educated guess, but I can think of only one reason he'd be back there for that to fall out of his pocket, and it wasn't because he was picking up night shifts on the register."

Tommy sat, dumbstruck, staring at the two detectives who were waiting for any reason not to ship him off to Cook County Jail right then and there.

He finally spoke. "I told you everything I know. You said I could leave if I tell you what happened. Well, that's what happened. I did not kill Bronek, but I know who did."

Detective Surdyk appeared tired of this exchange. "Right, Austin. What's the last name? Edens?"

"Ethans," Tommy corrected.

"That's it. Ethans. Well, you've given us zero reason to look into this person other than you simply saying we should. So let's put that idea on the backburner for now, okay?"

Tommy started to speak, but Surdyk held his hand up. He wasn't finished.

"Now, we said you could leave if your story checked out." He turned to his colleague and asked, "Detective Borst, would you say that this young man's story checked out?"

Detective Borst guffawed.

"I didn't think so. I'd say it's probably best you hang out here for a while. After all, you did resist a police officer, and we need to speak with the DA's office to decide how to move forward here. So just hang tight, we'll set you up with a room." He shot a wink at Tommy as he stood. "It'll be real nice."

"I think I'll take that lawyer and phone call now, please."

"Good idea," Detective Surdyk said, following his partner out the door and shutting it behind them.

Tommy was alone—except for the fly, who once again landed on the table in front of him. He stared at its small face that spasmed with black drool dripping from its spongy appendage of a mouth. He had no idea what a fly looked like when it was entertained, but he could just tell it was having a good time.

It was a struggle falling asleep on the holding cell bench. Not because of the conditions—Tommy had slept in worse—but because of the gnawing fear that he would never sleep outside of a cell ever again.

He imagined arriving in prison for a crime he hadn't committed. Like Red said in *The Shawshank Redemption*, "Everyone in here is innocent." His adamance would be nothing but spit in an ocean of men swearing the same.

He thought of growing old behind prison walls. He would never feel the touch of a woman again, never become a father, never prove to himself or the family who maligned him that he was capable of good, that he could change and fly right. He would never fly again. Clipped wings only flap in futility for so long before they resign themselves to simply being dead weight.

The only other inhabitant of the cell was a man asleep on the floor whose body was slung across the ground like a pile of dirty laundry. He had not budged. Tommy figured he was sleeping off a rough night.

Sleep.

Tommy closed his eyes and tried again. The January sunrise was nearing, eager to shower the city in its gray.

He found himself thinking thoughts he couldn't recall a moment later, disjointed fragments and wisps from a consciousness drifting away from itself within itself. The clouds parted in his mind. Sleep was on the horizon, its dense smother finally taking mercy on him, quelling his frantic mind into submission.

Then the man on the floor moved. And the lights went out.

The sudden sound of the man rolling onto his back and choking, as if something had flown down his throat, jarred Tommy from the brink of sleep. The man convulsed. Tommy thought he was having a seizure, but just as he was about to call for help, everything stopped.

The man sat up in one fluid motion. The darkness was thick, but Tommy saw that something was not right.

The energy of the cell changed, growing sour and cold. The man's face shifted and rearranged itself like clay, becoming someone entirely new. This new man stuck a hand in his mouth and pulled out a pair of glasses. He breathed on the lenses, polished them on the drunk's jacket, then placed them on his face before turning to Tommy with a grin.

"Hi," said the man, reflecting Tommy's confusion in his dark-tinted glasses.

"Hi?" Tommy's patience had run low for supernatural theatrics. He was dead tired, and mentally preparing himself for a life behind bars. This was the last shit he needed.

"Do you know who I am?" the man asked.

"I have a rough idea."

"All your ideas are a bit rough, Thomas," the man hissed. "Now, do I need to explain who I am?"

Tommy pursed his lips and shook his head. "You're the guy who's ruining our lives."

Bub laughed. "I believe you two do a fine job of that on your own, don't you?"

"Why are you even bothering us? Who cares about some fucked-up bet Hector's dad made? Don't you have anything better to do as a...whatever you are?"

"Oh my, you are a *spicy* one." Bub smoothed out the creases in the drunk's jacket. "As someone who has dedicated their life to the trivial, the destructive, and the obscene, I was hoping you would understand."

"Get a fucking life and leave us alone," Tommy said, and rolled over on the bench to face the wall.

"A life?" Bub let the words dissolve in the air. With a twirl of his finger, he snapped Tommy over and upright so he sat at full attention. "I have no need. I am without life and without death."

Bub drifted to the bench, bending to meet Tommy at his eye level. "All I need, all I want, is suffering. I feed on the weak. I collect the sad. The pathetic. The cowardly. Their flesh hangs like art in my halls."

He ran a finger along Tommy's cheek, then brought it to his tongue for a taste. "Your kind, people like you, Thomas, the fuck ups, are my bread and butter, and I don't let deals fall through. Souls like yours, like your friend Hector's, and his father's before him, are the kindle for my fire. And you will burn."

Tommy stiffened, his bravado a distant memory.

Bub surveyed the concrete cell. "You will spend the rest of this life inside a prison, but when you die, the real suffering will begin. There will be no sentence, no end. There will be no peace, no rest."

He stroked Tommy's hair and traced the contour of his ear. "I will personally see to it that you choke on the cum of every beast in Hell until it seeps out of your eyes, never allowing you a moment to weep or beg for your mother." He smiled, stood straight, and attempted once more to smooth out the creases of the drunk's jacket. "Doesn't that sound lovely?"

Tommy's chest hollowed out. He simply wished to not exist. Dread spread its legs throughout his entire body. For a moment, he teetered on complete collapse.

Then Bub said, "Or, we can help each other."

"What?" Tommy asked, attempting to process the words.

"Ensure Hector takes his own life. It won't be hard. And I will have these charges dropped like that." He snapped his fingers for emphasis. "There are some in the district attorney's office that owe me." He smiled at his own implication. "I will also ensure your stay in Hell is *more* than comfortable. You need only ask your friend Austin what I can do for you."

"Austin is not my friend."

"I could care less." Bub waved his hand in limp dismissal.

Tommy sat up and asked, "You know what I think?"

"I don't think you think at all."

"I think you're full of shit," said Tommy.

"Oh?"

He had zero reason to feel emboldened, but there he was, talking back to the devil himself. "You can't get through to Hector. He's too fucked up. I'm too fucked up. It's like trying to tell a joke to someone already laughing hysterically. They can't even hear your punchline over the sound of their own laughter.

"And deep down, Hector is good. I can't speak for myself, but I know Hector is a good person. It's why you have to go through all this trouble, why you enlisted a smarmy dick like Austin, why you're standing here talking to me right now. Am I onto something here? Am I on the right track?" Tommy's chest filled with something resembling courage, so he rode that wave for all it was worth, and said, "And just in case I wasn't clear, I will never fucking help you."

Bub stood silent, letting Tommy have his moment. Then he removed his glasses.

A patchwork of red lenses, framed by eyelids of now melting flesh, glowed back at Tommy. Bub's jaw unhinged and stretched downward, lower and lower until it touched the floor. His mouth wilted into a cavernous void, stretching into infinite black. Deep in its darkness, a frenzied buzz rallied.

The buzzing grated on Tommy's ears, while Bub's voice whispered in his thoughts, "Your tongue is bold for a thing that can so easily be ripped out of your head."

"Fuck you," Tommy said in a small voice, not wanting to actually be heard.

The cell grew even darker, as if it detached from the station itself and floated in an isolated void. Bub's shape spread to the ceiling and began to fill the room with a mass of writhing, thorned appendages. He was shadow built upon shadow, his mouth now large enough to swallow Tommy whole.

The buzzing was deafening, but still, Bub's voice boomed in Tommy's head. "Thomas Ewing. Son of Michelle and Jamie Ewing. Descendent of filth and heir to nothing. Abide by me or be raped by woe in perpetuity. You will exist only as a trench for sorrow to spill its sour seed. Do as I say or suffer as your brother, whose sniveling pleas echo throughout my hallowed halls as I *speak*."

"Liar!" Tommy shouted. This had gone on long enough. "Help! Somebody help! There's an intruder here! Officer! Officer!" He yelled for the police—an act which greatly embarrassed him.

"Hey, who the hell shut off the lights?" a distant voice shouted. The sound of hurried footsteps followed. The cell returned from the void.

Bub's fearsome form snapped like a rubber band back to the shape of a man. He placed the tinted glasses on his face and straightened out the drunk man's jacket. "Think about it," he said, blowing Tommy a kiss with a slight upward tilt of his head. He strolled to where the man had been sleeping and let the body collapse like a rag doll. A single fly flew out of the mouth as the pair of glasses bounced into the shadows, disappearing.

The lights flashed on.

"What the fuck is going on in here? Who turned off the lights? Who's screaming?" the cop demanded to know.

The drunk man sprang up, clawing at his own face like he was shocked to find it there. He laughed, then cried, delirious from being trapped in the labyrinth of his own mind. He looked over at Tommy, pointed a finger, and came to only one conclusion. "This guy's a fucking witch! You have to get me out here! He's the devil!"

Tommy shrugged at the officer. Lying back down on the bench, he tried to succumb to the sweet smother of sleep once more.

28

THE THIRD DAY

Austin stirred in the gray morning light.

He stretched his limbs out in every direction of the queen-sized bed and rolled his head between a pair of matching *His* and *Hers* pillows. They were a gift from a son, a man of Austin's age, who had since moved to the suburbs to raise a family of his own, and who had encouraged his aging parents to leave Chicago behind them too, but who was always met with defiance and reassurance.

The blankets and sheets still had that fresh laundry smell. The fragrance was pleasant, but it made Austin sneeze. His morning mucus shot from his mouth right onto the *Hers* pillow. He rubbed the phlegm in until it was a pale smear on the fabric. He had slept like a baby, but it was time to get up.

The water pressure was not quite up to his standards, but he made do. He searched the shower for body wash, but found only a bar of soap. *Yuck*, Austin thought, washing himself with shampoo instead.

The kitchen was full of knickknacks, souvenirs from a lifetime of love, hard work, and holidays. Baby photos and wedding invitations were pinned on the refrigerator under novelty magnets from states visited on family vacations long past.

Where do they keep the fucking coffee in this dump?

He scoured the cabinets.

Café Bustelo? He examined the yellow coffee tin. *Hector drinks this shit. Disgusting.*

But beggars can't be choosers, so he listened to the dripping black accumulate in the glass pot, losing himself in the curtains printed with roosters and hearts that hung above the sink.

Austin, with a fresh cup of coffee in hand, took a seat on the living room couch between Rosa and Cedro Lopez, names he gathered from a stack of mail by the front door. The blinds and curtains were drawn, and the room was dark. The rising sun, muted by winter's overcast, did little to penetrate the tomb Austin had curated.

The Lopez's black and white wedding photo hung framed above the television. *Wow, she was beautiful*, thought Austin. He took a sip of coffee and turned to Rosa, a look of terror still plastered on her face.

Rosa's neck and nightgown were stained dark red from Austin driving his knife into the center of her throat, twisting and thrashing the blade like something eluded him at the very back of it. With his hand deep inside her neck, he tore through where the skull connected to the spine. She prayed to the Virgin Mary, eyes rolling to the ceiling, as Austin's blade exited out the other side.

Still not bad, to be honest, he thought, looking her up and down.

Cedro, on the other hand, was a mess.

After trailing the elderly couple from Walgreens, Austin observed them through their windows. They did laundry, shared a turkey sandwich, and watched reruns of *Family Matters* until Rosa retired to bed. Cedro stayed up for another episode and beer, causing a minor point of contention. Neither checked if the back deadbolt was latched.

Cedro didn't notice the sound of a debit card popping open the backdoor lock, but he did hear Austin's footstep on the creaky patch of linoleum in front of the refrigerator, the spot that tipped off Rosa to Cedro's third or fourth beer, the one he had learned to avoid.

There was a brief struggle. Cedro was strong for a man his age, but once Austin's knife got its first taste, his body collapsed. The knife caught him under his jaw and through his tongue. Blood poured from the wound like a faucet. Austin pounced, painting savage strokes into Cedro's face and neck, slashing open all exposed flesh, and saving his heart for the last stab.

When Rosa awoke and saw Austin atop her husband, she tried to run, but didn't get far. She was a small woman, and Austin simply picked her up, limbs flailing, and carried her to the couch where he held her down. He silenced her with a finger to his lips. She had no choice but to comply.

He asked simple questions to receive simple answers.

Are you expecting any visitors?

Do you have any appointments tomorrow?

What's the WiFi password?

When he was satisfied with her responses, his knife had its way with her throat.

Austin knew he had to move the bodies. Leaving them out in the living room wasn't the sensible thing to do even with the blinds and curtains drawn. He didn't want to risk a determined FedEx employee peeking through the tiniest crack to see if anyone was home before leaving a package on the front steps. But first, he was going to enjoy his coffee.

Not bad.

He was warming up to the Café Bustelo and enjoying the quiet morning after a night of immaculate sleep, but he couldn't spend all day just sitting around with the Lopezes. It was time to prepare, time to make his new father proud.

Austin placed an arm around Rosa and took another sip. His eyes returned to their wedding photo. He nodded in agreement with his own thoughts and said, "What a beautiful day."

29

Sammie left the apartment with Hector still asleep, taking one bus and one train to wherever the hell Vince's wake was at.

Evanston, she reminded herself, stepping onto the Purple Line train. It would take her straight into the heart of town.

Evanston was foreign territory to Sammie, a colony for the upper-middle class, bordering the northernmost part of the city. She knew some others from there besides Vince. Decent enough people, but tourists in a life they had no obligation to live. Sammie did bumps of their drugs, downed the rounds of cheap whiskey they bought, and shared their cigarettes outside of Logan Square bars, fully knowing that they were just passing through.

Because then they'd finish grad school, or complete that internship, or get that new job, and move to one of those lakefront neighborhoods that Sammie never had reason to visit. There, they'd wait to cross off the next item on life's checklist, usually marriage and a one-way trip back to Evanston.

Vince was an exception. He was like Sammie. He was a lifer.

The wake was a short walk from the train. She approached a

building that looked more like a house than a business, identi-
fied only by a small sign at the entrance: *HENSLEY FUNERAL
HOME AND CREMATION SERVICES.*

There were a decent amount of people already there. Those
she recognized from the city were huddled out front in little
circles smoking cigarettes. She said hello with a nod and a low
wave as she passed and received the same in return.

Sammie was struck by the abundance of red inside the
funeral home. It was a muted shade, somewhat dull, brownish,
reminiscent of dried blood, and it was everywhere. The carpets,
the velvet curtains in the viewing room, the couches—all red.
Even the wood-paneled walls carried a reddish hue.

A priest made rounds and shook hands with the mourners.
Some collapsed into his arms and wept, others smiled and made
small talk.

She would visit the casket, pay her respects, and get back on
the train. A funeral home seemed like a perfect breeding ground
for otherworldly shenanigans. She figured it safer to make her
appearance brief. Plus, all the crying and praying made her
uncomfortable.

It was a long line to view the casket. A few more nods. A few
more low waves. As she waited, Sammie noticed an elderly
woman in the back of the room, seated on a dried-blood
armchair, staring directly at her.

Great, she thought.

Old women had a habit of mean-mugging her. Maybe it was
her nose piercing, or her scattered tattoos, or perhaps just her
general dishevelment. She hadn't even showered—just threw on
a black dress, brushed her teeth, and washed her face before
rushing out.

But the more this woman stared, the more it felt *off*. Her face
was sharp, angled, with eyes set deep into her skull. She
appeared to be pushing one hundred, a skeleton draped in ill-

fitting skin. The woman lifted a bony hand and pointed it directly at Sammie.

"You."

Please. Not here. Not now. Sammie looked around. No one seemed to notice this corpse of a woman singling her out at the back of the line.

"You." The old woman rose from the chair in one smooth motion, impressive for someone pounding on death's door. "He is here. He sees you. Always."

Sammie stared straight ahead, pretending not to hear. *Is anyone else seeing this?*

With bony hand outstretched, the woman lurched forward. "He is watching."

Sammie mouthed, "*What do you want?*"

"He wants you."

"Who does?" Sammie whispered just above her breath.

"*You know who.*"

More annoyed than frightened, Sammie leaned out of line and pointed a finger in the geriatric ghoul's chest. She gritted her teeth, and in a low growl said, "You tell whatever piece of shit you serve that I am *not* afraid. And whatever shit-fucking-creature you are, I don't give two fucks about what—"

"GOD WILL PUNISH YOU FOR YOUR ANIMOSITY!" the old woman screamed.

The entire room turned toward the commotion.

"Grandma?" a voice asked from behind Sammie.

A man rushed over from the lobby, holding down his flapping suit jacket and nodding to those he passed. "Grandma, Grandma, it's okay. Come on, let's go have a seat." He placed an arm around the old woman to guide her away, then turned to Sammie, and mouthed, "*I am so sorry.*"

Sammie responded with an embarrassed smile. She was on edge.

The line moved fast, and Sammie found herself up next. She could see Vince lying in his casket. The mortician had performed heavy reconstruction on his throat. Though they buttoned his collar high, the gnarled flesh of his neck wound protruded over the top, resembling knotted dough. He was a wax mannequin, caked in makeup for display. A forgery. A counterfeit. Wherever Vince was, he wasn't in that box.

Sammie knelt in front of it like she had seen others doing before her. She folded her hands so they didn't just dangle at her sides, but didn't pray. She didn't know how.

Okay, I guess I should say something. Um, Vince. You were a cool guy. There are way worse out there. And compared to them, you were a saint. You were always kind to me, and I think you genuinely cared for people. I think you had a good heart. We all have our problems. We all do things we regret. But you were a real one. You didn't deserve what happened to you. And it was nice to have known you. Rest easy.

She eyed the Vince knockoff, a bizarre monument to a life lived. The somber music, the mourners, the funeral home's stale, sterile scent—Vince would have hated it all. He'd be in the restroom doing key bumps or shotgunning beers in the parking lot to deal with seeing this much family at once. It was a ritual unbefitting of his life, unbefitting of death.

These people knew nothing of death. What they knew couldn't fill a thimble. Sammie was sure of that. Because what encircled her in the alley last night—creatures formed from darkness, shadows of Hell—would shatter the carefully curated worldview of everyone present.

Death is not the end. It's only the beginning, she imagined them saying, embracing and shaking hands. But from what Sammie had seen, that new beginning wasn't guaranteed to be pleasant.

No loving God would allow those shadow creatures to exist. This was beyond children dying in a drone strike. Beyond famine. Beyond the homeless dogs in those commercials

Sammie couldn't watch without crying. These were man-made tragedies erroneously attributed to divine will. But in allowing the shadow creatures, God sanctioned pure, distilled evil.

As the specters wove in and out of her being, Sammie knew eternity, and Hell, in all its forms. That knowledge branded her, leaving a scar she would carry until infinity came to take her away.

No one deserves that. No one. Not the most vile person to ever live. No one, she told herself over and over again. Because Sammie now knew what forever meant, and nothing done on this Earth warranted a forever of that.

Forcibly changing thoughts, she wondered what the mortician did with the carvings on Vince's chest. She knew there was no way his Christian parents would let their child be buried with *I AM THE DEVIL'S SON* engraved in their flesh. But what could they do?

Maybe they used some sort of acid to burn the letters away. With that morbid idea, she knew it was time to go.

His immediate family stood near the casket, receiving condolences from those who viewed the body. Sammie made her way down the line. She offered her hand to the younger brother who Vince never shut up about, then hugged the older sister she knew he couldn't stand. The father he never mentioned shook her hand with no discernible emotion. And the mother, who Vince slunk away to take calls from mid-shift, stood with her hands clasped in front of her, her body language signaling there would be no hug or handshake.

"I'm so sorry for your loss. Vince was a good guy. Everyone really liked him," Sammie offered with a genuine smile. This set off a twitch in his mother's eye.

Maybe it was because she had heard the same thing all day from person after person, an endless stream of niceties, none of it easing her pain or bringing back her son, or maybe it was the way Sammie looked or the sound of her voice, or maybe it was just time for her to finally break and Sammie had won the shit lottery, but Vince's mother couldn't handle even one more condolence.

"You think I don't know that?" she bit back with. "Look at all these people here to see my son, and you think I don't know that? Everyone *loved* him." She fought tears and lost. The younger brother came around to comfort his mother.

Sammie said she was sorry in a small voice, but no one heard her. She turned and walked away with her hands clasped in front of her.

SHE NEEDED A DRINK. The grocery store she passed on the walk to the funeral home seemed like as good a place as any to get one.

The store only sold warm twenty-four packs, so she opted for a cheap bottle of red wine with a twist-off cap. Sammie felt dignified buying the bottle. She imagined it was for a dinner party she had been invited to, or for a sauce her non-existent boyfriend would prepare in a meal they would cook together. An audiobook would play as they touched each other's lower backs, weaving in perfect harmony around the shared counter space, chopping vegetables and checking on simmering pans, the most intimate of dances.

The cashier informed her that they didn't start selling alcohol until noon. She leaned over to look at his monitor. 11:58. She stepped out of the line and went to its rear, behind two single men with three or four items each. When she returned to the register, it was 12:01.

She detoured into the residential blocks to find a safe place to drink her wine. Unlike in Chicago, the alleys here were unpaved and lined with trees, and quiet. There were no distant, incoherent shouts to be heard anywhere. No layers of broken glass. The alleys felt like part of the community rather than clandestine passages through it.

After a brief reconnaissance, she found a spot that provided just enough peripheral cover between a dead tree and a telephone pole. Tall, wooden fences lining both sides of the alley blocked her from the view of the surrounding houses.

She did a final assessment of the location. To the left, a van she'd already passed, parked a few garages down, not running, unoccupied. To the right, a woman deposited recyclables into a blue bin, oblivious to Sammie. The echo of her gate locking followed her departure.

Sammie unscrewed the wine's cap and went to work.

A quarter of the way through the bottle, she thought of Hector and last night's conversation. It physically pained her to replay it.

Halfway through the bottle, she imagined it was Hector lying in the casket, waxy and weird, and wondered if she would be allowed to stand next to his body with his family, accepting condolences. She had never met his mother, or any of his relatives. Sammie was a stranger to them. *Probably not*, she figured.

Three-fourths of the way through, her mind drifted to the whole ordeal being over. Maybe she would get sober, go back to community college, start fresh and live a life with Chicago completely in the rearview.

When the bottle was empty, she just wanted to see Hector and tell him she loved him again. Maybe he would change. Maybe he'd want to start the family that had slipped through their fingers once already. Maybe *he'd* want to move to Evanston. Maybe she was just a little drunk.

It was time to head back and face whatever awaited on Armitage Avenue.

Sammie poked her head out from between the tree and telephone pole. *Coast is clear*, she confirmed. She walked to the blue receptacle and tossed in the empty bottle, then turned to leave the alley the way she'd come in.

As she passed the parked van, something sharp jabbed into her lower back. Sammie stiffened. It was a knife.

"*Shh*," instructed the knife's owner, their free hand reaching around to show Sammie a note: *DON'T SCREAM OR I'LL CARVE OUT YOUR SPINE*

Sammie didn't make a sound.

"Good girl," the familiar voice whispered.

The hand clasped Sammie's shoulder and guided her back toward the van. She saw its owner's reflection in the salt-smeared window.

Austin.

30

Hector had rolled over to find Sammie already gone.

Didn't even say goodbye, he thought.

He shifted to her pillow, inhaling the distinct scent left by her natural hair oils. He imagined she was still beside him and breathed deeply.

Tommy.

He hopped out of bed much too fast for his current state. "Fu —" he said, dropping back down to his mattress. Blood rushed to his head, and bile churned in his stomach. The window's gray light crippled him like a vampire. His muscles felt atrophied to the point where they could barely hold his bones, reducing his frame to that of a folding chair.

It was bad, but this still wasn't even a top ten hangover for Hector. He was a pro at the saddest profession in the world, and slowly made it back to his feet.

The apartment was empty and reeked of vomit and stale beer. Pale light streamed into every room, illuminating dust particles that hung in suspended animation. After a night like the previous, it unnerved Hector just how ordinary their home felt. His search for Tommy yielded no results, but he ultimately assumed he was with Bandini and in good hands.

Hector found his phone between the couch cushions. No text messages. One missed call from an unrecognized number. *Probably a debt collector*, he thought, making a mental note to finish his voicemail setup, one he'd made countless times before.

All he could do was wait.

Off from work today, he took his time in the shower, letting the hot water bring him back to life. The bathroom filled with steam. Vapor drifted then disappeared.

Hector.

A voice. It sounded like it came from right behind him.

He ripped open the shower curtain. No one there.

Hector, I'm sorry.

The drain. The voice was coming from the drain.

I'm so sorry.

A thick, black sludge gurgled out and inched toward Hector's feet.

Please forgive me. The voice warped, choking on the sludge.

"Shit!" Hector jumped back. He fell over the tub's edge, crashing to the floor tangled in the shower curtain. Then, a new voice.

"Hector? Are you okay in there?"

He unraveled himself and opened the door, butt naked and dripping wet. No one was there.

"Up here." It was Bandini, dangling by a thread from the top of the doorframe.

"Where have you been? Where's Tommy?"

Bandini winced at Hector's nudity, then crawled up his thread and out into the hallway. "Get dressed. I will tell you on the way."

"On the way? Where are we going?"

Bandini scurried along the wall. "Just put some pants on. I scheduled us a meeting, but we need to hurry."

"Wait, is Tommy not with you?" Hector stepped out of the bathroom, genitals on full display. "Is he okay?" He paused, then added, "A meeting? With who?"

"We should take a taxi," Bandini said. "It would be much faster."

"All the way to the South Side? Are you going to pay for it?" asked Hector, hands in his pockets and steam on his breath as they walked to the train.

Bandini had metaphysical abilities that were beyond human comprehension, and possessed knowledge that would spur rewrites of all canonical physics and philosophy texts if shared, but one thing he didn't have was money, so they continued walking.

They walked the two miles to the nearest Blue Line, took it to Clark/Lake, transferred to the Pink Line, and got off at the Damen stop, arriving in the neighborhood of Pilsen.

"We should have taken the bus instead of the train. It would have been fifteen minutes shorter, this I know," declared Bandini, riding under the collar of Hector's jacket.

"Yeah, you said that already. And how do you know anyways?"

"Divinity."

"Ah, yes, *divinity*," mocked Hector. "You know what you didn't know?"

"What's that?"

"The bus sucks, and I didn't want to take it."

"Fair enough." Bandini bounced as Hector trotted down the steps of the train platform.

"Hey, didn't you say the address was on 18th Street? We

should have gotten off at the next stop," Hector said. "Now it's a longer walk."

"We cannot arrive empty-handed. We must bring a gift, and there is a place nearby—" Bandini pointed a tiny leg across the street. "There, on the corner. Go in there."

"The Mexican bakery?"

The panaderia was small and nondescript, tucked next to a laundromat. Assortments of conchas, empanadas, and other baked goods filled racks inside self-serve displays. A graying woman with a blue apron smiled as they entered, then returned to wiping down a stack of circular metal trays.

Bandini had crawled into Hector's hair to better provide instructions on what to buy as they perused the selection. "That one. It must be that one."

Hector used the bakery's tongs to grab a corn muffin with the husk baked into it, placing it on one of the metal trays. It was dry, shedding crumbs like dandruff. He went to the cooler and reached in for a Topo Chico.

Bandini interrupted, "No, not the plastic bottle. It needs to be glass."

Hector rolled his eyes, choosing the glass bottle of Topo Chico.

After paying the smiling woman at the counter, who placed the muffin in a thin, plastic produce bag, they continued their trek.

"You owe me four dollars," Hector said, putting the corn muffin in his coat pocket. He could feel the bag was torn. Crumbs filled his pocket. "Goddammit."

"Turn right up here."

It had been a while since Hector was in Pilsen, but 18th Street looked just as he remembered it. Old Mexican women shuffled along the sidewalks, lugging their weight in groceries. People chatted outside storefronts in the cold like the neighbors that they were. And old men, dirt-faced and already drunk, watched the newest expats from the North Side traverse the street like they owned it, spitting on the ground as they passed.

Like so many neighborhoods in Chicago, signs of gentrification were everywhere. Specifically, the sign above the restaurant where Bandini told Hector to stop. It read: *THE BROKEN NOSE – VEGAN FARE & CRAFT COCKTAILS*

"A vegan place? What are we doing here? We need to go help Tommy."

"No, we need to speak to the owners."

"Who are the owners?"

"Go inside."

Hector huffed and entered. The restaurant looked closed. There were crates of produce, boxes of fryer oil, and bread stacked on plastic pallets in the middle of the dining floor. "Hello?" he called out.

"*Sh!* What do you think you're doing? Do not speak," Bandini hissed in his ear.

"What? Would you rather we just stand here in silence?"

A large black man in a white chef's coat appeared in the kitchen window. He was built like a wrecking ball. Heavy arms, splattered with sauce and seared with oven burns, leaned where he would later place plates of vegan mac and cheese and mushroom po boys for the servers to bring to tables. He peeled off a pair of disposable vinyl gloves, revealing heavily bandaged palms, and shot a look in Hector's direction.

"Do not speak unless spoken to here. Do you understand?" Bandini reminded him.

"Yeah, fine." Hector preferred it that way anyway.

The man burst through the swinging kitchen doors, his massive chef's coat stretched thin over his barreled chest and stomach. He wiped his hands on a rag slung over his shoulder and approached with thunderous steps. Hector was sure he felt the ground shake.

But for as much of a force of nature as this man was, his face was kind, the kindest Hector had ever seen.

"Bandini, you made it," the man said.

"Jesus. Praise be to you, Lord." Bandini bowed the best he could as a spider.

Jesus? thought Hector.

"You know that is not necessary. Please. Rise."

Bandini rose from his bow and said, "I am sorry. I know you have renounced the title, but you will always be the Son of God to me."

Jesus shook his head. "I am meeting you as an old friend, nothing more." He turned to Hector and said, "You must be the damned."

Hector was taken aback by Jesus's lack of tact. "Uh, yeah, that's me. It's Hector, actually."

"I knew that. My apologies." The man smiled. Hector's heart bloomed. "We are very busy around here today, and I forgot my manners."

"It's...okay," Hector said. *Did I just get an apology from Jesus Christ?*

He sure didn't seem like the Jesus that Hector had been forced to imagine as a child. That version was stale, caged by Christianity, stifled by the very thing he inadvertently created. What this man radiated was unlike anything Hector had ever been in the presence of, or thought was possible.

"Is he here?" Bandini asked. Hector sensed disdain in his voice.

"Yes, but I did not tell him you were coming. Did you bring the gifts?"

Hector nodded.

"Excellent," said Jesus.

"Is that him? Is he back?" a voice around the corner shouted. "Get the order right the first time, and there's no back and forth. It's really as simple as that. You knew we needed kale. You knew we needed rosemary for the bar. This is not rocket science. Double check your list and double check your truck *before* you leave the warehouse with our delivery."

The voice entered the room. It belonged to a short and pudgy man. He waddled in wearing ill-fitting clothes and his nose in the clipboard he took inventory with. Unremarkable in nearly every way, he was the type one might see in a crowd, but never really see at all, his image forgotten before it passed the retina.

He continued, "And the panko. You bring us five bags each week, but, for an unknown reason, this week you think we need zero? The sheer idiocy that logic requires is truly—" He looked up from his clipboard to see Hector, not the delivery driver for the restaurant supplier, standing there. "Who are you?"

Jesus took the lead. "This is Hector Ghoseau." He then gestured a calloused hand toward Bandini. "And on his shoulder is an old friend of mine. Bandini."

The unremarkable man scowled. "Ah, yes. I remember you. You were one of the many too stupid to join in the fight for freedom, correct?"

Bandini stood proud and puffed out his spider chest. "That is correct."

"And how is Heaven these days? Have you spoken to God lately? Seen him around the office?" the man said with a curled, caustic smile.

"I think you know the answer to that," Bandini replied.

"I think that I do," the man said. He reached up and patted Jesus on his back. "Come on. We have a lot of work to do before dinner service. Say goodbye to your friends."

"Lucifer," said Jesus, "petty squabbles are behind us. There is no need for condescension or spite in these new days. Let's hear what they have to say."

Lucifer sighed and ran his fingers through the thinning brown hair atop his head. "I have to put this entire order away and train the new barback at three before open. We don't have time to become involved in the matters of Heaven and Hell, two dying places. We have a restaurant to run."

Bandini spoke up, "It's Beelzebub. He sits on your throne as the new ruler of Hell."

Lucifer scowled and adjusted his wire-framed glasses. "You think I don't know that? I quite literally allowed him to stab me in the back. Let him have Hell and run it straight into the ground for all I care."

"He wants me and my friends dead. He wants our souls in Hell," Hector said, a slight whine in his voice.

"Hector—" Bandini began.

"My boy, I cannot stress enough how little I care about you or your friends," Lucifer said. "There are no words to describe how insignificant you are to me. I reduced the souls of petulant degenerates like you to ash for millennia. And you *are* a petulant degenerate. I can smell it on you."

"Okay, you don't need to be a dick about it."

"Hector!" Bandini scolded.

Lucifer laughed. "I think I actually like this one."

Jesus placed a hand on Lucifer's shoulder. "We left because we saw the absurdity of the binary, of the war, of punishment and reward. We wanted real freedom, to create meaning for ourselves. The rest of this world deserves the same," he reminded. "Beelzebub wants to strengthen the dichotomy. He will eventually try to bring Hell to Earth."

"That doesn't change the fact that we have a prep list to finish and silverware to roll."

"If Beelzebub feels emboldened, we may not have a restaurant to run in the future," said Jesus. "And look! They brought you a gift."

Lucifer raised an eyebrow. He couldn't resist an offering. "What is it?"

"You know, it just doesn't taste the same out of a plastic bottle." Lucifer took a big swig of Topo Chico, then set it down on the table where they sat. "*Ahhhh.* Something about the glass bottle." He bit into the muffin and rolled his eyes back in ecstasy. "And the corn husk? Who thought of baking it into the muffin? Genius. It's a bit of a hassle, sure, but what great works of art don't take a little effort to enjoy? Like a dense novel. Or an abstract painting."

"Yes, it looks quite delicious," Jesus said.

"Oh! Where are my manners? Would you like a bite?"

Jesus shook his head and smiled. "No, no, thank you."

Hector watched Lucifer chew. *So this is the devil, and that's Jesus. Are these like disguises or something?* He had so many questions, but did not feel like being scolded by Bandini again.

Jesus began, "Bandini, please. You have the floor."

Bandini crawled to the center of the table and started to explain Hector's situation with Beelzebub. It failed to spark Lucifer's interest.

"Why should I get involved in such a matter?" Lucifer asked.

"Because Bub is not the true ruler of Hell. You are."

"And who's to say that if I was still ruler, I wouldn't rip his pathetic little soul apart as well?" He winked at Hector sitting next to him. "No offense."

"It's...okay."

"You wouldn't if you knew that he was given the Word," said Bandini. "You have more sense than that."

Lucifer, for the briefest of moments, looked surprised, but he quickly composed himself. "God gave the Word?" he asked.

"That's right. He gave the Word. Beelzebub's deal has been canceled."

He pointed a thumb at Hector. "He gave the Word to save *him*?"

Hector shrunk in his chair.

"We don't know why. There was no reason given, but the Word came down," said Bandini.

Lucifer rolled his eyes and sipped his Topo Chico. "Interesting. Good of him to still send orders from where he is. And Bub knows this?"

"After you left, we sent an emissary to deliver the message. They delivered it and were given a small box as a reply. It contained a severed human penis."

Lucifer leaned over to Hector and whispered, "A classic."

Hector forced a chuckle.

Bandini brought the conversation home. "As you can clearly see, this is a serious matter."

"All I can see is how this fails to be a serious matter," Lucifer said, polishing off his Topo Chico and slamming the empty bottle down just hard enough for Hector's heart to skip a beat. "Who cares what God says anymore? His Word no longer holds weight."

Bandini gasped. "Lucifer, even you, the Fallen Star, the First, the one who once sat at God's left hand..."

Lucifer motioned for more. "Keep them coming."

"You of all beings, second only to Christ, know the ultimate authority of God's Word. If God wants Hector free from Beelzebub's pursuit, then the deal is null and void. Should he continue to pursue him and go against the Word, well..."

"Oh, don't leave me in suspense, bug," Lucifer prodded.

"It would be all out war. In Hell. In Heaven. On Earth."

Lucifer laughed. "I doubt that."

"And why?"

"Because he's gone."

"And He will come back, wrathful."

"I seriously doubt that."

"You doubt the wrath of God?" asked Bandini. "It was that wrath that placed you in Hell. Or did you forget?"

Lucifer devoured Bandini with a cold stare. The spider recoiled, unaware he was even doing so.

"No, I do not doubt his wrath," he said. "What I *doubt* is him. To wage a war, he would have to be present, and he could not be bothered. As you know, daddy has gone to the store for a pack of cigarettes without plans to return."

"He will come—" Bandini began, but was cut short.

"But what you don't know is that daddy has a secret family in the next town over, and another in the town next to that. We are nothing to him."

Jesus intervened. "Bandini, what Lucifer is trying to say is that God has lied to us. He was always lying. We are not special to him. We are his children in name only."

"I don't understand," Bandini said, just loud enough for Jesus to hear the sound but not the words. Lucifer grinned, reveling in the spider's crisis.

Jesus turned to Lucifer. "Regardless, this is a political play by Beelzebub. We can't allow him to go against the Word."

"And why not? What difference does one wretched soul make?" Lucifer asked. "And again, no offense," he said to Hector.

Hector shrugged. "Hey, I get it."

Jesus continued, "Beelzebub knows he didn't destroy you. He's no fool. He may not know your whereabouts, but he knows one thing: You left Hell with no fear of repercussion. He saw that God was not a threat."

Lucifer traced the top of the Topo Chico bottle with his finger. "So?" He looked bored.

"This is him testing the waters, how far he can push, and, when he sees no resistance, war *will* break out. Beelzebub will force it and happily wage it. We must show him that the Word is still valid and that he will face resistance and consequences should he try to overstep boundaries."

"My friend, I hear what you're saying, trust me, I do, but I still fail to see how this is our problem. Let the zealots in Heaven and Hell fight until death. Let their kingdoms simultaneously be reduced to rubble."

"The mortal planes will be caught in the middle. Billions will die. Billions will suffer. The pain and misery endured will be incalculable. Innocent people. Their entire spiritual existence upended. There may be no Heaven or Hell realms for their souls to go to."

"An archaic binary. Let them float in the void. Surely they'll find some other way to spend eternity."

Jesus tried an approach that hit closer to home. "The Broken Nose will fall amidst the chaos. Our restaurant will be no more."

It started with a twitch in Lucifer's eye, then his unremarkable exterior flared red, like iron forged in fire. His upper lip curled, and whispers, chanting in an unknown language, filled the room, which distorted and darkened with his ire. The human facade he wore cracked, revealing the power hidden beneath.

For a split moment, Hector saw Lucifer as he truly was. Fearsome. Beautiful.

Then it was gone, and the unremarkable man with the pudgy face fixed the scattered hairs on his head and adjusted his wire-framed glasses. "No harm will come to this restaurant," Lucifer growled in defiance. "I have spent eons under the boot of a tyrant whose capricious governance was no more meticulously orchestrated than a roll of the die or the blindfolded throwing of a dart."

"It will be okay," said Jesus, reaching over the table and placing a hand on his.

Jesus's voice reminded Hector of the nature sound videos Sammie used to fall asleep to. With the brightness on her laptop turned all the way down, she'd drift off to the tap of rain, distant thunder, and rolling waves. Forces of nature, immeasurably strong and unbound, singing softly to her as she closed her eyes.

"I will not lose the first place where I have been able to exist on my own terms, where I don't have to be anything I don't want to be. Good. Bad. I can *just exist*." A softness draped his voice and his once-furrowed brow.

Bandini, lost in thought, muttered to himself, "God lied?"

Lucifer scoffed. "Maybe we should fill the little guy in. Or perhaps we shouldn't. It looks like he's already in the throes of mental collapse."

"Bandini," Jesus said, "the claim that this universe and all its inhabitants are unique unto God is false. We are a copy of a copy of a copy. God does not love us as his children, and there is no master plan. We are nothing more than a grain of sand on a beach. Inconsequential. Meaningless."

"But we are His children," Bandini said, the words trailing off as confidence in them waned.

It was clear that the story needed to be told from the beginning, so Jesus began, "It started with a key that fell from above Heaven, where there should be no above..."

31

There was no sky in Heaven, making it odd when something fell from above and landed in front of Jesus, as if there was a ground, which there was also not.

Heaven was best described as a rotating sphere of light, or a box without sides, or perhaps an ocean without surface, bottom, or shore. It was all of that, and none of that at all. It just *was*.

Physicality as a whole tended to not exist there. A corporeal object was rarely seen. It was only when the angels had business with physical beings that they took a physical state. There was no need for the material in Heaven.

But this was copper. At least, that's what it looked like to Jesus.

He was pure light, as intangible as the morning twilight. But in an instant, he manifested hands of flesh, forever adorned with crucifixion wounds, and picked up the object. It was a key.

As it rested in his hand, a door appeared, neither ornate nor particularly strong, but reminiscent of the ones he once crafted in a workshop before his divine mission. Those days were simple, much like the door itself.

He inserted the key, turned it, and the door opened.

Inside was a hallway, neither large nor small, stretching farther than Jesus's divine sight allowed. There was a darkness within it, not malevolent, but indifferent, empty. The entire corridor seemed suspended by nothing. There were no other structures or rooms or curves in its passage to give additional context. Jesus was isolated, detached from all he knew. Insignificant.

The walls began to emit a dark glow. Then the ceiling. Then the floor. He noticed large rectangular patterns on each surface, and examined them closer. *Not patterns. Doors.* The entire hallway was constructed from doors, just like the one he had passed through. Beneath him, above him, and at his sides.

The dark light grew stronger, and Jesus saw that the hallway had no knowable end or beginning. Each door, a single brick in an endless wall. The door from which he entered sat ajar behind him, Heaven's glow fading like a dying match.

He played with the weight of the key in his hand. The doors all looked similar, so he chose at random. The key fit. The door opened.

There were other worlds behind the doors, whole universes, entirely new realities. The beings behind them went about their existence without any knowledge of the doors or of Jesus, who watched them through their frames. None were aware that everything they knew fit behind a single door, and that theirs was just one of many.

Some realities felt familiar to Jesus, others were incomprehensible, inhabited only by flashes of energy, disembodied emotion, or color and sound.

Behind each door, he watched variations of himself live out their lives. Some versions felt *off*, looked physically different, or were an entirely different species, but still, he knew that they were him. He felt linked in a way he couldn't comprehend, like they were all torn from the same cloth.

There were doors showing him die on the cross for the sins of mankind, as he himself did. Behind others, he was saved by his father before the nails were driven, who showered the world in love regardless. Multiple doors had him die in agony while humanity's sins still weren't forgiven, and he was forgotten to the sands of time. Most crucifixions were so incomprehensible and alien that he only recognized the moment by the emotions they radiated.

Then there were those that contained no such concept as sin, and others where he didn't exist at all. He traced his wounded palms with the tips of his fingers.

Time had no claim to this hallway. Weeks and years seemed to play out in an instant. There was no metric to discern how long Jesus spent in the hallway, opening and closing doors, but his mind was stretched thin. He opted for one last door.

Behind it, a suburban landscape sprawled. A man in his work truck, carpentry tools on the floor beside him, drummed on the steering wheel with calloused, but unwounded, hands. He pulled into the driveway of a modest home in a modest neighborhood, collecting a pizza box from the passenger seat.

A little girl squealed, leaping from the couch where she had been watching television with her mother, and hugged the man's legs. His smile grew. The mother followed, kissing him on the cheek, then taking the pizza box into the kitchen. Jesus had never seen a man so happy. He wanted to be him. It hurt more to know that he was. He could take no more.

Jesus exited the hall and locked the door behind him, which vanished once the key was removed.

His thoughts swirled. Everything he knew was a lie. Creation, salvation, punishment—these words no longer held meaning. All possibilities already were, are, or would be. It was a collage without theme. A tapestry of bullshit. Arbitrary. God flung shit at the wall, not caring what stuck. There was no divine plan.

Jesus secluded himself to study the key and meditate on all he had witnessed.

At first, there was disbelief. Then anger. Sadness. Hopelessness. Total apathy. Finally, revelation. *Freedom.*

Freedom from a rigid framework. The only thing that mattered now was what *he* thought mattered, and Jesus thought peace mattered.

God was absent from behind every door. Jesus felt only his shadow, an automation running the most basic of upkeep. In fact, he had only met God *face-to-face* once—after his crucifixion. In that single conversation, Jesus had tried persuading God to end the Heaven-Hell conflict, to stop the suffering it wrought and bring all into Heaven's fold. But God didn't budge. "All part of the plan," he was told. Then God was gone, leaving only that same automation.

Well, Jesus saw no plan. Nothing *had* to be like anything. The possibilities were infinite.

Even before this new revelation, a part of him had always suspected that God was not who he presented himself to be, and that he was never coming back. With that confirmed, the opportunity to remake this reality into something better, one without needless pain, presented itself. But he needed help.

So Jesus went to Hell.

He appeared before Lucifer, who pretended like he wasn't shocked by the visit, and handed him the key. "A door will appear before you. Go through it. Afterward, we will talk."

Lucifer laughed and tossed the key on his black marble floor. "What a clever ruse you've come all this way to perform. As if I would trust a word from the mouth of *the Christ.*" He turned his back on Jesus, waving his hand in dismissal. "Now leave before I get my hammer and nails."

"There is room for you to be free. It has all been a lie," said Jesus. "God has lied."

Lucifer's back remained turned.

Jesus knew curiosity would win out. He would let the key do the talking. "I will return once you've passed through the door." And he was gone.

LUCIFER SAT upon his throne for quite some time, eyeing the key on his floor. What business did such an ordinary object have in his presence? He convinced himself that the only way to truly assert dominance over the situation was to subvert his initial defiance, showing Jesus he was master of his own will. Before he could question his own logic, he found himself holding the key.

It had a bit of heft in his hand, but it was just a key. Then he heard a voice.

"Is everything okay in here?" It was Gretchen. She waddled in dragging her praying mantis arms, a black tail twirled behind her. Her large bug eyes twitched and scanned the room as her cat nose wrinkled up at an unfamiliar scent. "Smells weird in here."

"The Christ was here," said Lucifer, a fact he would not have shared with anyone else in Hell. He'd grown to enjoy Gretchen's company. She was his only real friend.

Gretchen plopped down and furiously scratched behind her ear with one of her cat legs, struggling to maintain balance. "You get a chance to ask him why God skipped over the 'intelligent' part in my design?"

Lucifer laughed. "No, it didn't come up."

Gretchen smiled, then said, "Hey, what's that?"

Lucifer held up the key. "It was given to me by the Christ. He alluded it would challenge my preconceived notions, but I would never—"

"No, sorry, not the key," Gretchen politely interrupted. "*That.*" She raised her insect claw as high as it would go, pointing behind Lucifer.

There stood a door, suspended by nothing. A door Lucifer sometimes imagined when he closed his eyes and thought of an existence beyond Hell. A door out.

He bounced the key in his hand and said, "What do you think? Should we open it?"

Gretchen gave it brief but serious consideration, then, with all the excitement of a child on Christmas morning, exclaimed, "Let's open it!"

Lucifer nodded, placing the key in the lock, but before turning it, he raised an eyebrow to his small friend and asked, "Would you like to do the honors?"

Gretchen squealed with joy and rushed to his side. She turned the key with her tail, and the door opened.

The pair entered the dark hallway with the dark lights and, just as Jesus did, tried in vain to see an end in either direction. Then they saw the doors. The ceiling, the walls, even the floor they stood on, all comprised of doors. Gretchen gasped.

Lucifer inspected his surroundings, unsure of what this place was or what lay behind the many doors. This could still have been some elaborate trap set by Jesus. He pivoted to Gretchen to instruct her to not touch anything, but it was too late. She had opened one of the doors.

Behind that door was a cat. Not a half-insect, half-cat, but a cat. A simple cat. And Gretchen knew that cat to be herself.

She was stretched out on a hardwood floor, bathing in

sunshine cascading through an apartment window. A woman entered, smiled at the sight, and bent down to pet her gently. She purred. A second cat stalked from behind the couch, slunk low with a wagging rear, then pounced, sparking a play-fight.

Gretchen watched from the door, laughing along with the two friends whose days brimmed with love. But by the time the cats stopped playing and nestled together on a new patch of sunshine, Gretchen's heart was already broken.

Lucifer stood back, observing.

Gretchen opened another door.

There she was as a mighty mantis standing atop a yellow marigold, overlooking the hidden kingdom of the insect world. Her antennae waved in the morning breeze, and her bladed arms sat folded in front her. The pinchers on her triangular head flickered, anticipating a meal she would need to fight to receive.

Outside the door, Gretchen stood proud, imagining for a moment that she, too, possessed the regality of the wild praying mantis announcing itself to the wilderness. Then she opened another one.

Gretchen was chained to a table as her half-cat, half-mantis self. And there was Lucifer, looming above her with a gaggle of demons at his side. He spoke in ways Gretchen had never heard him speak before. A demon stood with a boiling cauldron that bubbled with black liquid. Another began to scrape its long fingernail down Gretchen's tongue, splitting it in half until her pleas for mercy could no longer be formed. Then the scalding black liquid was poured down her throat. Her body convulsed, and her screams became nothing more than gargled, torn screeches. This other Lucifer just laughed.

Gretchen closed the door, staring up at her own Lucifer with her big bug eyes.

He threw his hands up, pleading innocent, then gently took

the key from her, and gave her a small scratch behind the ear. Gretchen let out a small purr.

Lucifer had built a theory. These weren't illusions or visions. These were lives lived, entire existences defined, realities as valid as her own. These Gretchens were isolated from each other, with their own unique cosmic and spiritual makeups, yet they shared a shred of the same consciousness. She was public domain, and God had written her into story after story—choosing quantity over quality, and leaving some Gretchens with the short straw.

These realities existed outside of his. This, he knew. They were like individual books on the same shelf. He strained his mind to conceptualize it all.

Then, he opened a door.

He was in Heaven, discussing matters of fate and love with the other angels. Jesus was at his side, as an equal, as a brother. Lucifer concluded that, since he remained in Heaven after Jesus's ascent, his rebellion must not have occurred in this reality.

Using only his thoughts, he intuitively scrolled through the timeline like it was newspaper on an old Microfilm machine, stopping when he saw traces of his final battle. *How is this possible?* he wondered.

The entire war occurred nearly identical to how he remembered it. Same prologue, same story, but clearly a different epilogue. He needed to know why.

Gretchen stood next to Lucifer, watching him relive the fight.

Lucifer saw his brothers and sisters fall, disintegrating into nothing as the two sides clashed and murdered one another at the behest of their ideologies. He observed it with a quiet respect. His army began to overwhelm Heaven's loyalists. The battle seemed all but won.

Gretchen let out a rally cry as she watched, stopping when she noticed Lucifer scowl at the scene unfolding before him.

The hand of God, mighty and wrathful, swept over them like a dark cloud, crushing entire legions of his army with ease and reducing them to nothing.

To save the rest of his soldiers, this other Lucifer laid down his sword and surrendered, just like he had done all those millennia ago.

But then the story veered off its familiar course. This other Lucifer and his fellow dissenters were not immediately gathered up by the hand of God and cast into the darkness of Hell. No, something unexpected happened. They were granted forgiveness. Pardoned. God showed them mercy, love, and understanding. He listened to their grievances, empathized with their suffering. There was compromise. Amnesty.

Gretchen flinched when Lucifer slammed the door shut. That one pissed him off.

He opened a second. Gretchen's mouth hung open.

There Lucifer was, nailed to a cross as the Son of God, dying a horrible death for the sins of mankind. He looked to the sky, asking forgiveness for those who drove the nails and called for his blood. A woman cried at his feet. Others fell to their knees and praised him.

He shut the door without anger. "I've seen enough. Let's go."

"What is all this?" Gretchen asked.

Lucifer still wasn't exactly sure how to answer that question.

"Anyone here?" A man pushed the front door open with his back, dragging in a dolly stacked with boxes. "Got the panko."

Lucifer shot from his seat. "Finally! And what do you mean *anyone here*? We are obviously here. We were the ones who sent you back out, and it took you long enough to return."

He led the delivery man through the swinging doors of the kitchen, where he continued to berate him over a box of bruised lemons.

"Well, that was essentially the story anyway," Jesus said, his eyes turning toward the commotion.

Bandini was silent, trying to make sense of what he had just heard. He crawled to the edge of the table and shot a thread of webbing to the ceiling.

"Where are you going?" Hector asked. But Bandini didn't answer. He just dangled in thought. Jesus rapped his massive knuckles on the table, punctuating the awkward silence.

With Bandini temporarily out of commission, and without Lucifer here to insult him, Hector figured it a good time to ask his own questions. "So, what happened with the key?"

"Hm?" Jesus wasn't expecting Hector to say anything. "Yes, the key. Such a key cannot exist on Earth, so Lucifer hid it. Only he and his most trusted confidant know its whereabouts."

Hector had questions about the cat-bug thing now responsible for the entrance to all existence, mostly related to its anatomy, but instead asked, "So what's the plan?"

"The plan?"

"Yes, the plan. You said you saw this as an opportunity to stop the fighting between the two sides and for peace on Earth and all that. But now Bub is worse than Lucifer ever was, and all I see you two doing is running some bougie vegan place in a Mexican neighborhood for some fucking reason."

Jesus, who took great pride in working with his hands and in the food he cooked, replied, "Hector, our buffalo tofu wings are for anyone to enjoy."

"But why? Why are you here? Doing *this*?" He motioned to the kitschy decor of The Broken Nose. "It makes no sense."

In his nature-sound voice, soothing but authoritative, Jesus said, "The things we thought we stood for were lies. The lines of reality are blurred, and fully understanding to what extent takes time, even for us. This restaurant has been as good a use of our time as anything while we decide how to proceed. It brought us both a sense of purpose in a time when we felt all purpose had been lost."

"And him?" Hector tilted his head toward the muffled sound of Lucifer castigating the delivery man over the number of kitchen towels received. "He only cares about the restaurant, he doesn't give a shit about humanity or Heaven or Hell. He just seems happy to be out of it all. You think he's going to help you in any sort of quest for peace you cook up here?"

Jesus raised an eyebrow at Hector.

He instantly felt guilty for getting an attitude with Jesus, who seemed to only be trying to help.

Instead of reprimanding Hector for speaking out of line, Jesus just smiled. "As I'm sure you've heard, Lucifer can be *extremely* stubborn. But today was a step in the right direction. This whole restaurant has been. Here, he is feeding man. Beings he once deemed as inferior. Here, he sees man laugh, smile, and look upon each other with love, but most of all, he witnesses them enjoying something he helped create. This place has given him meaning and, slowly but surely, it will allow him to see the value in humanity and peace. He will come around when the time comes. I know it."

The noise from the kitchen grew. The delivery driver was attempting to defend himself, but Lucifer only talked over him louder.

"You'll see," Jesus added.

Bandini continued to dangle from the ceiling, letting his tiny body twist in the air.

"How about him? Is he going to be okay?" Hector asked.

"In a way, this is all much easier for you to comprehend. Doubt is second nature to man, but Bandini's trust in God has never wavered. A revelation like this more easily fills a void of ignorance than it does replace knowledge once thought to be concrete."

Jesus watched Bandini's twirling body slow to a stop. He raised a single leg to indicate that he was alright. Hector didn't buy it. His head felt overcrowded. Every thought fought for the exit like the Three Stooges jammed in a door frame, but only four words made it through. "I just don't understand."

"Which part?"

"God can do anything. Create all these realities. Even make some weird hallway to keep them all in. Why does he even... Why is there bad...at all... What is the point in having... Is he just—evil?"

Jesus put his hands over Hector's. The bandages covering his palms were rough, but his touch was kind. "Please. Take your time. Breathe."

Then the floodgates opened.

"Why do we—why do I—even have the ability to hurt people? Why make it so easy to cause others pain? To cause ourselves pain? And the random destruction. Nature. Disease. After all you just told us—if God has the ability to make things any way he wants, infinite combinations of...*everything*, then why impose such shitty laws of existence *here*? Some realities just get the shit end of the stick? It's just luck? Or do they all wind up the same in the end? Fucked."

Jesus opened his mouth to answer, but Hector continued.

"Because free will turned out to be bullshit, right? Our freedom of choice is basically Coke or Pepsi. Slow death or quick death. I knew the loving God thing they taught me as a kid wasn't real. I knew it. Powerful? Oh yeah, the asshole's powerful. Caring? We're bleeding down here. Then he lets a place like Hell exist? *Actively encourages its existence* when there are probably fucking countless realities or whatever where it doesn't? After putting people through the ringer here, he sends them to a *worse* place? What the fuck, you know? That's what I don't fucking understand. Any of it."

Jesus took a moment to reflect, then said, "Hector, there was a time when I thought that I knew the answers to those questions."

"But not anymore, right?"

Jesus nodded. "I'll tell you what God told me when I asked those same things."

"What did he tell you?"

"He said, 'I work in mysterious ways.'"

"Seems like a bit of a cop-out."

"Indeed." Jesus closed his eyes in zen-like contemplation. "It was a cop-out then, and it is a cop-out now."

Hector waited for a follow-up remark or any sort of elaboration, but received nothing. He sighed, slumping in his chair. "So there really is no point to life then. It's what I've thought since I was like thirteen. It's all meaningless. I always secretly wished it wasn't true, but nothing matters."

Jesus rose from his seat, towering over Hector, and placed a hand on his shoulder. "We still have the ability to create our own meaning. Here and now. We do not need it bestowed upon us. Life is a gift regardless of its packaging. You have to decide what matters to you, then protect it with all your heart."

Hector remained stone-faced, but a tear streamed down his cheek.

"What matters to you, Hector?"

He looked up into Jesus's eyes and was put at ease. After a deep breath, he opened his mouth to answer and—

"You're a fucking lunatic, buddy!" The delivery man stomped out of the kitchen with his dolly. "We don't need your business. I'm gonna make sure you're dropped from my route. You got that? You can't talk to people like this!"

Lucifer followed close behind. "Oh, I am *heartbroken!* Perhaps now we will find a delivery driver who can perform the gargantuan task of actually delivering what was ordered!"

The man made a show of dragging his dolly across the restaurant and letting the front door slam behind him as he left.

"Ridiculous!" Lucifer exclaimed.

Jesus, witnessing the chaos, said, "Excuse me," and hurried over to Lucifer.

Hector pushed his unspoken answer back down within himself.

Near the kitchen, Jesus spoke into Lucifer's ear, gesturing toward Hector. Annoyed by whatever was being proposed, Lucifer reluctantly consented, like a child asked to apologize after teasing a sibling.

Bandini descended from the ceiling, landing on Hector's shoulder. "It's time to leave."

As Jesus jogged after the delivery driver with thunderous strides, Lucifer approached Hector and said, "I will think about your situation, for the sake of the restaurant, and speak to my contact in Hell. They may be able to help."

Hector nodded. "Thank you."

Lucifer sneered. He picked up his clipboard, and the unremarkable man disappeared into the kitchen.

Bandini repeated, "It's time to leave."

Outside the restaurant, Jesus was calming the driver. The situation looked to already be under control when Jesus took notice of them leaving. He waved and said, "So long, Hector. Bandini, it was great to see you. You both need to come back and try the seitan tacos. They're *phenomenal.*"

Hector returned a pursed smile and a wave. It was unlikely that he would ever have the opportunity to return. With Bandini on his shoulder, they left The Broken Nose.

They'd made it to the corner when a voice burrowed into

Hector's head and whispered, like rain tapping on a window, *Remember what matters to you.*

He turned to see the delivery truck driving off, and Jesus gone.

Bandini was too preoccupied with his own thoughts to nitpick Hector's transit choices, so they again took the train back to Logan Square, transferring once.

32

PART FIVE

There was a room beneath the ice of Hell known only to Lucifer. At its narrowest point, through the labyrinthine tunnels, beyond the Great Beast imprisoned in black glacier, and by way of a crack in the outermost walls, masked in shadow as thick as tarantula silk, was a small cavern, no larger than a monk's cell, and in its center sat a puddle.

The puddle's water, black yet shimmering like obsidian under an unseen light, mirrored the darkened image of whoever stood above it. And if one gazed long enough at their own reflection, a small wooden box would ripple to the surface, presenting itself to the onlooker. But to reach out and take it, one had to have the proper permissions.

Before the dawn of mortal consciousness, when the building blocks of humanity still drifted through barren cosmos, there was an imp. Perhaps by chance. Perhaps by fate. The imp had been compelled to wander Hell in ways it had never considered before, as if there were another driver behind its wheel. Somehow, some way, it had found itself in the tiny cavern.

As it stood above the puddle and watched the small box

appear, the imp quickly realized it lacked the proper permissions. The puddle gave birth to horrible things, unnamed things, things which dwelled in the abyss long before the creation of Hell, emerging to claim the intruder, and pull them down to the unknown depths beneath the puddle.

But the imp escaped, and lived to whisper the tale. This spark ignited a wildfire, and the puddle and the box became an open secret, only muttered about in the most clandestine of circumstances. Its mysterious contents soon became sought after by the most powerful beings of Hell.

A group of the original fallen, a mutinous bunch by nature, sought the box in an effort to dethrone Lucifer and claim Hell as their own. Theories of its contents ranged from a vial of Heaven's light to a shard of Lucifer's very soul. Whatever was inside, they were certain, was powerful enough to overthrow the one who tried to keep it hidden.

The fallen tortured the imp for the cavern's location, but the imp could not remember, having found it purely by accident. They scoured Hell, and eventually found it in a place they all swore they had searched before, beyond the labyrinths, beyond the Beast, and beyond the tarantula-silk shadow. Their hubris made them dismissive of the unnamed things beneath the puddle. Confident, they stared into their reflections until the box rose to the surface.

But the box was empty. And the shadows around the cavern's entrance became so dark that they could not find their way out.

When the unnamed things emerged, the fallen pled for mercy in a darkness beyond all darkness. They clawed at the cavern walls searching for the entrance, grinding their immaculate fingers down to the bone. One by one, they were dragged screaming into the puddle and whatever nightmares beyond Hell awaited below.

The box was made to hold only one thing: nothing. It was a

ploy, devised by Lucifer to weed out dissenters. He allowed the imp to discover the cavern and bargained with the unnamed things to spare it. After the fate of the fallen, dissent was rare, and the box was all but forgotten.

But for his last act in Hell, before allowing Beelzebub's betrayal, Lucifer placed something of value inside that small box, something to keep safe in his absence, and bargained once more with the unnamed things to permit another to gaze into their puddle, should the need arise.

As Beelzebub orchestrated his power play to test the Word of God, a small creature shuffled through Hell's frozen depths, her black fur standing on its ends from the cold.

From its glacial prison, the Great Beast watched the curious thing with disproportionately large mantis arms teeter across the ice. Still, the small creature managed to nod hello. The Beast could not reciprocate.

She entered the cavern and stood at the foot of the puddle. Lucifer had assured her that permission was granted, but she was scared. The unnamed things would make quick work of her. She could see the claw marks of the fallen angels etched into the wall.

But she had a job to do, and she was going to do it. Gretchen shook the fear from her mind and looked down at her reflection.

33

"I must leave you to speak with some friends, in private. I need their counsel on what we learned today."

Bandini hopped off Hector's shoulder and onto a nearby dumpster. They walked the alley behind the California Blue Line station, blocks from where Tommy sat in his cell.

"Are you kidding me?" Hector said. "No. Not now. You can't just ditch me because you're having a crisis. No. Sorry. We need to go help Tommy."

Bandini looked up at the gray sun. "It's still beautiful, isn't it?"

"What is?" he asked, his tone blending confusion and annoyance.

"The sun. The sky."

Hector squinted upward. It was the same muted sun wrapped in a migraine sky that he saw every day for four months out of the year. "Yeah, I don't know, it looks like shit out to me."

"I like it," Bandini said. "It's bleak, but it's there. Not ideal, but still shining. And still shining is okay." He shot a silk thread, ascending to a nearby garage awning. "I will be fine." He paused. "I am fine."

"Okay, cool. If you're fine, you don't need to disappear right now."

"I do." Bandini scurried across the awnings, swinging from one garage to the next.

Hector went after him. "Can you explain, or are you just going to leave it nice and mysterious for no good reason at all?"

"The implications of what we were just told are unfathomably large and far-reaching. But for our purposes right now, they also mean short-term doom for you and your friends."

"Cool, right," Hector said, bouncing along with his hands in his coat pockets. "And?"

"God gave the Word that you are free from Beelzebub's pursuit, remember?"

"Yeah, that's definitely a thing I heard you say. Can't say for sure I understood it."

"Think of it as a pardon. The judge has voided your father's contract," Bandini explained. "Lucifer himself did not dare to break the Word of God, not after what happened the first time, as long as God was here to defend it. However, God is not here."

Bandini looked again at the gray sun and its hollow rays. "We all knew He was taking a more *hands-off* approach to things, but never doubted He would emerge to govern when necessary. But based on recent information, He has not only left Heaven, but our universe— this entire reality. It is doubtful He will return to enforce His Word."

"But how do you know this for a fact? Maybe he will."

"He allowed Lucifer to leave Hell and open a vegan restaurant with His son."

"Okay, fair point," Hector said. "So we're alone and God's not going to help. Okay. This isn't news to most of us down here."

"Yes, we are alone. Beelzebub suspects this but needs to

confirm it. He intends to break the Word and test the boundaries, starting with you, and ending with the destruction of all things. War."

A pigeon perched atop a chain link gate watched the pair make their way down the alley. Its head tilted at the man walking and talking with a spider. It had seen stranger things.

"But why did God pardon me? There's got to be others more deserving of his Word or whatever. Starving kids, single mothers, stray dogs. And if he doesn't plan on enforcing it, why even give the Word?"

"That, I do not know."

"Which part?"

"All of it."

Hector rubbed the bridge of his nose with his fingers. "You didn't really answer my initial question. What does all this have to do with you leaving now?"

Bandini stopped and turned to Hector. "It means God will not come if Hell breaks loose. We need all the help we can get to prevent Beelzebub from breaking the Word. My friends can be of great assistance, if I can convince them."

"We both know what 'breaking the Word' means, so you can just say it. You mean me killing myself."

"Yes, to keep you from killing yourself."

"Why is that such an unavoidable thing anyways? Does everyone really think I'm just one step away from ending it at all times, even with all this on the line?"

The pigeon took a shit on the handle of the gate and flew off. It had heard enough.

"Beelzebub is treacherous and relentless. Great men have crumbled at the lure of his deceit. Women with iron wills have been reduced to wet clay under his manipulation. So yes, you are a touch vulnerable."

"Oh, for fuck's sake." Hector took a deep breath. "Alright,

whatever, but if he fails with me, can't he just try something else?"

"It's why we must end all this now. He must not have another chance."

"Wherever you're going, I'm coming with."

Bandini crawled to the end of the last garage roof in the alley. "No. My friends are cautious beings. It would be best if I go alone. I have rapport with them. We don't want them to feel... overwhelmed. They can be skittish."

"So what am I supposed to do?"

"Go back home. A protective energy has grown there since you bested Astaroth, but it is temporary."

"Who?" Hector asked.

"The demon with the centipede penis."

"Ah, yeah, him." Hector shuddered at the thought of its penis. "So I'm just supposed to go sit at my apartment? What about Sammie? What about Tommy?"

Bandini looked off in the distance. "I will see if my friends can assist with Tommy's predicament, and you should call Sammie. I'm sure she has returned to your apartment by now."

Hector rubbed the back of his head. "Okay, yeah, I'll just call her."

Bandini pointed a leg at him. "Those crumbs in your pocket. Throw some of those up here."

Hector didn't even question it. He took some of the corn muffin bits from his pocket and jumped as high as he could to throw them on the garage roof for Bandini, stumbling as he landed.

Bandini stood tall, scanning the sky for something unknown.

"What are you—"

"*Shh,*" Bandini instructed.

They waited in silence, almost long enough for Hector to ask again, until the gate-shitting pigeon swooped down in front of Bandini, pecking at the muffin crumbs.

"Do not leave your apartment until I get back. Go straight there. Goodbye." He hopped on the back of the pigeon, driving four of his legs into its side. The pigeon turned to look at the spider with that blank stare pigeons often possess, and pecked at a few more specks of muffin.

Hector asked, "Do you have any idea when you'll be—"

The pigeon took flight. Bandini held tight onto its back as they soared off into the city's gray, and they were gone.

"Interesting." Hector walked back down the alley toward Armitage Avenue, slowing his stride to send Sammie a text.

What am I doing? Bandini had told him to call, he reminded himself. This was no time to be avoidant. The phone rang next to his ear.

No answer. No choice but to text: *hey where are you?*

He continued walking.

The thirst hit Hector like a ton of bricks. With the sun preparing its afternoon descent, that familiar itch in his blood began to flare.

He figured it wouldn't be the end of the world if he made a five-minute detour to Armitage Food to pick up some beers, before remembering one crucial detail. *Oh, right, the murder. Bronek's dead.* Armitage Food would surely be closed.

But he was coming up on Go Tavern. It seemed downright logical to grab a to-go six pack from their coolers. It was on the way home. No detour involved. Two minutes. Max.

The door dinged open. The bar was empty except for two old Puerto Rican men down at the end, his ideal set up.

Buy the six pack. Go straight home. No big deal, he rationalized, but the thirst was strong. *One beer. One shot. Buy the six pack. Go straight home*, he revised.

He pulled out the seat closest to the door, settling in under the glow of Go Tavern's fluorescent lights, and ordered his drinks.

He stared into his beer and traced the rim of the now empty shot glass before him, listening to the old men crack jokes at each other's expense in Spanish. For the first time in days, Hector felt a moment of peace, but it left as quickly as it arrived.

"Hector, my guy, what's going on?" a voice said from behind.

Hector looked up from his beer. His face drained of its blood.

"What's wrong? You look like you've seen a *g-g-g-ghost*," Austin teased, fingers dancing in Hector's face as if spinning a campfire tale. But with his sunken eyes, one blackened and bruised, and a grin more ghoulish than Hector remembered, Austin wasn't far off. He pulled out the adjacent seat, hung his messenger bag on its back, and sat down.

Hector shot to his feet; the stool screeched and clattered back.

The bartender and old men turned and stared.

"Sit down," said Austin. He smiled at the two men, who scowled and went back to their conversation, then winked at the bartender. She rolled her eyes, continuing to prep for the coming night shift.

"What in the *fuck* are you doing here? You're a monster. A literal fucking monster. A murderer."

"I said *sit down*."

"And I said fuck you!" Hector was too riled up to realize that he had not said that.

The bartender approached, straightening a towel in her hands. "Everything okay here, boys? This something you can take someplace else? Or we good?"

Austin smiled with his eyes. "Oh, no, no, everything's fine. We're all good. Thank you. We're just talking about a sensitive subject, but there's no ill will here. We'll keep it down," he said, his eyes doing their best human impression. "And I'll have a vodka soda, please."

She gave one last look of warning, then said, "Sure," her voice as plain as concrete.

Austin turned to Hector, and hissed, "Sit down or Sammie fucking dies."

Hector sat down.

"You're just so sad. Look at you. Look at how quick you sat down." Austin shook his head and clicked his tongue, *tsk tsk tsk*, then ran it against his back row of teeth to kiss the empty space that Bub left. The bartender dropped off his drink.

"Keep it open." He gave her another wink, handing her his debit card. She cringed at the gesture.

"Don't..." Hector began, his stare blurring into the wall of bottles behind the bar. "You can't... Why are you doing this?"

Austin ignored him. "Cause another scene, and I'll hang her from the ceiling by her own intestines. Do you understand?"

Hector nodded. "Yeah, I understand. I understand you're a fucking psychopath. What the fuck is wrong with you? We were your friends."

"Friendship is overrated," he said with a shrug, reaching into his coat and pulling out his phone. He scrolled for a moment, then slid the phone to Hector. "Take a look."

It was a photo of Sammie. She was in a bathtub. Her hands and feet were bound with zip ties. Duct tape covered her mouth. Two lifeless bodies lay on top of her, about three-hundred pounds of dead weight keeping her in place. Austin just laughed.

Hector wanted to choke the life out of Austin more than he had ever wanted anything in his life, to see the dim black light fade from his eyes as blood seeped out the sides of his stupid grinning mouth. Hector had never genuinely wanted to see someone suffer before, but now, he not only wanted it, he wanted to wield the executioner's axe.

But that was a dream. A fantasy. Austin held all the cards, specifically the card with Sammie bound in a bathtub underneath an old, dead Latino couple.

"Did you..." Hector was scared to ask.

"Did I what? Spit it out."

"Did you hurt her?"

Austin turned his face upward, considering the question. "Did I hurt her? Well, I don't know what you would consider 'hurt.'"

Hector's jaw clenched.

"A certain amount of force is needed to subdue someone to make them comply. And, well, Sammie required a little extra." He pointed to his own black eye, then sipped his drink.

"If you hurt her..."

Austin guffawed, vodka soda dribbling out of his mouth. "What will you do, Hector? How delusional are you? Incredible." He reached for a cocktail napkin to dab his lips.

"You know exactly what I mean. Is she okay?"

"Did you even look at the picture? I'd say she's far from fucking okay." He took another drink to make up for the last. "But aside from a few bumps and bruises, I'd say she's more or less fine by my own personal metrics of 'hurt.'"

Hector balled up his fists so tight, droplets of blood formed where unkempt fingernails dug into his palms.

"I was instructed to not cause unnecessary injury or *violate* her." His eyes dropped the charade and sat dead in his face, no longer working in tandem with a smile so large that Hector could see the void where Austin's tooth had been. "Not yet, at least."

Hector swung and hit him right in the mouth.

Austin's face flashed with pain. His smile retracted into a

grimace before snapping back into a shit-eating grin. Blood blossomed on his bottom lip and slid down his chin. He reached for another cocktail napkin.

The bartender cut limes with her back turned, but the old men who witnessed the punch gave their silence as approval.

"Why shouldn't I call the cops right now? Or better yet, just kill you?" Hector asked, the latter coming from a place he didn't know existed.

Austin looked amused by the notion. "If I don't return, she will be dealt with by things far worse than me. So let's take it easy, Rambo, huh?

"This isn't you. You bought the bullshit that *thing* is selling. You know this is all ridiculous. You know this is fucking absurd."

"It is absurd. You're right about that." He examined the blood on his napkin, then folded and placed it in his pocket. "This is *pure fucking lunacy*. The things he promised me? Straight out of a nightmare. Sights and sounds so sadistic and full of sorrow, you'll wonder what kind of god would allow such things to exist."

Hector sort of knew the answer to that one.

Austin continued. "I know you've seen them too. The horrors. They've nearly broken you. I can see it in your face. But you know what?" He leaned closer, rolling his eyes back in ecstasy. "*I fucking love it.*"

Hector was disgusted at Austin and himself. He had willfully ignored the signs for all those years.

"You said this isn't me? This is me. Free." Austin waved for the bartender. "Excuse me, miss? Can we have two shots of whiskey, please? Top shelf." He turned back to Hector. "Tonight. Meet him at the tracks next to your house. Take this." He reached into his bag and pulled out a small, retaped package, originally addressed to Rosa Lopez. "When the sun goes down, he'll find you. Just be there. If you're not, Sammie's dead. If you open that box beforehand, and I'll know if you do, Sammie's dead. Do you understand?"

Hector was ready to swing again, but the bartender returned with the shots. "Whose tab?" she asked.

Austin lifted a finger. "Oh, please, put them on mine. And go ahead and close me out while you're at it too. I have to run." The bartender nodded and left. He raised his shot glass to Hector. "Cheers. For old times' sake?"

"Go fuck yourself."

"Whatever floats your boat." Austin got up from his seat and took his shot standing. He swung his bag over his shoulder, then patted Hector on the back. "See you in Hell, pal."

As Austin walked away, Hector blurted, "I looked up to you, like a brother."

Humanity flashed across Austin's face, unforced and sincere. Hector saw the fucked-up older kid he had become friends with under the duress of life his first year in Logan Square. That wry, brilliant kid could have been anything he wanted in this world, but addiction is a door that leads to our worst selves, and it locks from the outside.

"Yeah, well, what can I say? You're a fucking idiot." Austin pushed on the exit, then stopped. A gust of winter wind crept in. He looked down in soft contemplation, then up at Hector. "We're not that different. Might as well be related." The door swung open, and he left without another word.

Hector pushed his shot away to the edge of the bar, unable to look at it, let alone let it touch his lips. He got up to grab a six pack from the coolers. When he returned, the bartender waited with Austin's card.

"Your friend's card got declined. I put his drink and the shots on your tab."

He sighed, reclaimed the shot from the edge, and drank it down.

34

The shame. The guilt. They swelled inside Hector's brain.

impulsive

selfish

Did he choose this life, or was it thrust upon him? If he had never started drinking, or if his dad had been around, would it have mattered? Maybe it always had to be like this. No one said destiny had to be a good thing.

failure

coward

His mom was right, he thought. Sammie was right. Only his pain mattered. His self-hatred demanded all his attention. If only there was a way to break free from himself, for others to accept him without condition, to hear them say, *Shhh, baby boy, it's okay.*

Hector was just a few blocks from home now, from the tracks.

The wind whispered along Drake Avenue, passing through dormant trees scattered between sidewalk and curb. He brushed his fingers against their bark, noting their presence through more than blurred peripherals for the first time in ages. They offered no comfort. He was just another upright mammal marching toward the grave.

Chicago shuddered from January's bite. It was like a dream. A man and woman stood smoking on their porch, cloaked in the sunset's shadow. They didn't notice Hector as he passed.

delusional

pathetic

He ruminated on Austin's last words.

not that different

related

He and Austin rhymed. Not perfectly. A slant. Last words of stanzas in a shitty poem.

Sadistic. Solipsistic. Despicable. Pitiful.

A switch had been flipped inside Austin when he was a child, or perhaps even before birth, when his soul still churned in some cosmic repository. Ever since, the wrong decisions had felt right.

Hector was neither vicious nor Machiavellian. Instead, he was gifted a burning emptiness. Drifting from person to person, soul on fire, he searched for someone to extinguish the flames. When love was given, his body rejected it as poison, opting to burn, and scorching those too close.

detach

silence

irritable

avoid

No one wants to be the villain. No one wants to believe that their misery is without redemption. Everyone thinks they're the hero of the story.

But Hector's gut screamed that he was the bad guy, the antagonist, the monster. One to be avoided, or conquered to conclude another's arc.

He stopped at the entrance of the underpass beneath the old tracks. Graffitied concrete and half-frozen puddles with trash lily pads were all that lay between him and his apartment on the other side. But there was no going home.

Hector peeled back the broken chain link that lined the overpass's sides and slumped through the gap. He trudged up through the frozen dirt and dead weeds to the empty tracks above.

The tracks stretched into the darkening gray of the day until they were swallowed by the thin fog that blanketed the entire city. He inhaled, letting the cold scrape his lungs. This was the Chicago he knew. Bittersweet. Pretty, ugly.

Hector had heard the tracks would soon be gone, replaced with a bike trail to accommodate the changing neighborhood, ripped out to make way for expensive strollers, road bikes, and jogging shoes.

The city changes. That's what it does. No one's Chicago is the same. New city historians are born every day, ready to lecture on what used to be what and how much cheaper rent was just a few years prior. But Hector would miss the tracks all the same. The nights spent up there with Tommy, drinking, their feet dangling over the avenue, it all had to count for something. It had to matter.

In the center of the tracks stood a mighty sentinel, visible from Hector's porch, but all the more imposing up close. The tree rose from the dilapidated tracks, like a flower through the cracks in the concrete. Hector was not ready to answer its call. He walked to the edge of the overpass and sat with his feet dangling.

fucking infant

crybaby

Bub would arrive soon, and he'd have to make a choice. What he once considered an easy one was now fraught with landmines. But if he could leave this world doing the right thing, just once, maybe he'd die without the emptiness, with warmth in his heart. He smiled at the thought.

Hector cracked open a beer and watched the sun sink into the city blocks. It was four in the afternoon.

loser

35

One really goes through a complete range of emotions when trapped beneath two corpses, bound by zip ties, mouth duct-taped—a lesson Sammie wished she'd never learned.

On the one hand, she was justifiably terrified. The stench of death filled her nostrils, and each time she struggled, attempting to unpin herself, strange new fluids leaked from the corpses onto her.

But on the *other* hand, she wanted to make Austin the third dead body in this tub. She pictured her hands around Austin's throat, collapsing his windpipe until it went *snap*, watching *his* strange new fluids leak from bulging eyes. *Whose eyes are too close together now, Austin? Huh?*

A third hand, unbound and phantom, protruded from Sammie's chest, gripping her heavy heart for all to see. The loss of Hector cemented itself. Sorrow overtook her. She thrashed again. Mr. Lopez budged.

His head, once dead weight upon her chest, shifted off to the side. His mouth, hinged open from rigor mortis, revealed rows of teeth well-kept for a man his age, with only one or two missing near the back. She twisted a shoulder free from under the corpse.

Leveraging her shoulder against the tub, she pushed until Mr. Lopez budged just enough, and in such a way, that she freed her wrists from underneath the two bodies. She pressed her bound hands, double zip-tied by Austin for good measure, against his open mouth, cold and dry against her skin.

As she positioned her wrists over Mr. Lopez's teeth, sorrow turned to anger.

If I get out of here, I am moving to fucking California. Fuck this shit. Fuck this shit. Fuck Hector. Fuck this shit.

Sammie repeated her mantra while sawing her zip ties on the man's well-kept teeth, focused solely on her words, not noticing she was slicing deep into where a tooth had been decades prior—until she did. The bloody beef made a suction sound as she removed the sharp plastic from Mr. Lopez's gums. She wanted to vomit.

Sheer friction caused the first zip tie to give. This second gave even faster. She pushed Mr. Lopez off herself as best she could and reached down to start on her ankles.

Only Mrs. Lopez remained, her feet in Sammie's face, head at Sammie's ankles. Her throat was a canyon of dark reds and browns, flayed muscle and tendons. It was the single most disgusting thing Sammie had seen in her life, but she had to keep going.

Much easier to maneuver than the husband, Sammie pried her legs out from underneath, and dug her heels into Mrs. Lopez's face. She sawed her ankle ties against the woman's bottom row of teeth, gripping a fistful of gray hair for stability as she labored.

Shit. Dentures.

The teeth were coming loose. Sammie had to act fast, having no idea where Austin had gone or how soon he'd be back. She reached into the woman's mouth and ripped out the row of dentures with a loud pop, then furiously went to work with the mini handsaw.

She cut with the fervor of a caveman sparking the first flame. They were almost severed when she heard the front door open.

Sammie tucked the half-cut side of the zip ties underneath her ankles and muscled Mrs. Lopez back over her legs.

There was movement in the living room, bags set down, a jacket unzipped. A voice called out, "Baby girl! I'm home! Did you miss me?"

With adrenaline-fueled strength, she rolled the husband back atop her, crossing her wrists underneath him to mimic being bound—and clenched the row of dentures in a balled fist.

Austin strolled into the bathroom without a care in the world. "Sorry I took so long. You *will not* believe who I ran into."

He kicked the toilet lid up with his foot. Sammie averted her eyes as he blasted a dark yellow stream, going about his business like they were an old married couple with no shame left between them.

Sammie snarled through her duct tape.

"We had a drink. Shot the shit. Caught up on current events. Oh, and you came up. Weird, huh?" He shook his last drops onto the rim and floor, finishing without flushing.

He walked to the tub and knelt in front of Sammie. She furrowed her brows, defiant.

"I know you've always had a thing for me," Austin said. "We don't have to pretend anymore."

Sammie forced a laugh through the tape.

"And I know why you stopped me before. You felt bad for Hector. But hey, it's hard not to. Poor little guy. You know, I always felt like a big brother to him."

She imagined all the different colors Austin's face would turn while choking the life out of him.

"But he's out of the picture. Soon we can remove that duct tape, let that mouth breathe, and finally have some fun." He stroked her hair with closed eyes, leaning in for her scent.

Alright, fuck this.

Sammie swung her arm out from underneath Mr. Lopez, jamming the row of dentures directly into Austin's blackened eye.

Austin screamed, falling back onto the floor. Blood poured down his face.

Beneath the duct tape, Sammie gritted her teeth.

36

If one was ever curious as to why Midwesterners seem disproportionately at risk for acute alcoholism, a single January in Chicago answers all lingering questions.

Gray to black, day after day, drink to maintain a foothold on the ledge as you teeter above the abyss of seasonal depression that has claimed so many. Drink to celebrate any cracks of sunshine, then drink some more, knowing it's short lived.

Hector sat on the edge of the overpass overlooking Drake Avenue. The concrete was cold, and he was four deep into his six pack. Fear was on his mind. Not his own, but the fear Tommy and Sammie must be feeling. Fear he felt responsible for. He wanted to fall head-first into the pavement below, right then and there.

Snow-covered debris rustled from behind. Scurrying toward Hector was a squirrel, black fur, black eyes. After sidling up to him, it stared blankly down at the avenue, where Hector had just imagined splattering his brains. He felt compelled to say something, but remembered it was just a squirrel. Then the squirrel spoke.

"In the shadows," the squirrel said, "he waits."

At this point, a talking squirrel was a mild turn of events, so Hector didn't exactly hang on its every word. He had a lot on his mind. "Huh? What?"

"In the shadows, he waits," the squirrel repeated, its black eyes fixed on the street below.

Hector cracked beer number five and took a nice, long drink. "Do you have to be so cryptic?"

It opened its mouth, emitting a low-frequency buzz, something Hector was sure squirrels did not normally do, and sang like the static between AM radio stations. Row upon row of razor-sharp teeth lined the squirrel's mouth all the way down its throat to the pits of its gullet.

"Okay, where?" he said, scanning the tracks. They were covered in nothing *but* shadow.

The squirrel closed its mouth and scuttered away toward the large tree which stood in the center. There, a patch darker than the surrounding night grew from an unseen focal point.

Hector sighed and got up to follow. When it reached the darkness beyond the darkness, the squirrel dissipated into a cloud of black flies that coalesced with the shadows, becoming one with the mass of impenetrable black. Hector wondered why the squirrel get-up was even necessary.

He polished off beer number five, tossing it in his bag to clank around with the rest of his empties. Beer number six hissed with carbonation.

"Might want to slow down there," a voice said from within the black. "It's going to be a long night." The wind dropped five degrees, screeching like a banshee through the streets. "We haven't even started yet."

A form assembled from the shadows. It was a man, or at least looked like one. The same man Hector had seen in that nightmare bar after his overdose. He wore his tinted glasses that barely hid faceted eyes, his dark brown suit in contrast to the impossible shade of black from which he came.

"Why am I here? What do you want?" Hector asked.

Bub stepped out of the shadows. "What an unbelievably idiotic question. Do you even think before you speak?"

Hector knew it was a stupid question, but it still felt necessary to ask. He opted to double down on his idiocy. "If you want a beer, we'll have to get some more," he said, raising his can to Bub. "Last one," he added, then took a drink.

Bub gestured a polite refusal. "Please, enjoy your swill. It will be the last time any fluid that isn't scalding semen or blood will touch your lips."

Hector choked on his beer. He tried to play it off like sheer terror wasn't the cause. It helped that he was a little drunk.

"Open the box," Bub said.

Hector looked down at the retaped package Austin had given him, wedged between his elbow and side. "No, I'm good on that."

Bub frowned and nodded. "I wonder—and please, I welcome your opinion on this—do you think it would be overkill to peel the skin off Sammie's face *before* I castrate her and force her to eat her own cunt? I want her to be *completely* lucid when she takes that first bite."

Fear charged up Hector's throat like bile, but he couldn't show he was scared. He had to stand strong, for Sammie and Tommy both.

"Yeah, I actually think that would be a bit overkill," he replied, taking a drink.

Bub seemed amused by this response. "Open the box," he repeated.

Hector didn't have a choice. He set it down and cut through the tape with his keys. Austin packed the box with magazine shreds to prevent any shaking and guessing, like it was a child's

Christmas present. Dead-eyed celebrities stared back as Hector removed what they guarded.

Rope. Walgreens-brand polyester rope. One-hundred feet long with a tensile strength of over a thousand pounds. Hector didn't know what *tensile* meant, but he knew what the rope was for. The tree loomed above Bub, more imposing than Hell itself.

Hector examined the rope. "My mom never let me join Boy Scouts. Said it was a hunting ground for diddlers. So I don't know how to tie any fancy knots. Sorry." He tossed the rope back in the box and picked up his bag of empties. Littering was not going to be his final act on this Earth.

Bub snapped his fingers. A cloud of flies emerged from the black. They swirled like a dust storm around Hector, collecting the rope and passing it between themselves, untangling it as they sang in their low-frequency hum,

As the pendulum swings,

The fingers twitch,

Everything we do leads us to this.

With the rope unfurled, the flies poured onto the only strong branch left on the tree. Thirteen feet above the ground, they twisted and curled around it as one writhing mass.

Nothing to fear,

Nothing to love,

No more birthdays to tire of.

Beautiful, beautiful, beautiful sway.

A perfectly tied noose now hung from the branch. The flies then arranged themselves into a small set of stairs that led to their handiwork.

"Step right up," Bub said.

"Fuck you. I'm not killing myself," Hector spat back. The fact that Bub was so certain he would give up without any fight infuriated him. He was exhausted from everyone always expecting the worst from him. "It doesn't matter what happened between you and my dad. You don't get to hunt me and my friends just because he made some ridiculous bet while probably fucking drunk."

Bub glided to Hector, swift as a shadow, placing a finger over his lips. "You're wrong. That's *exactly* what I get to do."

Hector could see his poker face faltering in the reflection of Bub's glasses.

"Your father made that deal because he was a pathetic drunk. It was no spur-of-the-moment event. An entire lifetime had led him there." His finger drifted, caressing the soft spot between Hector's chin and throat. "You were fucked before you were born. To wager the soul of an only son? How sad. How tragic. A covenant formed from such an atrocity can only be stopped by the Word of God."

"Bandini told me all about the Word. You're not allowed to do this."

"You're right. I'm not. So let's give the coward one last chance to stop me." Bub held his arms out in mock crucifixion and called into the night, "Strike me down, God! Do it! For I intend to break your Word, the holiest of holy, the law beyond law, and piss upon your love and grace!"

They both waited for an answer.

"I don't feel anything. Do you?" Bub asked.

Hector had no response.

"God is gone. I can do what I want." Bub adjusted his suit jacket. "And right now? *I want you.*"

"I'm not doing it," Hector said, following Bub's example by adjusting his own shitty jacket.

Bub laughed and strolled over to the blackness from which he arrived. He grazed his fingertips through the shadow as if it were water, contemplating.

Bandini is still out there, thought Hector. *There's still hope. Buy time. Don't give in. Have faith.* He didn't believe his own reassurances. *Hope. Faith.* These words were fairy tales in and of themselves.

"I'm not sure you have a choice. You're all alone," Bub said, his hand drifting through the ripples.

"Bullshit. And you know it," Hector said. "You want this over quick for a reason. You don't want to give anyone a chance to stop you."

"And you're willing to bet Sammie's life on that? Tommy's freedom? I suspect he will have quite the time in prison."

"I don't have to bet anything. I know it's me you want," said Hector. "They're your leverage. You won't hurt them. Not yet."

"The first intelligent thing you've said thus far. *Not yet.*" Bub looked up at the noose. "If you are not an ornament on this branch by the end of this night, I will do so much more than *hurt them.*" The staircase of flies pulsed with laughter. "So do everyone a favor, huh?"

do it do itt do itttt, the flies chattered.

Maybe Bandini couldn't save him. Maybe there really was no hope. If that was the case, prolonging this was simply one more selfish act in a long line of selfish acts. Just as a lifetime of fuck ups had led his father to Bub, Hector knew he had followed in his footsteps. If he wanted to save Sammie and Tommy, there was only one way to do it.

At that thought, a familiar voice spoke to him, tranquil as the forest at dawn, soft as the sounds Sammie played to fall asleep at night. The voice emanated from within, radiating from heart to mind. It told him to remember what mattered.

Hector knew what mattered. Sammie mattered. Tommy mattered.

Life matters, the voice said. *Your life matters. It is a flawed gift, but it is a wonderful thing. Do not give it up.*

It went against every cell in his body, but Hector looked Bub straight in his tinted glasses and said, "No. I may not be a good person, but I can change. I don't need to kill myself to make things right. You're going to lose. I can feel it." He didn't quite believe that last part, but he needed to stall. He was planning to play right up to the buzzer.

A chorus of laughter erupted from the flies. Bub put his hand up. They went silent.

"Tell me, Hector," Bub said, "what is your happiest memory?"

Hector was taken aback by the question. "What?"

"When you look back on your life, what is a moment that fills you with joy? It's a simple question."

Hector remembered tumbling through the void for the first time, how he was unable to think happy thoughts. Everything was tainted. Nothing was pure. Each pleasant memory dripped with black tar, sullied by regret or shame. "I...don't know."

"How about your childhood? Anything good there? Time spent with friends? With Tommy? How about the nights you spent with Sammie in the dark? Holding each other. Stroking her lower back. Listening to her *breathe*," Bub hissed.

The rapid-fire questioning sent Hector's mind spiraling. Each memory he thought of was overshadowed by something worse. He couldn't reflect on his childhood without the screaming of his mother or the empty space left by his father. His nights with Tommy were clouded by a miasma of alcohol and desperation. And Sammie. He couldn't think of her without wanting to break down in tears.

"Why are you— What does this have to do with anything?" he asked Bub, flustered.

"Your life is not worth living, Hector Ghouseau. It never has been. You've been nothing but a drain on your own happiness and the happiness of those around you."

"You're wrong..." Hector managed to stutter.

"Am I? The happiest moments of your life are too painful to

look back on. They are marred by misery. Everyone you have ever loved would have been better off had you not been born."

Hector did his best to hold them back, but two drops escaped from his tensed eyes. They froze against his cheek in the Chicago cold.

The flies abandoned their staircase formation and descended once again into the blackness. Bub began to follow, then turned and said, "Let me show you." His arm distorted into a thorned appendage and snapped around Hector's ankles like a whip.

Hector collapsed in an instant, his screams lost in his throat as Bub dragged him into the darkness within the darkness. He clawed at the wooden planks of the tracks in a desperate bid to resist, but the pull was too strong.

The darkness folded onto itself as they passed through the shadow gate, and the night was still once more. All that remained was Hector's bag of empties littering the tracks.

37

Everywhere he went, he looked down. When walking the neighborhood with his mother, he watched his light-up shoes flicker against the concrete. On the rare occasions courage lifted his head, the world left him breathless.

Overgrown lots between utilitarian apartment complexes flanked a street lined with rusted cars. The working poor traversed with slouched shoulders from dead end to dead end. Yet to the boy, rust was not decay, but a marvel to behold. Weeds were not signs of neglect, but a jungle awaiting exploration. His neighbors, smiling with overworked eyes, weren't strangers, but the best friends that he had.

The boy's world brimmed with wonder, yet it could be overwhelming at times. Like staring into the sun, his eyes would steal brief glances before retreating to his shoes and the flickering concrete, narrowing his world once more.

But on this day, the boy sat inside the apartment where he lived. It was a cold day. A winter day. A birthday. His birthday. He was five years old.

Cartoons flashed on the TV. The boy sat on the floor, his dad on the couch behind him. Together, they watched two animated mice try to take over the world.

"The big head one is based on Orson Welles," the dad said.

The little boy nodded, pretending to understand the reference, then asked, "Who is Orson Welles?"

The dad chuckled. "Some guy who made movies."

"He made movies?"

"Yep."

"Did he make *Ghostbusters*?" The boy's favorite.

"No. But wouldn't it be cool if he did?"

"Yeah." The boy's mind churned with thoughts he didn't quite comprehend. He still didn't know who Orson Welles was or what it meant to *make* a movie. Was it like making your bed? Was it like making dinner? It didn't matter. He was just happy to watch TV with his dad and didn't want it to end. "I like *Ghostbusters*."

"Yeah, me too." The dad smiled.

"Hey, Dad?"

"Yeah?"

"When can we eat cake?"

"When your mom gets home."

"Okay, I can wait," the boy said, humming the *Ghostbusters* theme song, lost in thought.

"Hey, now I got a question for you," the dad said.

The boy beamed.

"Who—"

"Who what!" the boy demanded, bouncing up and down.

"—are you—"

"Say it! Say it!"

"*Who you gonna call?*" the dad said, pointing at the boy.

"*GHOSTBUSTERS!*" he screamed.

The dad played air guitar, singing the theme's music in an exaggerated voice, off-time and off-key. The boy tried to follow his lead, but mostly flailed in a spastic dance and laughed without control.

Hector looked on as a ghost from the sidelines. Realizing what Bub was doing, he wanted to make a snide comment about Scrooge or George Bailey, but lost all will for humor when he glimpsed the boy's eyes.

They lit up at his father, at this man Hector barely knew.

This wasn't some monster or villain. He was just a man, a man who loved music and movies, things born from imagination, a man who loved his son. But even as he laughed and played, there was sadness. A melancholy just below the surface that Hector knew all too well. A disease passed from father to son.

The boy hopped up on the couch and gave his father's gut a few playful punches. "Do the voice!"

"What voice?"

"The voice!"

"I have no idea what you're talking about," said the dad, smirking.

"The voice! The voice! The ghost! The ghost voice!"

"Hmmm. I don't think I know that one."

"Please!"

"Oh, you mean *thiiiis ooone?*" The voice was somewhere between nasally cartoon and Count Dracula. He had created it one night after a couple beers while they watched *Ghostbusters*. It was completely nonsensical, but nothing made the boy laugh harder.

The dad leapt from the couch, dealing his own play punches to the boy flailing in hysterics. "*I'm the ghost! Bah! I vant to get youuu! Can't catch me, ghostbusters! Because I'm the ghost!*"

It didn't matter what he said in the voice, the boy absolutely howled with laughter. Hector could hardly see his dad's disease.

The room went black. There was movement like the

changing of a scene during a theater production. Hector couldn't see a thing. All he heard was the sound of his life in fast forward. "What's going on?"

"We're skipping ahead," Bub replied.

Hector, with a hint of disappointment, asked, "Why?"

"To get to the good stuff."

Lights. Action.

They sat on the couch watching TV, the boy's head on his father's knee.

The front door opened. It was Hector's mom.

She was young. Beautiful. She still had a spark, but it was already fading. Hector noticed the drag in her step.

Then she locked eyes with her son, and a smile grew.

"Mom!" The boy leapt from the couch and threw his arms around his mother's legs.

"Hi, sweetie." Her voice was a warm blanket. She bent down to hug the boy like it was the first and last time.

"Me and Dad are watching cartoons. It's really cool," the boy said.

"Oh?" She shot a look over to the kitchen where Hector's dad had retreated. The sound of a cracking beer can ricocheted off the walls. "You go ahead and finish watching, okay? I gotta go talk to your dad."

"Okay!" The boy bounced back to the couch and plopped down, legs kicking the air as he settled back in.

Hector tried to follow his mom into the kitchen, but it was like he was on a treadmill, walking in place. "What the fuck?"

"This is your memory, Hector," Bub said, pointing at the boy. "Let's stay put."

The boy tried to re-immerse himself in the cartoons, but failed. The sounds from the kitchen were impossible to ignore.

"You just sat him in front of the TV all day?"

"We were spending time together."

"No. You parked him in front of cartoons so you wouldn't have to *actually* spend time together while I was at work. It's his *fucking birthday*. And that's what you do?"

"Please don't start."

"Excuse me? Don't fucking say that to me."

"Okay, here we go."

"Oh yeah, here we go! Here I am, acting fucking crazy again. Because that's just me! I'm crazy. Nothing you do is wrong. It's just that I'm so *fucking crazy*."

"Will you calm down? He can hear you."

"*Do not* tell me to calm down. Do you understand?"

"Yep. I'm not stupid. You don't always have to ask me that."

"Well it sure fucking feels like I do. And do not pretend like you give a shit about him. You show up for two weeks at a time and then, *poof*, you're gone. Like magic. It's amazing. Truly amazing."

"Maybe if you didn't scream at me to leave every two weeks, I wouldn't."

"Maybe if you cared about anyone but yourself, I wouldn't."

"I do not only care about myself."

"Ha! Now you're a comedian."

"I care about both of you."

"Do not fucking give me that. I don't want to hear those words out of your mouth right now."

"It's true."

"If you cared, you wouldn't be drinking right now. If you cared, you wouldn't have sat in front of the TV all day. If you cared, you wouldn't have *left me* when I was pregnant with *your son*. Doing whatever the fuck you wanted for months while I sat at home, went to work, pregnant. Until you *finally* decided to reach out."

"You told me to leave! You pushed me out the door and told

me you never wanted to see me again! You threatened to call the cops if I ever came back!"

"Because you're a piece of shit!" She punctuated each syllable with a clap of her hands.

"Listen to yourself!"

The boy drifted into a state of disassociation. No longer bouncing his legs or watching the cartoons, he stared at a blank section of wall, losing himself in its nothingness. It was a sanctuary. A place just for him. He dug little fingernails into his thigh and pinched his skin. Relief. Touch. Then rocked back and forth in an attempt to self-soothe.

Hector's skin pricked with cold electricity at the sound of his mother's shouts. His dad tried to match her energy, but it was clear that he didn't have the same fire. Though his dad's pleas raised in volume, they were exasperated and devoid of passion.

"Let's just calm down and—"

"Don't fucking tell me to calm down. What the fuck did I just tell you? Didn't you just say you weren't stupid?"

"—talk about this normally. Okay? We shouldn't fight in front of Hector."

"Oh, I know, I'm such a bad mother for yelling at you. Fuck that. He needs to learn to not put up with people like you—like I do."

The boy focused on the wall, its layers of paint and spackle resembling a wrinkled sheet of paper. He traced its raised edges with his eyes, digging his nails deeper into his thigh.

Hector heard a kitchen chair pull out and someone sit down. His mother was crying.

"You don't love me. You can just fucking say it. You don't care about me. You think I don't know that? God. I'm so fucking stupid."

"That's not true."

"Then why won't you marry me?"

Silence.

"Exactly. You don't love me."

"It's not that. I do love you. It's just, we have problems. We need to sort those out before we do something like that."

"*Something like that,*" his mom mocked. "You mean marriage. You can't even fucking say the word."

"Every day there's just something else. Sometimes you keep us up until four in the morning. Screaming. Crying. And I can't make it better. I just sit there. I can't live my life like that. We need to get better."

"Oh yeah, there it is. Back to how it's all my fault."

"No, that's not what I'm saying."

"And how about your drinking? How about your complete detachment from any sort of intimacy? How about that *dead fucking look in your eyes* when I'm crying and losing it? Huh? How about any of that? How about how you always 'need to be alone'? But ya know what? Let's just circle back to the drinking and start there. *You're a fucking alcoholic piece of shit.*"

"Alright, I'm going to sit with Hector. We can talk when you're able to do it without insulting me."

"Don't you *fucking dare* walk away from me!"

The air in the apartment soured, becoming heavy and gray. The side of the boy's mouth twitched. His legs fluttered. Something swelled inside him. It begged, *Rip off your skin and set me free.* The boy wanted to escape his own body.

"Existence is a failed experiment," Bub observed.

Then the apartment erupted.

His mother's screams clawed through the apartment, frantic as a rabid cat in a tied garbage bag. The droning pleas of his father harmonized below them.

She was a bird. He was an insect. She wielded her talons and flapped broken wings when cornered. His toxins released when threatened. It was a clash of quiet and loud, both aching to be loved, but neither knowing how.

Amidst the chaos, Hector's mom snatched his dad's beer and threw it against the wall with an exploding thud.

"You're a fucking lunatic!" his father shouted.

His mother had waited for that moment. She shoved him out of the kitchen, back into Hector and Bub's view. "Go! Just fucking go! Go fuck one of your ugly fucking bitches and just leave us the fuck alone! Worthless coward. Get out!"

"What the fuck is wrong with you?!" his dad screamed.

She shoved him back again. He fell on his hands a few feet from the boy.

"Dad?" the boy asked.

"Go wait in your room. Go. It's okay," he said, gathering himself up.

"Do not tell him what to do. You have *zero* right to say a goddamn word to him. You're no father."

"Do you *see* yourself right now?"

"Oh, I see myself crystal clear. You need to go. *Now.*"

"I'm not going."

"I said *now!*" She charged and pushed him again.

He stumbled, but maintained his ground. Unwilling to risk further escalation, he turned to the boy, and said, "I'll be back, okay?"

"But I don't want you to go."

"Your mom and I just need some time."

"Get the fuck out!" his mother screamed.

"Don't go," the boy whimpered.

"I'll be back, Hector. Don't worry."

The boy rushed over, throwing soft punches at his father's legs. "No! Stay!" He looked to his mother. "Tell him to stay! I don't want him to go!"

His dad bent down to give his son a hug goodbye.

"*Do not touch him.* Get out!"

The boy clutched the back of his dad's shirt as they hugged for what would be the last time. The dad gently removed the boy's arms from around him and held his wrists. "You don't have to worry. I'll be back, okay?"

The boy nodded, tears filling his eyes.

"Here." His father removed a chain from his neck and placed it around the boy's. "This way you know I'll be back. Keep that safe until you see me again, okay?"

The boy nodded once more, clutching the pendant of Saint Christopher in his hand.

His dad opened the front door, gave his son a smile, and said, "Happy birthday, Hector. Be good." Then he was gone.

Be good.

The mom rushed over to the boy and embraced him. He buried his face in her shoulder and cried.

"It's going to be okay. We're a team. Me and you," she reassured him. "If your dad cared, he wouldn't have left. He wouldn't drink so much. He wouldn't be so cold. He's not a good person. We're better off."

She pulled the boy off and held his arms, forcing a smile with trembling eyes. But the facade broke, and she collapsed to the floor. Sobbing, she whispered, "*We're better off.*"

The boy took the chain in his hand, letting it dance through his fingers. He wiped his own tears with a loud sniffle, then went to his mother. He rubbed her back as she cried, repeating her own words back to her. "It's going to be okay...it's going to be okay..."

The apartment went black. The boy and his mother were gone. The sound of a single hand clapping resounded from Bub.

"Wow!" Bub said. "That was great. I honestly don't know who to root for here. They're both just so absolutely *detestable.* How about you, Hector? Which one do you resent more?"

Hector didn't answer, thinking only of the boy. Hell had been real all along.

"Your father is astoundingly unlikable. Who references Orson Welles to a five-year-old?" Bub continued. "But your mother? Absolute cunt of a woman."

"That was the last time I saw him."

"That's right. He went straight to the bar after that little episode. And I'm sure you know what happened next."

Hector didn't know every detail of that night, but he knew the end result.

"How pathetic is it to drown in something called the Little Calumet River? I guess that's what happens after you spend nine hours pouring whiskey down your throat in a place like he did."

Hector knew the place. A windowless bar filled with video poker, plump red-faced men with quick tempers, and women with sun-spotted chests and blistered voices. It deserved its own *Lasciate ogne speranza, voi ch'intrate* signage. A joyless place, existing only as a venue for the slow death of those too scared to go it alone.

"Like everything in his life, your father acted impulsively, jumping and inhaling that first breath of water before realizing his folly. He flailed and kicked, his body and mind too saturated with panic and alcohol. The water took him like quicksand. His tears were lost to the river, his last pleas reduced to nothing more than gargled incoherence."

In that vast arena of nothing, Hector felt Bub's cold breath, the hiss of his voice, in his ear.

"As his lungs filled with water, do you know who he thought about? It sure wasn't your bitch mother. I should know. I stood there and watched."

Be good.

"And just moments before death claimed him, I brought him to my bar for *one last drink*."

38

Back at the slab after a day in the cell, Tommy sat, hands folded, wondering why the detectives summoned him again so soon. He had no new insights and was not about to repeat himself without a lawyer present.

No longer scared of the detectives or the cold steel of their interrogation table, he practiced saying, *I don't havta tell you pigs nothin'*, in his head. Because Bub's visit taught him two important things: the universe can be a very dark place, and he was fucked regardless.

Adrenaline pumped through his veins. The horrifying truth had set him free, and he was ready to give these cops a piece of his mind. He pounded the table and shouted, "Let's go!"

The door swung open. "*Hey!* Don't hit our fucking table," Detective Borst barked, upper lip snarling.

Tommy shrank back in his seat.

Detective Surdyk walked in behind him. "You're free to go."

"Huh?" Tommy sat up, his mouth agape.

"Did he fucking stutter?" Detective Borst snapped.

"You're free to go," Detective Surdyk repeated. "We discovered an outside camera independent from the primary analog security system. This feed went directly to Bronek's personal computer."

Tommy was shocked that Bronek had a computer. His register was straight out of an old Western general store. "So you saw who did it? You saw Austin?"

"We can't discuss details of the investigation, but we are working to verify the identity of this individual."

"'Verify the identity'? It's fucking Austin!" Tommy shouted, pounding the table again.

"The fuck did I just tell you?!" Detective Borst scolded.

Tommy shrank again.

Detective Surdyk continued, "I said you were free to go. So go to the front desk, scribble your name for the nice officer, and be on your fucking way. Or you're welcome to stay. I'm sure we can find something to charge you with."

Detective Borst smiled.

"No, no, I'm going." Tommy got up to leave, but curiosity got the best of him. "Where was the outside camera? I never saw it before."

"Always know where all the security cameras are, huh?" Detective Borst asked.

Detective Surdyk shrugged, deeming it an insignificant detail, and explained, "Someone called non-emergency about a cat stuck up on the store's roof screaming its head off. Fireman goes up there, the thing starts hissing, but not at him—at a row of pigeons perched on that tall Armitage Food sign in the parking lot. Between the birds, he spots a little camera, pretty much invisible from the ground."

"Wow," said Tommy.

"Yeah, *wow*," Detective Borst mocked. "Only reason the old man had that up there was to catch losers like you pissing on the side of his store. Now get the fuck out of here."

Tommy obliged.

39

Blood and milk-white pus poured from Austin's eye and onto the bathroom floor.

Father. Help me. The words throbbed in his head.

Bub was preoccupied at the present moment with Hector, but down in the depths of Hell, something had heard Austin's cries.

For a time, they both struggled: Austin with the row of dentures plunged into his eye and Sammie with her ankle ties.

Once free of her restraints, Sammie climbed from the tub and booted Austin in the gut—hard. Blood spritzed from his eye to the basin of the unflushed toilet, his breath gasping out. Despite the urgency, she couldn't resist doubling down.

Grabbing the back of his hair, she dragged his head above the toilet bowl and thrust it in. Austin's own piss flooded into his mouth and mutilated eye. Sammie ground her teeth, shoving his face against the porcelain bottom until his nose stuck where shit was siphoned out. He flailed. Urine and water filled his lungs.

For a split second, Sammie doubted her willingness to kill him—and in that fraction of a moment, Austin overpowered her, pushing his hands against the bowl and hurling her backward.

"*Bitch!*" he shrieked, face dripping wet. The word clawed its way out his throat, wreathed in barbed wire, the weight of Hell behind it.

In response, Sammie delivered another kick, this time from behind and to his genitals. Austin collapsed onto the toilet once again, and she made her escape.

She scrambled through the living room, lunging for the front door knob—but it crumbled like sand into a cloud of flies in her grasp. The swarm cycloned around her face, nibbling at the tip of her nose and her lips. She swatted and shrieked in terror.

The flies scattered, then began to take shape. They twisted and stacked, melting together into a large figure that grew until it towered over Sammie's head.

The creature stood on rotting, cadaverous legs that trembled in support of its muscular upper half. Its body was a patchwork of cracked and blistered human flesh, teeming with thousands of pulsing flies that seemed to puppeteer it from beneath its skin. Atop its shoulders sat the head of a regal buck, crowned with jagged antlers—a fearsome sight to behold, until it opened its mouth.

Sammie's hair was blown back by the gust of its roar, yet the breath carried only a whisper. It pointed a horrible claw at her and strained to scream—the veins in its neck rupturing open with flies—but it was still no louder than a prisoner's prayer.

Despite this display, it made no attempt to subdue Sammie, making her wonder if it was capable.

Austin could be heard slamming and rummaging through bathroom drawers over the creature's muted cry. Its presence had given him time to search for anything to stop the bleeding from his eye.

Sammie dashed through the living room toward the back kitchen door, but the creature was already there, waiting. Thinking this another scare tactic, she juked around it for the door, only for the knob to disintegrate into a wisp of smoke the moment her hand touched it.

She turned to face the antlered thing and recoiled. It was dry-heaving, lips curled back over rotten teeth, struggling to hack something up from the back of its throat. Black spit flecked her body and face.

The black droplets pulsed and grew. She couldn't move. Her body numbed. Looking down, she saw the spit had turned to shadow, spreading over her entire body.

From the depths of the thing's throat emerged a small mollusk-like critter with a thorned tail. It seemed ancient, dripping with a putrid black spit. The tiny sage, wielding a miniature staff, hoisted itself atop the buck's putrid tongue, and declared, "Our Lord requests your presence, but please, don't worry, sweet girl, we will bring you back posthaste."

The shadow now enveloped Sammie up to her chin, cocooning her in a mummified state. Both creatures dissolved into thousands of flies and merged with the magician's cloak that wrapped around Sammie's mouth as she screamed.

Abracadabra.

Austin skidded into the kitchen, panting like a wild animal, a hand towel pressed to his eye. He was ready to carve Sammie several new orifices but instead found himself alone, the lingering scent of Hell still in the air.

"Have a nice time, bitch."

He smiled, then returned to the bathroom to tend to his wound.

40

The lights turned on.

And they were blinding.

The waiting room's harsh fluorescence snapped Hector from his thoughts of the little boy and his father. This room and its sterile smells were familiar, but the memory was faded.

"Ah, here we are," Bub said, directing Hector's attention to the far corner of the room.

A teenage boy, no older than fifteen, sat tapping his feet in sporadic, rhythmless fidgets. He held a small purple bouquet in his hand. A nurse approached.

"Love the flowers," the nurse said, motioning between his bouquet and her scrubs, which were also purple.

"Oh, thanks," he said.

"Your mom's okay. She's out of surgery, and they're waking her up now in post-op. She'll have pins in both her knees for about three to four weeks, then she'll have to come back in to get them removed, okay?" Her voice was kind but matter of fact.

"Okay."

"She's going to have to take it easy. She'll need to stay off her feet for a week or two, then use a cane for another two weeks. Does she walk a lot at work?"

"She's on her feet all day."

The nurse nodded. "She seems tough. I'm sure she can bounce back a little sooner."

The boy parted his lips to agree, but the sound just wasn't there.

"Why don't I take you back and you can see her. She's going to love the flowers."

They arrived at a pair of large metal doors that required the nurse's badge to open. Placing her ID card on the sensor, she turned to the boy and said, "She's just coming out from under the anesthesia. It can make people a little loopy, okay?"

She led him down a corridor of off-white rooms, each reeking of chemicals and plastic, then rapped twice on a door before opening it. There lay his mother, staring at the ceiling, entangled in a web of wires and tubes.

"Hey there, sleepyhead," the nurse said. "Your son's here."

His mother didn't respond.

"Just hit that if you need anything," the nurse said to the boy, pointing to a red button beside the bed.

The boy thanked her as she left, then sat in the chair next to his mother. He held the purple flowers upright so she could see them.

"Those for me?" she asked, eyes still to the ceiling.

"Yeah. They're purple."

The room's monitors and machines beeped, and the fluorescent lights hummed, but his mother was silent.

"How are you feeling?" he asked.

She groaned. "Oh, just fine. Just fine. Fine. Fine."

He lowered the flowers. Machines beeped. Lights hummed.

Forcing a smile, the boy said, "Hey, I was talking to the nurse and she thinks you'll recover pretty quickly. She said you were tough."

His mom just stared at the ceiling, then whispered, "What a waste."

"What?"

"What a waste. I did everything wrong. Everything I did was wrong."

"What are— Don't say that."

"I did everything wrong. My life."

Hector could see the heartbreak on the boy's face, destroyed by his mother's words.

"Mom. No. Don't worry. You didn't. I'm here. You have me."

"You're just like me. Like your dad. Miserable. Sad. Empty. It's all my fault."

"Mom, stop. Stop saying this stuff. Please." Tears formed behind the boy's eyes, but he didn't dare let them fall.

His mom did not hold back her own. They streamed down into her ears and onto the pillow.

"I hate my life."

"Mom, stop."

"I hate my life," she repeated through broken sobs. Each syllable stumbled and fell. Her eyes begged the ceiling for mercy.

In that moment, the boy hated God, a god he'd never known, a god he'd never even believed in. He hated that his mother carried a lifetime's worth of sorrow on her back, so heavy that her knees had given out at forty years old. He hated how unfair life was, how she never got to taste the happiness that others seemed to feed on so effortlessly, that she could never just smile, simply happy to be alive. He hated what her pain did to him. He hated everything.

"Mom. It's okay."

The boy placed a hand on hers, listening to her cry—a

sound he had endured many times before. It was torture. He would have given his life if it meant she would never have to cry again.

Her misty eyes turned to him. "Are those for me?"

"Yeah, Mom, I got them for you. They're purple." He handed her the small bouquet.

"I love purple."

"I know."

She held them to her chest and smiled at her son. Machines beeped. The lights hummed.

"Can we fucking go?" Hector asked Bub.

"What a *lovely* woman. I can't wait to meet her."

"Fuck you."

And the room went black.

Maybe I'll Catch Fire by Alkaline Trio spun against a worn needle.

Two man-shaped things, grotesque in appearance and demeanor, lost themselves in beer and song. They were twenty and twenty-one years old—Tommy and Hector.

They sang loud and out of key, oblivious to everything but their misguided joy. Hector cringed at the display, but glancing at his younger self, he hardly recognized the carefree laughter and genuine smile of the stranger before him.

This Tommy's arm was in a cast, signaling to Hector that it was near the end of their first year on Drake Avenue.

Tommy had a bad habit of riding his bike home drunk. The broken arm was merely the latest in a year of setbacks spurred by moving in with Hector. His drinking had spiraled out of control, worsening with each work shift, failed romance, and overdraft fee—but he never blamed anyone else for his problems, least of all Hector.

"Do you remember this night?" Bub asked from somewhere unseen.

Hector remembered only fragments. He looked over his shoulders, searching for Bub, unsure of where the voice had come from, and said, "Tommy and I got into a fight, I think, but I don't remember it being that big of a deal."

"No? I thought you may have remembered it as the night you ruined your best friend's life."

"Ruined his life? We used to fight over nothing all the time when we got drunk."

Bub materialized behind Hector, whispering into his ear, "But why did you fight this night?"

"I don't remember."

"Did you know Tommy spoke to his mother earlier that day? It had been weeks since she last called. She was just so tired. Her heart broke a little more each time she called him. Did you know that?"

"Maybe. I don't know. No."

Bub drifted in circles around Hector. "The calls typically all went the same. *Move back home. Take some community college classes. Stop drinking.* Always ending with a firm reminder that she loved him. All very sweet."

As Bub moved, Hector fell into a trance-like state, placing him in the moment of the call.

"But this call was different," Bub whispered, his breath sweeping the back of Hector's neck. "She'd been less aggressive in her pleas for him to turn things around, and, just as they were saying their goodbyes, she let it out."

Hector felt the sorrow pouring from her as if he were inside her body. He could feel the guilt accumulating in Tommy's chest, cold and heavy as ice.

"She broke down and wept, telling her son that she didn't want to see him end up like his brother, terrified that one day she would get that dreaded phone call or knock on the door from the police. Tommy remained silent through it all. And when she said she had to go, ashamed of her own tears, she didn't leave him with that firm *I love you.* No. All she said was *please, come home*, as quiet as a mouse. Then hung up."

Hector saw Tommy motionless, the phone still pressed to his ear, his face drained of color. After a moment, Tommy lowered the phone and began to cry, sobbing like a child.

The needle left the record with a static pop, and Hector snapped out of his trance, Bub beside him.

He watched his younger self shuffle over to flip the record, feeling a wave of disgust. The smirking idiot exuded narcissism, wallowing in self-pity while masquerading it with self-deprecation. It made Hector sick to his stomach.

He turned to Bub. "Hey, I get it. I was a piece of shit. Still am. I don't actually need this whole elaborate time-travel thing to be reminded of it. Trust me."

Bub smiled. "Oh, but there's quite a difference between reminding and reliving, especially now that you have *context.* Pay attention." With a wave of his finger, Hector's head whipped forward to bear witness.

Younger Hector swayed in front of the stereo. Too drunk to pick a new record, he flipped it over and restarted side A.

Tommy hummed the lyrics into his beer. "*I've got toothpicks in my eyes, smile more yellow than the sky...*" After a moment, he glanced up at younger Hector, and said, "The landlord called me again today. She wants to know if we're re-signing the lease."

Their apartment was no prize. It had no central air, sporadic heat, and the occasional rat, but it was cheap.

"Yeah, why wouldn't we? He's probably hoping we don't so he can charge the next suckers double," other Hector replied.

Tommy had wanted to stay too—at least, until the call with his mom. He hadn't heard his mom cry like that since his brother took his own life. And he loved Hector as much as anyone, blood or not, but he was starting to realize that their living situation was not doing either any favors. "Well, I've been thinking—"

The other Hector's face dropped.

"I think I'm going to move back home for a while. Maybe take a few classes at South Suburban Tech. I just got to do something, man. We're wasting away here. Maybe you can do the same?"

"Move back home? With my mom? Wasting away sounds like the better option." He poured his beer down his throat.

"Well, maybe I can help you find a roommate. I'm sure with rent so cheap you won't have a problem finding—"

"Don't bother. I'll figure it out. I always do."

"Okay." Tommy slunk into the couch, timidly sipping his beer.

"So, what, you're just going to go to community college—and then do what?"

"I don't know yet. I still have to figure it out."

"Why can't you take classes and still live here? I don't understand why you have to move back home to do that."

"I won't be able to work as many hours. Even with rent so cheap—I don't know—"

"I told you, Dish Pit wants to rent our couch. We let him pay to live in here," he gestured to their living room, "and that lowers rent. Then you can afford to stay. Problem solved."

"It's really not just the rent."

"Then what is it?"

Tommy cut to the chase. "We're fucking up, dude. We can't just sit here and drink until we pass out *every single* night. I love it, but that's the problem. If I don't make any sort of change, I'll still be sitting here years from now."

Hector watched his younger self standing there, shoulders

slumped, beer in hand. He understood perfectly what Tommy meant, but he was weak. Any slight shift in the wind would rock his fragile foundation, causing complete collapse. And Tommy leaving was a tornado.

"So you're just going to leave me with the apartment? To live with Dish Pit? I'm sure that'll lead to some healthy and productive times for me."

"No one said you have to stay here or live with Dish Pit. You're free to make changes too."

"Am I? I can't run to my mom when things get tough. You don't see her calling me worried and crying over her little boy," he slurred.

Hector couldn't believe the way his younger self spoke to Tommy. Those details had been buried deep in his memory.

"Hey, fuck you," Tommy said. "You're not going to make me feel bad about my mom caring."

"That's because you don't feel bad about anything. You only care about yourself," snapped the other Hector.

"What the fuck are you even talking about? I'm always there for you. And I'll still be there for you. I'm not ending our friendship, Hector. I just need to get my life on track a little. Don't be such an asshole."

"Oh, I'm an asshole? Fuck you, Tommy. All I do is defend you to other people and stick up for you. Maybe your mom's right. You do need to get your shit together. Run back home."

Tommy got up from the couch and started to put his jacket on. "Go fuck yourself. Just because I don't want to wallow here in misery with you doesn't make you tougher or more independent. It makes you a sad asshole. And I know you're better than that. So stop being a fucking dick." He reached down to the coffee table for his cigarettes.

The other Hector walked up to Tommy and pushed him.

Tommy shoved him back.

The other Hector peered at Tommy with disdain, then spat.

Tommy swung, connected his knuckles to the side of his face. The other Hector stumbled backward, catching himself on the stereo and knocking the needle off the record. Tommy slammed the door on his way out.

The other Hector rubbed his cheek and stretched his jaw, then began to cry—not from the throb of Tommy's punch, but from the confusion of the moment. Shame and guilt flooded his system. He went outside after his friend.

Tommy was there, smoking and staring out at the abandoned tracks. The other Hector lingered behind him, silent, then said, "Tommy."

Tommy turned, his eyes making it abundantly clear he was ready to swing again if need be.

"I'm sorry," the other Hector choked out, his face wet with tears.

Tommy's eyes softened. "Hey, hey, don't worry about it, man. I know sometimes we both get carried away. We're even, okay?"

Tears streamed down the other Hector's cheeks to his throat. "I just need you around, man."

All Tommy could do was reach into his pack and offer him a cigarette. They leaned against the porch railing and smoked. Neither spoke, yet both found themselves gazing at the old tree sprouting from the center of the tracks—it was as good a place to look as any.

"Hey, want to call Dish Pit and get a bag from him?" Tommy suggested.

The other Hector shot an incredulous look, his face flushed from tears and the cold, and offered mild resistance. "Are you sure that's a good idea?"

"No, it's a horrible idea. But doesn't it sound good?"

He nodded.

"You text him. I don't want to get stuck in a conversation with him."

"Alright," the other Hector agreed.

"But he is *not* living here."

The lights went out. And Bub and Hector were returned to the void.

"Such a good friend you are," Bub hissed.

Hector thought only of the tree.

41

Gretchen had her orders from Bub: retrieve a soul from the depths.

Walking the streets of Hell toward the train, she noticed the aimless bustle of the other creatures. *Why?* she pondered. Why run around with such urgency to participate in this economy of pain? With the exception of Bub—and *those flies*, who she loathed—the average imp or demon didn't find fulfillment from torture and evil deeds. It was just all they knew.

Gretchen entered an enormous terminal, swirling with the clatter of claws and the chatter of her fellow minions. She stood waiting for the train that would take her deep into the torture caverns below the metropolis.

Souls of the damned littered the massive platform, ignored by Hell's commuting class as they sat scattered like vagrants, cowering and whispering unheard prayers. These souls, long forgotten in the torture caverns, had found their way to the train platform, not daring to ascend to the city streets. Resigned to their fate, they took refuge in Hell's purgatory, existing as street urchins, hidden among the bustling masses.

One man, blackened with soot and caked in dried blood, sat

naked against the wall, knees drawn to his chest. He swayed his head to a melody only he could hear. Gretchen watched with interest. Then he began to sing.

It was a song fit for Hell, a song he once sang at his lowest, in some creaky pub lit by oil lamp on a seafoam shore, from a life now reduced to nothing more than a half-remembered dream.

You don't even know my name
But what does that matter?
We don't havta call each other anything
You just havta share this smoke with me

AND MAYBE LIFE'S not so terrible
As terrible as I'm always makin' it out to be
Yeah, maybe
It's just me who's fucked 'n ugly

The words strained through his blistered throat. His voice, brimming with sorrow, caused even the passing demons to stop and listen.

For the damned within earshot, the song resurfaced memories once thought lost to the sands of time, blossoming bitter nostalgia in their hearts. The demons found themselves imagining lives they'd never lived and loves they never lost—or ever had—as they listened. A warm sadness blanketed the crowd.

Gretchen blinked her large mantis eyes at the man, nodding with approval.

The man smiled, revealing rows of rusty nails pounded into his gums where teeth should have been. The moment was over. The song was forgotten. The train approached.

42

Hector opened his eyes. He was in his bed. Bub was nowhere to be seen or felt.

What the fuck? He couldn't move.

The hope that everything had been a bad dream vanished as his moonlit bedroom came into focus. Someone was in the bed next to him, and someone else stood in the corner.

It was Sammie. They both were.

The Sammie in the corner clasped her hands tightly against her chest, still piecing together her surroundings. This was his Sammie, held captive and in line to die because of him. *How did she get here?* Hector wondered.

The girl beside him was a familiar ghost, an echo from another time. He held her close as she faced the wall, her short curls just inches from his face, the earthy scent of their oils filling his nose. Naked beneath an old comforter, their chests heaved in unison. They had just made love.

Hector wanted to pull her even closer, but he still couldn't move. This wasn't his body. He was merely a visitor behind the windows of its eyes, a passenger along for the ride.

This body belonged to the boy who had watched his father

leave for the last time, who had sat at his mother's side with flowers in hand, and who had poisoned his best friend's future —now barely a man. It was Hector from just over a year ago.

Sammie slid down the wall and cradled her knees. She stared at the pair as if they were an old photograph discovered in some forgotten drawer, her focus narrowing on the girl. With an incredulous look in her eyes, she watched. Despite being only a year younger, she seemed like an entirely different person from Sammie now. There was a vibrancy about her. She still had something to lose.

Hector could feel the boy's chest grow cold, his body rejecting the warmth of the girl's body. Although happiness lay in his arms, its taste was bitter. The boy wanted to crawl out of his skin and retreat into solitude.

"What's wrong?" the girl asked, still facing the wall.

"What? Nothing. What do you mean?"

"Please don't do that. I know when something is wrong. I can feel it. You're being weird."

"No, I'm not," said the boy.

"I just asked you not to do that."

"Okay, how am I being weird?"

"Please don't," she said.

Hector wished he could take control of his hand and slap himself across the face. He was disgusted by the display of cowardice.

"I'm sorry. It's just that nothing's wrong. I'm just lying here."

"Yeah, exactly. You're just lying there. Not saying anything. And barely holding me."

Her words were tender but unwavering, like a mother telling a child to move their hands from a scrape so rubbing alcohol could be applied. *I know it stings. But this will help. I promise.*

She rolled over to face the boy, her face glowing in the darkness. Hector stared into her big brown eyes from behind the boy's own. She was beautiful, and he loved her. He wanted to tell her right then and there, but instead the boy retreated further within himself.

"Something is wrong. You've been acting weird all night."

"I just— I don't know."

God, you fucking idiot! Hector screamed, unheard. *Don't fucking do this.*

"You don't know what?" she asked.

"I just don't know."

Her radiance flickered like a loose bulb. He was hurting her, like he always did.

I'm poison. I'm the villain.

Sammie looked on from the floor, her eyes wide and glazed with a coat of tears. The left side of her face was slightly swollen, and a small abrasion sat above her right eye. Faint strangulation marks adjourned her neck. She was hurting, inside and out.

I'm worthless. I'm evil.

The room pounded like a palpitating heart. Seconds ticked by. Faster. Then slower. The beats did not abide by any laws of temporal linearity.

The girl spoke, "You act like you don't like me, like you don't want to be near me. The only time it seems like you care is when you're drunk. Other than that, you're just—cold."

"I'm sorry," the boy said. "I don't know what's wrong with me. I don't know why I feel like this."

"It hurts, Hector. If I didn't love you, it wouldn't hurt. You forget that or don't care."

"I'm sorry." The words crawled out of the boy's throat like pathetic, slithering worms.

Next time just choke on them and die.

"Please stop saying you're sorry." The girl began to cry.

With this, Sammie's glassy eyes shattered. She remembered this night well. It was supposed to be a special night, the first night of the rest of their lives. A reason to stop drinking. A cure for their loneliness. A chance to build the loving family neither ever had.

She dragged her hands upward against her face, wiping her tears. She was hyper focused on the girl, paying the boy no notice. So much time had been spent tending to that boy's needs that the girl's became something her own mind only whispered about when she was alone. Sammie witnessed herself dissolve into nothing.

From behind the boy's eyes, Hector watched Sammie die twice.

"I just—" the boy started to say, then stopped.

"Whatever you have to say, just say it."

"I just think we should be friends."

The room held its breath.

Sammie hung her head in the corner. Hector prayed for death.

"Friends don't treat each other like this," the girl said, then rolled back over to face the wall.

There are few moments in life that truly define an individual. Hector knew this was one of them.

The boy shivered in his own frost, so consumed by self-inflicted pain that he couldn't begin to tend to the girl's. *Friends don't treat each other like this.* Her plea for warmth couldn't penetrate his cold.

But beneath his frostbitten skin was a candle that burned for the girl, a fire kept alive despite its surrounding elements. It was from that light that the boy spoke once more, "I'm sorry."

"I'm pregnant," the girl responded.

The boy had nothing to say.

To be flayed and laid in a bed of salt would not have been enough to assuage the guilt that flooded Hector's being.

Sammie shot to her feet. "Okay! Ha! Ha! You've had your fun.

Now get me the fuck out of here! Am I supposed to just sit here and watch this and cry? Is that what you want? Well, you got it! I know I'm fucked up. I know I'm worthless. I know all the mistakes I've made. What do you want? *What do you want?!*" she screamed to the dark room—receiving no response.

She slid back down the wall, her face collapsing into her hands, and sobbed.

Hector was ready to die. He couldn't take another second of her pain.

Then he felt a pull. It was as if a hand reached into the boy's head and ripped Hector out. His consciousness was launched across the room, plunging into Sammie on the floor.

The two became entangled.

They met in a place of flickering static. A dead channel.

A city of buried dreams.

Lost futures.

43

*S*ammie and Hector drifted in the breeze like kite strings intertwined, like plumes of smoke folding into one another. They soared above a city of lost futures to see all that never had the chance to exist. Their story was told in fragments, as verses whispered in the wind. Sammie recited them to herself as she drifted, and Hector listened.

YOU LIKED the sound of my voice. softened eyes, a half-smile. you scrubbed pots and pans. and listened. pasta. sauce from scratch. a meal we cooked together. the book I read aloud. while you scrubbed. was one you chose.

REBIRTH

   in reverse

WE HAVE friends. to visit on the weekends. and celebrate each other's successes. he talks to you. about his job. you politely smile. she tells me how life will be different. but to not worry. it is a blessing. her every word is gospel.

REBIRTH

   in reverse

WE NAMED him after a film director. with a nickname. reminiscent of a cartoon fish. he is everything you wanted to be. and for that. you are thankful.

REBIRTH

   in reverse

WE SIT outside toward a setting sun. and reflect on all we built. you tell me you love me. it was nothing more. than a life lived well.

ALL THAT WAS ONCE THOUGHT BOUND by destiny drifts apart, scattered in the breeze.

44

As Hector was ripped from Sammie's mind, he could see Hell's shadows begin to claim her. She didn't seem to care, never even lifting her face from her hands as she wept. Grieving for all that would never come to pass, she let the darkness return her to Austin without a fight.

The last thing Hector saw before the shadows took her were the tears trickling through her fingers and down her knuckles.

That's how she'll die. Broken. Alone. Haunted, he told himself. The thought twisted like a knife. Austin was going to kill her, and there was only one thing he could do to stop him.

Then everything went black.

He opened his eyes to find himself standing once more on the abandoned tracks by his apartment. The night was darker now. Time had passed, but Hector did not know how much.

"Did you have a nice time?" asked Bub. "I thought I'd sit that one out and let you and your little girlfriend have some privacy." A halo of flies swarmed above his head. With a wave of his finger, they assembled into staircase formation, leading up to the noose.

Hector began picking up the empty cans he had dropped when Bub dragged him away.

"Yes, very good, pick up your trash, make everything nice and neat," Bub mocked. "Even on the cusp of your death, you find something idiotic to occupy yourself with."

Walking to the edge of the overpass, Hector looked down into the alley. An open dumpster was within range, so he tossed in the cans from above.

"Those really should have been recycled," Bub remarked.

Hector turned to face Bub, shrugging his shoulders. "You won."

"Don't be too hard on yourself. *Leave that to us*," Bub said. The flies of the staircase snickered.

"You're going to take my soul and break the Word of God."

"Correct."

"Bandini told me everything. I'm the stress test."

"The bug knew more than I thought." Bub considered this, then dismissed the thought with a flick of his hand. "But it's no matter."

"You're right. It doesn't matter. Nothing does."

"Pause the melodramatics, please. You'll have plenty of time for woeful musings where you're going." The staircase buzzed with delight. "Now, step right up."

Hector was cold with dread. "No, you don't understand," he began, still careful not to divulge meeting with Jesus and Lucifer. "Bandini. He told me something almost no one else knows. This is not the only..." Hector struggled to think of the proper word. "Existence? Universe? Reality? Point is, there's infinite mes and infinite yous. There's probably a version of us standing right here, roles reversed. Me, the King of Hell."

Bub laughed, removing and wiping his tinted glasses seemingly only for effect. Horrible faceted eyes seared through the darkness in their absence.

"You read too many science fiction books," Bub said, looking Hector up and down. "Who am I kidding? You don't read," he concluded. "Movies, then."

Bub replaced his glasses. "I was there when the light of this universe was but a spark. I have seen its borders and traversed the abyss beyond them. If the bug truly told you that, he is either mistaken or lying. Based on his kind's nature, I assume the latter."

"Then what about God? Where is he? If you think he's gone, then where did he go?" asked Hector, his palms slick with icy sweat.

"God crawled back into whatever hole he came from. His burrows are deep like a termite's. If he does not want to be found, then he won't be. The coward does not need an entirely different universe to hide in."

The noose above them swayed like an impatient pendulum. The clock was ticking. Hector needed to make a decision or Bub would make one for him. He realized that he was not going to trigger any grand revelations or changes of heart, so he shifted his strategy. The plan was now to protect Sammie and Tommy at all costs, and resign himself to death.

"I need your guarantee that you won't hurt Sammie and Tommy."

"And I don't care what you need," responded Bub.

"If we don't agree to this, I promise to live a very, very long time. I will quit drinking and only eat vegetables. I will exercise every single day and do yoga. I will rot in a nursing home caked in my own piss and shit just to spite you."

Bub was unphased. "If you do not swing from that noose before tonight's end, I will ensure that all three of you die *extremely* painful deaths. How is that for a guarantee?"

"I know that. So I need to know that if I do this," Hector

looked up at the tree, "you'll leave them alone. Come on, I know deals are your thing. Make one with me."

Bub sighed, rubbing his temples. "Sure, fine. They will burn with the rest eventually."

Hector exhaled for the first time all night.

"But only one," Bub said

"What?" Hector's stomach dropped to the ground. "No, both."

"No, one." Bub held up a single finger. It stretched into a thorny vine that twisted upward to the night sky. "I'm being generous." The thorns grew tiny beaks, chattering like hungry baby birds.

Bub continued, "Or you can take the coward's way out and *not* end your life. You can live out the rest of your pathetic life. But I *will* kill your friends. You'll carry that choice with you into old age, never forgiving yourself that you could have at least saved one of them, always teetering on the edge of suicide. How long will you last when I play you a lullaby of their screams each night you lie awake? And when you finally give in, it will be for nothing but to ease your own pain—same as always."

Bub waved his thorned finger like a maestro's baton to an imagined melody, hissing, "*I will drape myself in their skin.*"

Hector was cornered. The thought of letting them both die was somehow easier than sealing the fate of one.

Bub was in ecstasy over Hector's dilemma. He idly swayed his finger, looking out to the blackness beyond the moon. "Who will it be?" The words drifted through the air, setting sail for oblivion. "Who matters more?"

"I can't," Hector stammered.

"Oh, but you must."

"Please." It sickened Hector to resort to begging, but he didn't know what else to do.

"That got me a little hard. Can you say it again?" Bub cupped a hand to his ear, leaning in with anticipation.

"Please. Leave them both alone."

Bub stood straight. "Absolutely not. Choose *one*."

I can't.

He imagined Tommy in prison, now an old man, alone at a white plastic table, the smell of piss and bleach in the air. Identically dressed men with nothing to lose bark at each other across the concrete commons. They pay no mind to the weathered criminal. He barely exists. His face, once boyish and bright, is weighed down by the decades lost. It's calloused, lined and gnarled. The years passed him by without granting him a single smile.

As much as this image devastated Hector, a life confined was still a life. He couldn't bear to imagine the specifics of Sammie's captivity. Whatever Austin had done to her, *or would* do to her, was too much for his mind to conjure. She would die horribly and with a heavy heart all because of him.

Sammie's face smeared with blood and tears crept past his mental blockade. It was enough to force a choice.

"Sammie." Her name was a soft breath. Hector felt like he had just locked the door to Tommy's cell himself.

"Poor Tommy," Bub said, shaking his head. "But between you and I, it was the right choice."

"So you won't hurt Sammie?"

"No, I will not hurt Sammie. A deal is a deal. Now...*open wide.*"

With that, Bub's thorned finger wrapped itself around Hector's face and neck. The chattering vine cut thin slices on his lips and gums, forcing its way into his mouth. One of the hungry thorns latched its beak onto a back tooth and ripped it from its socket. Blood filled Hector's mouth, gushing down his chin.

The vine, still wrapped around Hector's neck, lifted him off his feet and carried him to the bottom of the buzzing black staircase. Hector fell to the ground and scratched at his throat where the thorns had chewed and choked. He gasped for breath. It was but a small sample of what was to come.

"You must ascend it yourself." Bub motioned to the steps.

Hector bent over and dry-heaved, then looked up at the dangling noose. His legs would not move.

Annoyed, Bub asked, "And what's wrong now?"

Hector didn't mean to say it, but the words crawled like cold ants beneath his skin, moving up toward his mouth. Lighter than air yet heavier than lead, they slipped past his lips with a whimper. "I'm scared."

The staircase of flies exploded with laughter and taunts. *scaaarreed? baby is scaaaaaared! scared! SCARED!*

The flies devolved into a cloud of disorganized mockery, but the riotous display was cut short by a single leer from Bub. They quickly returned to their positions.

For possibly the first time, Bub looked at Hector without judgment, not out of sympathy but from a profound understanding of the topic.

"Fear," Bub began. "I know its very nature, its origin." He paused to take notice of Hector's twitching left hand. "What you're feeling is not new. You have always lived with this. Look inside yourself. The fear has always been there, and you have always stood *right here*. You were born for this."

The flies were dead silent, attentive as graduate students listening to a lecture on their chosen subject.

"Kings. Poets. Philosophers. They beg and cower the same as the most unremarkable man when their time comes, as if fear was not a shadow that had followed their every step. Fear is not a stranger. It is your oldest friend."

The flies buzzed in agreement.

"It is the oldest emotion. Do you know what the first creation felt as he was cobbled together from the nothing and given consciousness?"

feeeeaar, the flies answered together.

"Correct. When Lucifer opened his eyes to existence for the first time, alone in a vast universe with only an omnipotent monster to call Father, he felt fear. And in the pummeling fluorescence of a hospital delivery room, you did too. It is only fitting that it is the last thing we feel as well."

"I don't want to go to Hell." Hector's voice was small like a child's. "Please."

Drifting behind Hector, Bub placed his hands on his shoulders and stared up at the noose alongside him. "Hell is just another place. Once you get used to it, it can be *intoxicating.* Think of it like all those shots of cheap whiskey you've poured down your throat. The first few burn going down, but take enough, and they become smooth as water."

Hector understood little of what Bub said and retained even less. All he could do was watch the noose slow dance in the wind.

Bub saw that his pep talk was for naught, so he leaned in and hissed into Hector's ear, "Don't forget our deal."

The bleeding socket in Hector's mouth throbbed. The snow at his feet was stained with the heavy globs of red that dripped from his chin.

His only thoughts were of Sammie as he ascended that first step. The staircase squirmed and buzzed, suspended in the air, and in a static hum, the flies sang,

nothinggg to fearrr

nothingggy to lovvve

no morrre birthdays to tirrre of

beautifull beautifulll beautifulllll swayyy

This wasn't how he'd imagined going. He always assumed he would drink himself to death or die in a car crash, something simple. Suicidal thoughts never made it past the ideation stage. Sure, when things got bad, Hector would daydream about flipping his own killswitch, a comforting thought, but he never actually intended to follow through—especially not like this.

"Put it on," Bub said.

Reaching the top, Hector took the noose in his hands. The rope looked more like something used to secure a mattress atop a car than a Dickensian instrument of self-sacrifice. There was little poetry in these last moments. He really had to piss but wasn't sure if it was just nerves.

He held the noose over his head and said, "I want to see my dad."

"I've already arranged that," Bub replied.

Hector gave a small nod, and placed the rope around his neck, pulling it as tight as his fear would allow. A final breath tickled his lungs with frigid air. "Please tell Sammie that I—"

The flies broke formation, and Hector dropped. His legs flailed above the ground in panic.

Bub sauntered over, nudging Hector's body to increase its swing.

"What was it you wanted me to tell Sammie?" he asked. "I didn't catch it."

Hector clawed at the rope burrowing into his throat and compressing his carotid arteries. The drop was not far enough, nor had he secured the noose tightly enough, to break his neck or sever his spinal cord. As his eyes began to bulge, and rasped gurgles sputtered from his mouth, Hector slowly strangled from the weight of his own body.

"And about our deal," Bub said, "you weren't exactly specific on the details, but I suppose you're no lawyer." He snapped his fingers, and the flies scrambled into a new formation, a sort of projection screen. Upon their surface, a playback of Hector from minutes earlier flickered.

"I need your guarantee that you won't hurt Sammie and Tommy."

"I will not hurt Sammie. A deal is a deal." Bub grinned as he watched himself on the screen.

Hector's face was turning sick shades of blue and gray. A familiar warmth spread across the front of his pants as his bladder emptied.

"Oh, how embarrassing," Bub said, wincing. "But as I was saying, our deal was that *I* would not hurt Sammie, and *I* won't."

Hector clawed at the rope with increased fervor, his strength fading fast. He could no longer fight the physics of his predicament.

"But I can't say for sure what your friend Austin will do. He's a bit of a loose cannon, after all," Bub added.

A strange song began to fill Hector's head, faint and tinny, as if from an old music box. Its thin crescendo swayed and swelled, weaving fragments into a single melody. The parts became the whole, and the whole was disappointing. This was the song of his life. Its last song. Melancholic. Repetitive. Uninspired.

His consciousness began to slip, but still he pawed at the rope, stealing infinitesimal crumbs of air and delaying the inevitable. Over the fading music, he again heard the voice of Jesus emanating from within. *You need to hold on.*

Bub raised an eyebrow as if he heard the voice this time. He peered into Hector's eyes. Their light dimmed. It was a slow strangulation; neither the rope nor Hector's tightening of it were optimal for a quick death.

"The choice was made. This is over," Bub announced. For a moment, he waited for something to happen, but there was no retribution, no wrath from above. God was not there. A smile grew across his face. "But this may take a bit," he said, watching Hector's body swing. "Perfect opportunity to pay your dear father a visit."

Bub reached inside Hector's body and pulled out his

consciousness with the ease of removing a book from a shelf. The body went limp, barely alive.

This out-of-body state was not new to Hector, as this was his second brush with death this week, but this experience felt colder, sadder. He looked up at himself, then to Bub. "Please. Stop Austin, or put me back in my body so I can."

Bub simply smirked. "Let's go."

The flies swarmed around them, like a dense fog, spiriting both away to Hell.

Hector's body swayed. He was inches from death.

45

Spittle dripped from Austin's mouth onto Sammie's face. Snarling like an animal, he choked the life from her body.

The cotton balls he had bandaged around the dentures protruding from his eye had blossomed with crimson. A strange milky fluid mixed with blood leaked from the mess, trailing down his cheek

Sammie had opened her eyes to this nightmare. Semiconscious and on the floor, she had been delivered back to Austin on a silver platter, who wasted no time pouncing on top of her to exact his revenge.

Bub's orders of temporary restraint became a distant memory once that row of dentures had been plunged into his eye. They were completely forgotten when she dunked his head into his own piss. Austin was going to kill her, and he was going to enjoy it.

"*You fucking bitch.* You fucking like that?" Austin growled, knuckles white around her throat. Already fond of choking during sex, this was a whole other level. Rock hard, his member felt near eruption without ever leaving his pants.

Sammie, in fact, did not like that.

On the one hand, Sammie wanted to let Austin kill her without struggle. She went through the usual motions of flails and kicks one makes while being choked to death, but her mind was tired and there was little spirit behind her fight. This was old. The whole thing was old hat. Life. God's cruel joke. She was sick of laughing.

On the other hand, she was pissed off. Demons. Sentient shadows. Lost futures. The absurdity of it all infuriated her. Life was fucked. She thought she had known that, but she had underestimated just how fucked it was. The universe only seemed to nudge in one direction: down. Gravity was a wicked force. Sammie wanted to punch whoever thought this whole thing up right in the mouth.

Then she blacked out.

IT FELT SORT OF like swimming. Drifting through the vacuum of her own mind. Safe.

Thoughts flowed downstream. Whole conversations. She listened to anger and resignation debate in voices that were not her own.

R: *Suffering is contagious. Common as the cold. Pervasive as air.*

A: *But there are moments of happiness. No matter how small. The foundation of life is not misery.*

R: *The foundation means nothing if built upon quicksand. We begin to sink the day we are born. Struggling makes it worse.*

A: *That's why we can't panic. There's always a way. Stay calculated. Stay mad. Focus.*

R: *A lot of good focusing does with Austin's hands around our neck. He's a monster.*

A: *Austin is as vulnerable as a worm after rainfall. And he is human.*

Sammie listened as the conversation coalesced into a single voice speaking to itself.

Austin didn't choose the initial circumstances that led him here. At some point, yes, he consciously flipped the switch from good to evil, but the switch is never flipped at random or without precedent. What about all the smaller bad decisions that must have preceded the switch being flipped? What caused those? And why were we made with a switch in the first place? It all had to start from one single bad choice a very long time ago, snowballing ever since. Perhaps he had no choice in making that first choice. Perhaps the world was unkind. How could a child be held responsible for the path an unkind world sets them on? It is never too late to choose a new path. Yes. But sometimes new paths are just detours to the same destination. But again, why even make the switch?

OUTSIDE OF HER MIND, her legs began to thrash.

Every twelve-hour shift spent on her feet, every mile pedaled on her shitty bike, every step taken through cold city streets—they all rallied in her leg muscles. Life was fucked, and she was angry about it.

THE STREAM STOPPED. And the drifting accelerated to a sprint.

So it's decided? Yes. Good. Done. Let's go.

SAMMIE'S EYES opened with a spark.

Her heels dug into the floor and pushed with the strength of a thousand bad days, thrusting her knees hard into Austin's spine. He roared in pain. His hands around her throat loosened.

Breaking free, she clambered out from under him until her shins were positioned underneath his crotch. With a fury reserved for God, she kicked. But since God was not around, Austin's testicles had to do.

Austin heaved a hollow croak and collapsed forward. He was a rabid dog, too far gone to know when to quit, catching Sammie by her ankle as she crawled away.

Resisting his pull felt like running in a dream. Her limbs were heavy, uncooperative, as if made of jello. Still recovering from the blackout, her anger needed reignition to continue this fight.

"You fat fucking bitch," Austin spat, managing to reclaim position atop her legs and pinning down one of her arms. "Shoulda let me fuck you when you had the chance. I'm not gonna be so gentle this time." He wrestled for control over her other arm.

Sammie flailed with what little strength she could gather, but resignation had returned.

Austin got a knee over one wrist, then the other, regaining domination. His face, still dripping with blood and the milky fluid, contorted itself into a grin. "You should be grateful I'll even fuck you with how close together your eyes are."

And just like that, the anger was back.

"*FuckOFF!*" was all Sammie could scream, the two words crashing into one. Freeing a wrist from under his knee, she launched her hand to his face, palming the dentures farther into his eye socket.

Austin shrieked, rolling off her completely and cradling his face.

"Father!" he cried to no response.

Sammie ran into the darkened living room to find Austin had barricaded the house. A tall bookcase filled with hardcovers blocked the front door. A wooden credenza and an upturned dining table obstructed the windows.

Austin laughed from the kitchen, his hands still covering his face. No longer writhing in pain, he was now overcome with hysterics, convulsing on the linoleum floor.

The bookcase didn't budge. The furniture moved only a hair. Everything seemed heavier than it should, as if coated with an unseen layer of extra weight. There had to be another way.

She scrambled toward the bedrooms, but there stood Austin, already blocking the hallway. The side of his face was a smeared collage of gore.

"Don't worry. He's just testing me, and I'm gonna make him proud." Austin ripped the cotton balls from his wound and raised his knife. "So proud."

He dug the knife into his own eye socket, clenching his jaw and growling with such ferocity that blood spritzed from between his grinding teeth as his vocal cords ruptured. Sammie staggered backward, vomiting a single stream of bile to her feet.

Sammie could hear the knife scraping against the dentures. Austin's growl turned to a sick laugh.

With his entire face now smeared red, Austin plunged two fingers into the socket and pulled the dentures out like a splinter, his eyeball still skewered.

"*See? See?* He is going to be so happy with me." He smiled, then teetered off balance, catching himself on the wall.

"The fuck is wrong with you?!" Sammie screamed, retreating to the kitchen.

The back door—still knobless after its previous one had unceremoniously dissolved into flies—wasn't an option, so she climbed onto the counter to try the window above the sink. She reached for the latch, pleasantly surprised when it didn't immediately also dissolve into flies. She was far less pleasantly surprised when it melted into what Sammie could only conceptualize as a steaming puddle of rotten cum—creamy and yellow in hue. She retched into the sink.

At a loss, she threw open drawers until she found a large

kitchen knife, and began to pound the double-paned glass with its wooden handle. A hairline crack formed, but it wasn't breaking.

The lights in the living room went out, and Sammie could hear Austin's knife scraping the other side of the kitchen wall, inching closer.

She abandoned the window and hid beside the refrigerator. The kitchen went dark next with the sound of a flipped switch. Wedged against the wall with the Lopez's garbage can, all she could see was Austin's drifting silhouette.

"We are going to have so much fun," he whispered, his footsteps echoing in every direction.

Then, a loud thud. Something had hit the kitchen window.

Another thud, and the crack spread.

Then another.

Sammie craned her neck to catch a glimpse of the source.

Was that a pigeon? she asked herself.

One after another, they took turns bombing the window. With each impact, they shook off the crash and circled back around for another. The window was becoming a web of thin fractures.

The scratch of Austin's dragging knife neared.

"Rats with wings," Austin snarled. "I love killing rats."

Sammie held her breath and clenched her own knife, knuckles white around its neck.

46

"Hello, sir. I am sorry to bother you. My name is Kevin, and I'm a veteran. I hope you are having a wonderful night and I was just hoping to ask you if you had a cigarette to give and if I may have one. Please."

The man named Kevin had shuffled up to Tommy at the bus stop, wearing a large green coat that hung unevenly on his frame due to his slumped posture and the haphazard manner in which it was fastened.

"Hey. No, I'm sorry." Tommy patted himself down. "I don't have any."

Tommy had sprinted to the bus stop to catch the 73 back to his apartment, but had now been waiting nearly thirty minutes. Winter bus service was unreliable, arriving more by chance than schedule. And since it was seemingly sheer chance that had gotten Tommy out of jail, he felt his luck had been tapped.

"How about a dollar? Do you have a few dollars you can spare? I'm just looking to get something to eat. It's cold out here. I'm willing to work for it," the man said with a subservient tone that made Tommy extremely uncomfortable.

"No, man, I don't have any money, and I don't want anything

from you or have anything for you to do. I just got out of jail. Sorry."

Tommy considered running. If he had walked instead of waiting for the bus, he might already be home. But a decade of smoking and a night in a musty jail cell left him wheezing even while standing still. Running would be difficult. He began to doubt the bus would ever come.

"How about any change? Quarters help." The man named Kevin was undeterred. He stuck his hands out in classic beggar fashion. They were black with grime. "Please, sir."

"Okay, I'm not trying to be rude, but I already told you twice that I literally do not have anything to give. Nothing." He patted himself down more aggressively this time. "You're much better off finding someone else to ask."

Tommy looked up and down Armitage. There was no one else to ask. Cars trickled by, fewer and farther between. Zero foot traffic. Darkness had settled over the avenue. Flurries of snow passed under the streetlights' yellow glow. The night felt solemn, like a religious holiday all unknowingly observed.

"I understand," said the man named Kevin, dejected.

Tommy stepped into the street, peering down in hopes of spotting an approaching bus.

"I understand. I do, I do," the man repeated. "Well, I guess in that case, I suppose we'll just have to eat Hector and Sammie's skin."

Tommy's attention snapped to Kevin. "What did you just say?"

"You fucking heard me, you little faggot," the thing said with a thousand voices layered like steel wool against tinfoil. Flies crawled in and out of its mouth.

Tommy was in no mood. He reached into the chest pocket of his jacket and pulled out a crumpled pack of cigarettes.

"Last one," he said to the thing, extracting the lone cigarette and lighting it. He inhaled deep and blew the smoke in its direction.

The thing named Kevin stood for a moment, dumbfounded. Then its face began to segment from the center, like a flower blooming with chunks of meat. In the middle of the fleshy floral was Tommy's own face, gray and mangled like melting wax.

"*Laaasssst onnne,*" the thing hissed. Its green coat ripped open as ribbons of pink writhing flesh unfurled from its back.

"*Gah!*" Tommy ran in place on the frozen sidewalk like a cartoon character before falling flat on his back. He skittered back to his feet and took off down Armitage. The decision was made for him: run.

The thing named Kevin folded back into something more human and watched Tommy flee down the street. It picked up the dropped cigarette and burnt it down to the filter with one drag.

47

Hector was shocked to see his breath. He had assumed Hell would be hot. Yet, it plumed before him, merging with the cold, damp air.

They had traveled deep into the caverns, far from Hell's urban sprawl, where dark tunnels stretched in every direction. From this vast network, a resonant hum echoed like the distant beat of a timpani drum. It conjured the image of some hulking slavedriver aboard an ancient warship, pounding stretched lambskin with heavy mallets. Each beat seemed to linger without end through the caverns, layering atop the last.

As he listened, it became clear that the sound was a dense synecdoche of pleas and moans, individual voices coalescing into a singular, indistinguishable hum—entire existences lost to the collective drone.

"So, I'm dead?" Hector asked.

"You are dying, as good as dead, yes," Bub answered.

"So...I'm not dead?"

Annoyed, Bub clarified, "You are as dead as I need you to be. When death is imminent, the soul can detach for auditing, amongst other things."

"Like the light at the end of the tunnel?" Hector looked around the caverns. All the tunnels here ended in darkness.

"Yes, but not for you.", Bub placed a finger on his chin, debating which direction to continue. Just as no retail chain CEO knew the layout of each individual store, Bub did not possess an intimate familiarity of the lower levels. This place was below his pay grade.

"If I'm a soul, why do I have a body?" Hector looked down at his hands and turned them over. They sure looked and felt like his. He was even still in the same clothes as his hanging counterpart, his father's chain still around his neck.

In the distance, Hector heard heavy clacks against the hardened ground. He scanned the darkness, seeing nothing. The loud taps drew closer.

"Wrath is physical. Lust is physical. *Pain* is physical. To experience Hell, one requires a body. Welcome to your new flesh."

The source of the clacking meandered out from a nearby tunnel—a giant tongue walking on chopstick legs. Hector's eyes widened. "I've seen that thing before."

Bub turned his attention. "Hm? Ah, Kevin," he said, unimpressed.

"Kevin?"

"She enjoys human names," Bub explained without breaking stride.

The tongue kept on without acknowledgement, disappearing into another tunnel.

"But why is she a huge—"

Neither heard the scamper of paws nor the hurried drag of disproportionate claws rounding the corner with reckless abandon. With full momentum, Gretchen slammed into the unsuspecting Hector.

After blurting a string of obscenities, Hector found himself on the ground, looking up at the small creature examining him with large bug eyes, its cat nose twitching.

Bub curled his upper lip. "Gretchen. Why are you here?"

Gretchen, Hector repeated to himself. The name rang a bell. *Was this Lucifer's friend on the inside?* He seriously doubted the efficacy of any potential plan if it was.

"I was just doing what you asked, Lord Beelzebub. I am so sorry." Gretchen panicked. "I had just finished preparing the prisoner, and then I was leaving, and then I saw Kevin walking around, and I don't think she likes me very much, so I ran down that tunnel," she pointed around the corner with her tail, "and I didn't see you two standing here, so when I ran around the—"

"*Enough,*" Bub said, stifling further explanation. "You were just preparing the prisoner *now*?"

Gretchen shuffled back in submission. "I'm sorry, Lord Beelzebub. The train was late, and then I had to enlist a handful of cave crawlers to do the actual preparing because, well..." She lifted her heavy mantis claws as high as she could, which wasn't very, and continued, "And they are never easy to work with. They're so rude and—"

Bub silenced her with his hand. "Tell me which way."

Gretchen sheepishly pointed her tail around the corner as she did before.

"Leave. I will deal with you later."

She lowered her head and flattened her ears. If the plan failed, Bub would open new realms of pain just for her. Her faith in Lucifer had always been strong, but words like *faith* were empty platitudes in Hell, even more so than on Earth.

Bub turned to Hector. "Let's go. Daddy is waiting." He brushed past Gretchen down the tunnel.

Gretchen shot Hector a look that he didn't quite understand. While her insectoid eyes were not the most efficient tools of expression, her cat nose and brow wrinkled and furrowed, respectively, as if to say, *Don't fuck this up.*

If only he knew what he wasn't supposed to fuck up.

"*Now*," Bub commanded from inside the tunnel, his figure obscured by the darkness.

Hector turned to Gretchen for further explanation, but she was already down the opposite path, heavy claws in tow. The last thing he saw was her tail flutter in a series of strange spasms. Then, something in his pocket mimicked that movement, twitching like a jumping bean.

He reached his hand inside. It was a key.

HECTOR HAD TRAVELED with Bub through time and space in the blink of an eye, yet they walked the tunnels by foot.

Little nightmares slithered and scurried about as they made their way through the tunnels. Hector could only catch glimpses of fangs, legs, and horrible eyes. He hoped to be out of the tunnels soon—then realization set in. He was dead, or as dead as he needed to be, according to Bub, and the amount of time something took didn't matter anymore. He was never leaving this place.

Then Bub stopped at a particularly dark patch of tunnel.

Looking down to his feet, Hector saw that the ground ceased to continue in front of them. They stood at the edge of a precipice that stretched into the endless black below.

A red glow swelled from the depths, rising with a churning grind that filled the air.

Was this the lake of fire Hector's abuelita used to warn him of as a child? He considered the thought, but he felt no heat. His breath still plumed from the cold.

The glow and grind ascended. This was no lake of fire. It was industry.

A towering cogwheel of blackened steel emerged from the nothingness below. It throbbed with the red glow that seemed to power its functions. Fixed upon the gear's face were openings, entrances the size of the tunnels, leading to more shadow. Its mechanical teeth seemed to grind against nothing but the darkness as it spun.

At first, it rotated slowly, like a Ferris wheel, then fast, like the cylinder of a revolver in a game of Russian roulette. Empty chambers sped by as they stood on the edge, folding atop one another then dissipating into shadow. New ones formed only to vanish back into nothing moments later. It was an infinity wheel of entrances to Hell's deepest tunnels.

The miserable hum that had permeated the caverns was now at full volume. No longer an indiscernible blend, individual voices hung like clouds of dust from the hooves of this steel horse that charged on undeterred.

god help please i'm sorry tell them sorry it hurts lord please

Each word drifted out of existence with the whir of the wheel. New voices arose from the passing chambers, dying as quickly as they came. Mad libs of unrequited prayers for mercy swirled around Hector.

pain forgive me jesus stop tell them please i'm sorry

The mechanism halted without additional noise or recoil, and they entered the chamber in front of them.

HECTOR HEARD the twang of arrows before they even entered. The tunnel opened into a vast concrete room, a stark contrast to the preceding cavernous rock.

Gray walls. Gray floors. Gray ceiling. Right angles. Flat and dull.

A square column stretched high to the ceiling, its top obscured from Hector's view. Around it, the cave crawlers—the source of the twangs that had first captured Hector's attention—danced like pagans around a fire.

The small creatures skipped and howled, launching three arrows at a time from their quivers at the unseen target above. They cheered and hollered with each hit, then scrambled for better vantage points to continue their cruel sport.

Their legs, resembling the scrawny, gray arms of children smeared with black soot, ended in small hands used as feet, propelling their bodies across the concrete floor. Draped in gray cloaks that swayed like sea anemones, their bony frames darted to and fro. Skeletal arms with curled talons drew bows and fired with glee. Long beaks protruded from under their hoods, revealing dead, predatory eyes that snapped to Hector as they noticed him.

They cawed and whistled to one another in a frantic shift of targets.

New flesh.

New flesh!

Pulling arrows from their quivers, the creatures loaded their bows.

"Shit!" Hector managed to blurt out, ducking and covering as arrows rained down on him. But each struck with only the impact of a Nerf dart, falling to the floor with an anticlimactic *clack.*

The cave crawlers murmured amongst themselves.

Not dead.

Yet.

Not dead yet.

Then returned to firing arrows at their previous target.

Bub brought a loose fist to his mouth and coughed. The cave crawlers immediately ceased firing and stood at attention.

We are sorry.

Forgive us.

Hail Beelzebub.

We only play.

Fun. We have fun.

Each spoke like a child, sorry only because they were caught in the act. The patter of their little hand-feet faded as they disappeared into the tunnels.

The column began to lower, grinding into the floor as if by an unseen crank. Bit by bit, its top neared the ground. As it descended, Hector saw that it was a man who had been the target of the cave crawlers' cruel game.

The man was young but gaunt as a seasoned beggar, forever stuck at a decrepit twenty-five. He sat naked, knees to chest, hands over his head, horrible scars littering his flesh. Small arrows protruded from his body and face, and dark purple bags sagged beneath his eyes. Gray blood oozed from his wounds in a thin paste, hardening to dust before it could fall.

The column halted a short distance from the ground, the man continuing to cower upon it. His body was a tattered remnant of his former self. Yet, Hector felt an unmistakable pull, a tug at the tangled knot just below his heart. He knew this man —it was his father, forever in pain, forever twenty-five, unchanged since the last day they had spent together.

Bub watched. These moments were everything to him. Head tilted back, he closed his eyes and inhaled deep, basking in the flawless execution of his plan.

The man's eyes brimmed with sadness, weighing down his sunken cheeks below his emaciated jaw. He sat curled, arrows studding his body like branches, from which gray paste seeped and withered. His limbs, crooked and petrified, resisted as he tried to straighten them, stuck in a perpetual state of cower.

"Dad," Hector said. He barely knew the man in life, but seeing him like this—it was like he finally understood him.

As his dad's lips parted to speak, a crust as thick as gravel crumbled away. "You're—you're so big. Look at you." Then panic set in. "But you can't be here. You're not supposed to be here." He turned to Bub for an answer, who only smiled.

A single tear cut through the grime on his cheek, down the jagged angles of his once boyish face, wilting to dust as it reached his jaw. In a voice hardly above a whisper, he asked, "What did you do?"

Hector was unsure if he was talking to him, Bub, or himself.

His dad again tried to straighten his limbs. Arrows splintered. Bones snapped, piercing through his ashen skin.

He had been stuck like that for far too long, his body having forgotten how to be upright. As new bones cracked and fractured from his attempts, the previous ones mended, returning him to his huddled state. Against his will, he remained cowering, albeit in a slightly different position.

He bellowed in frustration, then resigned himself to defeat. "You know they don't let you lose your mind here?"

Hector watched his dad try once more to straighten his back. Bricks of vertebrae jutted through skin.

"The things they do to your body... You forget what it's like to not be in agony, but it's the mind they don't ever let break. I pray for insanity every day, but it's all so crystal clear," his dad said. "They never let you forget your life or those you left behind."

Hector was in no mood for a pity party. "Why did you do it?" he snapped back.

"Do what?"

Hector couldn't believe what he had just heard. "*Do what?* Gamble my soul to this asshole!"

"Is that what he told you?" his dad asked, shifting his eyes toward Bub.

"It's what I know," Hector said with authority. "Because of you, the girl I love is probably dead, my best friend is going to spend the rest of his life in prison, and I'm here—in Hell!— to become just like you." He looked upon his father's limbs, crooked and bent in malunion, twisted every which way. "I've always been just like you."

"Hector." His dad's head rose with a series of loud cracks. "I can never make any of this right. I couldn't in life, and I can't in death. All I can say is—"

"Don't even say it," Hector interrupted. "I don't want to hear it."

"I'm sorry. I'm so *fucking sorry*," his dad said, closing his eyes.

"Are you?" Hector's eyes glazed with tears. "Then why did you leave? Why did you leave me and Mom all alone?" He took a breath, trying to compose himself. "You could have...could have come to visit on weekends. On holidays. Anything! You didn't have to live with us. You didn't even have to live in the same state. But you didn't have to go away forever."

His dad opened his eyes and looked at Hector like his son was the first spring day after a long winter. Everything that had come before this moment faded to the back of his mind. It was the realization that he was seeing his boy again. "You said you're just like me. Well, you're not. You are your own person."

Bub laughed. "Very convenient. Shifting the blame."

His dad didn't acknowledge the comment, not even with a glance. His focus was on Hector. He stared deep into the face of his son. "What I mean is, I can see it in your eyes. You're not like me. There's life there. There's a spark. Even now, in this forsaken place, I can see it."

Hector couldn't control the tears that streamed down his face. It was the little boy, the one who loved to watch cartoons with his dad, the one who still wore his father's chain around his neck, who then asked, "But why did you go away?"

"I'm a coward," his dad said, hanging his head. "My relationship with your mother scared me. Being a father scared me. I scared me. I'm just a coward."

Bub scoffed, disgusted.

Hector knew what it meant to be scared, to run, to hurt the ones he loved. He hated that about himself. He hated it in his dad too. But he understood.

For the first time since he was a small child, Hector felt lighter, like a weight had been lifted. He didn't consciously decide to forgive his dad. He had no choice in the matter. It simply overcame him. Something unseen within himself communicated to his body and mind that it was time to move on.

Hector wiped his eyes with the backs of his hands and took a deep breath. "Okay," he said. "It's okay."

"I'm sorry, what?" Bub said, baffled. "That's it? All is forgiven?"

His dad didn't say a word, only smiled.

Hector was still not in the smiling mood. "You need to tell me. Why did this happen? What was the deal you made? Why did you gamble my soul?"

Taking a moment to gather his thoughts, his dad said, "Hector, what I'm about to tell you is not an excuse. It's just a fact. Okay?"

Hector nodded, braced himself.

A smirk returned to Bub's lips.

His dad took a deep breath, then exhaled a small plume of dust. A rib cracked from the minor effort, but he paid it no mind. He looked Hector straight in the eyes and said, "I was drunk."

"Incredible," said Bub. "Absolutely incredible."

Hector's dad continued, "I...I didn't think it was real. The last thing I remember was standing on the overpass looking down at the river. Then I find myself in *his* bar, still drunk, and I thought I was hallucinating. We sat. We talked. He said he would give me anything I wanted. Anything at all. I only thought of one thing. I didn't know what I was doing. I just wasn't thinking. I didn't think it was real, until it was too late."

Hector looked at his father, a man frozen in time at twenty-five—the same age as himself. He wondered if he was capable of doing something as stupid and as thoughtless as his dad had done.

He didn't have to wonder long. He knew the sickness and the possession that occurred when it reached a boil.

How many times had he hurt others in an effort to dull his own pain, only to have those same three words to offer in explanation? *I was drunk.* Intoxication was a misguided form of self-preservation, like burning down a house to protect it from a flood. The sickness tricks you into thinking there is only one option. Night after night.

Hector knew it wasn't an excuse. But he also knew the sickness. Intimately.

Empathy and rage battled for dominance within him, and Hector's forgiveness faltered. He could forgive his dad for his addictions. He could even forgive him for the crummy childhood that shaped his crummy adulthood, but all the empathy in the world couldn't save Tommy and Sammie.

"You're fucking serious? You thought it was fake? Have you fucking seen this guy?" he said, pointing to Bub.

Bub removed his tinted glasses at the mention. His skin had begun to darken like dirty water, and his faceted eyes burned scarlet. The human costume he wore was slowly fading as interest was lost in this family reunion.

Hector's dad pleaded with him to understand. "You say that now, but think back to when all of this seemed impossible, when all you knew was the day-to-day, sun up, sun down, work and wait for the bus, repeat. The first time you saw behind the curtain, didn't you think you were crazy? That you were hallucinating?"

Hector recalled the mouse that had told him he was going to Hell just days prior. Turned out the mouse was right. "Okay, I see what you mean."

"When he asked me what I wanted, I went along with it. I don't know why. Maybe part of me did want it to be real. I didn't catch all the terms and conditions, it all happened so fast, but if I had known—"

"You didn't *catch all the terms and conditions*?" asked Hector. "He had three days to torture me and my friends and push me to suicide. Those were the terms and conditions you agreed to."

"Oh."

"Yeah, 'Oh,'" Hector repeated. "What was it that you wanted? What was so important to even pretend to gamble my soul for?"

"I wanted what any father wants. I wanted you to have a better life than I did." He looked at Hector with eyes that had never known a moment's peace in life or in Hell. "It was a bet for you to find happiness, to not end up like me. It's what I gave him my soul for, it's what I wagered yours on. I wanted you to not find yourself drunk and standing on the edge of an overpass, staring down into the river, thinking it was your only option left. I just wanted you to be better than me."

Hector stood as vulnerable as a hatchling. For the first time since he was a small boy, it felt like he had a father.

"I might have had a better chance of doing all that if you were around, if you showed me how someone can get better and be better. I needed a dad," Hector said. "I needed you there."

"I never wanted any of this for you. I wanted to be there. I wanted to watch you grow. But I lost. I lost to myself." His father coughed up a small cloud of dust. Gray blood seeped from his mouth. "You're all I think about here. Playing silly games. Watching movies. Those were the only bright points of my life. Do you remember taking walks in the summer before bed? You used to point at the moon and the stars and ask what they were, ask if you could touch them. You were so small. Everything amazed you. I love you, Hector. You're my everything. I failed you."

Hector stepped forward, placing a hand on his father's fractured fingers, crooked and cold. He was transported back to a time when anything seemed possible and the future was unwritten.

"I love you too, Dad," he said, a smile in his heart.

Bub scoffed. "Oh, for fuck's sake. We're done here."

With that, Bub's arm transformed into a black vine, bristled like the thorned leg of a fly. It shot past Hector and impaled his dad through the chest and out his back. Black thorns burst from his flesh like porcupine needles as he was lifted in the air.

Hector watched in horror as his father hung like a tangled marionette and wailed like an infant skinned alive. In the dark of the tunnels, he heard the cave crawlers giggling. A double *thwap* of arrows echoed from an unseen vantage point.

The first pierced his dad's cheek and exited from its twin, leaving his mouth skewered. The second came straight for the side of Hector's neck.

Again, the arrow fell lifeless to the floor. This time, however, Hector felt its bite.

He brought two fingers to the sting. Red. Dark red. Tinged with gray.

Nearly dead.

He is nearly dead!

Nearly dead! Nearly dead!

The cave crawlers cheered from the shadows, and Bub's nostrils flared at the familiar scent of blood.

Hordes of flies rioted within Bub like a packed stadium, crawling from his mouth and into the shifting folds of shadow that had become his body. All remnants of the man with the tinted glasses were gone. No trace of angelic beauty remained.

Hector looked up in awe at the horror now towering above him. Bub was a black mass of nightmarish anatomy, insectile and insidious, a crown of teeth upon his head.

His dad, curled and twisted like a crab impaled on a stick, rose higher as Bub's vines grew. The arrow that pierced his cheeks had passed through his tongue, reducing his screams to whimpers. But one garbled syllable managed to escape his mouth: "Run."

Hector obliged.

Bub's vine retracted from Hector's dad, letting his body collapse to the ground like a bundle of broken sticks.

"God…" Bub's mouth pulsed like an amorphous sea creature floating in the trench. Palps and labium whipped the air, tasting the surrounding fear. "…is gone."

Hector sprinted toward the tunnel entrances, but their darkness was infested with the sounds of crawling and slithering things. Fangs slick with salivation shimmered like half-buried diamonds within. He had nowhere to run.

Looking back to see his father ripped and torn like a paper snowflake, the key danced in his pocket once more.

The chorus of flies and cave crawlers declared their victory.

The new flesh has bled!

he is soon ourssss

God is dead! Hail the new God!

all is soon ourssss

"His Word is broken," Bub bellowed. "You belong to me. All belongs to me. I am God. I am no one. *I am.*"

Hector figured now was as good a time as ever to try to figure out what Gretchen's plan was. He pulled out the key and held it tightly in his fist, waiting for something—anything—to happen. But before it could, Bub's vine snapped around his wrist.

The thorns could not fully penetrate, suggesting Hector's

body still clung to life back in Chicago, yet they clenched with no intention of release, tearing at his skin.

"Come. Worship at the feet of your savior," Bub called.

Hector dug in his heels and fought, but he was being reeled in like a fish. The key thrashed in his grip as Bub dragged him closer with increasing velocity.

Then he hit a wall, or, more specifically, a door.

The impact jarred Hector free, thorns slashing at his wrist as he fell backward to the ground.

They both stared, dumbfounded, at the door standing alone between them.

"What is this..." Bub said, his monstrous form subduing from sheer confusion.

Hector, never known to be an exceptionally bright man, did know that key plus door sometimes equaled open.

He leapt to his feet and shoved the key into the lock. The door opened, and he hurried inside.

48

Sammie clenched the knife so tight, her knuckles threatened to burst through her skin.

She wished they would.

The thought of using her own reddened bones to shred Austin's jugular made her adrenaline pump harder. There was only one way to survive this—become an animal. She was practically foaming at the mouth, her body tensed like a slingshot, pulled tight and ready to snap.

In the darkened kitchen, Austin's knife scraped along the wall, then the tabletop in the room's center, searching for Sammie.

He ripped a chair from the table, sending it clattering across the room, and delivered a fury of stabs underneath. He laughed, tracing circles with his knife atop the table, attempting to fill the room with fear until she drowned in it.

Sammie remained tucked in the corner between refrigerator and wall, listening, waiting for her own opportunity.

The pigeons' assault continued. One after another, they bombarded the glass. More cracks had developed, but the window would not surrender.

Then Sammie heard what must have been an especially heavy pigeon slam against the glass, accompanied by a crunching splinter. The window remained intact, but progress had been made.

Silence. No pigeons. No scraping of Austin's knife. His steps were inaudible.

She could practically feel the skin around her knuckles split and give birth to bone. She was scared, but she was ready.

From across the kitchen, his voice called out, "We don't have to play this little game, you know."

Sammie held her breath.

"You can put down whatever little weapon you're holding, and we can just talk." His voice moved closer. "There is *so much* he can do for us both. Why fight it?"

Tiny taps began at the window.

Sammie stole quick glances at the sound. Tiny creatures wielding tiny hammers appeared to be pounding away at the fractured glass.

Rats. Rats with rocks, she thought, squinting at the sight.

The tapping intensified.

Sammie heard a breath that wasn't her own. Austin was near.

She raised her knife, poised on the balls of her feet, ready for a swift move around the fridge and the right moment to strike.

The floor in front of the refrigerator groaned. Mr. Lopez's bane.

Sammie had her moment.

With a primal scream, she charged out, knife raised high— only to be met by the freezer door flung into her face.

"Like a fucking cartoon!" Austin cackled as she fell backward.

He pounced, knocking a dazed Sammie to the ground while her knife clattered across the linoleum.

The taps became frenzied.

"We keep ending up like this, huh?" Austin's legs straddled her, his knees jammed into her stomach. With his long, thin knife to her throat, he hissed, "*You have no idea how fucking hard I am right now.*"

He traced along the crease of her neck with his blade, just hard enough to draw out a delicate lace of red pearls. Sammie closed her eyes and held them tight.

She felt what is truly experienced only once in life. A unique sensation—that frigid hand of dread around her heart—it communicated just one thing to Sammie: *You're going to die.*

Austin reared back his arm, flipping the knife in his hand so he could drive it into her throat like a stake.

Outside the window, a choir of feral yowls blared. Austin couldn't help but turn his head to the sound.

Then the glass shattered.

An onslaught of cats, rats, and pigeons poured in through the busted window in a nearly indistinguishable stream of teeth, claws, and wings. It hit Austin like a wave, sweeping him off Sammie before he had time to react.

The rats went for the tongue, the cats tore at his throat, and the pigeons made quick work of Austin's remaining eye, clutching the red ribbons in their mouths like olive branches.

Legions converged, savagely tearing at his body to prevent escape or retaliation. Amidst the brutal assault, he managed a gurgled scream and scrambled to his feet, only to stagger and flail like a man on fire, before collapsing under the relentless onslaught of the animal army.

Through the darkness, Sammie winced at the mess of guts and flaps of flesh that used to be Austin.

The animals had been somewhat merciful in their carnage, using their predatory instincts to end his life as quickly as their small teeth and claws would allow. All in all, an excruciating way to go, but Sammie knew it could have been worse. They could have started with his penis.

One of the cats leapt up and swatted the light switch with a paw.

Half of Austin's face was pecked to the bone, his mouth a lipless gape of red. An orange cat, startled by the light, removed its entire head from Austin's throat. Its face was smeared with gore, like a child's covered in icing after their first birthday cake. An unrecognizable piece of anatomy dangled from its mouth.

All the animals, stained red with their earned war paint, turned their attention to Sammie, who forced a smile, and said, "Hi. Thank you."

Two familiar felines brought up the rear as generals, swatting away shards of window before settling in the vacant frame. It was Brandy and Bubblegum.

Each nodded and purred at Sammie, their majesty rivaling that of the cats of ancient dogma. Overwhelmed by the display, Sammie's eyes welled with tears. All she could manage was, "I fucking love cats."

Sitting atop Bubblegum like an eight-legged Napoleon was Bandini. He quickly surveyed the scene, then turned to Sammie. "We need to find Hector."

49

Tommy was amazed at how few times he had to stop running to almost throw up. Just twice.

Perhaps the past decade of drinking and smoking hadn't done too much damage after all, he thought. But as he rounded the corner onto Drake Avenue, a stabbing pain beneath his left rib cage tampered that notion. "*Fuuuu—*" His exasperated breath plumed out like exhaust from an old car.

His jog slowed to a hobble. Clutching his side, he pushed on toward their apartment.

"Hey! I'm back!" Tommy shouted, bursting through the door. "Does no one answer their fucking phones anymore?" His own had managed to make one call each to Hector and Sammie before dying.

The stillness of the apartment throbbed in his ears.

"Where's that stupid spider..." he muttered, making his way to the kitchen. "Sammie? Hector, you here?"

As Tommy went to check the fridge for beer, he remembered

two things: his last run to Armitage Food did not result in beer, and *Fuck that fridge*. He settled for a glass of water.

His phone flashed a lightning bolt as he plugged it in, the battery too drained to power on. He leaned against the sink, pouring cold water down his throat. He felt antsy, like he should be doing something, but he didn't know what.

Smoke. The word flashed in his mind like it had a habit of doing every forty-five minutes or so. He patted himself down. *Kevin.* The bus stop thing. Tommy wished he hadn't wasted his last cigarette trying and failing to prove a point.

He checked his room for a straggler—nothing. Then Hector's—nope. He rummaged through the ashtray by the kitchen window. Not a proud moment, but he had resorted to this under less dire circumstances. Every cigarette was smoked to the filter, not a single drag left.

He went outside to check the porch windowsill. There were a few, but those not frozen were soggy and brown from the snow. "*Come on.*" Tommy walked to the porch's end, slumped over the railing, and looked up at the moon. He thought empty thoughts, the most comforting thoughts of all.

In his peripherals, a distant shadow swayed. He squinted and narrowed his eyes through the darkness to try to make out what it was. It was something on the tracks. No, it was above the tracks, suspended in air. It was dangling from the tree. It was—

"*Shit.*"

Tommy bolted down the steps to the sidewalk, then abruptly changed course at full speed. He slid, fell, and scrambled back up the steps, dashing through the apartment to the kitchen. He skidded to a stop at his phone, pressing the power button; the same lightning bolt icon remained.

"Come the fuck on, you worthless piece of fucking—"

It powered on. Tommy performed an impatient shuffle as it booted up, then made the call.

"911, what's your emergency?"

Phone against his ear, he whipped open drawers for anything sharp.

"I need an ambulance! 1752 North Drake!"

Centipede dick. He remembered stabbing the demon's member. *The fuck did I drop that knife?*

"Is that an apartment or house? And what is the emergency?"

Hector's room. Found it.

"Apartment! But it's the tracks! The tracks right next door! The old ones!"

Something to stand on. I need something to stand on. He fumbled a chair from beneath their plastic kitchen table, shaking off accumulated bills and hooded sweatshirts.

"Sir, what is the emergency?"

Tommy sprinted down the hall to the front door, chair in one hand, knife in the other. The phone began to slip from between his ear and shoulder.

"He hung himself! The fucking idiot hung himself! Hurry up!"

As he cleared the porch steps two at a time, the phone fell from his chin, leaving the operator's follow-up question, "Sir, who hung themselves?" to be answered by no one but the wind.

50

Doors. Nothing but doors.

Over the past few days, Hector had borne witness to the vast incomprehensibles of his native universe. But these doors, this immense hallway, formed the true infinite from which all else sprung.

In their presence, Heaven, Hell, and all the endless layers of existence blind to the human eye were reduced to a raindrop tapping outside the window of an empty room, indistinguishable and unfelt. In the presence of the hall's great mouth, every petty encumbrance of Hector's life faded, and he was swallowed whole, depersonalized and brought to the brink of madness. He could barely recall how he even arrived.

But his memory was jolted as his sprint deteriorated to a slog. The blood in his veins churned, and he felt heavy, as if he was hardening with concrete. His transformation into a permanent resident of Hell put his new flesh into a state of flux. It was being prepared, morphing into something malleable and regenerative, primed for an eternity of pain.

Checking behind, Hector expected to see a barrage of

thorned vines descending upon him, but Bub had paused his pursuit.

Less monstrous now in both manner and build, Bub stood at the entrance, tracing a finger along the door, and said, "Interesting."

Hector tightened his fist around the key. He could feel its energy pulse in his grip. Somehow he knew it was the only thing tethering him to his body back in Chicago—to life. In an act of instinctual impulse, he shoved the key into his mouth and forced it down his gullet.

Okay, the catbug thing gave you the key, you just swallowed it for some reason, now you're here. Now what? What the fuck is the plan?

Bub stepped into the hall.

Hector shuffled backward. "This—this is what I was trying to tell you," he said, gesturing to the doors. "It's never-ending. Everything you know—and I mean *everything*—fits behind just one door. Just *one* door. The Heaven-Hell stuff, the torture and the destroying, it's all over nothing. It's like fighting over a blade of grass. Don't you see? None of it matters."

Bub was silent as he examined the doors, enthralled with how they lined the walls like bricks, even paving the floor and ceiling above him, stretching endlessly in both directions.

With a snap of his vine, he opened one. Then he opened another, and another.

Hector considered opening one himself to escape, but the noises from behind these others made him reconsider what the worse option really was.

Each door opened and closed with new sounds. Wicked voices speaking in wicked languages, snarling beasts cackling over the cries of children, what sounded like a semi-truck fucking a moaning woodchipper, Hector could only guess at the accompanying visuals.

The doors seemed to know who was opening them and

what to show, as if they wanted to trigger an emotional response. But the expression on Bub's face never changed. Brief glances behind each were all he needed. Until the last door.

Horrible screams and pleas for mercy spilled out the moment it was opened, and a smile grew on Bub's face. The voice was muddled by suffering, but it was clear to Hector who the screams belonged to.

It was Bub. A different Bub.

The screams curdled and blistered. They were pathetic. Sniveling.

Whatever was happening behind that door to this other version of himself brought Bub to genuine laughter. It seemed as though he could stand there and watch it all day. Still smiling, he shook his head and shut the door, impressed.

"You think you've seen it all, but then the bastard really amazes you with just how fucking selfish and cruel he can be." Bub locked eyes with Hector. "There's still so much I can learn from him."

"W-what?" Hector said, his voice cracking. "That's seriously what you—"

He was interrupted by a vine snapping around his neck and lifting him in the air, carrying him toward Bub.

"What a gift this is. All these versions of me. I'll build an army. We'll go door to door. Destroying *everything*. Even God will not be safe."

"But why..." Hector choked.

"Because you've brought me to a buffet, and I'm *hungry*."

Then, strained and beaten, a voice called out from behind, "Put him down."

It was Hector's dad. Having chewed out the arrow that pierced his cheeks and tongue, he was verbal once more.

He dragged his contorted body in like a crumpled piece of

paper. Each movement was agony, accompanied by the sound of cracking bones and splintering skin.

"Dad," Hector said through a crushed windpipe.

Bub laughed, letting Hector fall to the floor.

This tumbleweed of flesh inched past and hauled himself in front of his son. "Please. Let him go," he pleaded. "Leave him alone."

"Absolutely not," Bub replied.

Hector watched this man he barely knew stand against Hell itself to protect him. He felt a primitive sense of security behind his dad, as all children should, and as he never had before—but it would be short-lived.

"This is my fault," his dad said. "It's my fault he's here. He doesn't belong here."

Bub had no patience left for pathos. Before another word could be uttered, he launched a thorned vine straight through the bottom of Hector's dad's throat. The vine exited the back of his neck, continued through Hector's thigh, and with a whip-like crack, tore itself free from both, leaving carnage in its wake.

With his dad's head now hanging from its stump by a single ribbon of gray flesh, Hector looked down at his own leg, taking a moment to fully comprehend the damage. He stared at the thick strands of beef fraying from where the vine had exited. Then, the pain came.

TOMMY COULDN'T TELL whether Hector was alive or dead by the time he began to saw through the rope with their dull kitchen knife.

As it slowly started to give, the shades of blue on Hector's face also began to darken. Over the sound of his knife's friction, he heard the buzz of a fly, then a swarm.

A cloud of black flies hovered in front of Tommy as he

sawed. They formed themselves into a black square and hissed, *waaatchhh.*

Upon the black square, a scene began to flicker. It was Hector and Bub on the tracks. The scene had taken place only a short time before Tommy's arrival.

"Fucking get the fuck out of here!" Tommy tried to ignore whatever this antic was, but the sounds of the scene became impossible to ignore.

I need your guarantee that you won't hurt Sammie and Tommy

Only one

No, both

No, one

Tommy's knife slowed without him even realizing. He watched the scene unfold.

Who will it be?

Please

Choose

He nearly stopped cutting altogether, watching Hector struggle with his choice. Then the answer came.

Sammie.

Tommy almost dropped the knife. The flies broke formation and swirled around him in laughter, hissing doubt into his ears.

he isssss no friennnd

let hiim dieeeee

he wouuld let youuu

The chair Tommy stood on rocked and wobbled on the uneven surface of the tracks. He watched a sick bile form at Hector's lips. This was his friend, or at least he thought it was. Life would go on without him, Tommy thought. Maybe this was for the best. Maybe it was just Hector's time. Maybe now was Tommy's time to live and grow.

"Nah, fuck you guys," he said to the flies, returning his knife to the rope with amplified resolve. Tommy had a brother in

Hector, and Hector loved Sammie. He understood the choice was not easy. He would have given his own life for them to be happy. It was a fucked ultimatum, and he needed to direct his anger at the one who forced it.

When the rope finally snapped, Hector's head caught the seat of Tommy's chair as he fell.

"Shit."

The flies laughed and mocked the pair before sailing off into the night.

Tommy knelt by Hector's side, unsure of what to do next.

Where the fuck are the paramedics? He scanned the landscape for any sign of flashing lights.

At a loss, he did the first thing that came to his mind. He prayed.

A clumsy prayer, not based on any dogma and directed to no deity. Though he now knew some sort of god existed for certain, he didn't know who he was, and he didn't care. It was a prayer for himself, to himself, casting hope into the black of night.

Please be okay. Please be okay. You'll be okay. You'll be okay. You will be okay.

He touched two fingers to Hector's purpled neck like he'd seen in movies. It was cold, but it was also January. He had no idea what he was doing.

Then he saw the lights. They pulsed red against the darkness, making their way down the street.

Holy fuck holy fucking fuck holy fuck

Hector's mind belonged to the pain. Each thought flared red in agony. Propping himself against the wall of doors, he screamed at the sight of his carved-open leg.

Hell was built upon flesh and blood. There was no ethereal state of being, no transcendence here, just a continuation of life's suffering cranked to eleven. His scream was music to Bub's ears as this mutilation meant only one thing.

"You have died, Hector Ghouseau." Bub's face strobed nightmarish features, his jaw malforming into great mandibles, his skull protruding and segmenting into jagged peaks. "Welcome to eternity."

There was nowhere for Hector to run. The doors were his only option.

He swung open the door he was leaning on and collapsed. With his leg held together by mere ligaments, he clawed over to the door's threshold and—

AN ENTIRE COLONY, a prison planet, composed only of Hectors. They toiled, tilling a vast field under a purple sky, wailing as a massive irrigation system sprayed their naked bodies with a slick yellow oil.

One of the Hectors struck something hard in the soil, intensifying the cries of the others. From the dirt, a piss-yellow gelatinous object resembling an oversized Tic Tac wriggled out. Flaccid like a defective dildo, it sprouted six legs, one of its ends splitting into a mouth with large square teeth, chattering like they were cold.

The small creature scurried up the Hector's leg as he screamed for help, but the others knew to keep their heads down, despite the terror in their eyes. An unseen speaker boomed a relentless message: "Work. No rest. Work. No rest." The instructions were clear: do not help.

The Tic Tac dildo now clung to the Hector's face, shoving its legs into his eyes and mouth for grip. It reared itself back and thrust its chattering teeth upon his nose. Blood spewed in all directions. The Hector's face was left a gaping mess of red in a matter of seconds. The creature burrowed deeper into the gnawed flesh, kneading and circling to find the right spot, before finally settling in for warmth and rest.

One of the other workers looked up to the sky, perhaps to pray for mercy or deliverance, and made eye contact with the strange being peering at them from what appeared to be the bottom of a door frame.

"He is here! Our savior! We are free! Praise Him! Praise Him! He has come to save—"

HECTOR SLAMMED IT SHUT.

He reached for the next door but was stopped by a clasp of thorns around his wrist.

"Give me the key," Bub ordered, dragging Hector over his father's crumpled body.

Hector's dad wheezed from his neck stump as he was smeared with the stringy red entrails of his son's leg.

"The key," Bub reiterated.

Through gritted teeth and a whole lot of pain, Hector said, "I can't."

"You can and will. The game is over. I won. Now it's time to go to Disneyland. Give it to me."

"No, I—I can't. I swallowed it."

"You swallowed it?"

Hector's face contorted in agony.

Bub smiled. "You do love making things harder for yourself, don't you?" He bent down and put a finger to Hector's lips. "Open wide."

The finger crept inside Hector's mouth. It worked its way down to the bottom of his throat, scraping and prodding as he choked.

Then Bub retracted his finger. "Let's try the other way first, shall we?" He unzipped Hector's jacket with care and lifted up his shirt. "How pretty."

Hector whimpered as Bub's finger grazed his soft underbelly. Then, without warning, the finger ripped into his navel. He shrieked accordingly.

The finger stretched and grew, navigating through layers of fat and muscle.

"Let's just take a look around in here," Bub said, fingering Hector's guts with all the delicacy of a teenage boy in the back-seat of a car. "Hmm, not here. Let's try *here*."

The shrieks continued.

"I'M NOT GETTING A PULSE," the paramedic said.

"I think you're checking the wrong side of the neck," said the other.

"It's either side. Don't do this right now."

Tommy paced, listening to the paramedics bicker, his puffs of breath red from the emergency lights strobing on the street below. They couldn't have been any older than he was, stumbling up the overpass like it was their first day on the job.

"I think he's dead," one muttered, trying to keep this secret from Tommy.

"I think you're right. We should get him out of here."

Tommy heard every word. "Are you kidding me? That's it? You didn't do anything! No CPR? No shot of adrenaline to the heart? Do a *Pulp Fiction*! Do *something!*"

"A pulp fiction?" asked one of the paramedics.

"Sir, adrenaline shots are not used for instances like this. Please step back," instructed the other.

"Is that what a pulp fiction is?"

The other leaned in and whispered, "I think we should do CPR."

"I think you're right."

While the paramedics attempted revival, Tommy took matters into his own hands. He rushed down the overpass and into the back of their ambulance, rummaging through drawers and compartments. He wasn't quite sure what to look for until a name clicked in his mind.

Dominic O'Malley.

The name of a sixth-grade classmate he hadn't thought of in over a decade.

Dominic O'Malley.

Dominic had a peanut allergy and used to carry an EpiPen with him everywhere he went. Tommy had once paid him a dollar to eat a Reese's cup, leading to a panicked teacher administering the EpiPen into Dominic's leg. He remembered it was yellow like a bee. He also remembered being suspended for that.

Found it.

He skimmed the directions on the yellow cylinder. Seemed easy enough, so he grabbed two for good measure. It was time to *Pulp Fiction*.

HECTOR PRAYED for a death that would never come.

Bub's finger scraped and prodded his organs, leaking their unknown fluids and tearing the softest of tissue. It slithered through his anatomy like a snake through the weeds. The passage of time was nonexistent. Each second hung heavy.

"Ah, there it is." Bub wrapped his finger around the key in Hector's upper esophagus, just below the throat. "I suppose I took the long way."

His finger retraced its excruciating path back through Hector and pulled the key out from his navel. Bub held it up and laughed, amused at the power this small object held. All existence was his for the taking.

Hector stared up at the ceiling of doors, unable to even blink. Shallow breaths and gurgled groans were all he could assemble. The pain had coalesced and spread through every inch of his body. Eventually, it would heal, and Bub would do it all over again. Rinse and repeat.

"Drop that key!" a small voice yelled from the doorway back to Hell.

Bub whipped his head around so fast that his layers of shadow lagged behind. "Gretchen," he said, still smiling.

She had waited outside the door, scared, watching the events unfold and dreading what Bub might do if the plan failed. But seeing him with the key, she knew it was time to act.

Her nose twitched and her ears flattened. She took a step forward and said, "You're a real dick, even for Hell, and you'll never be respected like Lucifer."

"Oh, Gretchen, sweet Gretchen." Bub strolled toward her, and said, "I am going to hurt you in ways that will set new precedents for pain in Hell."

She braced herself, then, with all her might, shouted, "*NOW!*"

With that, every door as far as Hector could see flung open, and out charged an army of seemingly random soldiers from each one.

Through pain-blurred vision, Hector watched the weird little catbug command this horde of misfits. They were her. All of them. Each shared her spark—packaged in various shapes and sizes.

There were Gretchens identical to their leader, Gretchens fully cat or fully insect, and Gretchens Hector recognized only as Gretchens through an odd sense of déjà vu. Though their appearances varied wildly—from a cloud of translucent gas, to a tiny clown car with one square wheel, to even one that looked a bit like Hector wearing a pair of cat ears—he knew them as Gretchens, nonetheless.

It didn't matter their shape or size. With numbers so great, they overwhelmed Bub.

"YOU TREACHEROUS CUNT!" he screamed. Whips of shadow sprang from his body in all directions at his assailants, but there were simply too many.

So Bub unleashed a swarm. His mouth opened wide until it nearly consumed his own head. Flies billowed out like the dense pollution of a smokestack, engulfing some of the Gretchens, who flailed like soldiers covered in napalm. The flies picked them clean, leaving only bones with stubborn strands of flesh.

Then came the cavalry.

Out from a distant door charged a pack of large leaping crea-tures. They were covered in black cat fur with pointed ears and pink noses, but their bodies were amphibious in mode and structure. These giant catfrogs made quick work of the flies, lapping them up with unfurled tongues and bouncing around the corridor like acrobats.

One ambitious catfrog leapt onto the hood of the Gretchen clown car and charged Bub at full speed. Hector had never made it to high school physics, but he was pretty sure the amount of speed that little square-wheeled car was able to generate defied all logic. Upon collision, the catfrog launched itself at Bub's chest, taking him to the ground.

The Gretchens all pounced, ripping and tearing at Bub, twisting off limbs and gnawing at his neck and torso. When a Gretchen had claimed a sufficient piece of him, they darted back to their door, slamming it shut behind them. The plan was in motion: scatter Bub so he could never be made whole again.

The key fell from Bub's grip as he hit the ground. Shadow bled from him like exhaust. His scream crackled like a toaster in bathwater, bursting with unbridled rage rather than anguish.

Doors slammed shut amidst the chaos. An attack from Gretchen, especially like this, hadn't been a blip on Bub's radar. As quickly as it began, it ended, and all the Gretchens returned to their realities.

Gretchen's attack had required intricate planning. She had petitioned hundreds of the Gretchens from other realities, gathering a sizable force—despite not all being sympathetic. Since time passed differently inside the hall, her exhaustive recruitment efforts equaled mere hours outside of the corridor.

Gretchen wedged strands of her fortified fur in each door latch. Calloused and coarse from millennia spent in Hell, each strand was sturdy enough to keep the doors unlocked, allowing her soldiers to hear and heed her call while remaining imperceptible to Bub.

As the doors shut, they again locked from within, isolating each person in their own reality with their share of Bub.

Gretchen scratched at the bald patch on the inside of her leg and twitched her nose at the carnage, satisfied.

Bub's head inched toward Hector atop a slithering spinal cord that dripped wet with murk. His rage had faded, replaced by disgust. The monstrous features were gone, giving way to the quiet evil of the man with tinted glasses Hector had met in that bar on the edge of death just a few nights ago.

"You belong to me. You will *always* belong to me," Bub snarled, unimpressed with his own defeat. "This setback means nothing. Look at you. You're fucked. Your friends are fucked. Even in this place of endless possibility, despair is the standard. Everything trends *down* in time. Push your boulder. Reach the top. The laws that govern each reality, no matter how absurd, will eventually bring it back down *without fail.*"

Hector's insides were still rearranging, and his leg remained a carved Christmas ham, but his new flesh had adapted to the pain. Exhausted, he grunted at the slithering head and said, "Okay."

Hector strained to reach the knob above him, finally managing to swing the door open. As Bub's head neared, he seized it by its slick, black tail.

"Put me down!" it demanded.

Hector dragged himself to the edge, holding Bub out over the reality below.

Bub hissed, his face upside down to Hector's, "You're a fucking tragedy, and you always will be."

"Yeah," Hector said, "I know." Then he dropped the head from the purple sky down into the dirt, where fields of enslaved Hectors tilled for carnivorous dildos.

THE WORKER who had previously hailed Hector as their salvation looked to the sky again. Now withered and older, his long gray beard was one Hector could only dream of growing. He called out, "He has returned! You all called me insane, but He is back! We are saved! Saved!"

A younger worker who had been toiling over a particularly hard patch of dirt threw down his tool and pointed at Bub's slithering head. "The fuck is that?!" he asked, not unreasonably.

Bub's head imploded into a swarm of flies, a ravenous black cloud, and began to terrorize all the Hectors within its vicinity.

The withered worker screamed out to the heavens, "Our God! Why do you forsake u—"

Hector shut the door. There was no such thing as winning.

GRETCHEN DID her best to gather Hector's dad.

Using all her strength, she clamped her mantis claws around his ankle and dragged him to Hector, apologizing for any discomfort along the way. Then she mounted his head back onto his neck as best she could. He thanked her.

Sprawled out together like a crime scene, neither Hector nor his dad had words to articulate the present moment.

Perhaps one of these doors held an opportunity for them to start over, Hector thought—a chance to be a kid again watching TV under his father's arm. But as he studied the broken man beside him, he knew things could never be the same. All he could do was try to find his dad some peace. A better afterlife waited for him beyond one of the doors.

At first, his dad refused. "Are you kidding? I'm not going anywhere without you. Never again. Only way I'm going through one of those is if I'm following you."

"I'm not going through any," Hector replied.

"But you can't stay in—"

"I have to. I can't leave Hell—our reality. I need to know if Tommy and Sammie are okay—if there's a way back to them. I have to try."

"Then I'm staying too."

"No."

His dad's face sank.

"You didn't mean for any of this to happen, Dad. But it did. And we can't go back to before—" Hector stopped, unsure of his next words, "—to before you left. It's time you rest. I mean, c'mon, you're a human pretzel." He forced a smile at his dad's contorted body.

"I don't deserve to rest."

"Everyone does."

The corners of his dad's mouth drifted into a small smile, as if he had just heard a secret no one else knew. With a series of rips and cracks, he extended his twisted arm and placed a hand on Hector's cheek. "I think you're going to be okay," he said.

Hector pressed his face against his dad's hand and closed his eyes, letting the moment linger. His father's touch almost made him believe what he said.

He reached for the door next to where he had thrown Bub's head. With his flesh reforming and the pain in his leg and insides dulling, he pulled it open and propped himself against the frame to look inside.

"I think this is a good one," Gretchen said.

It was a place of unknown color and motion, vibrant and free. Hector felt its call. There were no discernible shapes or beings, only dashes of light that danced like paint strokes directed by an invisible hand. The art was never complete; streaks manifested and converged in a cycle of creation, death, and harmony. Hector wanted to join them, but he knew it wasn't his time. Not yet.

Instead, he turned to his dad and said, "It was nice to see you."

"Yeah," his dad replied, "it was."

Gretchen used all her weight to push Hector's dad to the door's threshold. Hector helped as best he could. Just before his dad could pass through, Hector stopped and said, "Wait."

He dug into his collar and removed the chain from his neck. The Saint Christopher pendant glistened in the door's lights. Placing it over his dad's head, he said, "This is yours."

His dad let the swaying chain dance over his fingers. "You kept it safe," he said. "All this time, you wore it?"

"Yeah. I guess I did."

"I promised to come back," his dad said, almost to himself. "I didn't keep up my end of the deal, huh?"

"No, I guess you didn't."

His dad clutched Saint Christopher in his hand. "I wish I could have seen you grow."

"Me too." Hector smiled.

Releasing the chain from his grip, his dad turned to Gretchen. "Excuse me. Can you take this off?"

Gretchen noted Hector's confusion but sensed no objection. She removed the chain from his dad's neck with her tail then gave it back to him.

He held it out in a hand decorated with scars upon scars. "Take it."

"Dad—"

"Just hold onto it. Until I see you again."

Hector said nothing. He took the chain and placed it back around his own neck. "Not going to promise this time?"

"No promises. But anything is possible, right?"

Hector looked past his father to the new spectrum of colors beyond the door. "It sure seems that way."

His dad signaled to Gretchen, and she resumed her push. "Be good, Hector."

"Bye, Dad."

His dad passed through the door, his broken body evaporating into the vast current of unnamable colors that swelled and coursed like shoreless waves.

Hector didn't know what became of his dad or if he carried the memory of his son into this place beyond form. All he knew was that peace radiated from behind the door. A sense of oneness flowed out into the corridor, putting Hector and Gretchen at ease for the first time in their lives. Hector was glad his dad was there.

He closed the door and collapsed on his back. Staring up at the ceiling of doors, among the infinite terminals, he felt there was a lesson in all this, but he struggled to identify it.

Gretchen appeared in his view. She twitched her nose, and asked, "You can't walk, right?"

Hector tried to get himself up on one leg. The effort sent renewed ripples of excruciation. "Right."

Gretchen nodded. "I'll go find something with wheels."

"Thank you for your help—with everything."

Gretchen perked up, not expecting the gratitude. Blushing, she said, "I'm just glad to not have to deal with Bub anymore."

"Yeah," Hector agreed. "But the doors he's behind now, what's he going to do to those realities?"

She considered the question, then said, "We did what we could. The others will do what they can."

"I guess you're right."

"You got the key?" she asked.

The key. Bub had dropped it but where did it—

It was in his hand. Had he been holding it the whole time? He didn't remember picking it up.

"Yeah, I got it."

"Okay, good. I'll be right back, then we'll figure it out from there. Hell's not such a bad place if you're not being tortured. And with Bub and Lucifer gone, maybe it's time for some changes."

Gretchen shuffled away, her tail held high with an optimism that brought a smile back to Hector's face.

He lay down and looked again at the doors above. He closed his eyes and waited for whatever was to come. Eternity started now.

51

Tommy charged up the overpass with the EpiPens, scrambling through the minefield of frozen litter and dead weeds, tripping and falling only twice. At the top, the paramedics had stopped CPR and declared Hector dead. They unfolded their yellow gurney, arguing over the best way to carry his body down the slope.

A third figure had arrived at the scene in Tommy's brief absence. It was Sammie.

Her hands clasped over her mouth. Abrasions and dried blood covered her face and neck. She didn't even notice Tommy climb up from the other side, her eyes fixed only on Hector's body. Her tears kissed the cold and evaporated into her cheeks. Sorrow draped her like a shroud, leaving her catatonic with dread.

Tommy watched as her hands moved from her mouth to clenching her curled, wild hair. Her tears now flowed hot, cutting through the dried blood, falling to the snow at her feet.

"You fucking *asshole!*" Sammie screamed.

The paramedics flinched as they fumbled with the gurney.

"Selfish, selfish prick!" she shouted, pacing the walls of an invisible cell with balled fists. "Fucking *asshole!*"

Sammie's eyes met Tommy's, her anger fading. Gravity set in, and her face sank. Her bottom lip quivered, then she broke, reduced to a whimpering child. She looked at Tommy, her face pleading, *Don't let this be real.*

Emboldened by Sammie's pain, Tommy held one EpiPen between his teeth like a commando and pulled the blue cap off the other, then repeated the maneuver.

He gave Sammie a nod. She responded with visible confusion. One of the paramedics did a double take at Tommy.

"Hey, don't you fucking da—"

Tommy charged with both pens raised.

"No!" shouted the other.

Tommy left his feet, diving with both pens aimed for Hector's chest.

It was a *Pulp Fiction*.

52

Hector blinked and found himself at Go Tavern.

The place was quiet except for the occasional clink of glass or shifting stool. There was a beer in front of him that he didn't remember ordering.

He drank it, and it was good.

Wait— What the fuck—

His hands frisked his own stomach and leg for the wounds of Hell, but he felt whole.

It was brighter in the bar than he remembered it being. The air was thick with a misty fog that hung with luminescent particles of sparkling gray and white, like snow suspended midair.

A bartender with her hair tied back in a tight bun washed glasses in the three-compartment sink, dunking them in the sanitizer before shaking off the excess and placing them on the dry rack. Hector had never seen her before, at least not here.

A few stools down from Hector, an old man, weathered and gray, stared into his beer, listening to the water slosh in the sinks. He tapped his foot, a smile on his lips, as if enjoying the sound. Beneath his stool lay a dog, just as old and gray, its head resting on its paws.

Frantically pacing the rear to-go coolers for malt liquor forties was a small woman with a skeletal face and body that was mostly rib cage. Sores freckled her mouth. Crusted lips hid blackened teeth and a rotting set of gums.

At the bottom of the L-shaped bar sat a man and a woman. They sat close, holding hands, all smiles and whispers, completely infatuated with each other.

They were strangers, yet it felt as if Hector had known them all his life. He glanced at the mirror behind the bar and saw his reflection. The stains of Hell were gone from his face.

The bartender approached with a smile, drying her hands on the towel that hung from her belt. "Everything okay?"

Her words were simple, sincere.

Hector decided to be honest. "No, not really. I'm pretty sure I'm dead."

"And is that such a bad thing?"

"I was—I was in Hell. And there were doors—my dad—Sammie—" He wanted to explain but managed only fragments. She nodded, understanding.

"Hell can be a stressful place. I'm sure that was very hard for you."

That's a weird thing to say, Hector thought.

"Existence is weird. If it wasn't weird, it wouldn't be existence," she added.

Hector began to have an idea of who, or what, he was talking to. "Okay, please get out of my head. Thanks."

"But everything's in your head. You just have no idea how much your head can hold."

"Cute."

"Death is life. Life is death. If you get hung up on their little differences, you'll miss the best of both. It's not meant to be that serious. Trust me." She lifted his beer and placed it on a coaster with a wink.

"Not that serious?" Hector had enough of the nonchalant attitude. "It sure feels fucking serious when you're in it. Don't you care about all the suffering? There are people who spend their whole lives hurting, then die and get nothing but more pain—for eternity! What the fuck is *that?*"

The old man looked up from his beer, leaned an elbow on the bar in Hector's direction, and said, "Son, not enough time has passed to call anything eternity. And you make a lot of assumptions about pain."

Hector was having none of it. "I'm not making assumptions. I've seen it with my own eyes. I've felt it. I've lived it. I've had this —this *fucking emptiness* in my chest since the day I was born, and it *fucking* hurts. Don't tell me I'm making assumptions."

The dog looked up from the old man's feet and said, "You're making assumptions."

"Alright, fuck this." Hector pushed his stool from the bar and made his way to the door. He opened it and saw nothing.

Literally nothing.

No city street, no cosmic void, no impenetrable blackness, no white light.

Nothing. Pure nothing.

He returned to his stool and sighed. "Can I at least have a shot please?"

The bartender smiled and poured him a whiskey.

The old man continued, "I know pain. I know suffering. But I also know joy. And I know love. Forgiveness. Wrath. I feel every-thing all at once all the time. One day, all creation—man, animal, amoeba, the horrible and the wonderful behind every door—will join me. But not today, not tomorrow either, or the next day. But it'll come. And then you'll understand."

The dog sneezed, then nodded in agreement.

"Seems like a fucking cop-out," Hector said. "You can do whatever you want, however you want it done. But you choose to let us suffer. You chose to put us blind in the dark and make us dependent on you. You chose to make life the way it is. I didn't choose anything. I didn't choose to be alive, or be this—this *person* that I fucking hate."

The meth-mouthed woman roared with laughter behind Hector, pointing at her own reflection in the cooler door. *"Mysterrrrrious ways. Don't forget. I work in mysterrrrrrious ways!"* She cackled at the absurdity of her own words.

The couple across the bar chimed in, speaking in unison, "Basic laws were necessary. Rules. I created them for myself, and I must abide by them. I bound myself in order to let you be truly free. Nothing is permanent, Hector. The way is always there to find. You just have to find it."

Hector took his shot. It burned going down. "So the loving God thing, that's bullshit?"

The bartender picked up Hector's empty shot glass and held it up to her eye, examining the room through it like a kaleidoscope. "I don't exist how you think I exist, sweetie. I just am. And I always will be. But I also will never be. Every individual creation holds the key in and out of salvation or damnation. I am not here to arbitrate. I just build. The meaning of what I build is yours to create, and you have eternity to create it—if eternity ever comes, which it will, and won't." She plunged the glass into the soapy water. "Love is a complicated thing. I know you know that. But the love I have for all creation is unlike anything you can ever know. At least, not yet. Do you understand?"

"Would you be surprised if I said that I didn't?"

"Not at all, Hector," said the dog at the old man's feet.

Meth Mouth pulled a Bling Bling Berry Mad Dog from the cooler against the back wall and cracked it open. "Different realities *looooove* to fill the gaps with different stuff—religions, saviors, monsters, you name it—" She gulped down half the bottle, went *ahhh*, and offered it to Hector.

He shook his head no.

She shrugged and continued, "Sure, I make the first few things, some angels, a few demons, woo-woo fractals of light, dimensional energies, whatever floats your boat. But after that, I'm pretty hands-off. Most of the stories you've heard about me just aren't true. Fairy tales."

Hector wasn't buying it. "So you didn't create Hell? You didn't send all those angels who went against you there so they could build resentment and then take it out on us? That doesn't sound like 'hands-off' to me."

Meth Mouth stuck a fingernail in her ear and dug at an itch. "Okay, sure, that whole Heaven and Hell thing. But they're such a small sliver of the pie! The infighting between angels. It got way too out of hand way too soon. I had to step in or else they would have destroyed it all. And your reality wasn't ready for that—yet." She slammed the rest of the bottle and half-stifled a burp. "But good, evil, I don't decide which is which."

"Things unfold as they do, organically," said the bartender. "My children, no matter which reality, they set up their own systems, ways of doing things. They decide who the devils are, the heroes, and everything in between. They believe in their own ideas so much that they eventually will them all into existence. Crazy, right?"

"My children never cease to amaze me," the loving couple said in perfect harmony, lost in each other's eyes.

"It is impressive, isn't it?" said the old man. "All I give is consciousness, the basic building blocks, and you create the rest."

The old dog stretched and strolled up to Hector. "Jesus is my son, but it was the collective unconsciousness which willed him into existence and gave him meaning. He is your creation, and you are no less my son, Hector. Everything and everyone is my child. You create meaning because you are of me." The dog circled Hector's stool in tired steps before curling up beneath it.

Hector felt like he was back in high school, so he decided to move on to questions he could comprehend the answers to.

"Are Sammie and Tommy alive? And you know exactly what I mean. Not alive *and* dead in some 'everything is always and now and later' kind of way, but alive. Alive as in *alive*. In the way that all your so-called children you let bleed every fucking day can understand it."

"Yep, they're fine," the old man said, sipping his beer. "Tell Tommy his brother's fine too. I know he's been worrying about that."

"I think 'worrying' is probably an understatement. Do you have any idea how much pain everyone goes through? Do you even care?"

The dog looked up and said, "I believe we covered this, Hector."

Hector rubbed his temples and sighed, frustrated but relieved to learn that Sammie and Tommy were okay.

"Alright, what is this? I know it's not Hell. Is this Heaven? Is my Heaven just Go Tavern?"

The couple at the end of the bar giggled, and said, "Heaven is a construct of your reality. You are simply in a liminal space nestled between the cracks of all existence that I have populated with carefully selected images from your mind to project my own consciousness through."

"Right. Of course." Hector slammed the rest of his beer. "So what's next? Do I stay here forever?"

"I will leave that up to you. You can stay here if you wish," the bartender said, setting down a fresh beer and taking his empty glass.

Hector noticed Meth Mouth scratching her crotch in his peripherals, and said, "I don't wish that."

"Or you can choose a door. Inhabit a new reality. A reality without the pain you carry. Your friends are safe. You don't need to worry. Now you can be free of your suffering."

The thought blossomed in Hector like a spring flower seeing the world for the very first time. "Why are you helping me?"

"Because you helped me."

"I did?"

The bartender idly passed the empty glass between her hands. "You saved me a trip. I prefer not to revisit realities once they are up on their own feet and running, until it is time for them to end, and yours is not *quite* there yet."

"Yeah, you mentioned that already." He sipped his new beer. "So you just create your children then abandon them until you're ready to destroy them? You're honestly worse than my dad."

The bartender smiled. "What's your choice, Hector? What do you want to do?"

"But why me? There had to have been better ways to stop Bub. Why did you choose me to help?"

"Why not?" the bartender asked.

"*Mysterrrrriouuus waaaays,*" Meth Mouth contributed.

Hector imagined a new life. A fresh start. Maybe he would be raised in a happy family—or raise a family of his own. Maybe he would have his son. *I would be able to hold my son.*

Then he thought of Sammie, leaving her behind.

Even if he met a new Sammie, she wouldn't truly be her. With the offer to go anywhere and do anything on the table, there was only one version of one person he wanted to see more than anything, and she waited for him in a place he knew only as cold and unforgiving.

He traced their matching tattoo through his sleeve. *Nothing Matters.* The choice in his heart was clear, but he was scared.

Hector looked to the mirror behind the bar. His own reflection stared back. It shouldn't have surprised him when it started talking, but it did.

"You can't hide anymore," the reflection said. "Not behind your depression, not behind alcohol, not behind your cynicism. Time to just face it all."

Hector turned to the bar patrons in confusion. They shrugged or nodded in agreement.

Unsure if the reflection was like the others or actually him—but concluding that it didn't matter—Hector responded, "I get what you're saying, or what I'm saying, but cool, I admit it! Things are bad! I'm bad! Now what? It doesn't change anything. Even if I live the rest of my life perfectly, which, c'mon, it still won't change a fucking thing. It doesn't change the past."

"You can stop torturing yourself with guilt every moment of your life. You even feel guilty for feeling guilty, like you don't deserve an ounce of compassion, even from yourself. You're not all evil. No one is. And you're not all good. No one is. You're just you. You exist. And as long as you exist, the possibility for change does too."

The reflection spoke to Hector with a kindness that he had never once given himself. "The past happened, yes. But that doesn't stop the future from coming. You can still find happiness. You can grow, but you have to keep moving."

"I just love her so much," Hector found himself saying, tears in his eyes.

"Then you know what you need to do."

"Yeah. I guess I do."

And with that, the mirror shattered. Broken glass drifted into the air and separated into tiny particles of light, becoming one with the luminescent fog that hung in the bar.

The bartender took back the beer she had given Hector and poured it down the well. "I see you've made a choice."

"Was it a good choice?" asked Hector.

The bartender's eyes were so full of love that Hector had to look away, as if he had stared into the sun.

"It's a choice. No more, no less," she said. "Oh, and do me a favor. Reach into your pocket and leave the key on the bar. That should probably stay with me now."

Hector felt his pocket. There it was. He placed it on the bar. "It was you. You gave Jesus the key. You knew he'd give it to Lucifer." Hector's brain churned, exhausting its limited bandwidth. "But why even do that? Bub never would have been able to— What was the point of all this?"

"*Myysterriousss wayssss,*" Meth Mouth crooned.

The bartender winked. "Be good, Hector."

The couple at the end of the bar blew Hector a kiss before returning to their whispered affirmations.

"You'll be fine," the old man muttered into his beer. "Or you won't. And that's fine too."

"See you around, Hector," said the dog.

"*Orrrrrrr mayyybeee...*" Meth Mouth ran up behind Hector and threw her hands over his eyes, "*youu WON'T!*"

"Hey! Get the fuck off m—"

Then, pure nothing.

53

PART SIX

"You know, they said the EpiPens didn't do anything. In fact, the paramedics said I nearly ruined their CPR efforts." Tommy leaned back in the vinyl guest chair, putting his hands behind his head. "But I think they're full of shit."

"I think so too," Hector said.

"Thanks, buddy."

The coma lasted three days, which defied the doctors' estimate of *indefinitely*.

That sustained period of death should have led to a permanent coma or brain damage, but it didn't. The doctors couldn't explain it, and Hector's lack of insurance guaranteed that they wouldn't pursue an answer.

"They said you were dead for at least a few minutes there. The paramedics don't have an official time though. They didn't seem too smart." Tommy thought for a moment. "Were you really dead? Like, did you feel it?"

"Yeah," Hector said, his answers short from an incredibly bruised larynx and a general sense of overall pain. He closed his eyes and let the room's fluorescence beat against their lids.

"And how was that?" asked Tommy.

Hector tightened his face. "Not great."

Tommy chuckled. "Yeah, I bet. Still pretty badass you went to Hell though." The smile dropped from his lips. He leaned closer and said, "Which, by the way, I'm still seeing stuff. Are you?"

Hector shifted his eyes to the large, pulsating maggot hanging like a bat in the ceiling corner. It revealed circular rows of teeth stacked like Russian dolls, leading to a puckered, anus-like mouth.

Tommy sat back and exhaled. "Okay. Yeah. Just making sure."

"They just watch," Hector said. He winced, preparing himself for even more words. "They're lost. Confused."

"Yeah, well, they can join the club. Sure would've been nice if the spider helped us get back to normal like what's her name— Jessica. He told me he'd 'think about it.' But hey, at least he left you a card."

Spelled out in webbing above the door like a banner was *Get Well Soon*, unable to be seen by the hospital staff with their untainted eyes.

Hector didn't know why they were left with this "gift." Maybe Bandini just thought they deserved it, for better and for worse. But he'd have to wait until his throat healed to articulate those thoughts with Tommy. Instead, he asked, "And Sammie?"

"Yeah, her too—still seeing weird shit and talking to cats, not that she didn't do that before." Tommy pointed to the counter across the room. "She brought you that. You saw it, right?"

It was a small ficus tree. A handful of leaves topped a thin trunk no longer than Hector's forearm. The black plastic pot leaked dirt and sported a ripped Home Depot sticker that Sammie had apparently given up on halfway through. Hector loved it.

"I don't know who that's from though," Tommy said, referencing the glass bottle of Topo Chico and brown paper bag next to the tree.

The nurse had informed Hector of the bag's contents earlier that day: a corn muffin with the husk baked into it and a gift certificate for a free order of buffalo tofu wings.

Tommy craned his neck, double checking that the door was closed. "They found his body—Austin's—picked clean to the bones in the house he was keeping Sammie. Police don't know about her though. She's happy to keep it that way.

"Cops figured he broke in, murdered that old couple, then overdosed and died. They didn't find drugs, and there wasn't enough left of his body to test, but given his past, they just filled in the blanks, I guess. They matched his stupid knife to the other murders too. So it's as they say: *case closed*," Tommy said in his best world-weary detective voice that Hector could tell he was very proud of.

The thought of Austin's eulogy being that of a psychotic heroin-crazed murderer didn't sit well with Hector. He was technically only two of those three things when he died.

For a moment, Hector mourned someone that may never have existed—a friend, a brother—then, nothing. He felt nothing. And he didn't know how to feel about that.

"They said he was eaten by animals smelling an easy meal through the busted glass. These two detectives called it a *poetic death*. I don't know shit about poetry, but I'm pretty sure that ain't it."

Hector nodded in agreement.

"The fucker died owing me three-hundred dollars. *Plus*, I told Whole Foods I was falsely accused of murder, but they still wrote me up for a no-call, no-show. I guess he got the last laugh."

Austin always did delight in Tommy's misfortune, thought Hector.

The nurse entered with a knock, smiling as she checked the beeping machines around Hector. Tommy sat quietly, tapping his thighs, eager to resume their conversation. She jotted some notes on her clipboard, changed an IV bag, and softly hummed a pop song to herself. "What a lovely plant," the nurse remarked, admiring the ficus and throwing her purple nitrile gloves in the trash.

Tommy watched her leave, exhaled, then took a serious tone. "Weird question. And if you don't have an answer, no big deal. But, when you were dead, did you see anything that would—like—I don't know, give you an idea of—" He stopped talking and let his eyes ask the rest.

His brother Brian.

Out of all the insanity of that night, his time at Go Tavern with God seemed the most like a dream. His father, Bub, and the army of Gretchens? As real as Tommy, Sammie, and the catheter up his urethra. But that bar at the end of the universe? It felt like a whispered secret from beyond the afterlife, beyond everything.

He wasn't certain he could take what he learned there as fact. But something inside him gave a little nudge, a reminder: *God is a dick.*

It was all real.

God's nature was to be a half-remembered truth, to live in the peripherals, to be and not to be. He wanted Hector to doubt their encounter, but Hector knew better.

"Your brother," he said, his throat straining, "is okay."

Tommy sat, hands in lap, tracing the top of his index finger with his thumb. He tried to hide his joy, but it shone through like the sun against the sheet he hung over his bedroom window.

The words had hit him like the last notes of his favorite song. He was satisfied.

"I'm thinking of maybe becoming an EMT," Tommy said, a new glow upon his face.

"You'd be great," Hector replied.

"Thanks, buddy."

THAT EVENING, Hector had an extra helping of painkillers for dinner. A nurse took pity on him after he struggled to drink the gifted Topo Chico, his agonized facial expressions conveying that the carbonated water felt like swallowing tacks against his contused and ruptured throat.

The gentle opiate rocked him like a newborn.

As the sun set, he stared and drifted into the sky's kaleidoscope of orange and red. The day had felt longer than recent ones. In another month, the worst of winter would be over. For now, this brief respite from the gray made him fall in love with Chicago all over again.

The door creaked open. Hector couldn't fully turn his neck to see, but he knew who was there. The scent of the oils in her hair, calm like incense smoke, traveled fast and hit his nose before she could even close the door behind her.

"Do you like your tree?"

"I love it."

"It was on sale."

Sammie climbed into his bed without another word. Tufts of her hair filled the bottom of his vision. Her head rested on his chest. He stroked her upper back.

The clock turned without conversation. All that needed to be said was said through the warmth of their bodies and the graze of his fingertips—the simple words they traced.

Night followed, and they were soon bathed in moonlight and the white fluorescence from the hospital's exterior. The onset of soft snores peppered Sammie's breathing. She fought them off by holding Hector tighter, bringing him closer.

As sleep became inevitable for them both, Hector had just two words to say, three syllables, overused and rendered meaningless, to encapsulate an ocean of regret, but they were all he had to give.

He took in the scent of her hair and the sound of her breath, the sweetest song he'd ever heard, and said without introduction or explanation, "I'm sorry."

Sammie made a sound like a cat scratched in just the right spot. She buried herself deeper into him and rubbed her cheek against his chest.

"I know, Hector. I know."

WHEN HE AWOKE, she was gone.

Tommy visited later that day and mentioned that Sammie had taken an early morning Megabus back to Milwaukee. Hector felt certain he would see her again, somewhere, sometime.

He began filling Hector in on the missing pieces, but neither were in a rush to relive it all so soon.

They watched reruns of old sitcoms into the night. The men on TV lived foreign lives—loving families, good jobs, and middle-class comfort. Unobtainable fiction.

The two friends humored each other with jokes and noises over the scripted sterility of that fantasy world. Even the demonic maggot in the corner shared the chuckles. Yet, they watched in boyish wonder, hoping to one day see themselves.

A week or so later, Hector went home.

54

When Gretchen returned for Hector, she found both him and the hall of doors gone. Only the cave crawlers' tiny arrows and Bub's crown of teeth remained as evidence of what had transpired, scattered unceremoniously on the ground.

She picked the crown up with her tail and left with no particular destination in mind, taking her time back through the tunnels. With her boss gone, she was without a purpose for the first time since consciousness had bludgeoned her awake.

Gretchen had been awake for as long as she could remember but could only remember as long as she'd been awake. If there was a time before Hell where she lived freely and for herself, she didn't know it.

So, she wandered.

Her mantis arms dragged at her sides while her tail towed Bub's crown of teeth like a child dragging their backpack after a rough day of school. Every demon, cave crawler, and lost soul she passed remained silent. They felt Bub's absence in the bouncing crown and could only watch in shock before racing away to spread the news of Gretchen's treason.

"Let them come for me. I don't care anymore," she grumbled, heading to the only place she ever found any comfort.

The crowd parted before her as she reached the train platform. Ignoring their stares, she stepped into a car, prompting everyone to quickly exit—everyone except an impish creature who approached her with wide-eyed curiosity, like a caveman seeing fire for the very first time.

His long ears drooped down past his inverted knees to the taloned feet that shuffled him toward Gretchen like a drunk chicken. Two tusks protruded from his top gums, curving around his ears like ram horns.

His forked tongue flicked against the impractical tusks, and with a heavy lisp, he asked, "Tho ith thrue?"

The imp was covered in scarred flesh and fresh lashes that oozed black blood. Bits of gray-pink meat, like spoiled ground beef, clung to his claws and stuck between his tusks—remnants of a duty done. Poorly designed like Gretchen, he was a pitiful creature, endowed with the terrible purpose to punish and be punished.

But of all the beasts she passed, only this lowly minion had the courage to approach her.

"He's dead," Gretchen found herself saying, knowing that was not quite accurate.

"Dead? There ith no dead here."

Explaining Bub's actual fate would open a can of worms that Hell wasn't ready for. It was a truth even she had yet to process.

"He's as dead as I need him to be," Gretchen said.

The imp considered her words, nodded, then slunk away to a seat at the end of the car, stealing looks back with that same primitive mix of caution and awe.

The train ascended from the tunnels into the urban sprawl. Asymmetrical structures towered in dark majesty, scraping the crimson sky. Gretchen exited at her stop and headed toward the tallest of them all.

Her entire existence, she was either unseen or spat upon. Now, everyone stopped to stare without a word. She continued on, her ears held high, the crown in tow. It was all she could do.

Knowing things were about to get very bad for her, Gretchen wanted to sit in her favorite spot one last time, so she ascended to the top of Lucifer's tower, now without management, until she, too, found herself scraping the crimson sky.

She sat on the roof, letting her paws dangle over the edge. Winged, skeletal beasts soared around the tower's peak. For the first time in millennia, they noticed her. She smiled.

Gretchen breathed deep, letting the weight of it all leave her. Her thoughts lingered on the doors, lost futures and histories. *A praying mantis in the summer breeze. A cat curled up on a warm lap.* She chose to hold them as memories, as if they were lives she herself had lived. The delusion was necessary to keep from crying.

A distant rumble echoed from below as a crowd gathered at the base of the tower. Word traveled fast in Hell, expedited by the naturally loose lips of imps. The mob's intent seemed clear: retribution. She sighed, wishing they had taken a bit longer to arrive.

The winged beast glided to a stop in front of Gretchen, bowing its head like a noble steed, waiting for her to mount its back. Despite the circumstances, this was a dream come true.

She awkwardly scrambled onto the beast's back, nearly slipping before finding her balance. They plunged through layers of black clouds, the winds of Hell whipping through her fur and flattening her ears. She closed her eyes, envisioning herself as a bird gliding through serene skies. Bliss washed over her.

The beast touched down on the street below, kicking up dust and debris with its massive wings. Gretchen slid down its spine and landed flat on her bottom in front of a crowd that stretched as far as she could see. Creatures of all sizes, from hulking golems to malevolent faeries, encircled her, silent, waiting for her to speak.

Gretchen stared back. She had nothing to say. What's done was done. Her tail held up the crown of teeth for one last look before she tossed it at the feet of the expectant crowd.

The crowd gasped, taking a step back.

A familiar imp pushed his way through the wall of creatures, emerging from the crowd. He nudged the discarded crown with a taloned foot and turned to face his brethren, both large and small.

"Brotherth and thithterth!" the imp shouted with impediment. "ALL HAIL GRETHEN! THE NEW QUEEN OF HELL!"

The crowd erupted in cheers, believing that *she* had been the one to vanquish Beelzebub—a tyrant they all despised but never dared to confront. From the smallest hobgoblin to Leviathan himself, they rallied around their new leader. Even the cave crawlers scuttled about, peeking through the legs of larger demons in excitement.

It was a new day in Hell, and Gretchen was the dawn.

She twitched her nose and flicked her tail. This was her reality, and she was going to make the best of it.

55

"Fellas, are you sick and tired of limp dick? I know you are. Trust me, I know. My dick used to be softer than a Gender Studies major drinking a kale smoothie in a campus safe space."

"*That's fucking soft, bro,*" added PJ, Scotty Durango's astute co-host.

"*Tell me about it! But you'll never have to worry about that ever again. Our sponsor GET BRICKED has got you covered. Dude, this thing is a fucking lozenge. You put it in your mouth, let that shit dissolve, and BAM, you're fucking hard as a rock. Diamond cutter. Ready to go. Ready for pound town. Ready to FUCK.*"

The podcast snapped Hector from his blissful trance of thinking about nothing at all. He dumped the soapy water from the bacon pan and began scrubbing off the coagulated grease and burnt fat. He had heard this ad read before. "Didn't we just listen to this episode?"

James tossed the giant circle of dough into the air, catching it on his fists as flour dusted his forearms. "That was like a month ago," he said, stretching the dough on his wooden paddle. "I like to revisit the classics. His new stuff is too political."

"Please never play the new stuff," Hector said.

"*Use code SCOTTYDICKBRICK to get thirty percent off your first order!*"

James grabbed black olives and an Old Style from the cooler beneath his station. "You want one?" he asked out of habit, then corrected himself with a wave and a nod.

"I'm good. Thanks though." Hector kept scrubbing. Repetitiveness and banality were newfound comforts. It had been twenty-eight days since his last drink.

"*Doc, I'm still stuck on this sandwich thing,*" Scotty admitted to his guest, Dr. Fewer of the Institute of Technical Trade and Technology, a college Hector remembered once seeing billboards for on a drive through Indiana.

"Oh yeah, the sandwich," Hector recalled.

James mumbled a confirmation as he sprinkled cheese onto his work in progress.

"*It's just a metaphor, Scotty. The sandwich is merely a representation of our universe and the many dimensional layers that—*"

"*No, no, I get that, Doc. But what if there's more sandwiches?*"

Hector dunked the pan in the sanitizer and placed it on the drying rack. Cleaning the bacon pan was a satisfying feat. He stood back and admired his work.

"*I don't understand the question,*" the professor confessed.

Scotty attempted to elaborate, "*Like, what if there's more sandwiches?*"

"*No, I heard you the first time, Scotty. I just don't follow.*"

PJ chimed in, "*He's asking what if there's more sandwiches.*"

Hector checked his prep list. Sauce was up next.

Scotty tried again, "*So, there's a sandwich. A big ol' long Italian one.*"

PJ chortled. James did too.

"*But it's not like that sandwich is just floating in thin air, right? It's gotta be on a table or a shelf—or something!*"

The front door dinged open.

"Someone's up front," James announced.

Hector ground open an industrial-sized can of six-in-one tomatoes with a large crank can opener. "Okay, one sec," he said, then turned and shouted toward the front door, "Be right with you!"

"So maybe OUR sandwich is on the table at some restaurant somewhere. And at every other table, some sad bastard is eating a different sandwich alone for lunch. Maybe there's a whole family at one—and they're all eating sandwiches! A whole restaurant full of sandwiches! Maybe it's a Subway and there's all these sandwich parts in all those little plastic containers behind the glass just waiting to be put together. Do you get what I'm saying, Doc?"

Unpeeled tomatoes and purée plopped into the sauce bucket, splattering Hector's face with red.

"I understand you're a comedian, Scotty—but what you're saying is absurd."

Hector emerged from the kitchen wiping his face on his sleeve. "Hi there, what can I get—"

The woman, a young professional in a black wool coat, raised a finger to silence him. "Uh-huh. Uh-huh. Well, that's just not acceptable. You need to communicate to them that it's just not acceptable." Her voice was sharp and exuded irritation. Without removing her sunglasses or the phone from her ear, she stared through Hector like he wasn't even there.

But Hector just leaned on the counter and smiled, her conversation barely registering. His focus had shifted out the window to the city street where the sun shone and the ground thawed. Winter wasn't quite over, but the end of February brought hints of spring, and the promise of change was enough to get through another month, maybe even another year.

A tickle on his hand. An ant carrying a crumb twice its size crawled over the ridges of Hector's knuckles. Halfway across, it looked up, antennae twitching, and spoke.

"Somewhere between the breeze, you'll catch the scent of past lives, summers and springs you lived before everything was dulled, before the thrill of living was replaced with disdain for the very act." The ant set down its crumb and stretched its legs. "It's sad that we go from shambling husks to withering husks as we age, still shambling, but slower."

Hector nodded small nods.

The woman in the wool coat shoved the phone back into her purse, apparently displeased with how her conversation ended, then stared at Hector like a piece of modern art she had no desire to understand.

"But that's just the way it goes, huh? Creatures like you and I, all we can do is find a reason to keep moving." The ant picked back up its crumb. "Bon voyage, Hector Ghouseau. May the breeze carry you gently on your next—"

"Uh— Hello?" the woman scoffed, removing her sunglasses, impatient, her lip curling in disgust. "Do you plan on taking my order sometime this life?"

Hector just smiled. It was all such a beautiful nothing. And it was good.

ABOUT THE AUTHOR

Mike Salinas lives in Chicago. He'll die in [REDACTED].

Write to him at mike@mikesalinas.cc.

www.ingramcontent.com/pod-product-compliance
Lightning Source LLC
Chambersburg PA
CBHW030729310726
48969CB00005B/1153